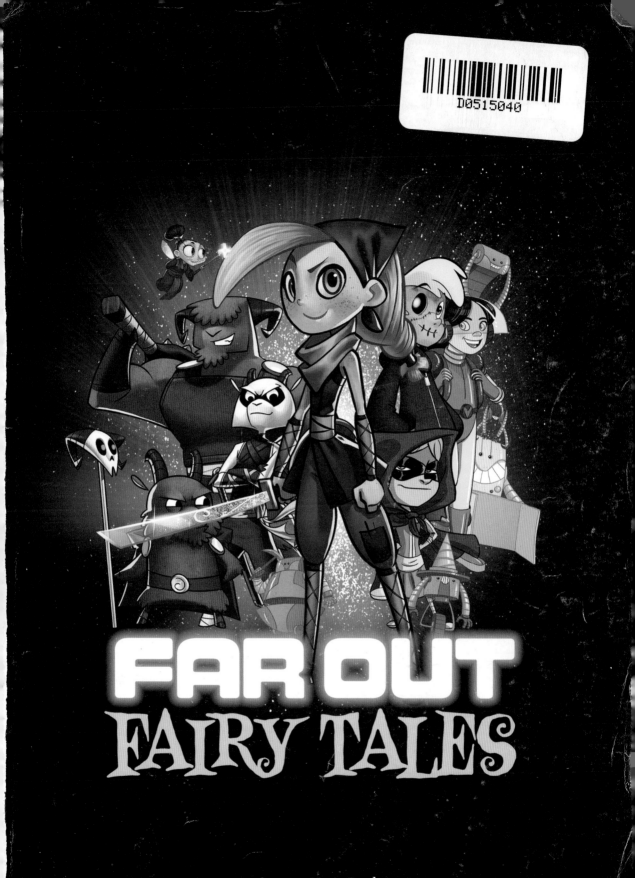

FAR OUT
FAIRY TALES

Capstone Young Readers
a capstone imprint

Ninja-rella 5

RED RIDING HOOD, SUPERHERO 39

SUPER BILLY GOATS GRUFF 73

SNOW WHITE AND THE SEVEN ROBOTS 107

HANSEL & GRETEL & ZOMBIES 141

FAR OUT FAIRY TALES

Ninja-rella

A GRAPHIC NOVEL

BY JOEY COMEAU
ILLUSTRATED BY OMAR LOZANO

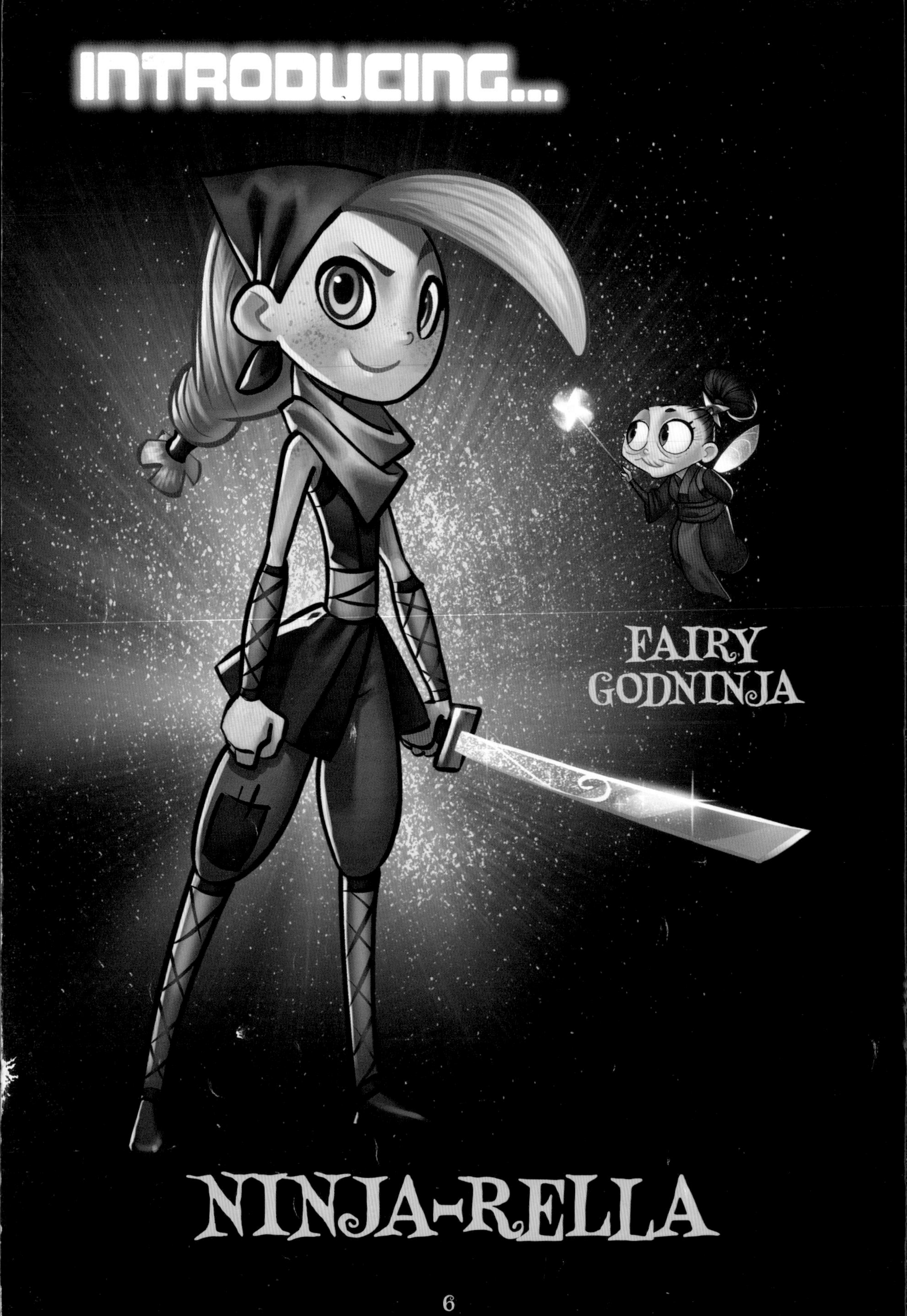
INTRODUCING...
FAIRY GODNINJA
NINJA-RELLA

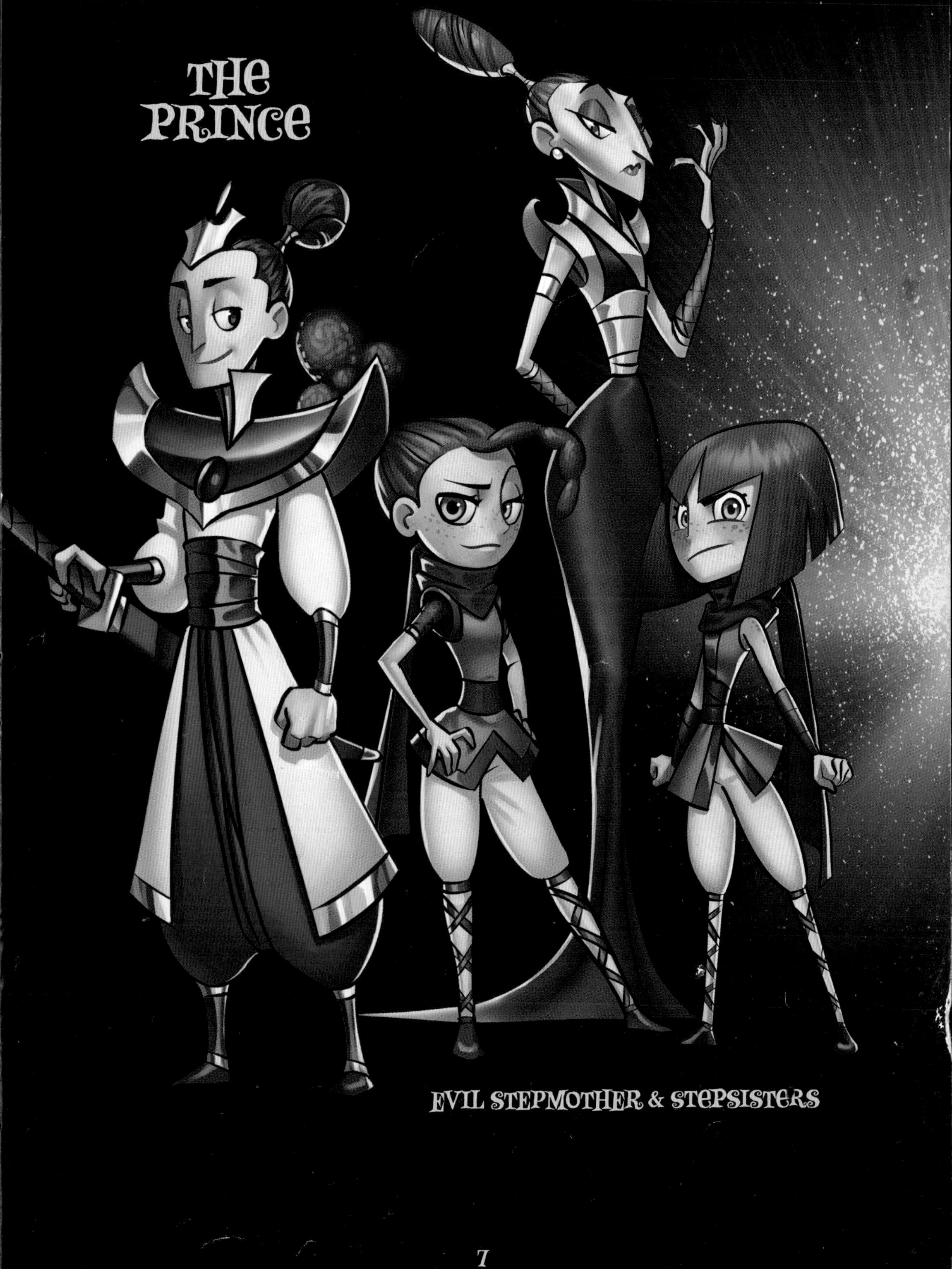
THE PRINCE
EVIL STEPMOTHER & STEPSISTERS

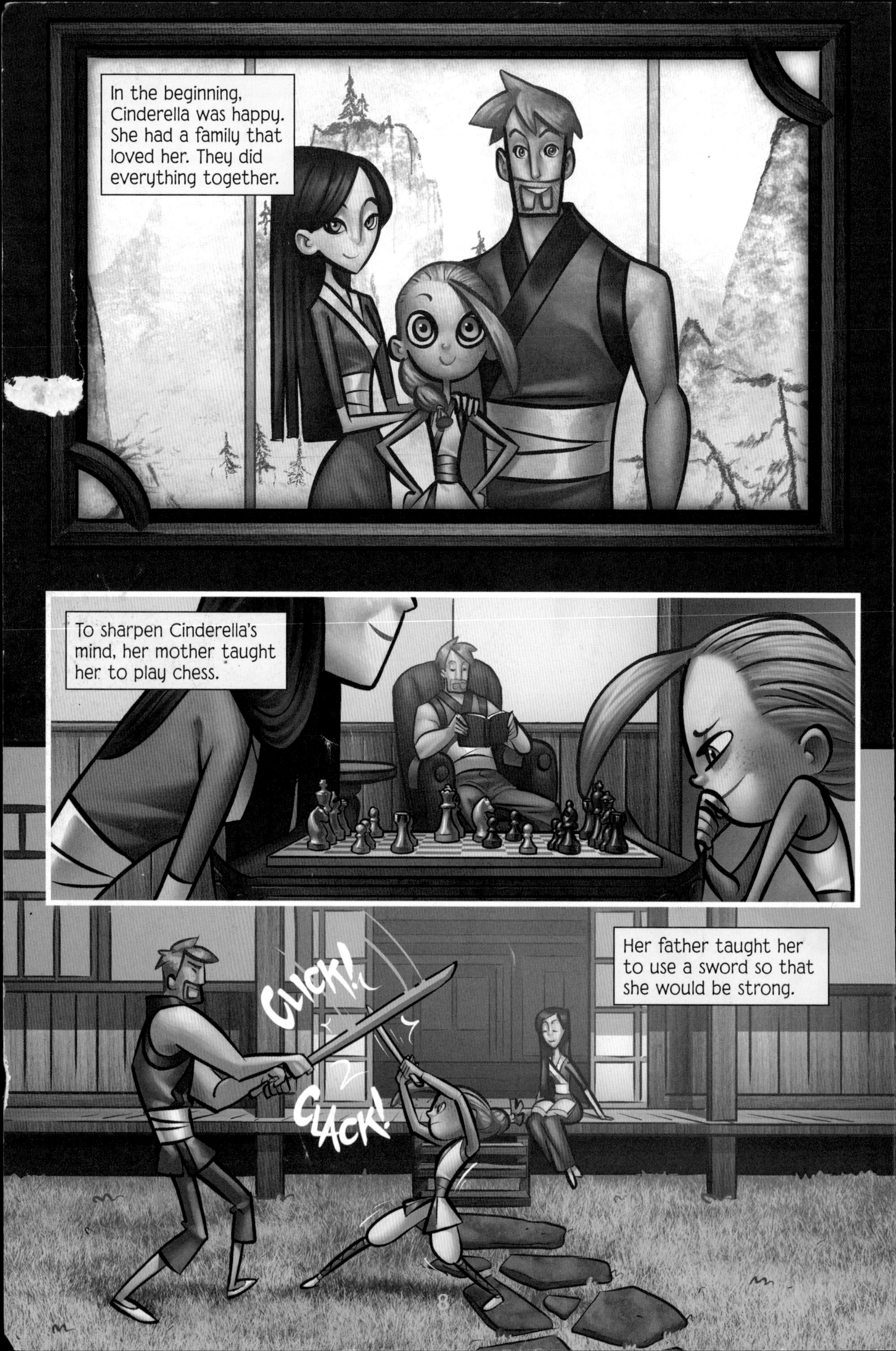
In the beginning, Cinderella was happy. She had a family that loved her. They did everything together.
To sharpen Cinderella's mind, her mother taught her to play chess.
Her father taught her to use a sword so that she would be strong.
CLICK!
CLACK!

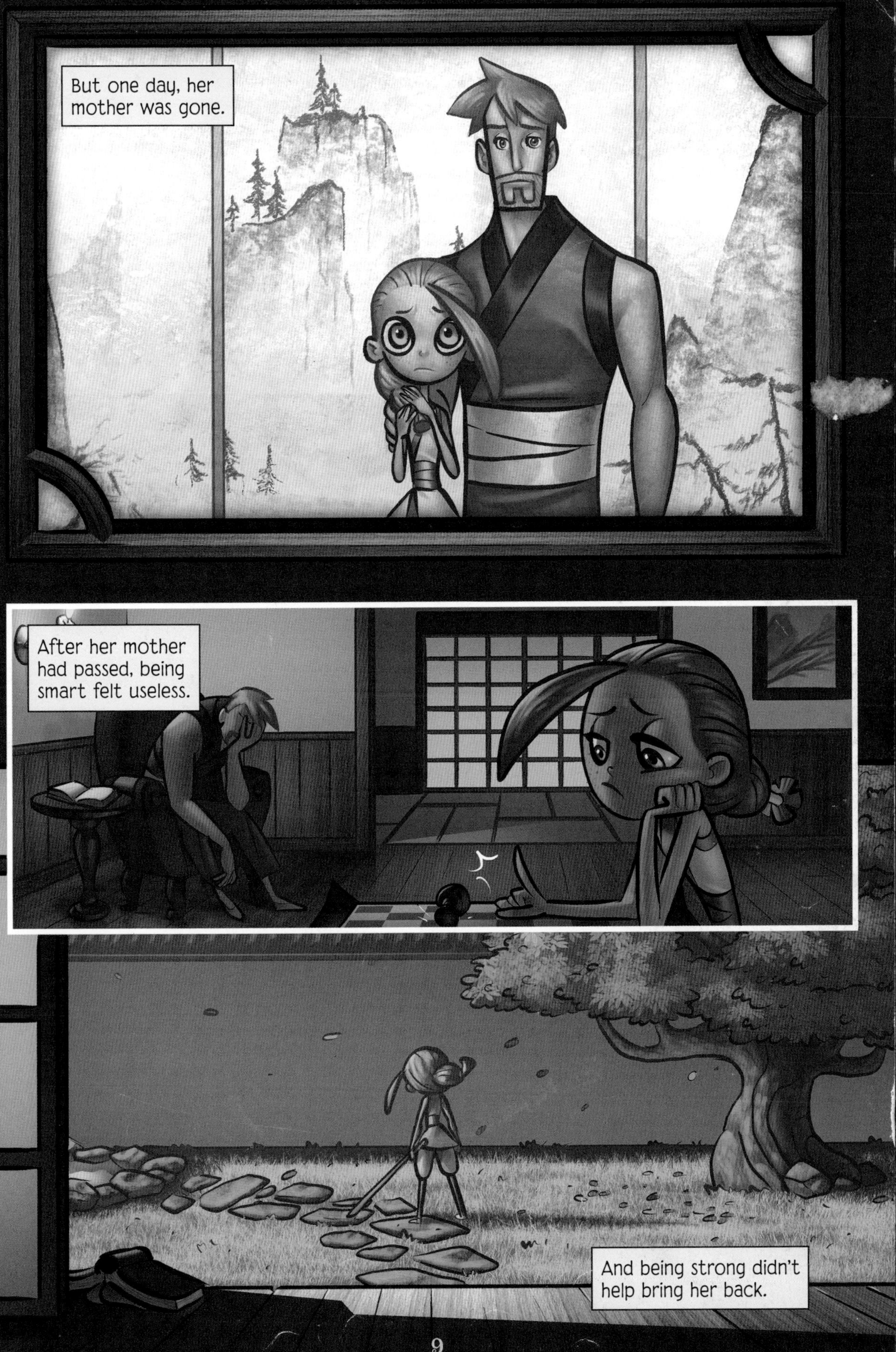
But one day, her mother was gone.
After her mother had passed, being smart felt useless.
And being strong didn't help bring her back.

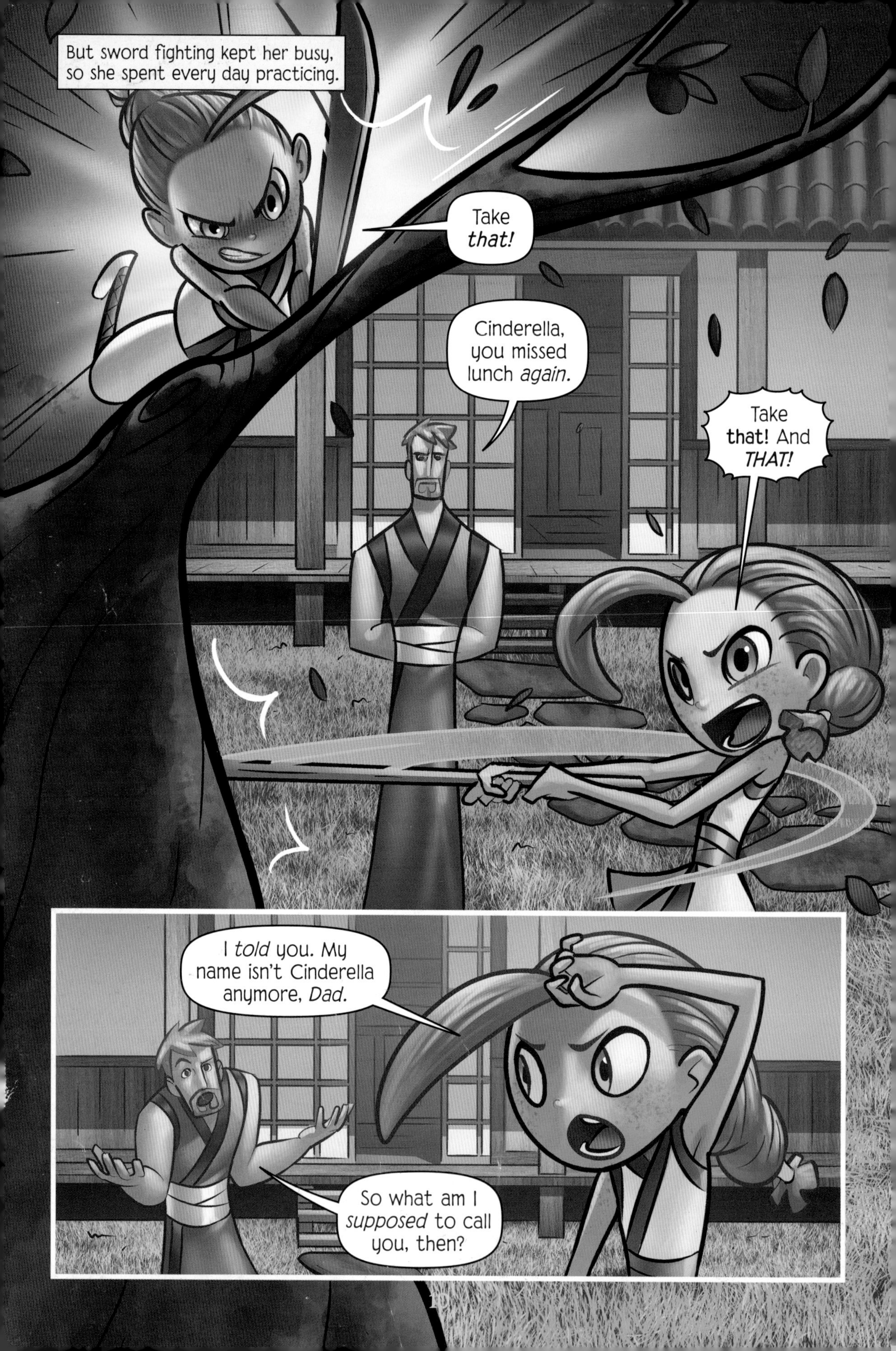
But sword fighting kept her busy, so she spent every day practicing.
Take *that!*
Cinderella, you missed lunch *again*.
Take **that!** And *THAT!*
I *told* you. My name isn't Cinderella anymore, *Dad*.
So what am I *supposed* to call you, then?

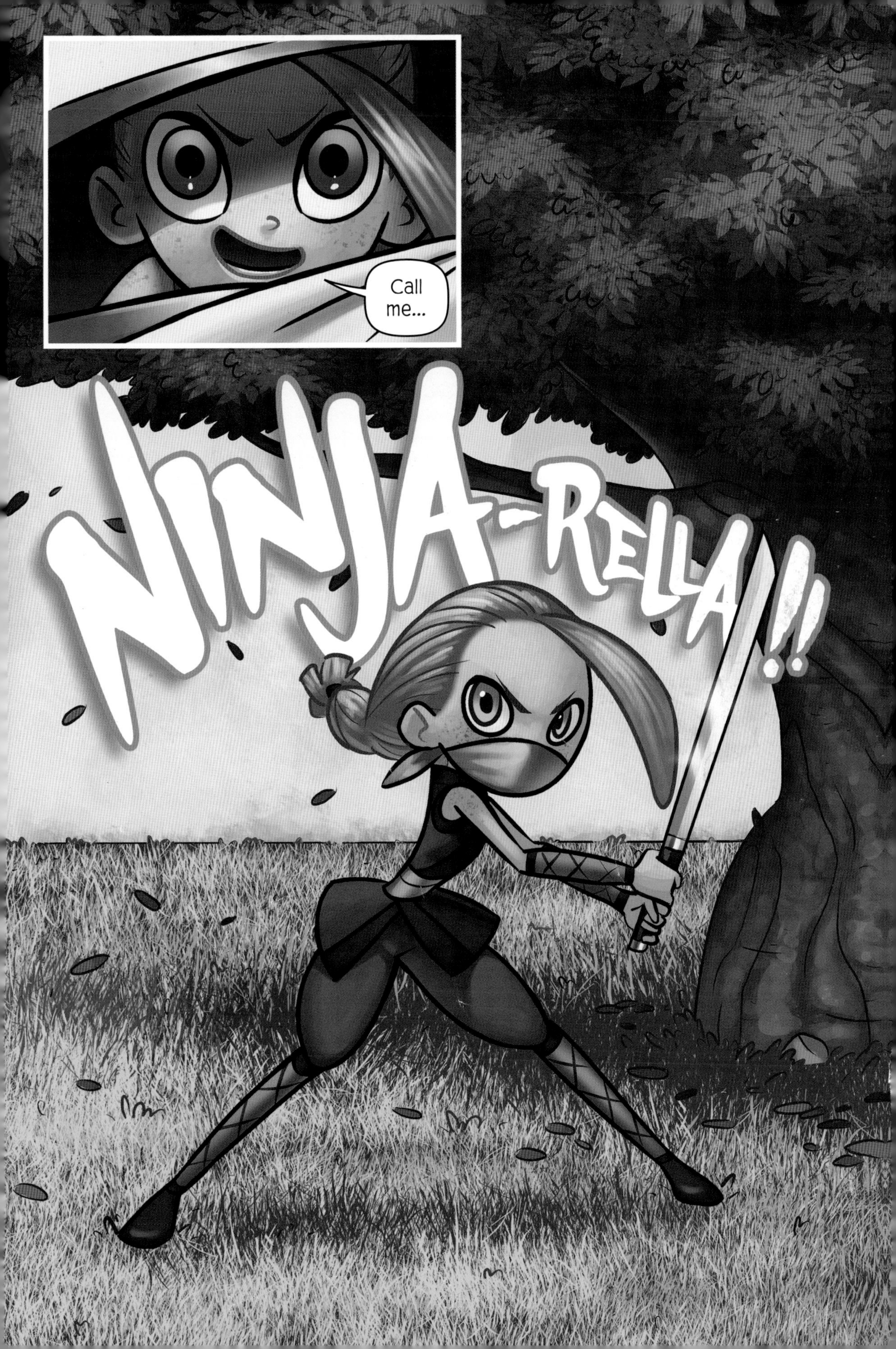
Call me...
NINJA-RELLA!!

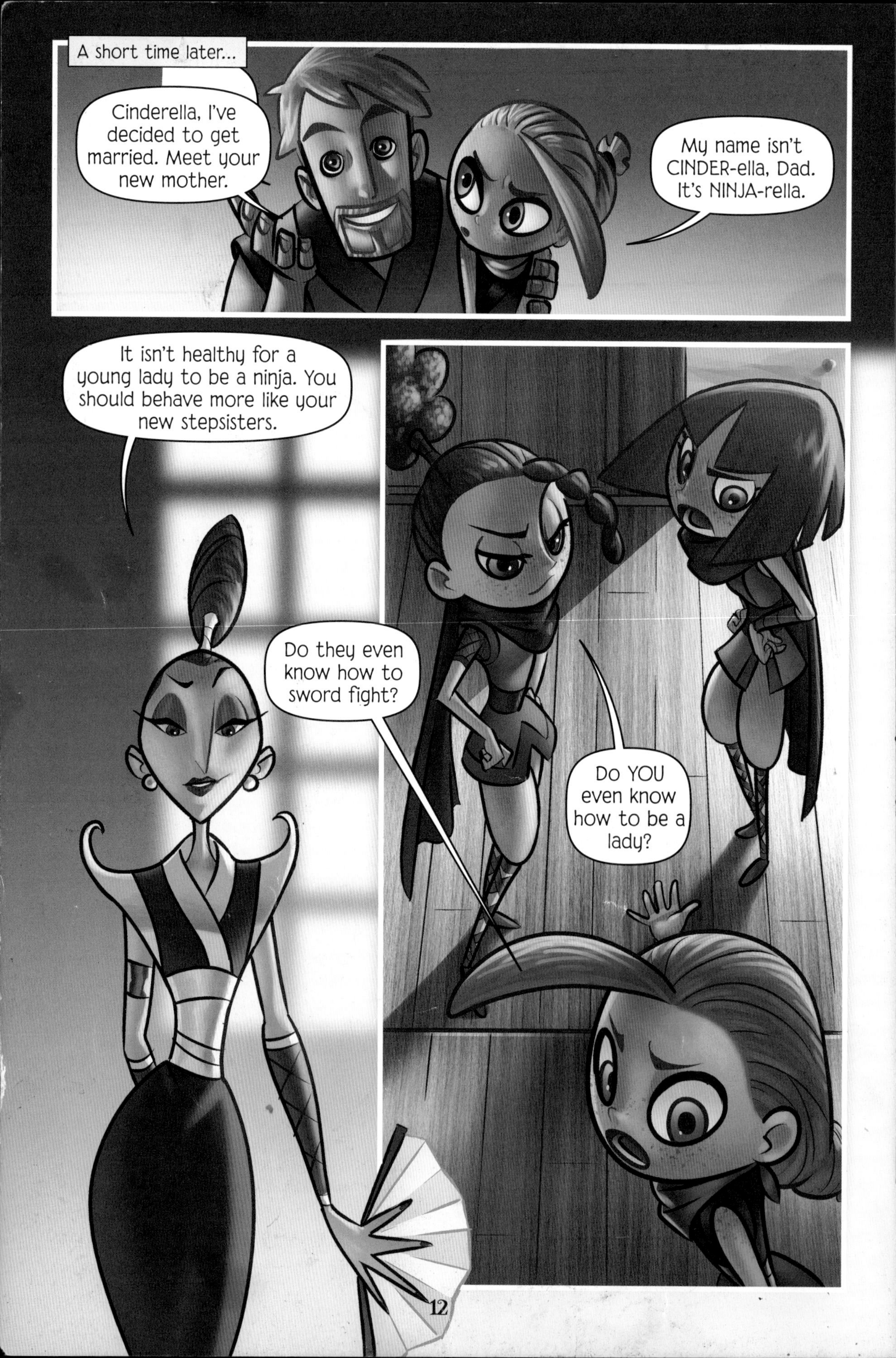

A short time later...
Cinderella, I've decided to get married. Meet your new mother.
My name isn't CINDER-ella, Dad. It's NINJA-rella.
It isn't healthy for a young lady to be a ninja. You should behave more like your new stepsisters.
Do they even know how to sword fight?
Do YOU even know how to be a lady?

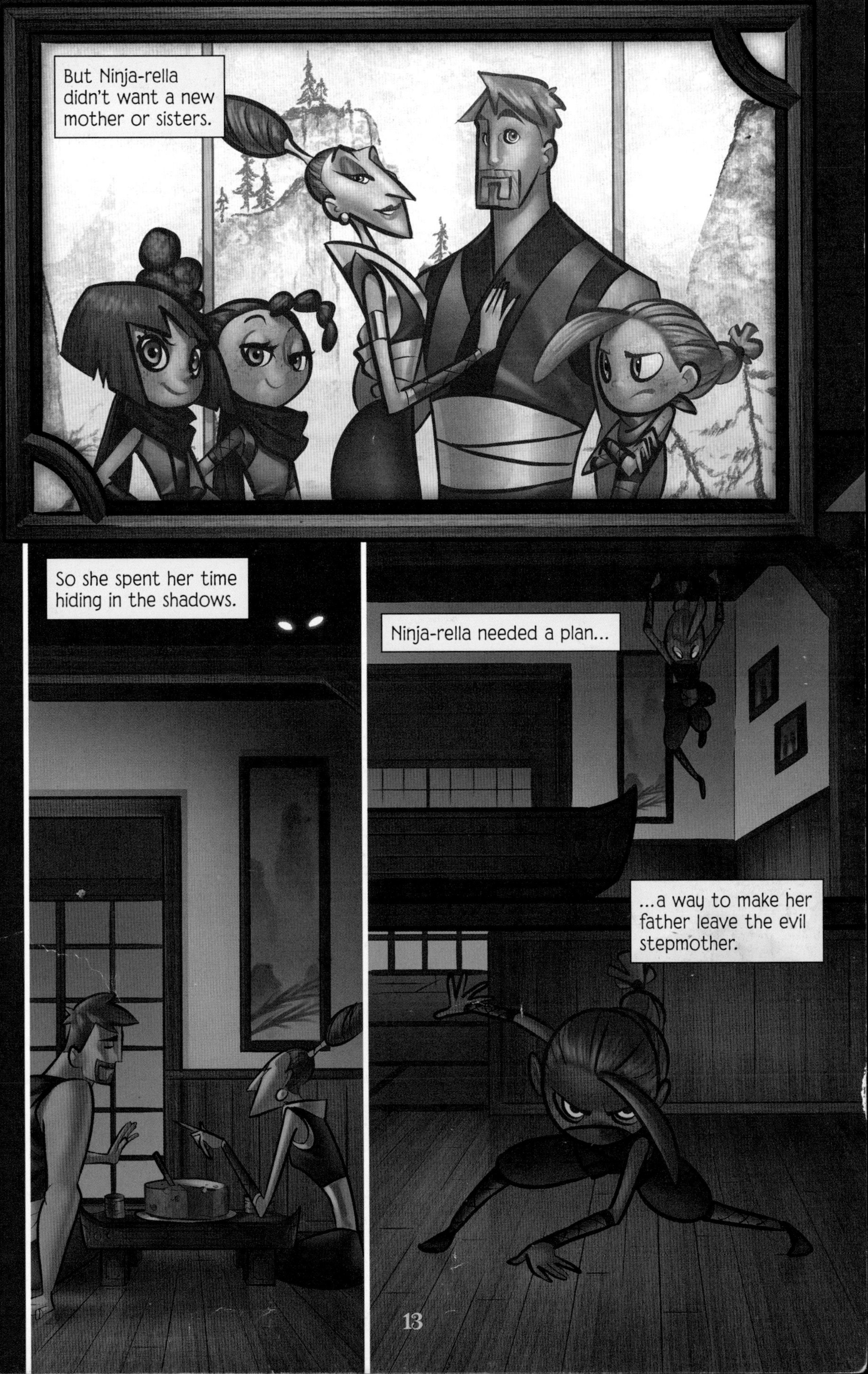
But Ninja-rella didn't want a new mother or sisters.
So she spent her time hiding in the shadows.
Ninja-rella needed a plan...
...a way to make her father leave the evil stepmother.

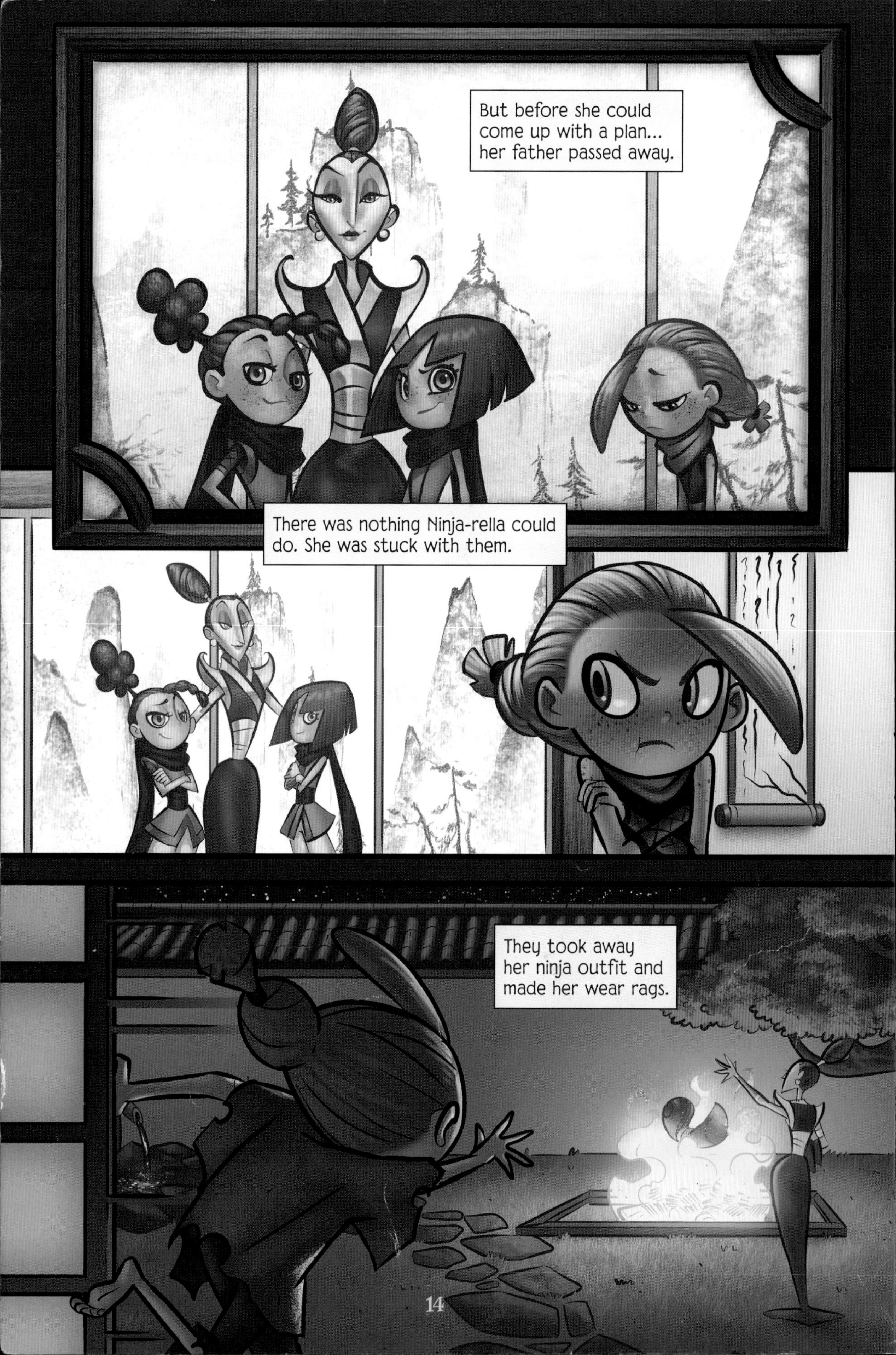
But before she could come up with a plan... her father passed away.
There was nothing Ninja-rella could do. She was stuck with them.
They took away her ninja outfit and made her wear rags.

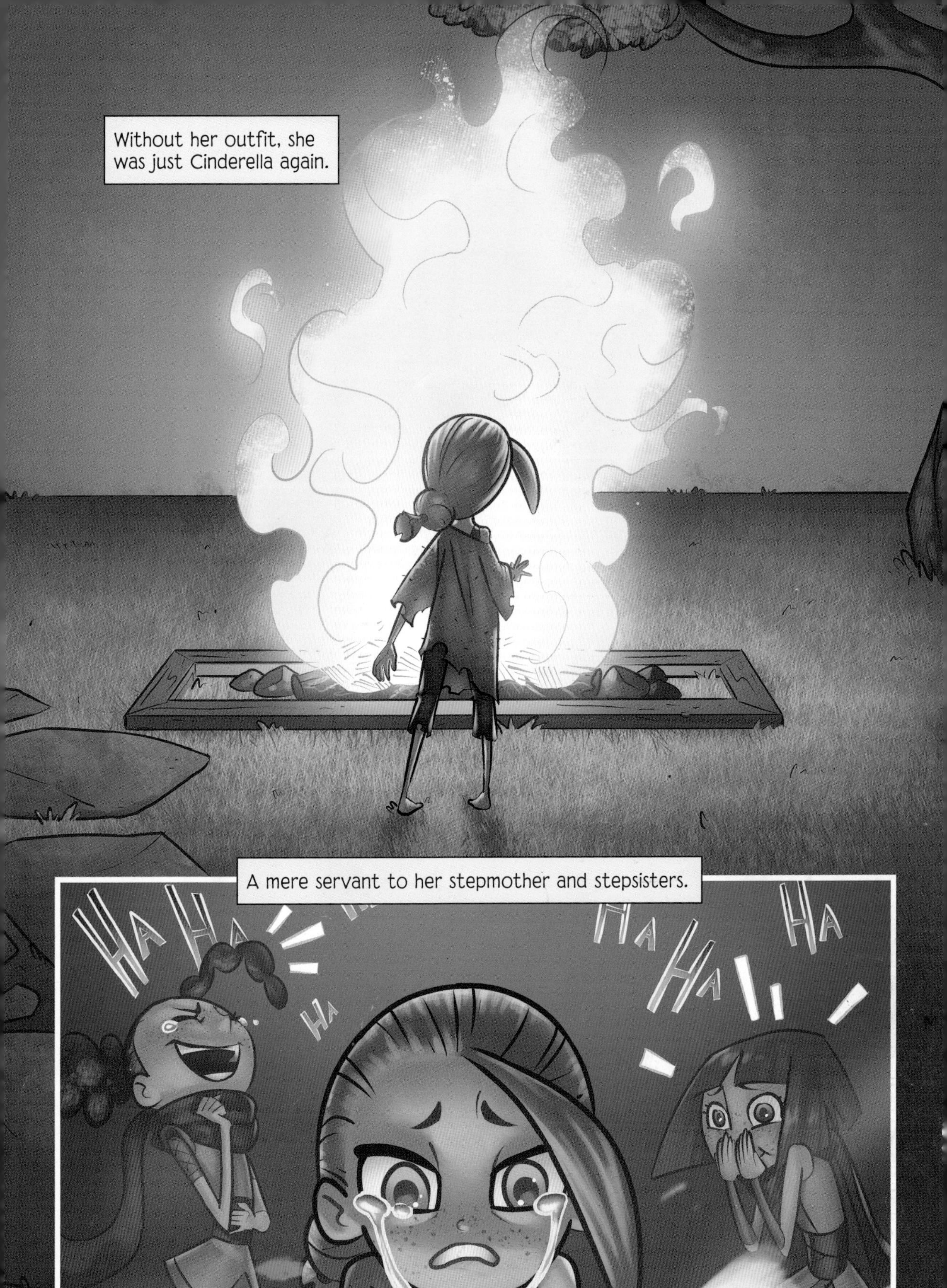
Without her outfit, she
was just Cinderella again.
A mere servant to her stepmother and stepsisters.
HA HA HA
HA
HA HA HA
HA

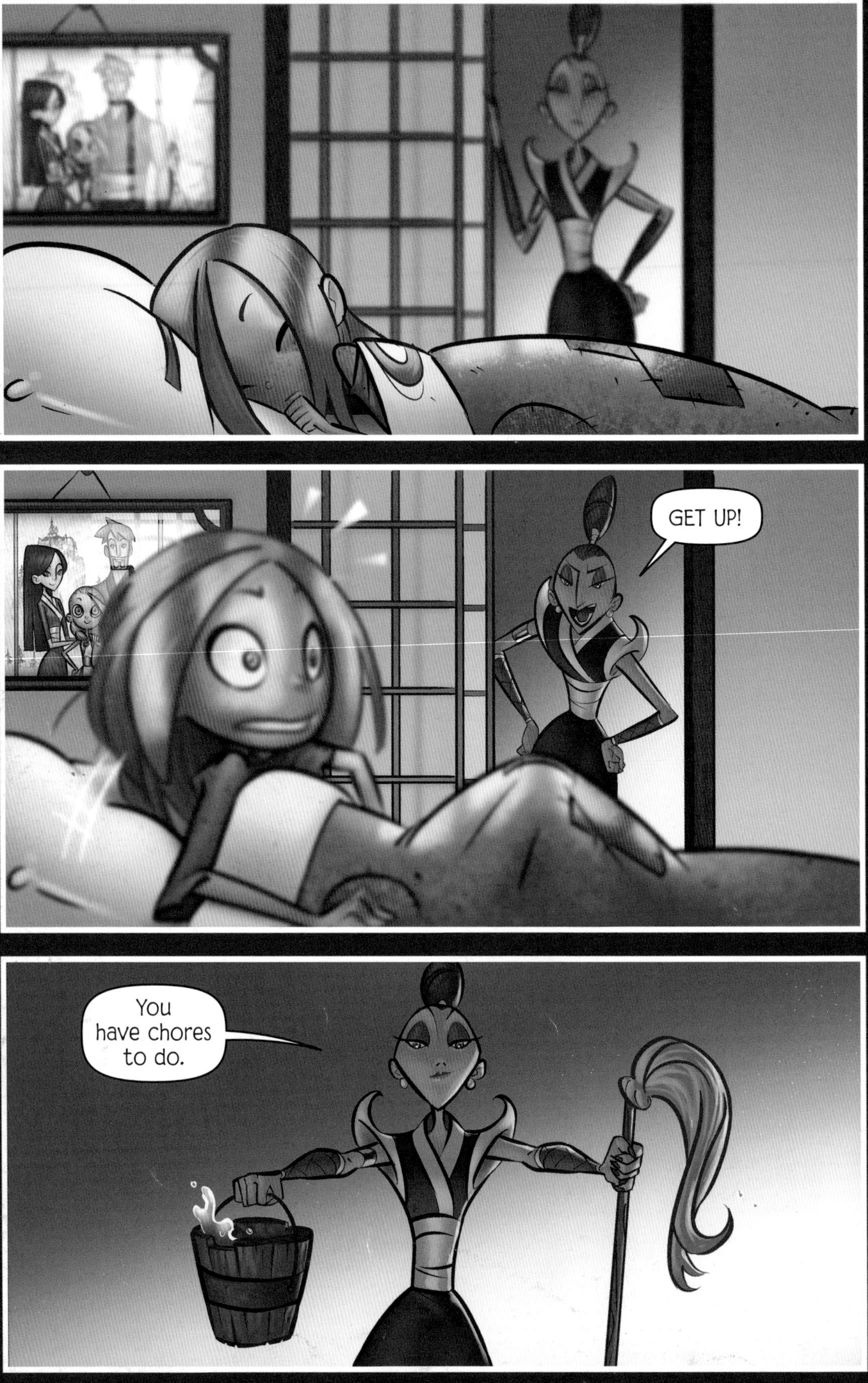
GET UP!
You have chores to do.

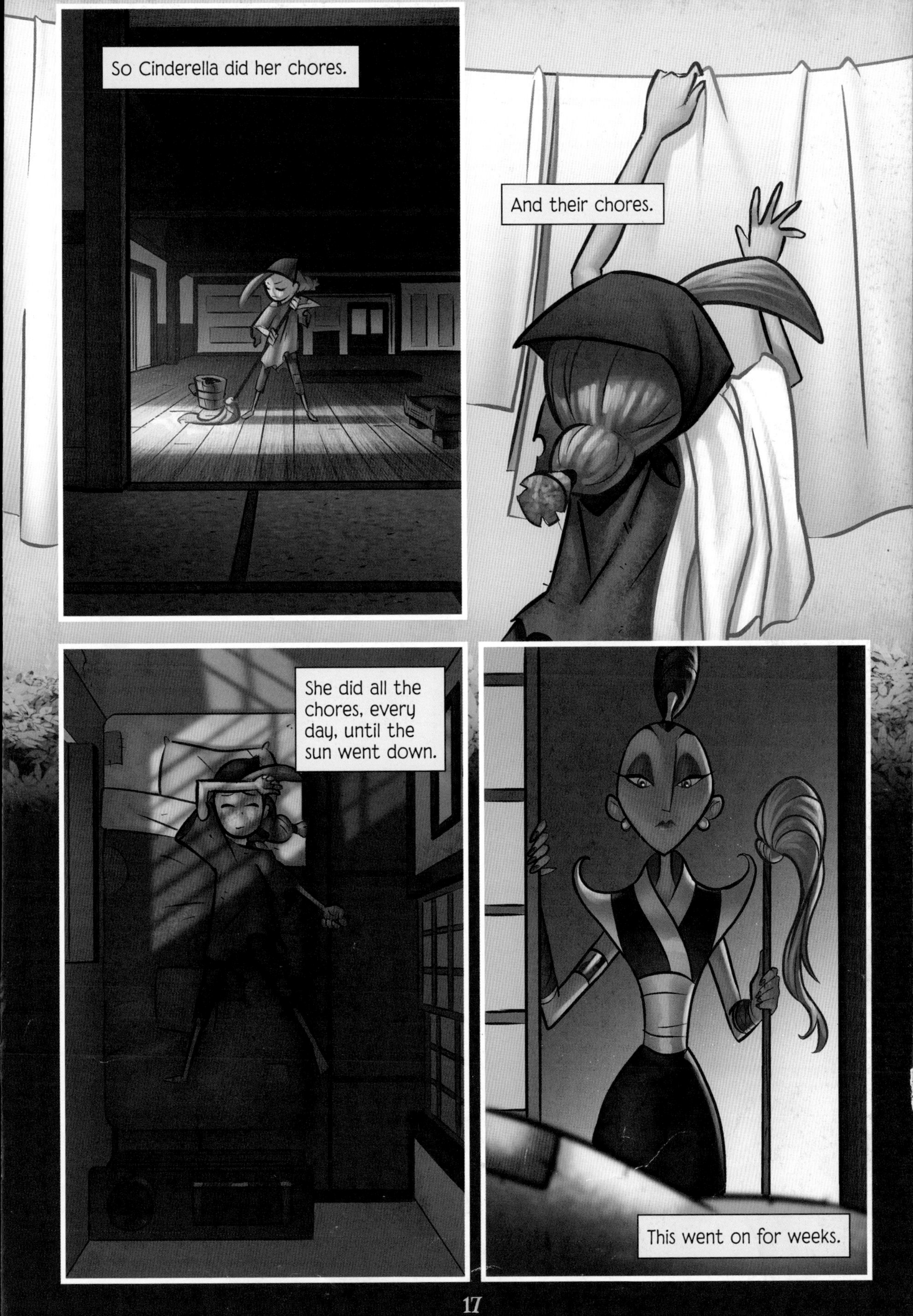
So Cinderella did her chores.
And their chores.
She did all the chores, every day, until the sun went down.
This went on for weeks.

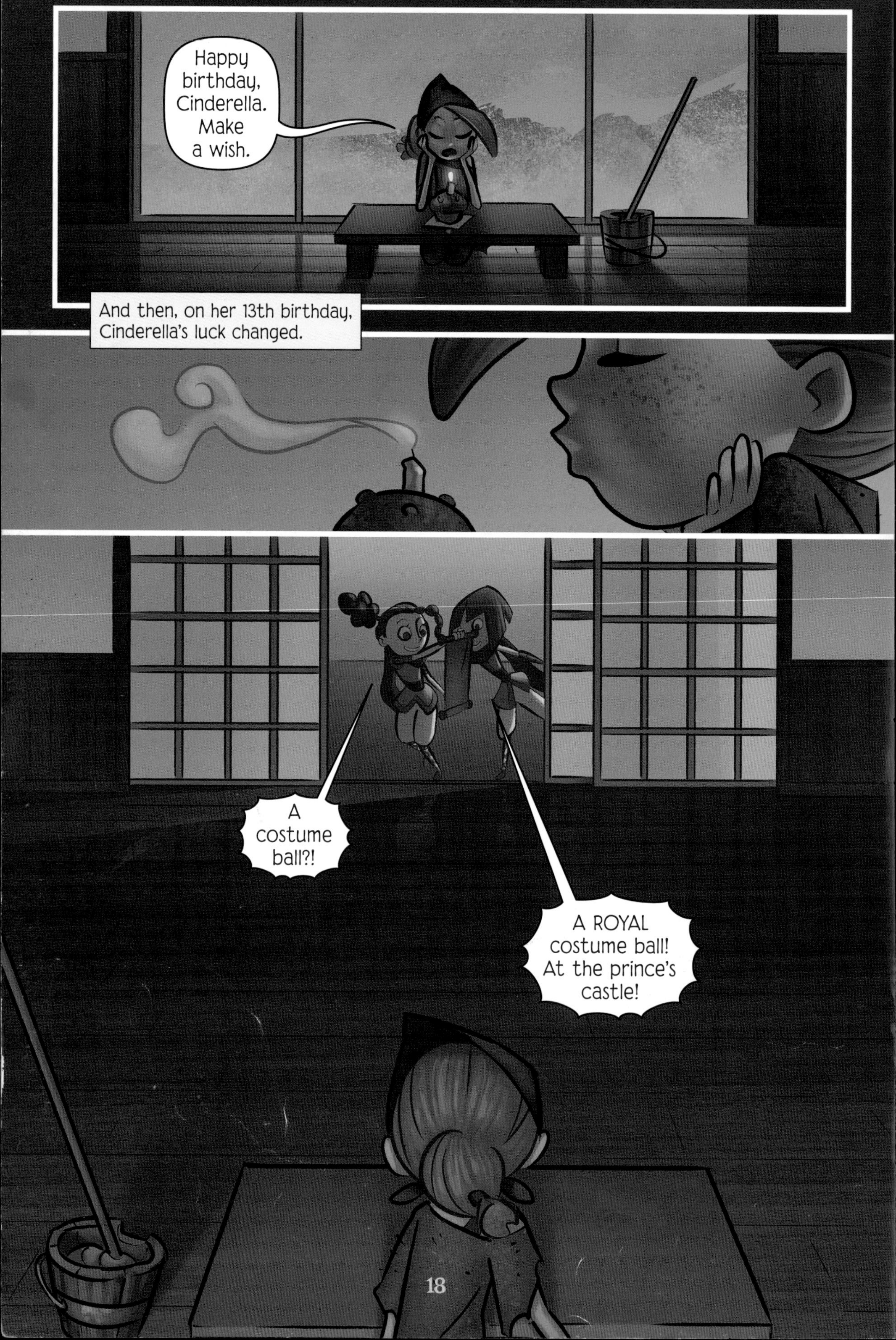
Happy birthday, Cinderella. Make a wish.
And then, on her 13th birthday, Cinderella's luck changed.
A costume ball?!
A ROYAL costume ball! At the prince's castle!

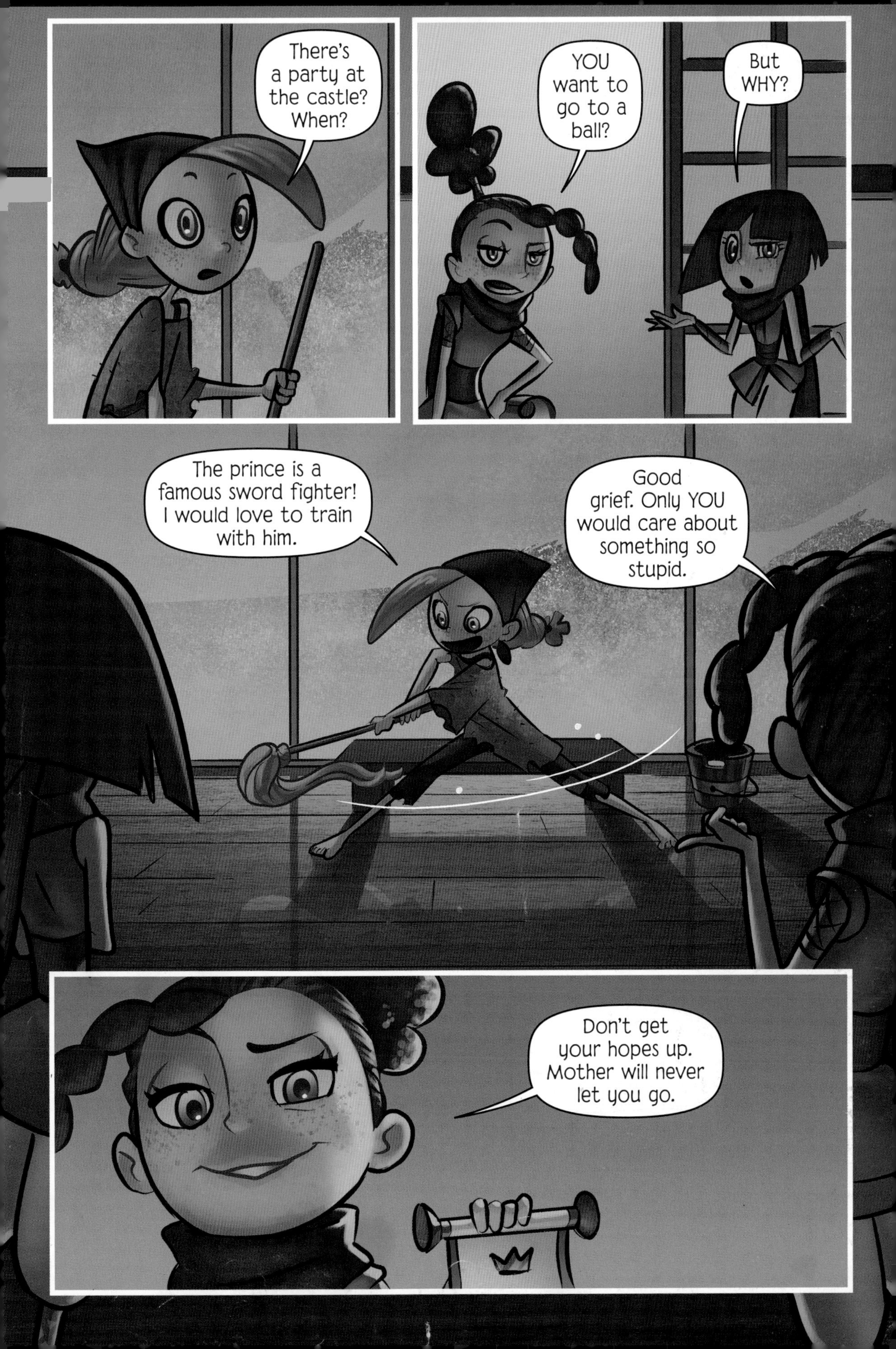
There's a party at the castle? When?
YOU want to go to a ball?
But WHY?
The prince is a famous sword fighter! I would love to train with him.
Good grief. Only YOU would care about something so stupid.
Don't get your hopes up. Mother will never let you go.

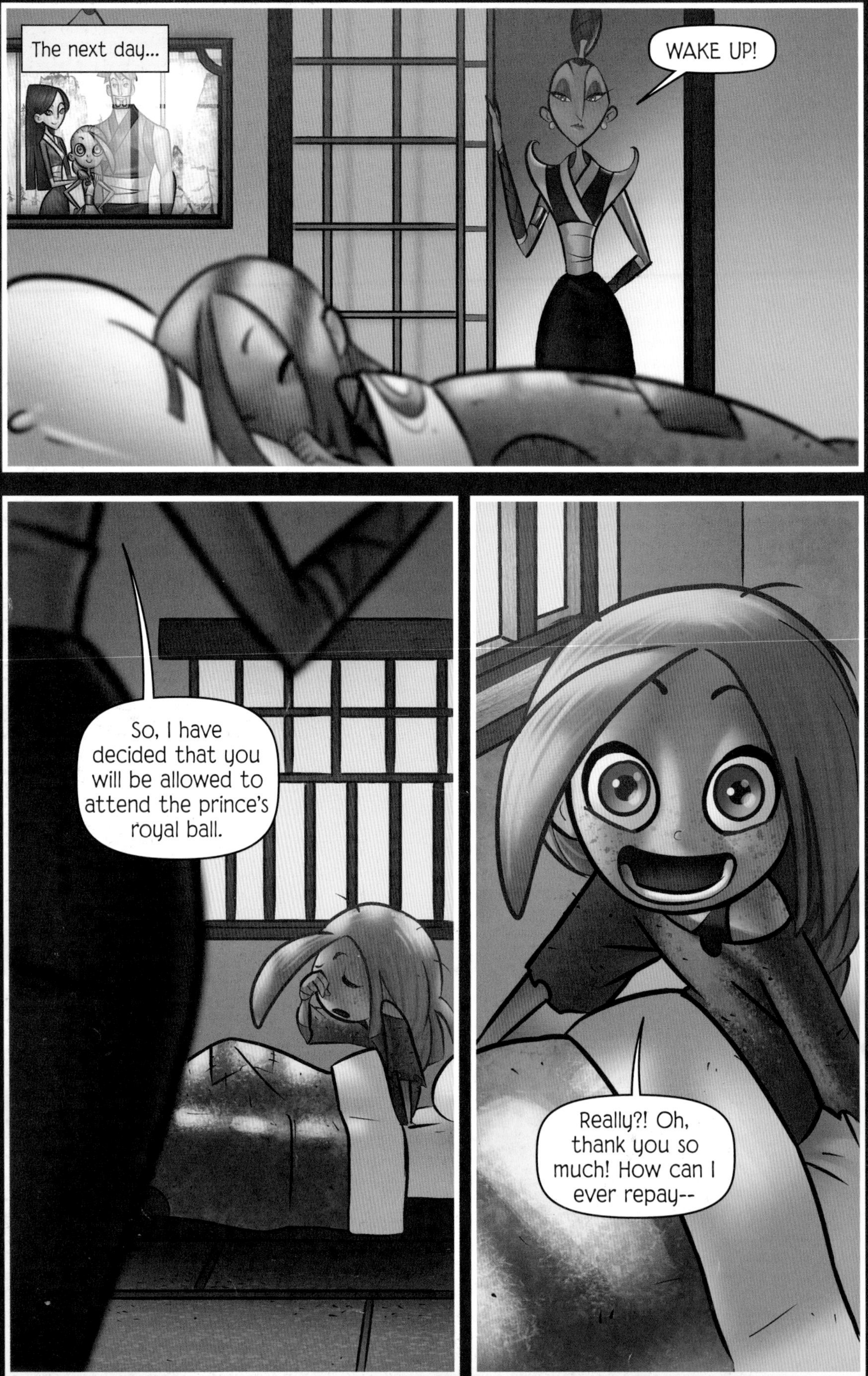
The next day...
WAKE UP!
So, I have decided that you will be allowed to attend the prince's royal ball.
Really?! Oh, thank you so much! How can I ever repay--

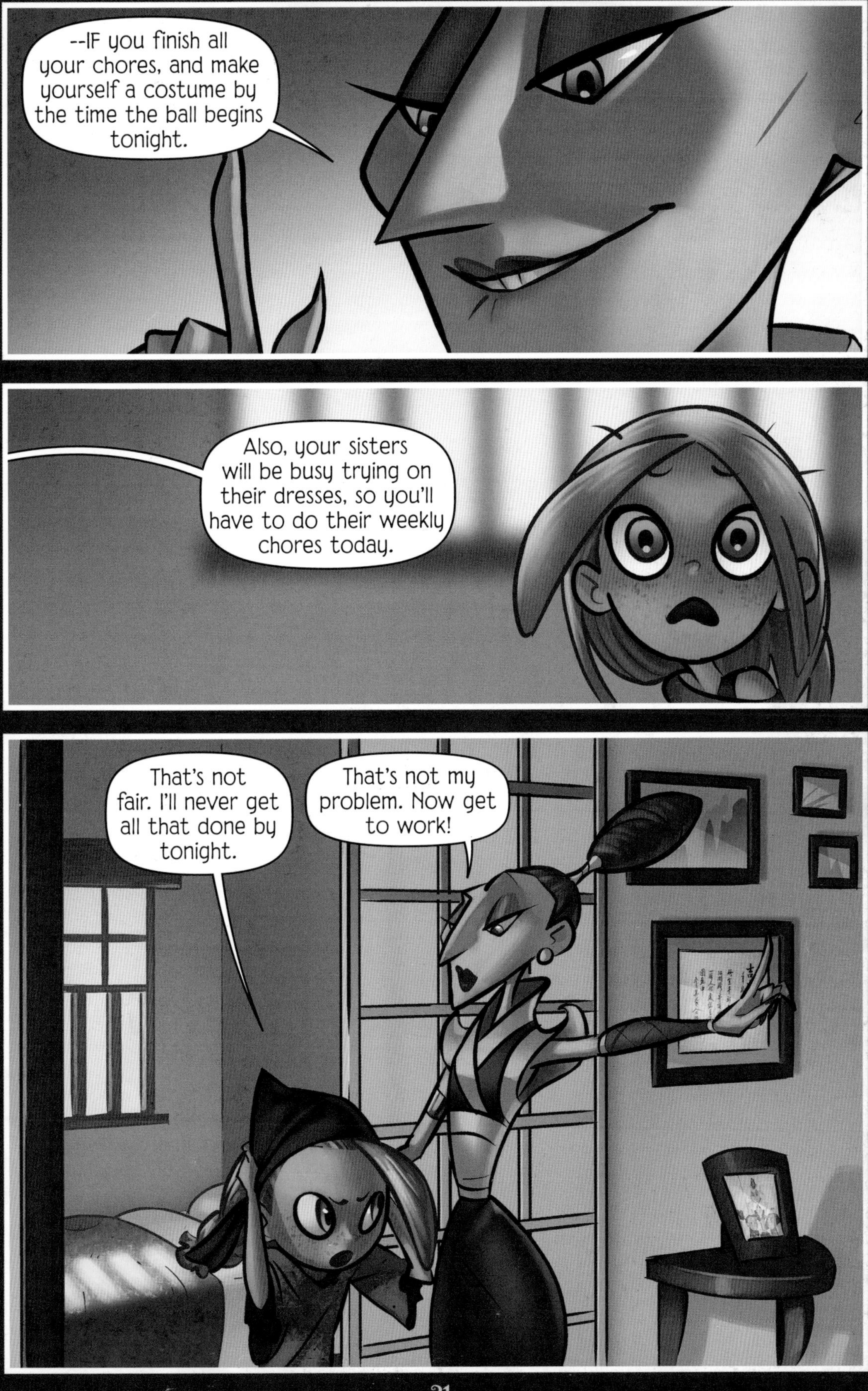
--IF you finish all your chores, and make yourself a costume by the time the ball begins tonight.
Also, your sisters will be busy trying on their dresses, so you'll have to do their weekly chores today.
That's not fair. I'll never get all that done by tonight.
That's not my problem. Now get to work!

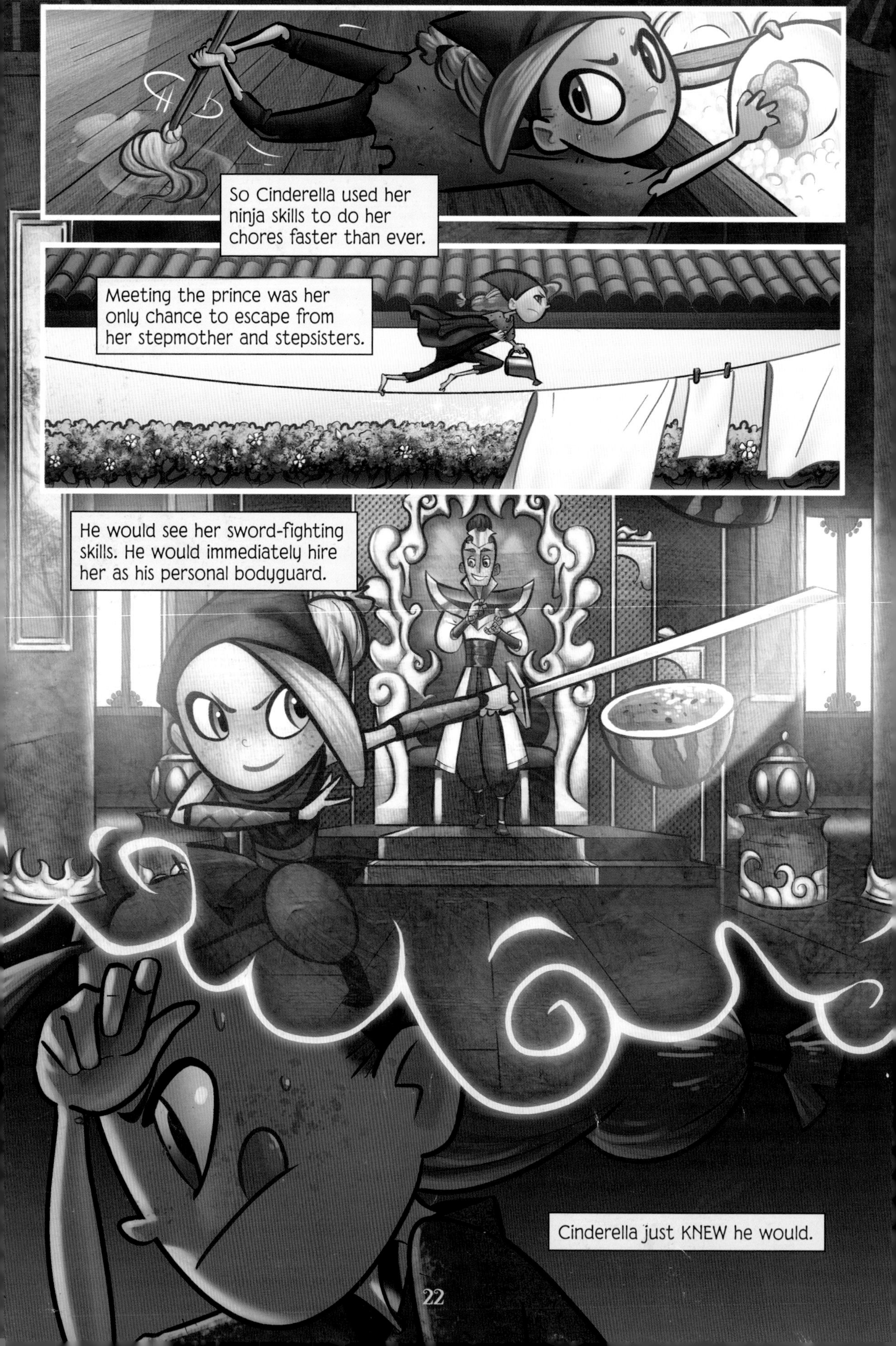
So Cinderella used her ninja skills to do her chores faster than ever.
Meeting the prince was her only chance to escape from her stepmother and stepsisters.
He would see her sword-fighting skills. He would immediately hire her as his personal bodyguard.
Cinderella just KNEW he would.

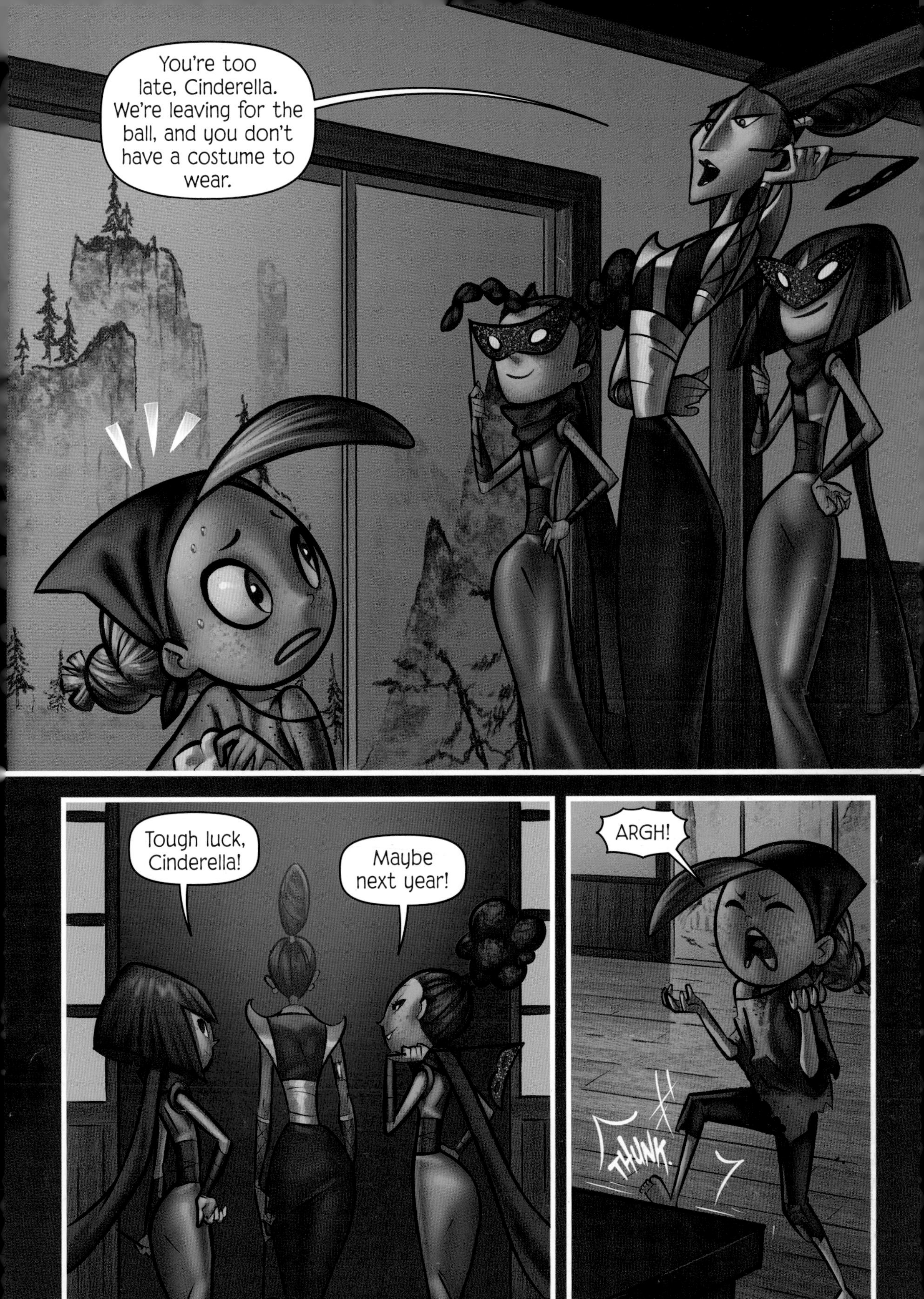
You're too late, Cinderella. We're leaving for the ball, and you don't have a costume to wear.
Tough luck, Cinderella!
Maybe next year!
ARGH!
THUNK.

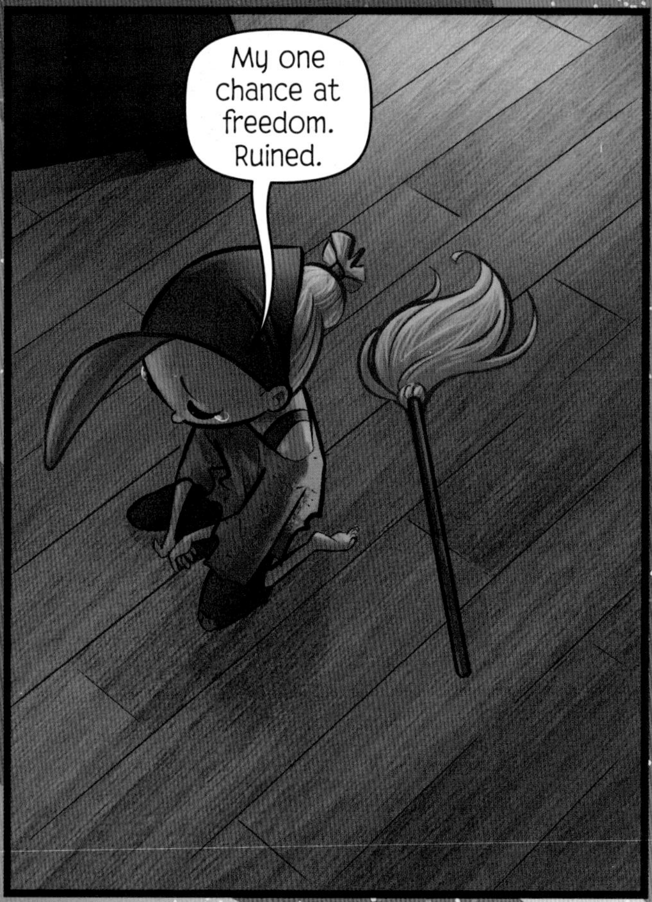
My one chance at freedom. Ruined.

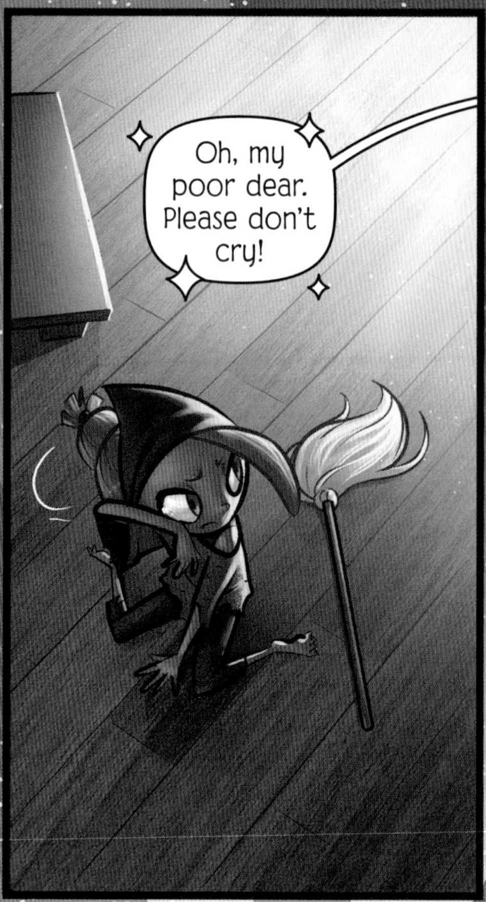
Oh, my poor dear. Please don't cry!

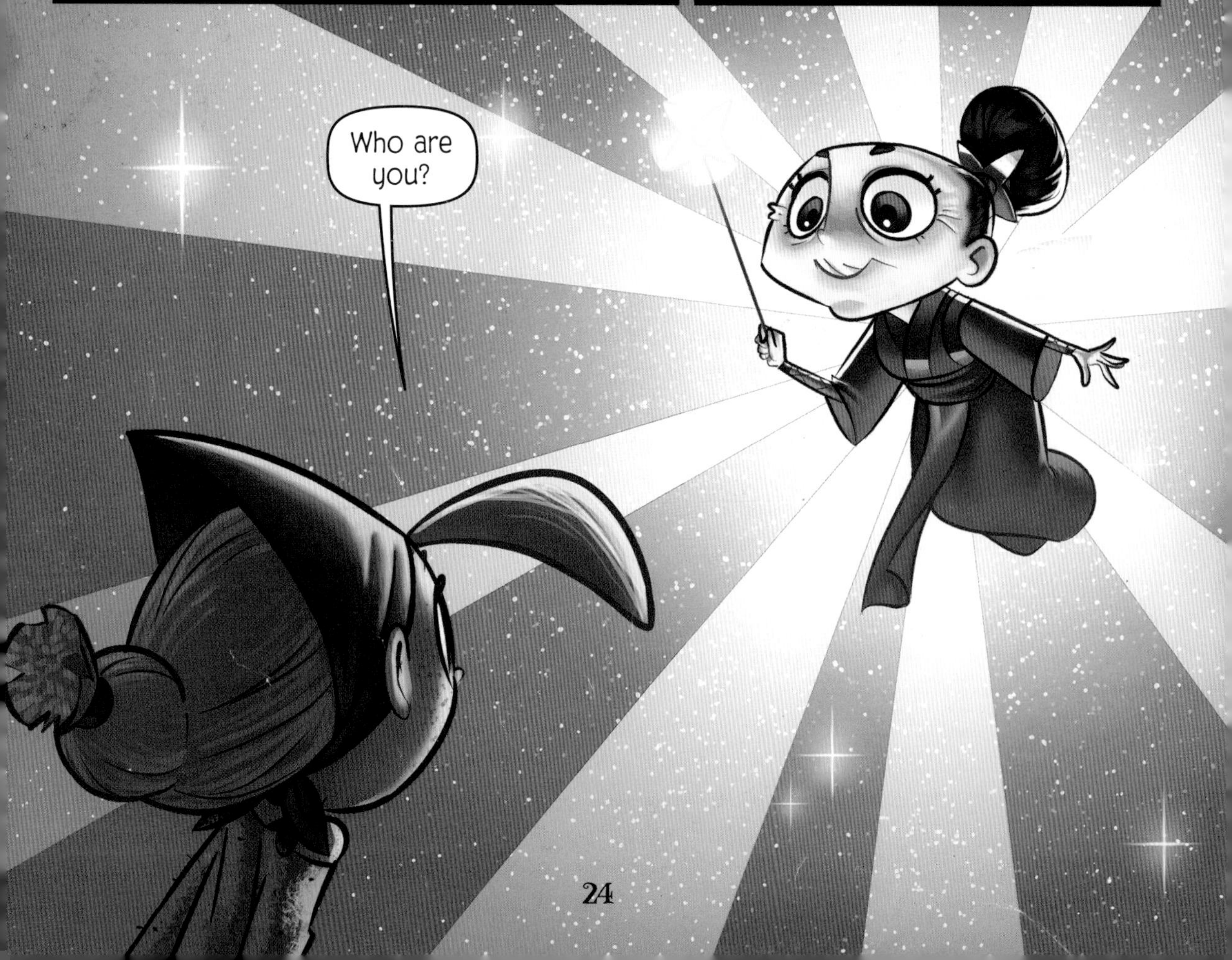
Who are you?

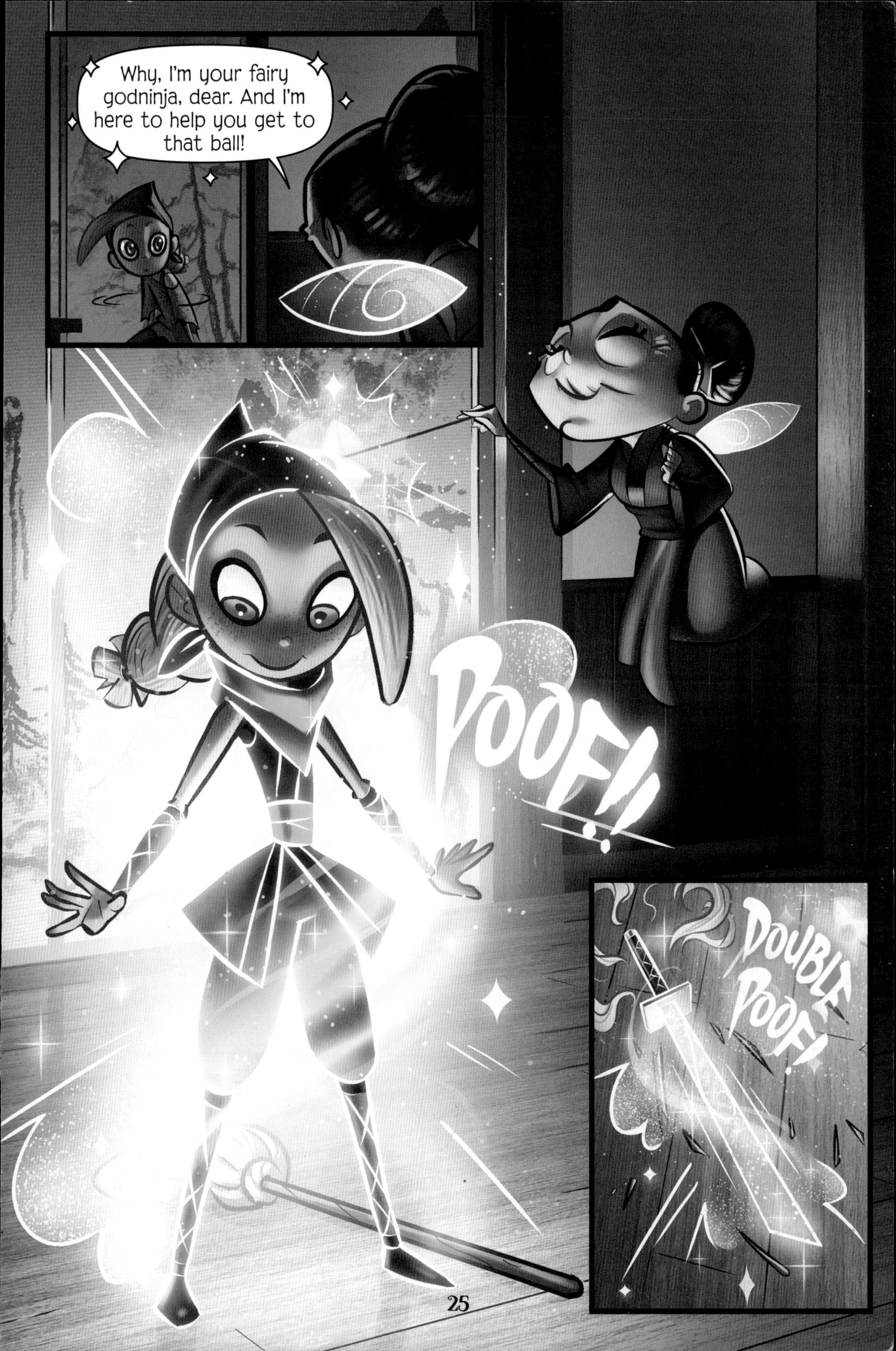
Why, I'm your fairy godninja, dear. And I'm here to help you get to that ball!
POOF!!
DOUBLE POOF!

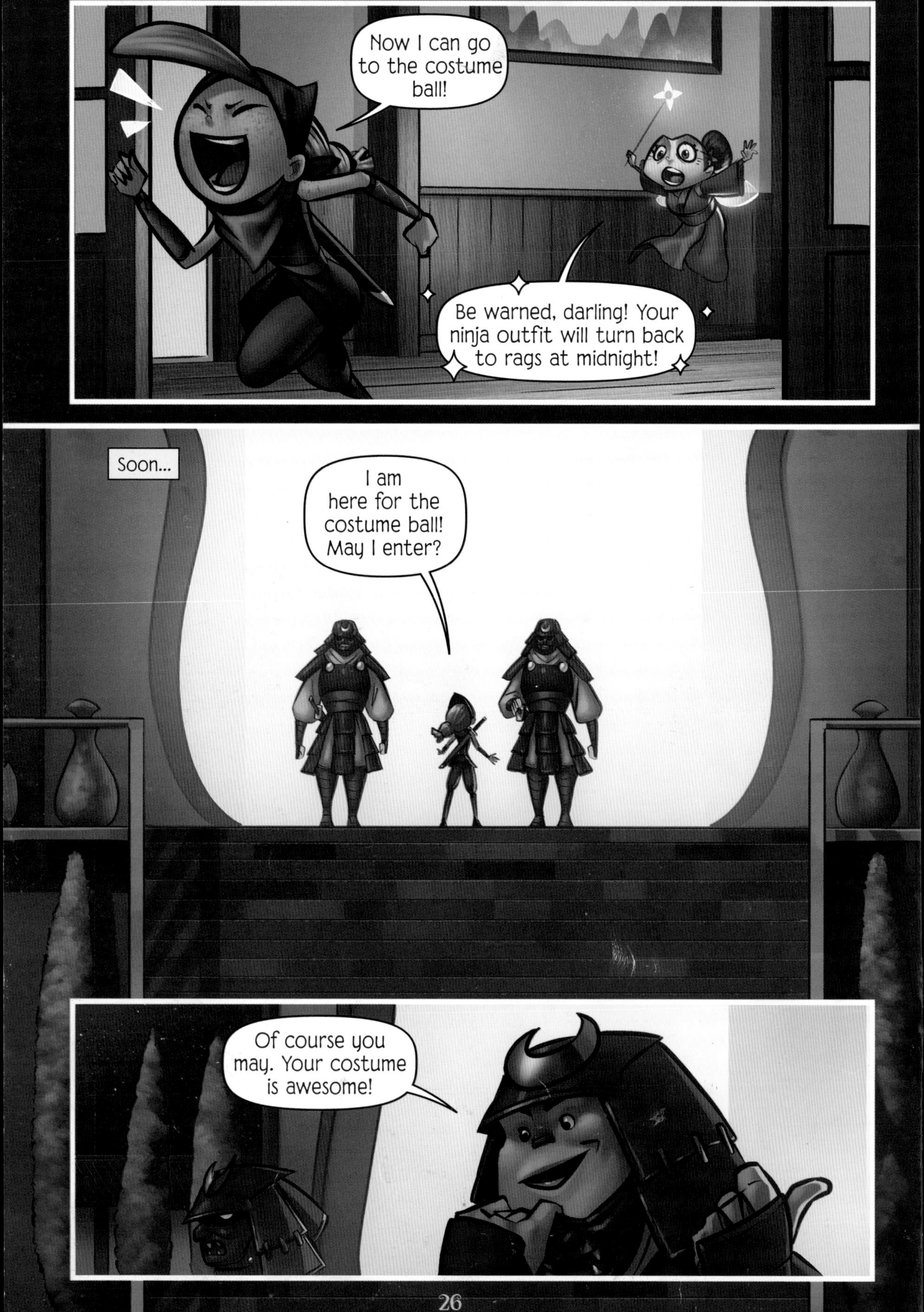
Now I can go to the costume ball!
Be warned, darling! Your ninja outfit will turn back to rags at midnight!
Soon...
I am here for the costume ball! May I enter?
Of course you may. Your costume is awesome!

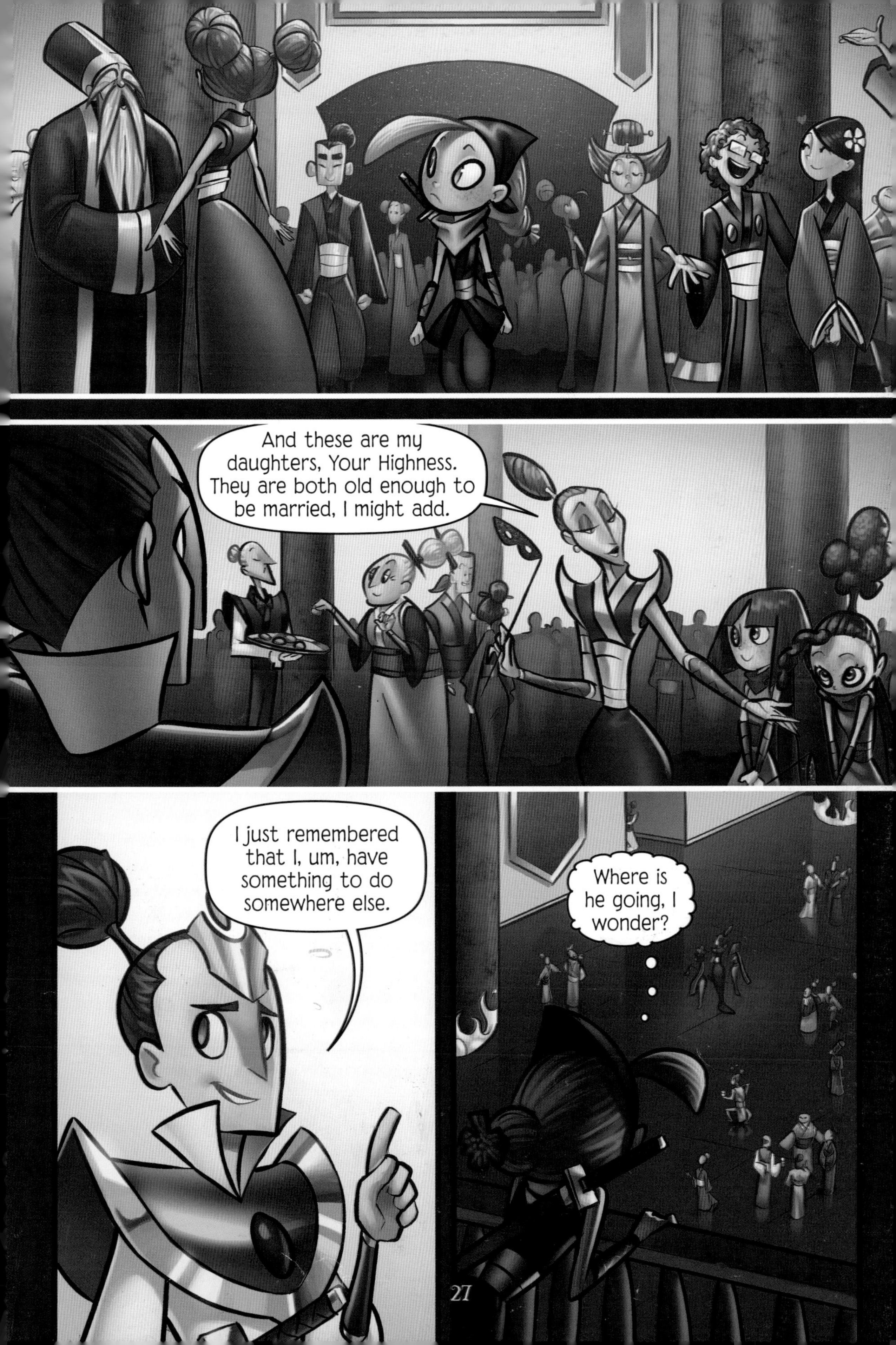
And these are my daughters, Your Highness. They are both old enough to be married, I might add.
I just remembered that I, um, have something to do somewhere else.
Where is he going, I wonder?

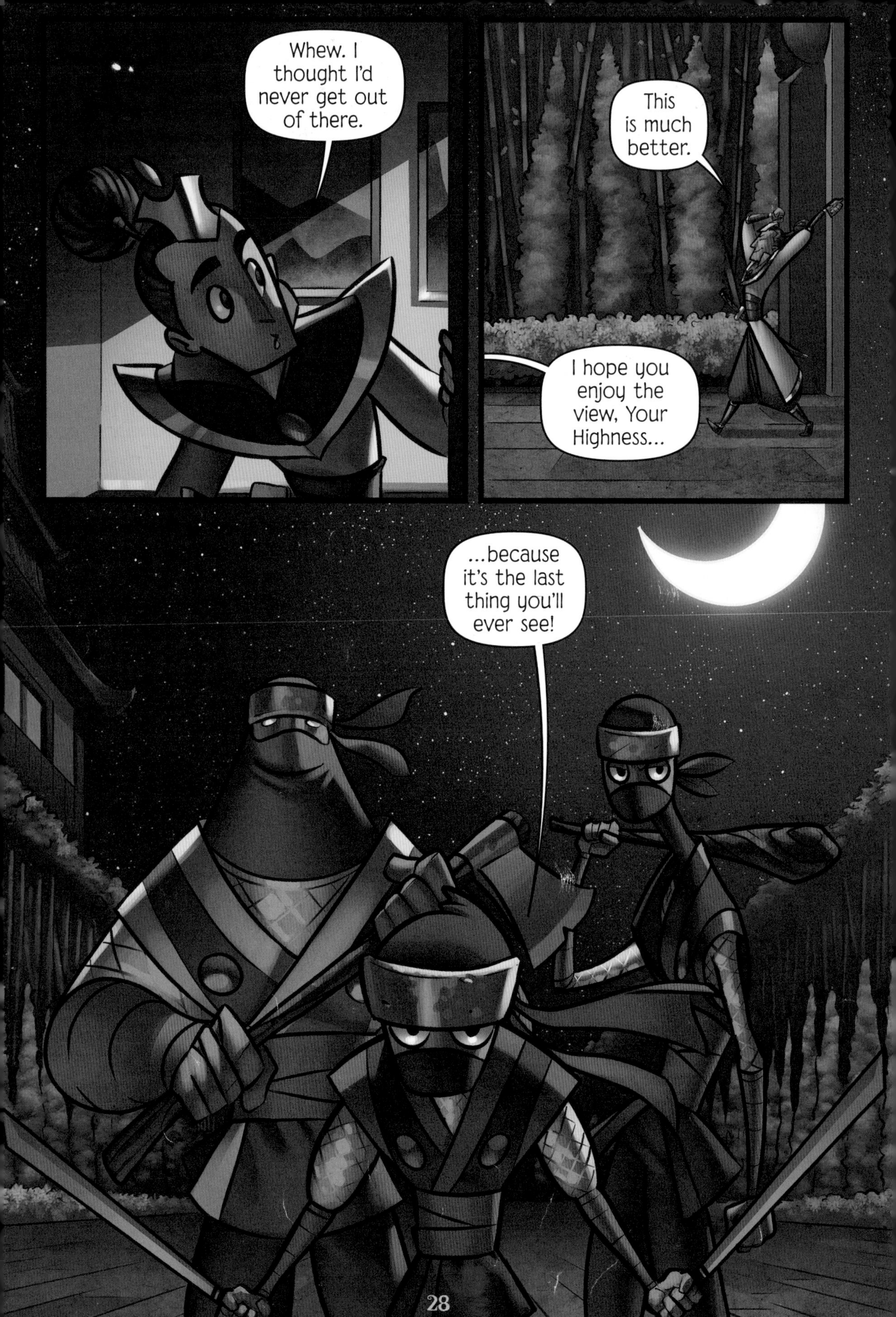
Whew. I thought I'd never get out of there.
This is much better.
I hope you enjoy the view, Your Highness...
...because it's the last thing you'll ever see!

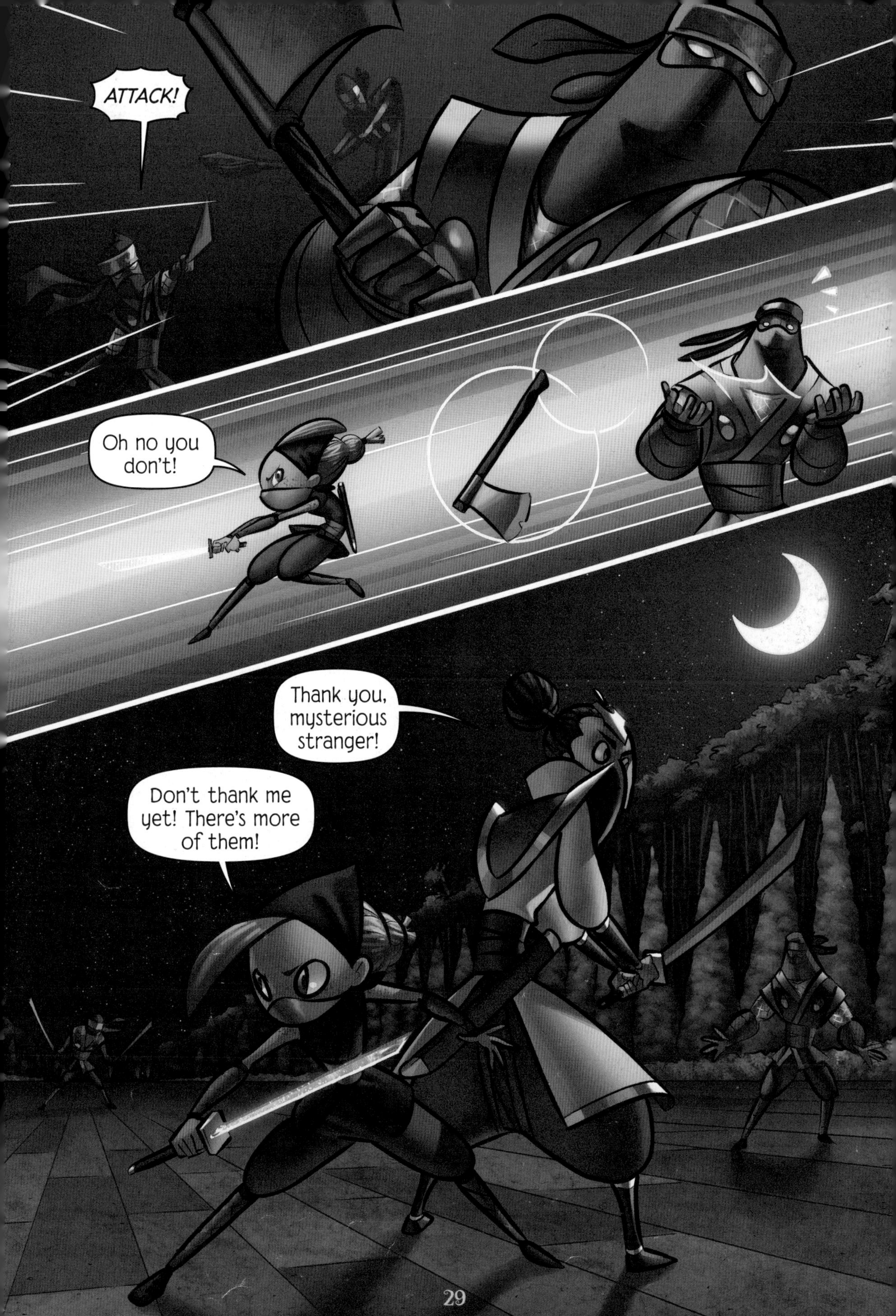
ATTACK!
Oh no you don't!
Thank you, mysterious stranger!
Don't thank me yet! There's more of them!

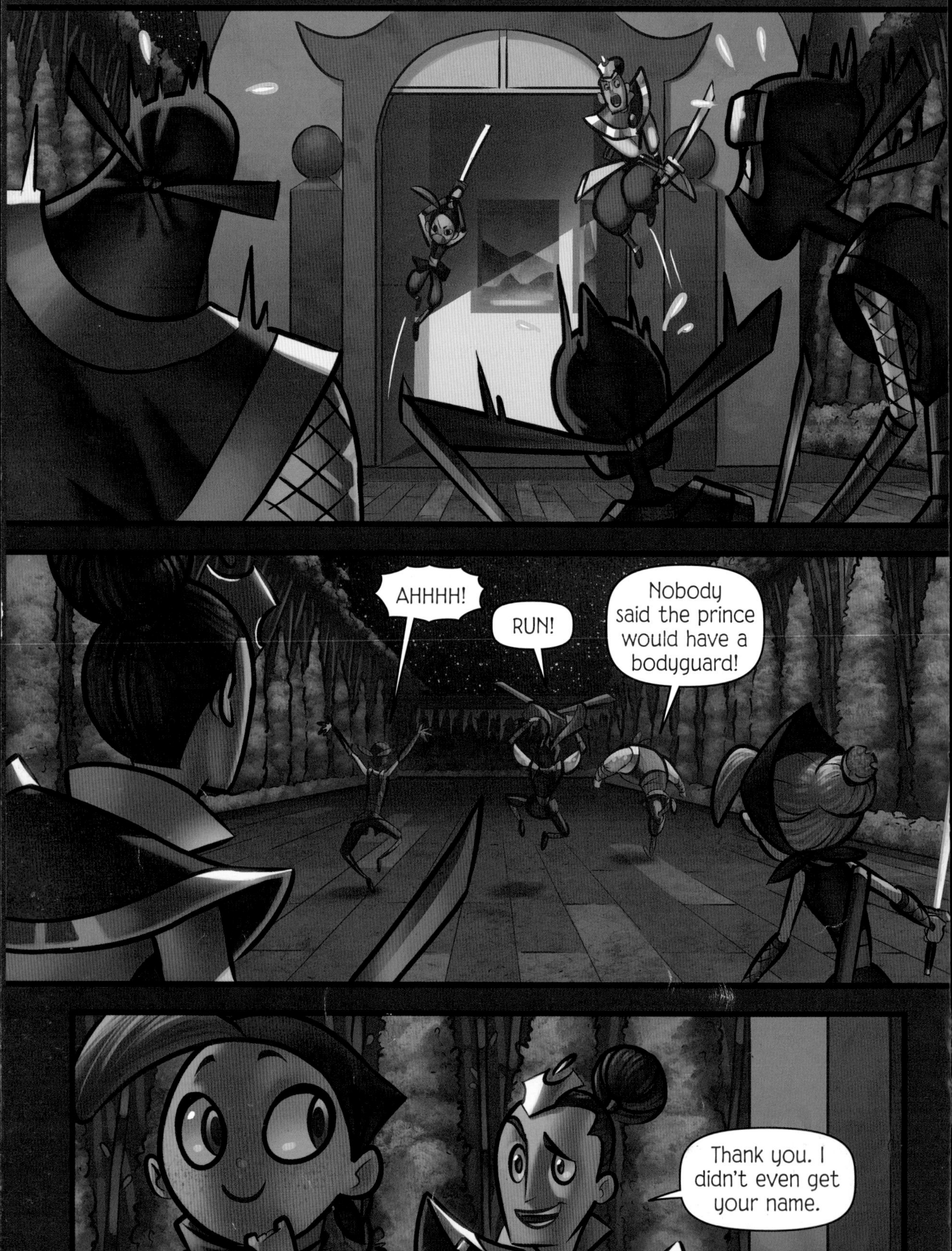
AHHHH!
RUN!
Nobody said the prince would have a bodyguard!
Thank you. I didn't even get your name.

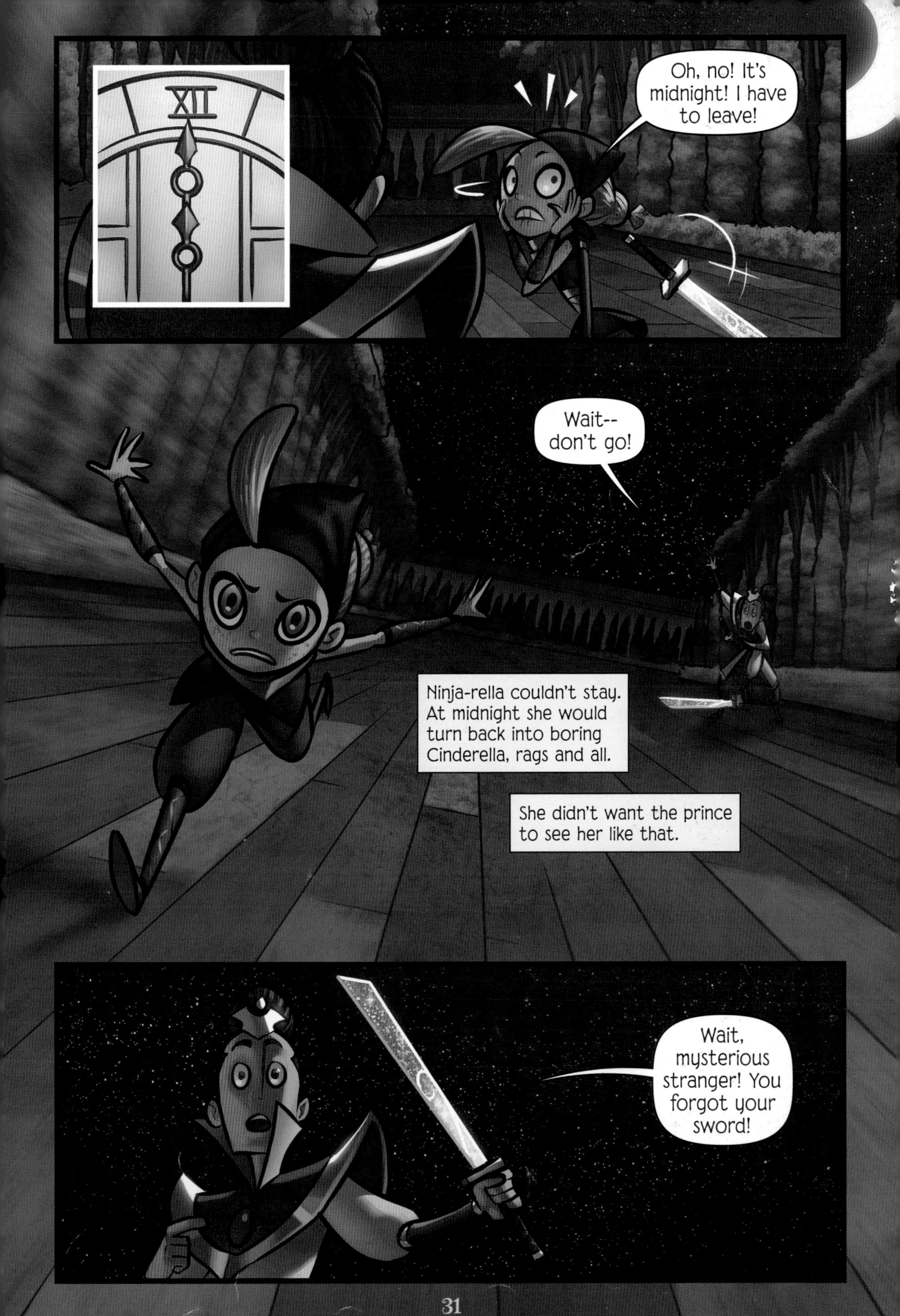

Oh, no! It's midnight! I have to leave!
Wait-- don't go!
Ninja-rella couldn't stay. At midnight she would turn back into boring Cinderella, rags and all.
She didn't want the prince to see her like that.
Wait, mysterious stranger! You forgot your sword!

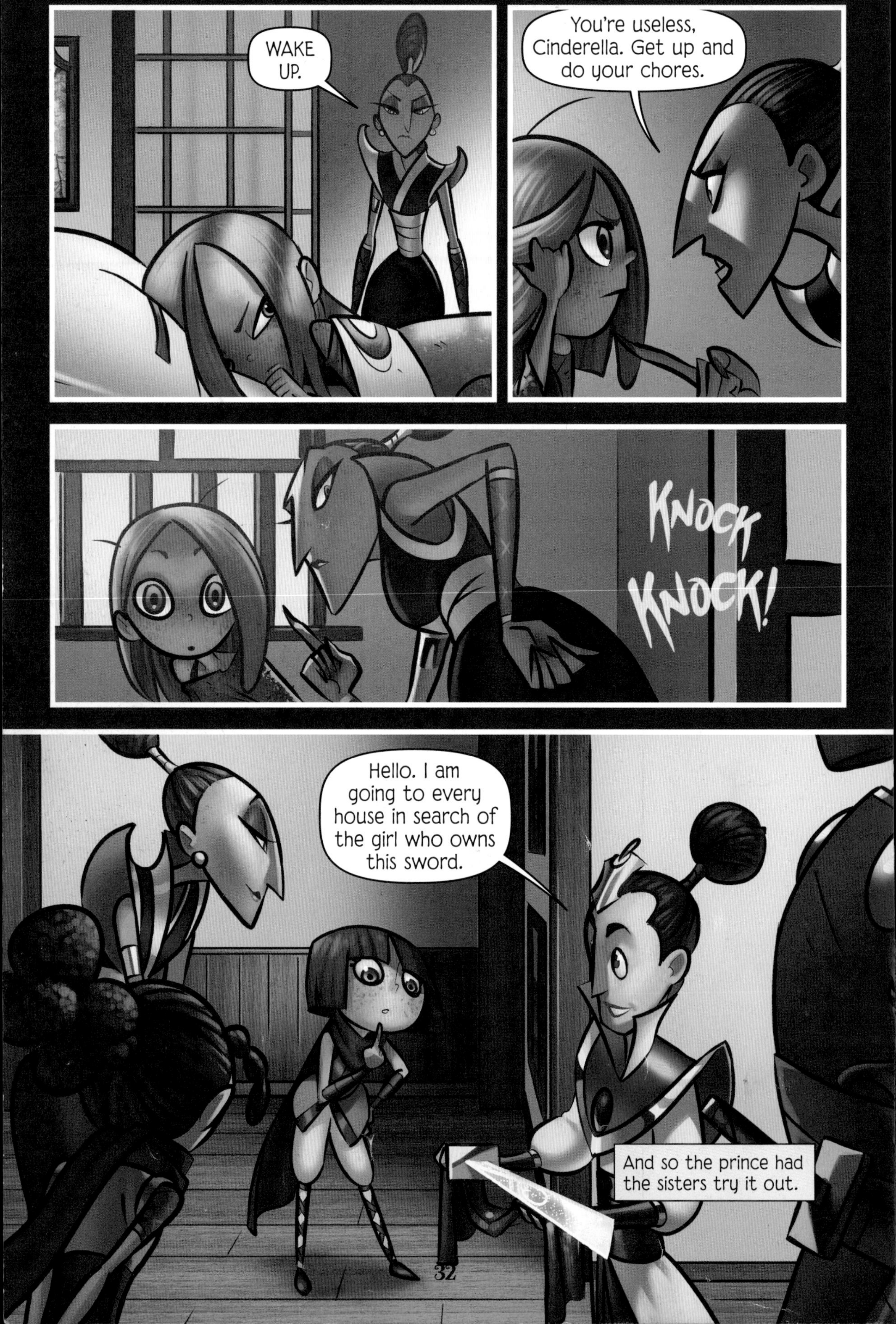
WAKE UP.
You're useless, Cinderella. Get up and do your chores.
KNOCK KNOCK!
Hello. I am going to every house in search of the girl who owns this sword.
And so the prince had the sisters try it out.

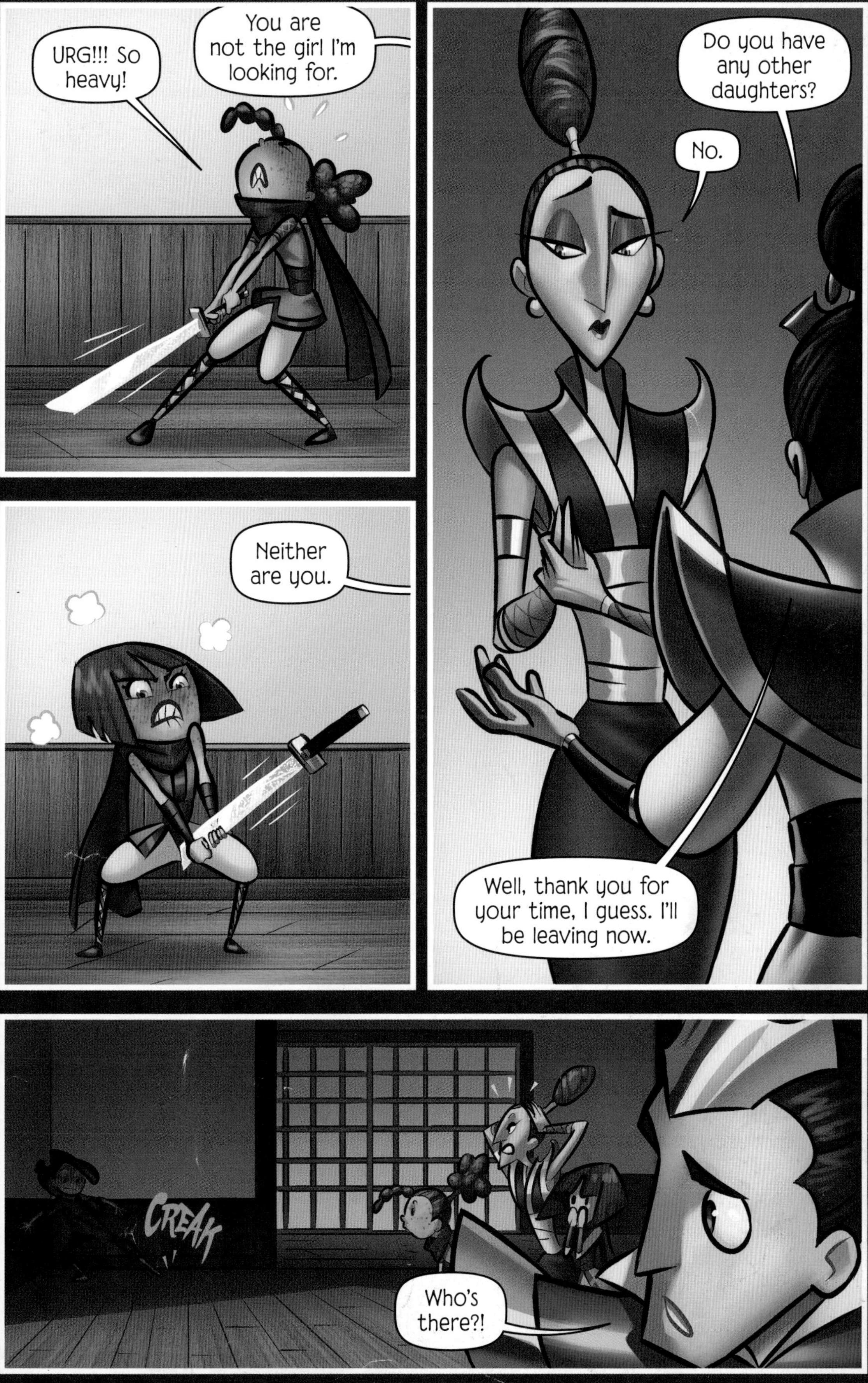
You are not the girl I'm looking for.
URG!!! So heavy!
Neither are you.
Do you have any other daughters?
No.
Well, thank you for your time, I guess. I'll be leaving now.
CREAK
Who's there?!

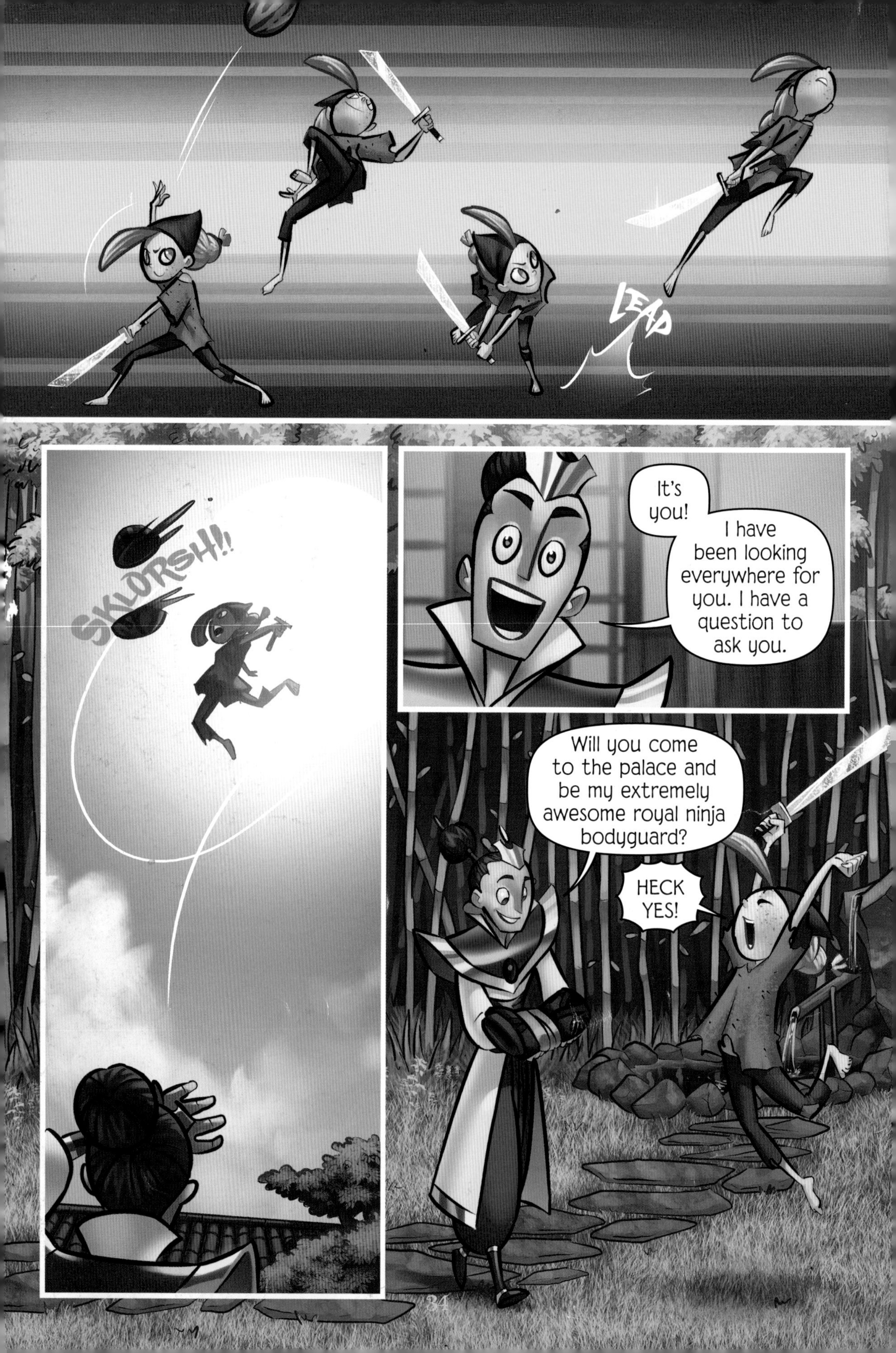
LEAP
SKLORSH!!
It's you!
I have been looking everywhere for you. I have a question to ask you.
Will you come to the palace and be my extremely awesome royal ninja bodyguard?
HECK YES!

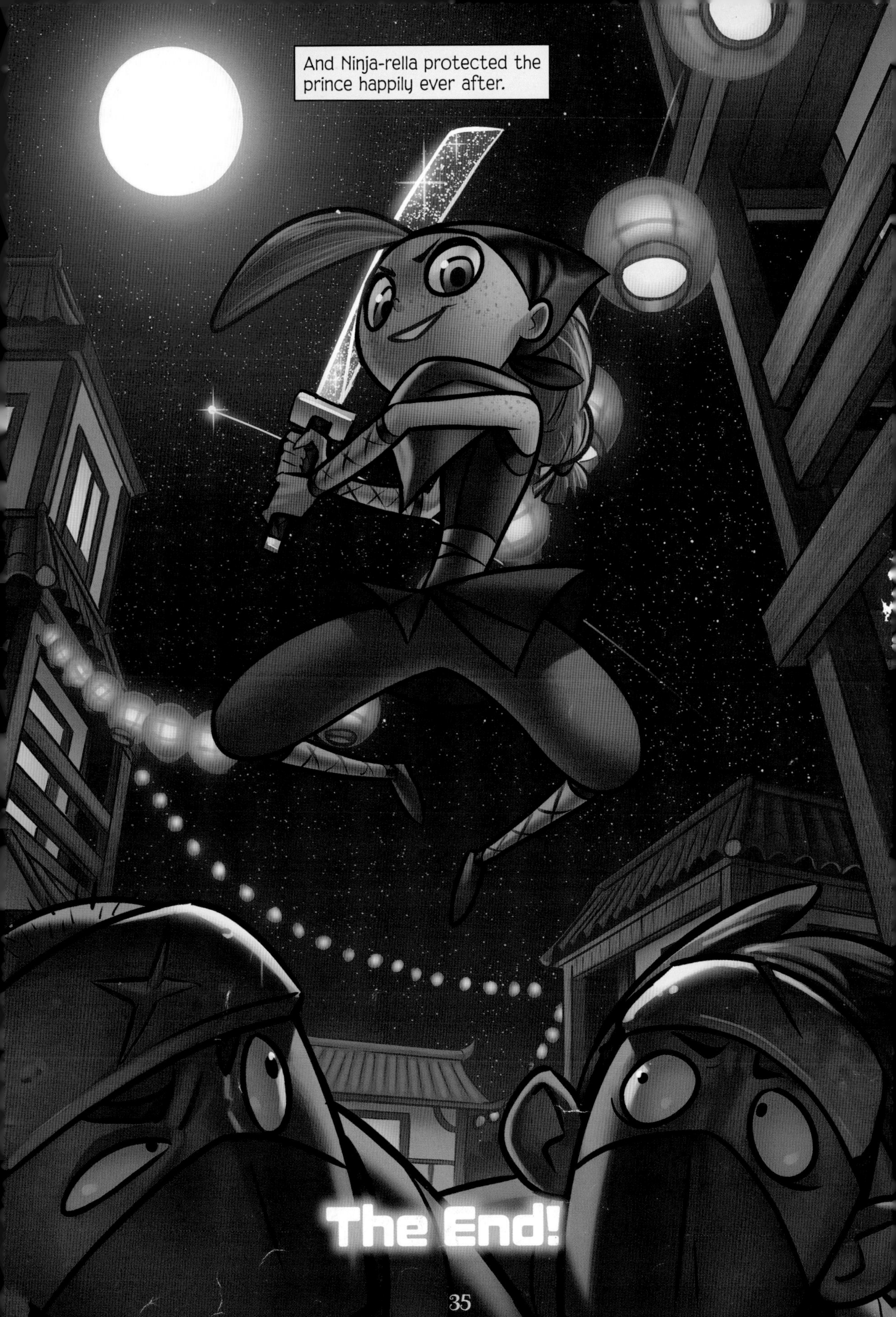
And Ninja-rella protected the prince happily ever after.
The End!

ALL ABOUT THE ORIGINAL TALE!

The story of Cinderella has been around for ages. The first popular version of the tale was *Cenerentola* by Giambattista Basile, published in 1634. This Italian tale tells the story of a widowed prince who has a daughter named Zezolla (Cinderella) who convinces her father to marry her nanny. After the wedding, the nanny moves in with all six of her own daughters. The stepsisters treat Zezolla like their own personal slave, making the girl miserable.

While traveling, Zezolla's father meets a magical fairy who gives presents to him for Zezolla. He gives her a golden spade and bucket, a silk napkin, and a small tree. Zezolla plants the tree and cares for it. One day, a magical fairy emerges from its branches. To thank Zezolla for taking care of her home, the fairy dresses Zezolla in beautiful clothes and slippers so she can attend the king's royal ball.

At the ball, the king falls in love with Zezolla at first sight, but she runs away before the king can find out who she is. Eventually, the king's servant discovers one of Zezolla's slippers that she left behind. So the king invites all of the ladies in the land to try on the special shoe. When Zezolla draws near, the shoe jumps from the king's hand onto her foot. They marry and live happily ever after.

Charles Perrault's version of the tale, *Cendrillon*, was written in 1697. It includes the following additions: a magical fairy godmother, a pumpkin-turned-carriage, and special slippers made of glass instead of fabric!

Perrault's additions to the tale likely made it more popular. To this day, most adaptations use his version of the tale, including this one.

A **FAR OUT** GUIDE TO NINJA-RELLA'S TALE TWISTS!

Instead of wanting to marry the prince, Ninja-rella wants to be his bodyguard.

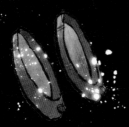

The fairy godmother of old is replaced by a fairy godninja, of course.

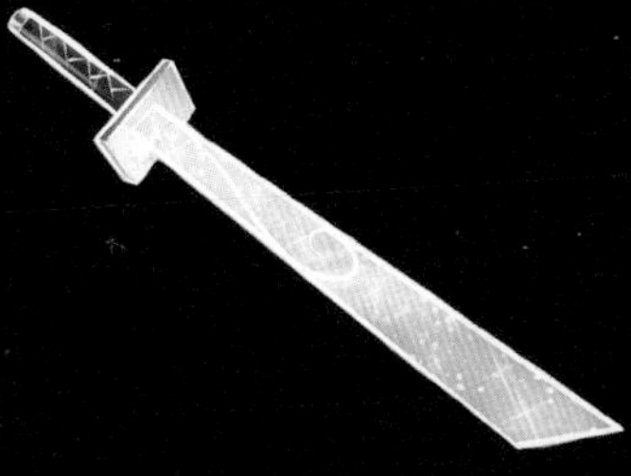

Instead of glass slippers, Ninja-rella gets a special glass katana sword!

And in place of a beautiful gown, Ninja-rella is given a sweet ninja outfit!

Red Riding Hood,
SUPERHERO

A GRAPHIC NOVEL

WRITTEN AND ILLUSTRATED BY
OTIS FRAMPTON

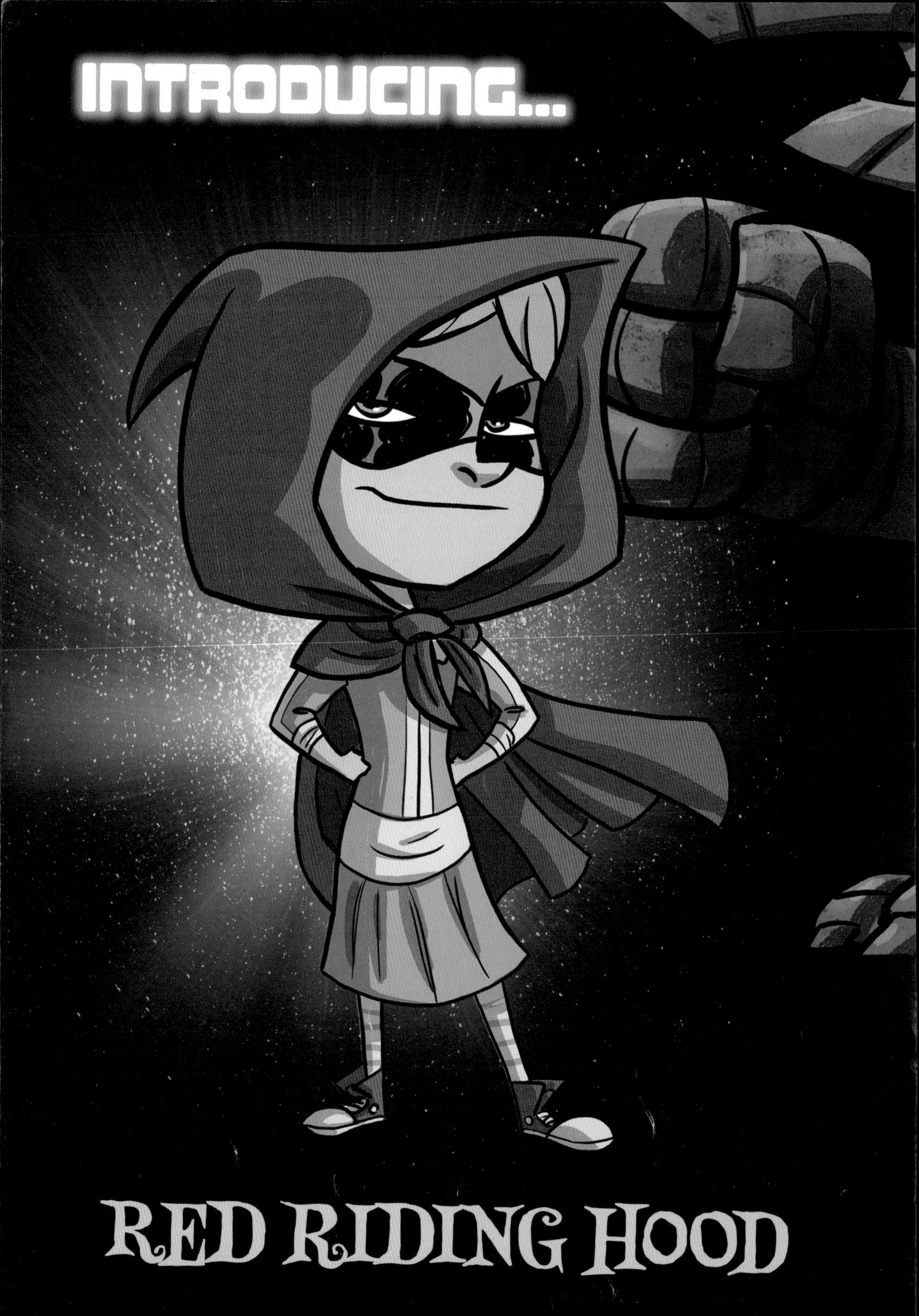
INTRODUCING...
RED RIDING HOOD

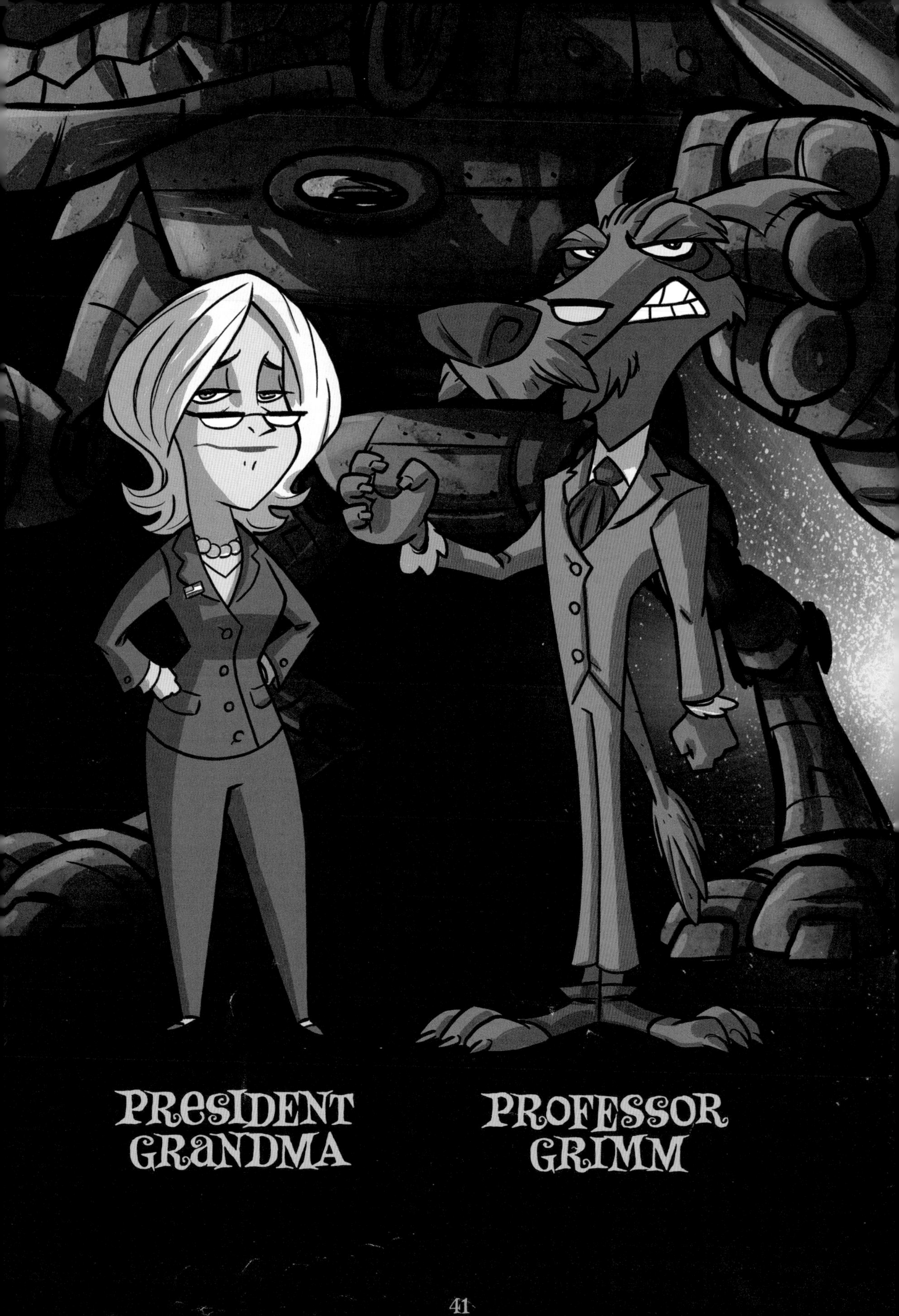
PRESIDENT GRANDMA
PROFESSOR GRIMM

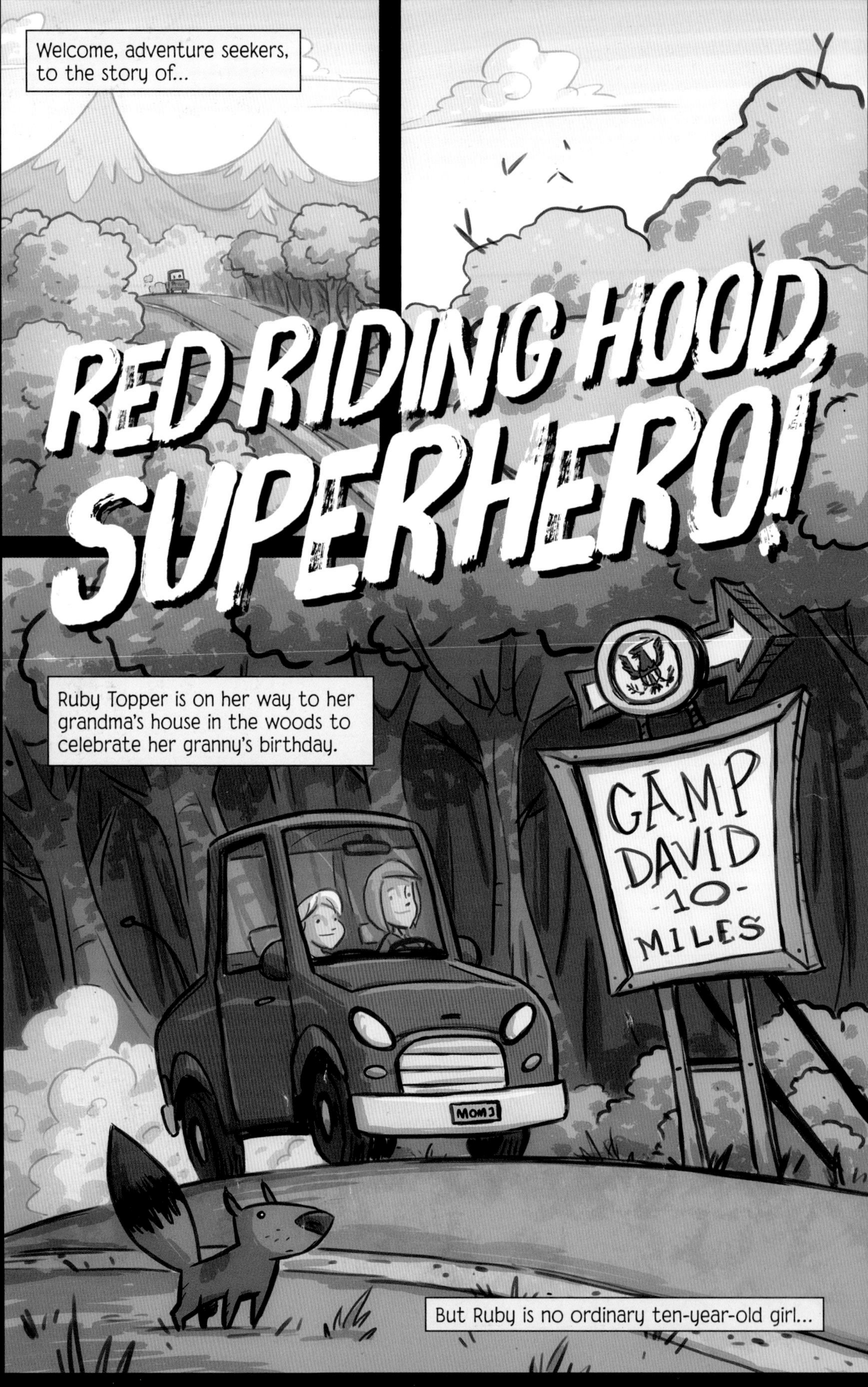
Welcome, adventure seekers, to the story of...
RED RIDING HOOD, SUPERHERO!
Ruby Topper is on her way to her grandma's house in the woods to celebrate her granny's birthday.
CAMP DAVID -10- MILES
MOM 1
But Ruby is no ordinary ten-year-old girl...

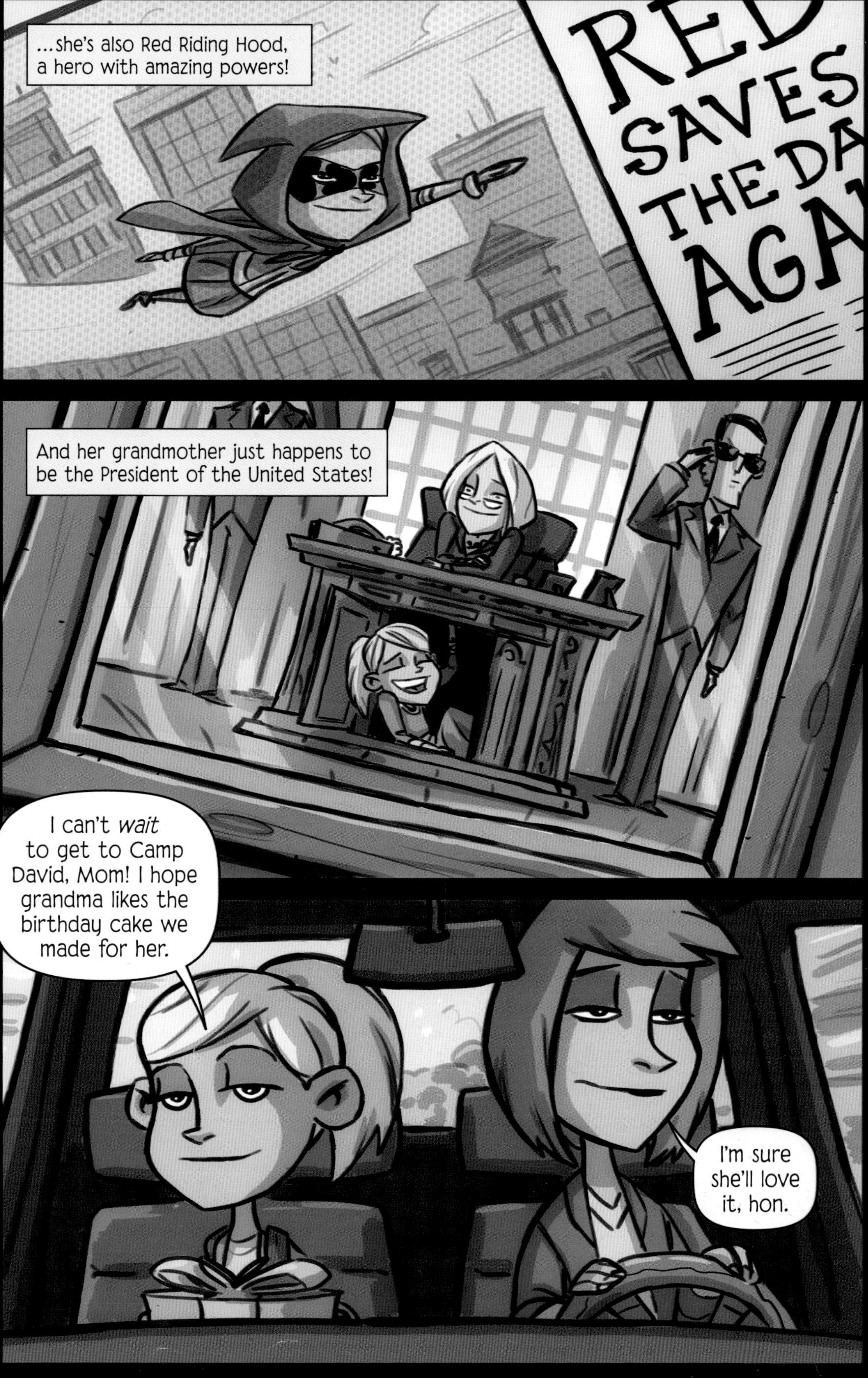
...she's also Red Riding Hood, a hero with amazing powers!
RED SAVES THE DA AGA
And her grandmother just happens to be the President of the United States!
I can't *wait* to get to Camp David, Mom! I hope grandma likes the birthday cake we made for her.
I'm sure she'll love it, hon.

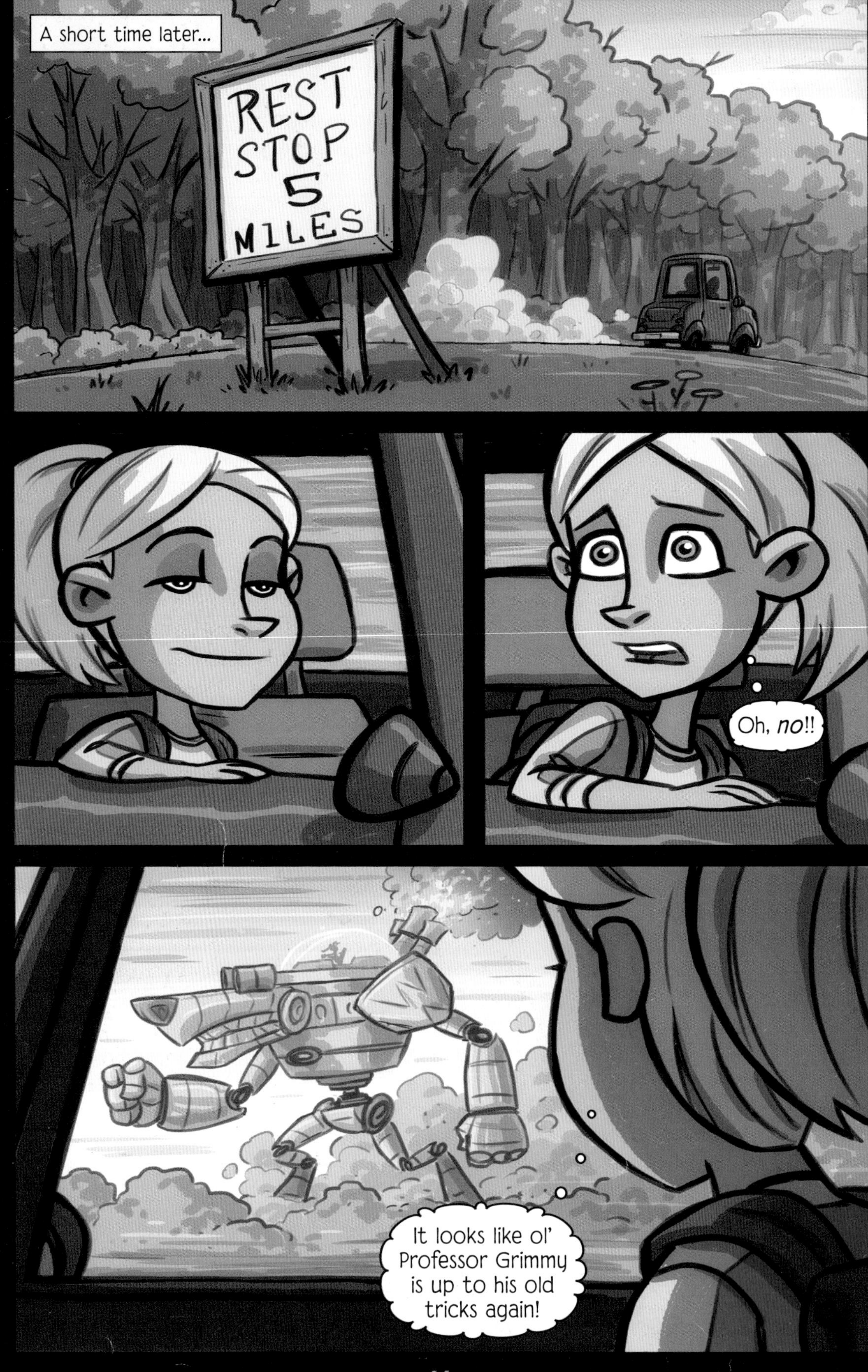
A short time later...
REST STOP 5 MILES
Oh, *no*!!
It looks like ol' Professor Grimmy is up to his old tricks again!

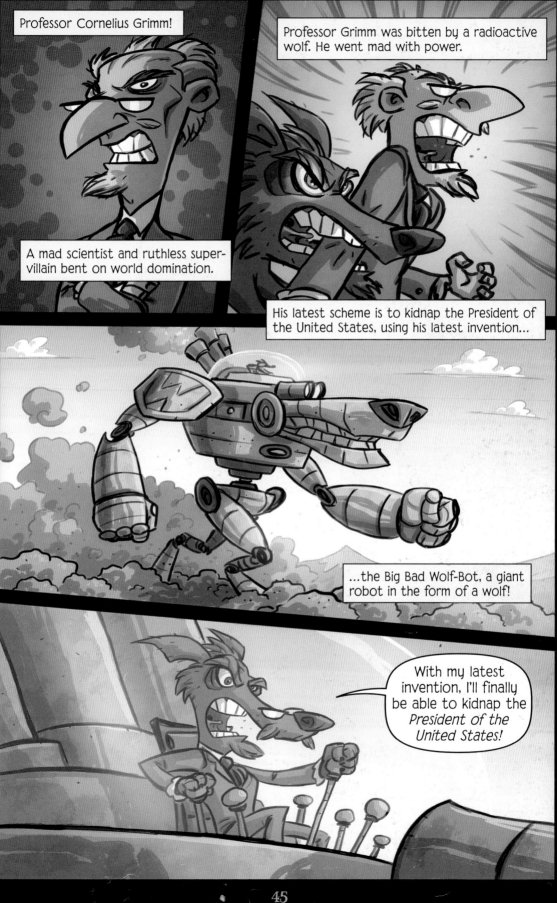

Professor Cornelius Grimm!

A mad scientist and ruthless super-villain bent on world domination.

Professor Grimm was bitten by a radioactive wolf. He went mad with power.

His latest scheme is to kidnap the President of the United States, using his latest invention...

...the Big Bad Wolf-Bot, a giant robot in the form of a wolf!

With my latest invention, I'll finally be able to kidnap the *President of the United States!*

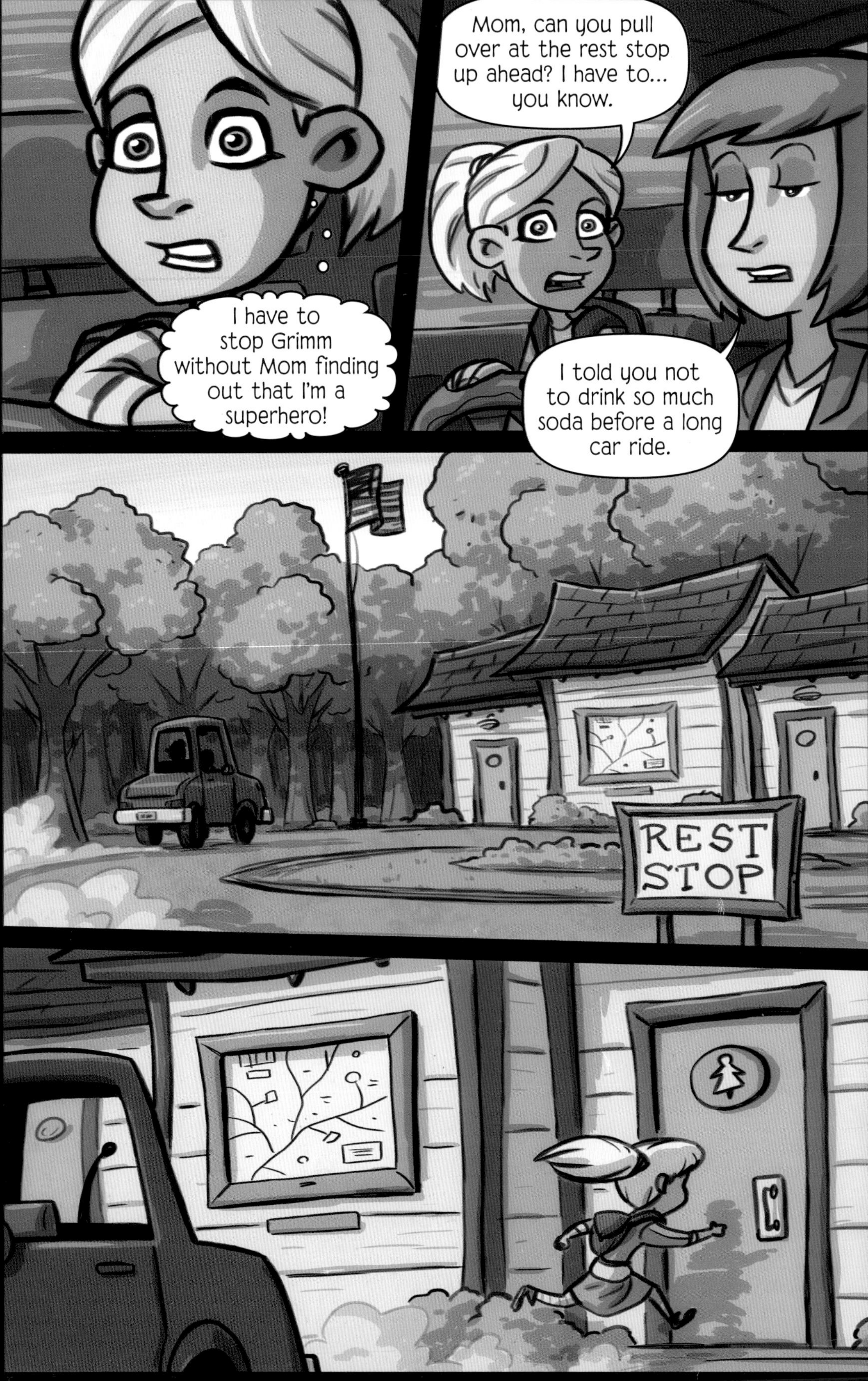
Mom, can you pull over at the rest stop up ahead? I have to... you know.
I have to stop Grimm without Mom finding out that I'm a superhero!
I told you not to drink so much soda before a long car ride.
REST STOP

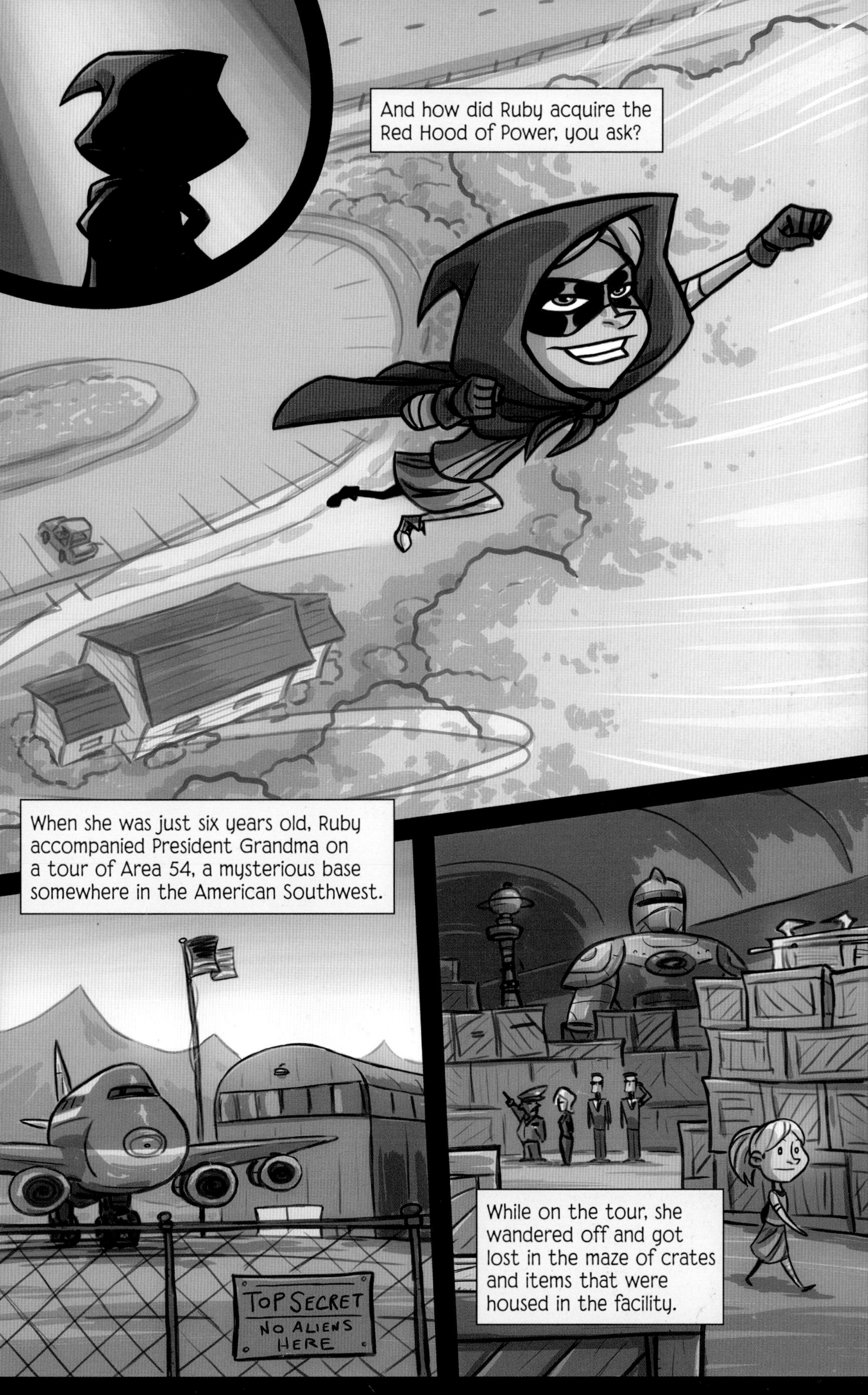
And how did Ruby acquire the Red Hood of Power, you ask?
When she was just six years old, Ruby accompanied President Grandma on a tour of Area 54, a mysterious base somewhere in the American Southwest.
TOP SECRET
NO ALIENS HERE
While on the tour, she wandered off and got lost in the maze of crates and items that were housed in the facility.

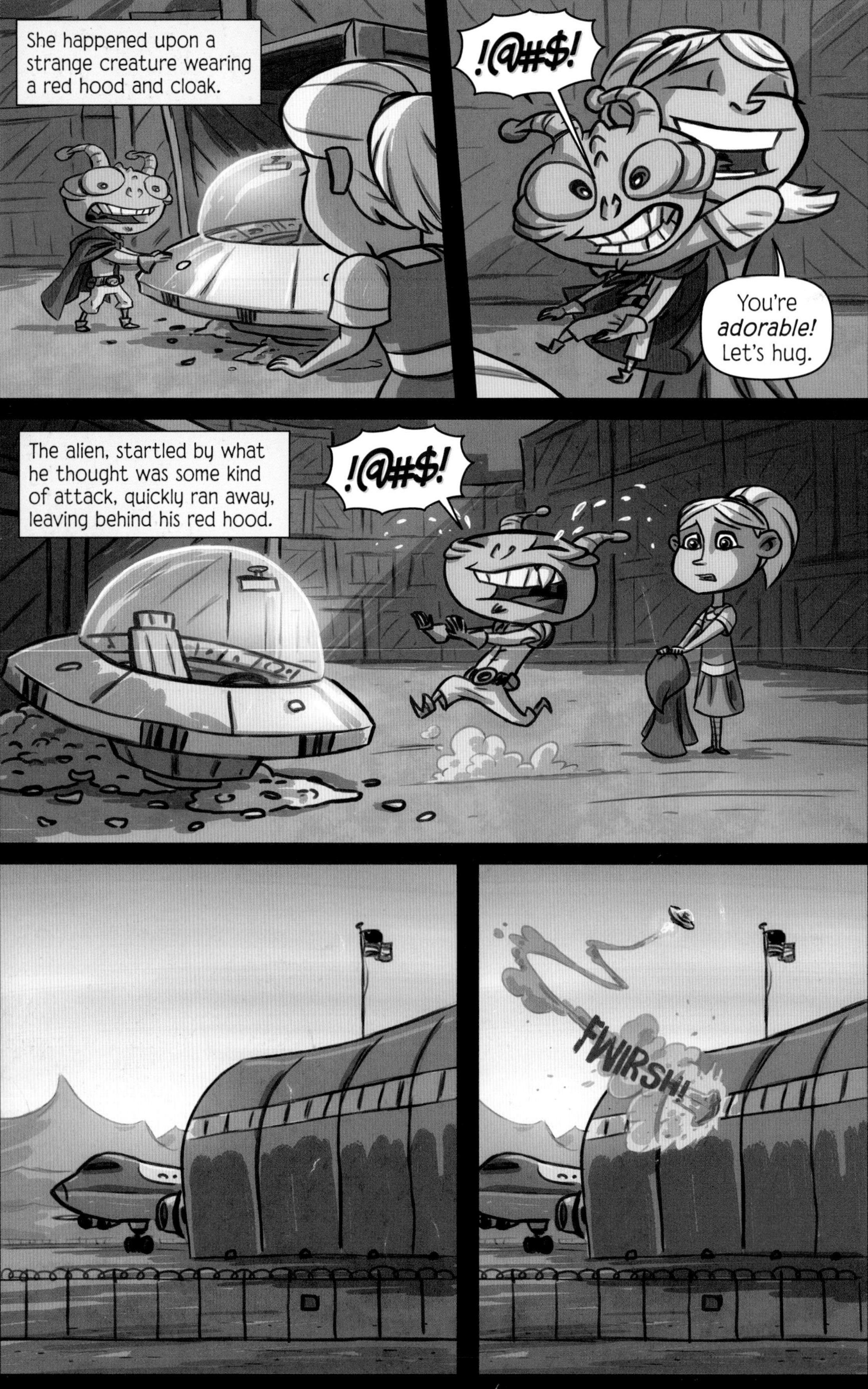

She happened upon a strange creature wearing a red hood and cloak.
!@#$!
You're *adorable!* Let's hug.
The alien, startled by what he thought was some kind of attack, quickly ran away, leaving behind his red hood.
!@#$!
FWIRSH!

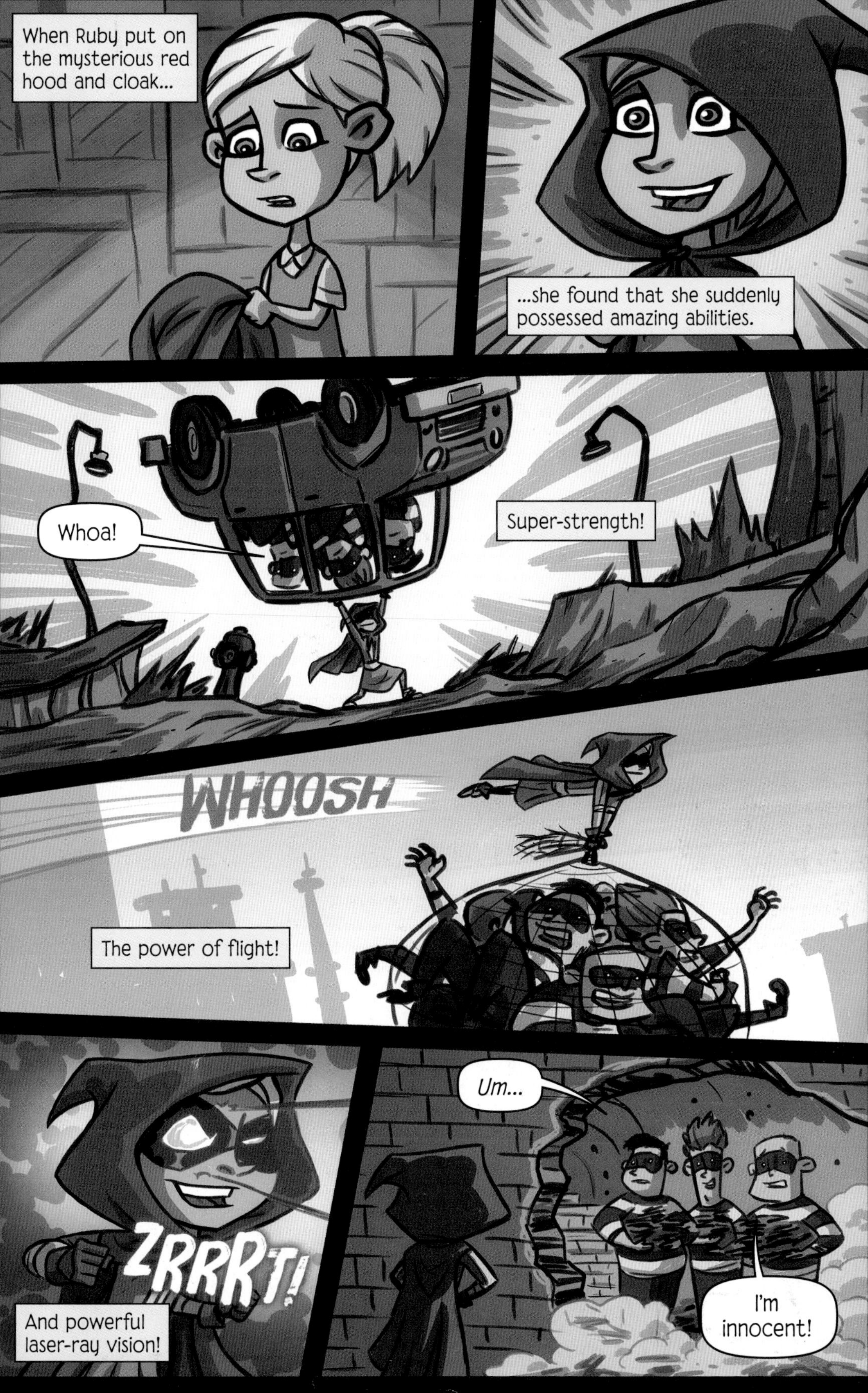
When Ruby put on the mysterious red hood and cloak...
...she found that she suddenly possessed amazing abilities.
Whoa!
Super-strength!
WHOOSH
The power of flight!
ZRRRT!
And powerful laser-ray vision!
Um...
I'm innocent!

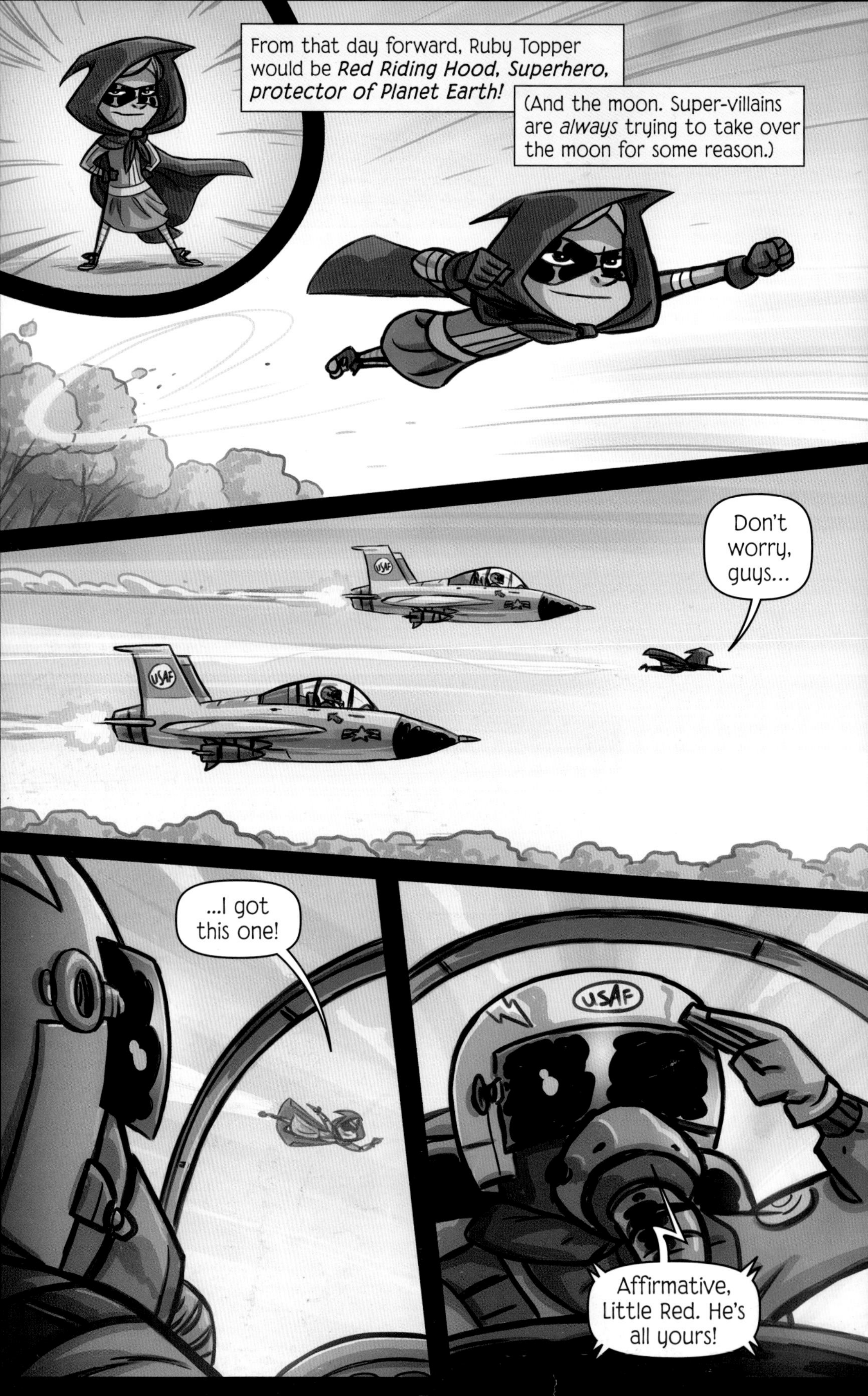
From that day forward, Ruby Topper would be *Red Riding Hood, Superhero, protector of Planet Earth!*
(And the moon. Super-villains are *always* trying to take over the moon for some reason.)
Don't worry, guys...
USAF
USAF
...I got this one!
USAF
Affirmative, Little Red. He's all yours!

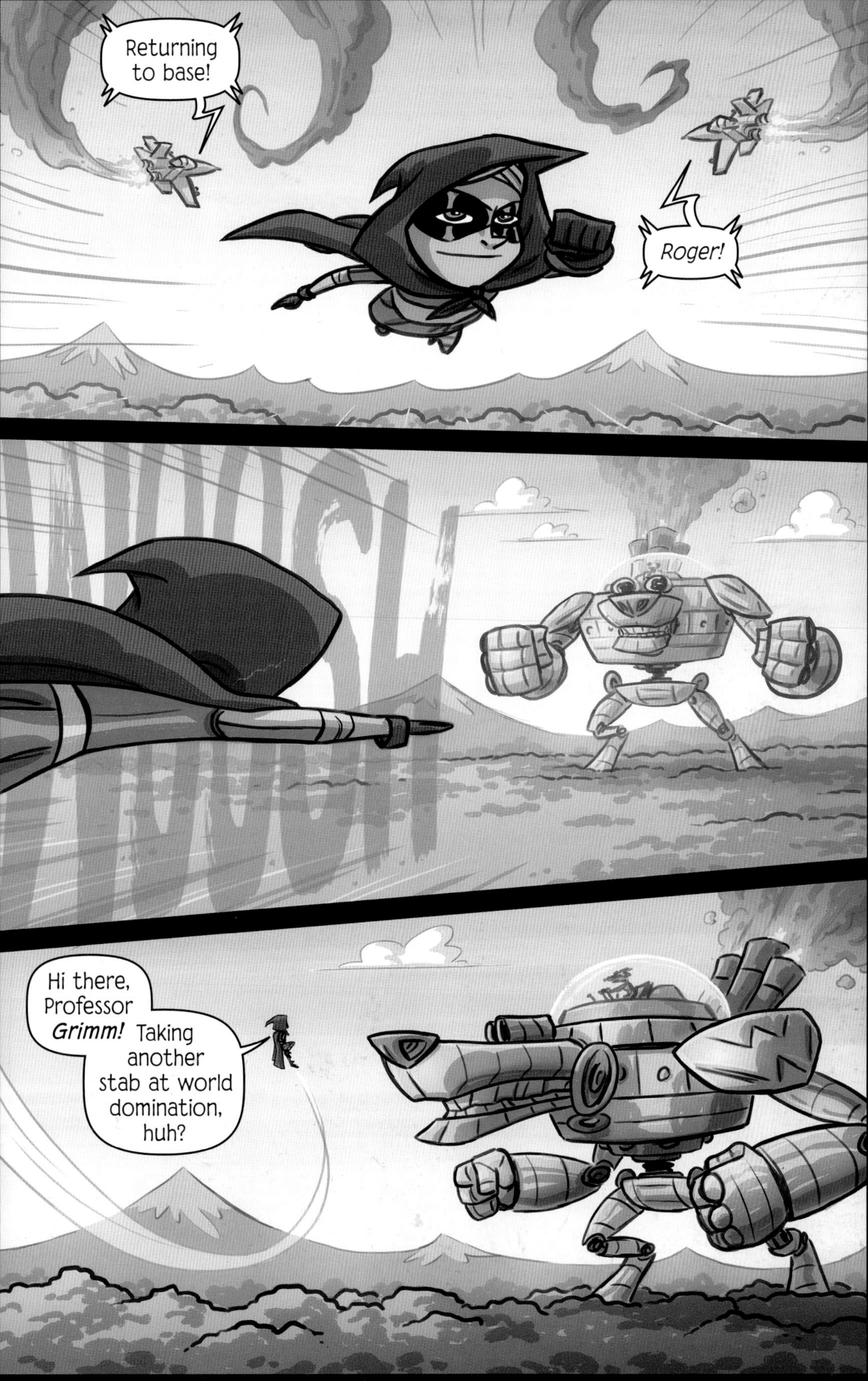
Returning to base!
Roger!
WOOSH
Hi there, Professor *Grimm!* Taking another stab at world domination, huh?

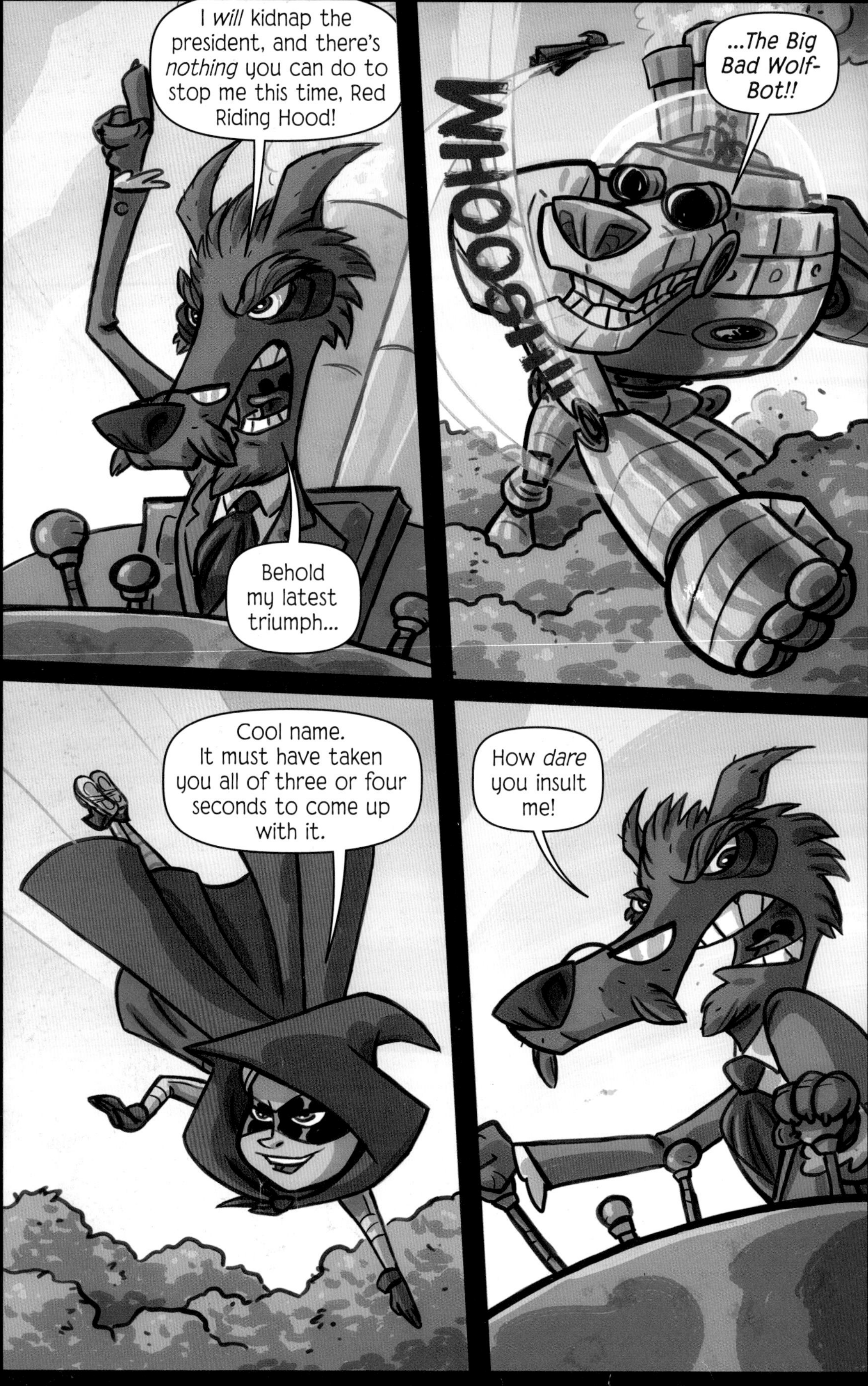

I *will* kidnap the president, and there's *nothing* you can do to stop me this time, Red Riding Hood!
Behold my latest triumph...
WHOOSH!!
...The Big Bad Wolf-Bot!!
Cool name. It must have taken you all of three or four seconds to come up with it.
How *dare* you insult me!

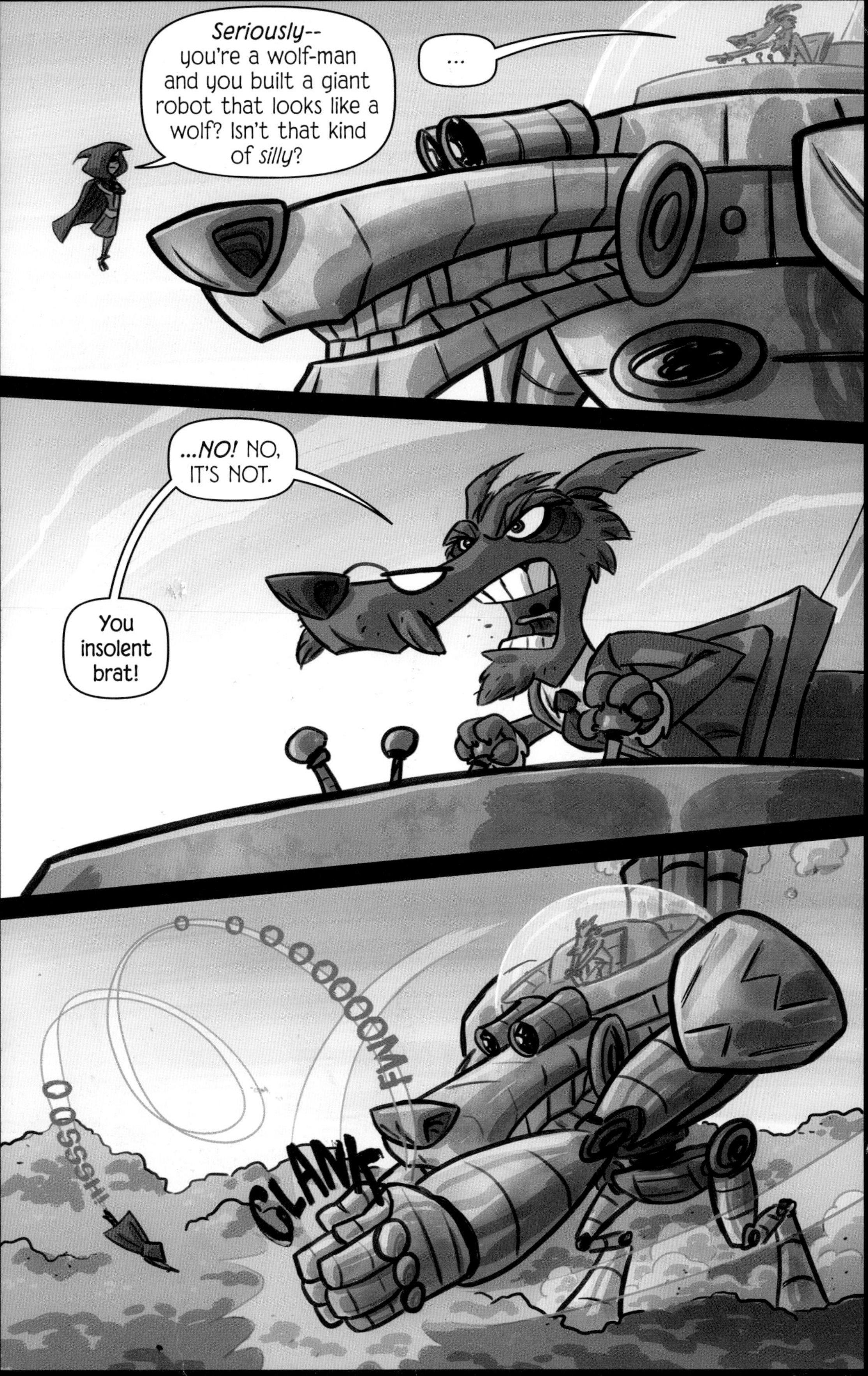

Seriously-- you're a wolf-man and you built a giant robot that looks like a wolf? Isn't that kind of silly?
...
...NO! NO, IT'S NOT.
You insolent brat!
OOOOOOOOOOOM!
CLANK
WHOOSSSH!

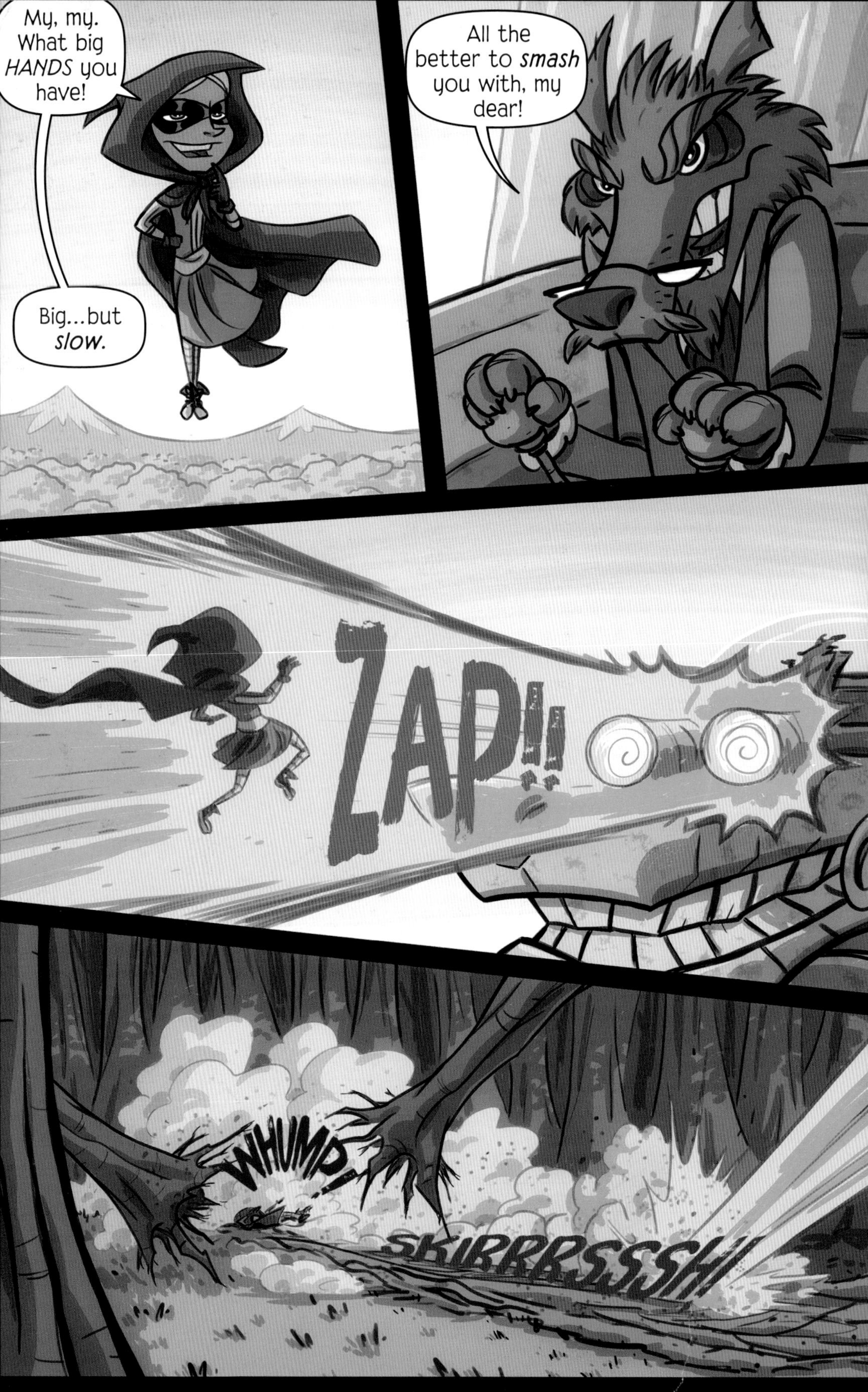

My, my. What big *HANDS* you have!
Big...but *slow*.
All the better to *smash* you with, my dear!
ZAP!!
WHUMP!
SKIRRRSSSSH!

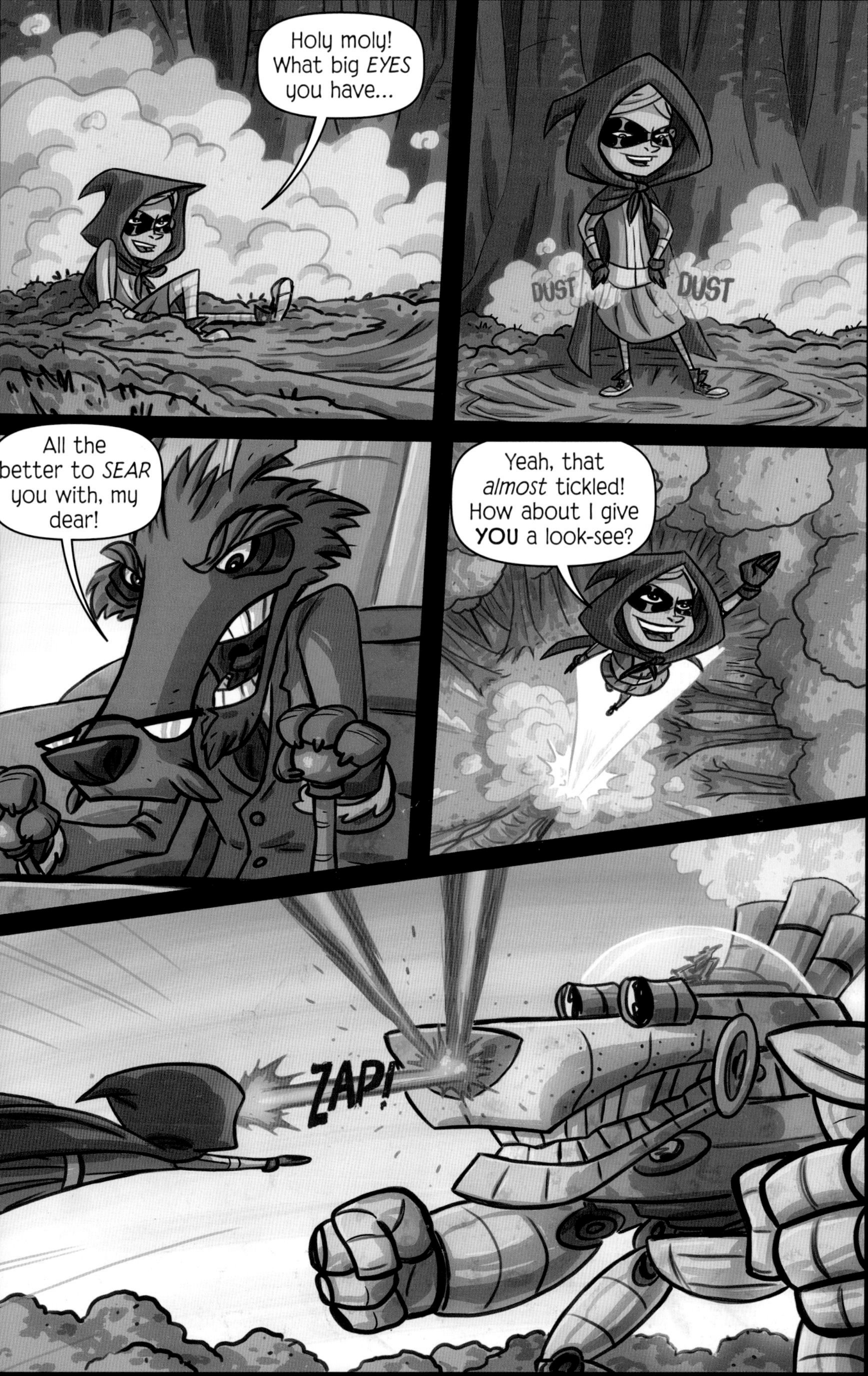
Holy moly! What big *EYES* you have...
DUST
DUST
All the better to *SEAR* you with, my dear!
Yeah, that *almost* tickled! How about I give **YOU** a look-see?
ZAP!

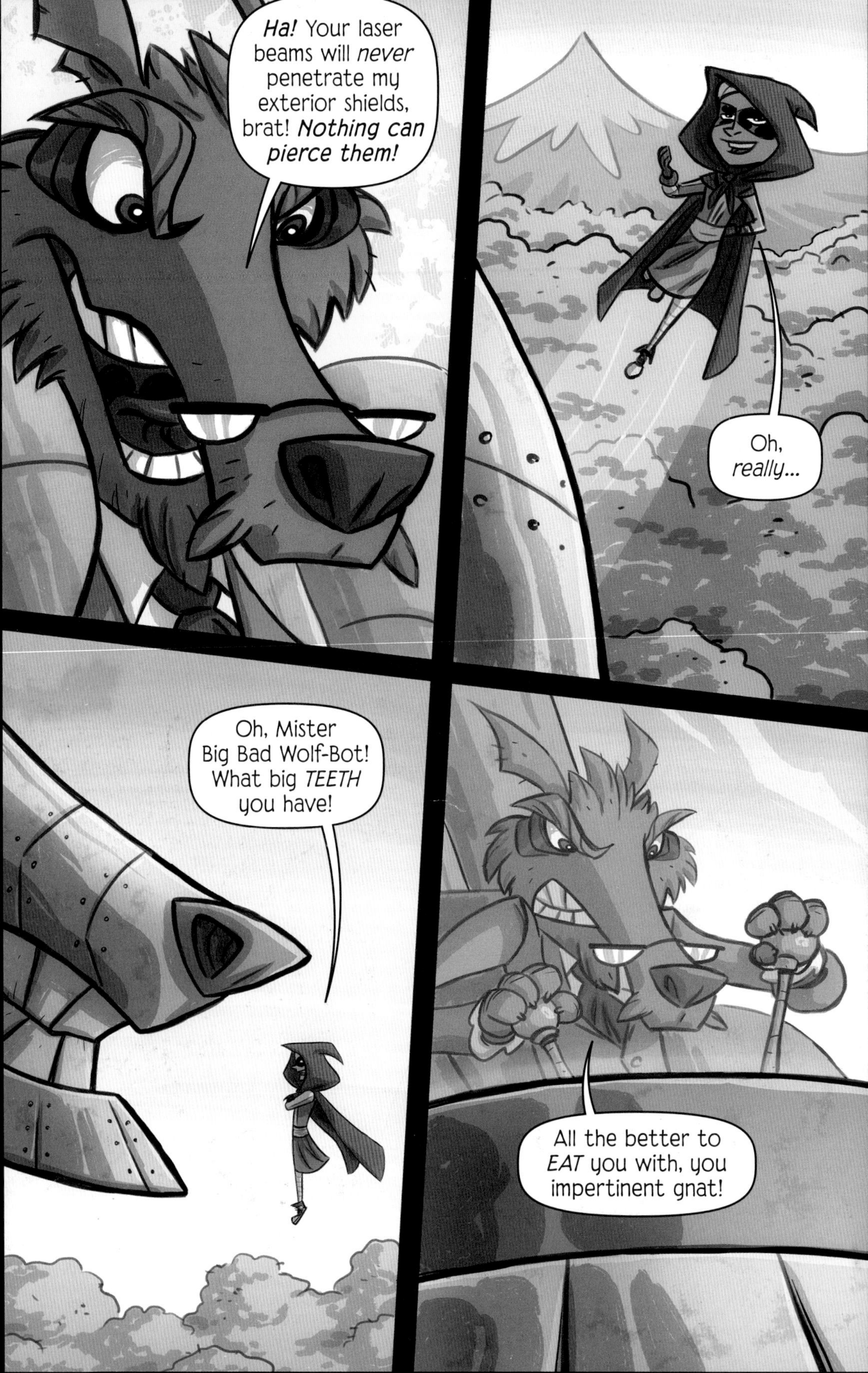
Ha! Your laser beams will never penetrate my exterior shields, brat! Nothing can pierce them!
Oh, really...
Oh, Mister Big Bad Wolf-Bot! What big TEETH you have!
All the better to EAT you with, you impertinent gnat!

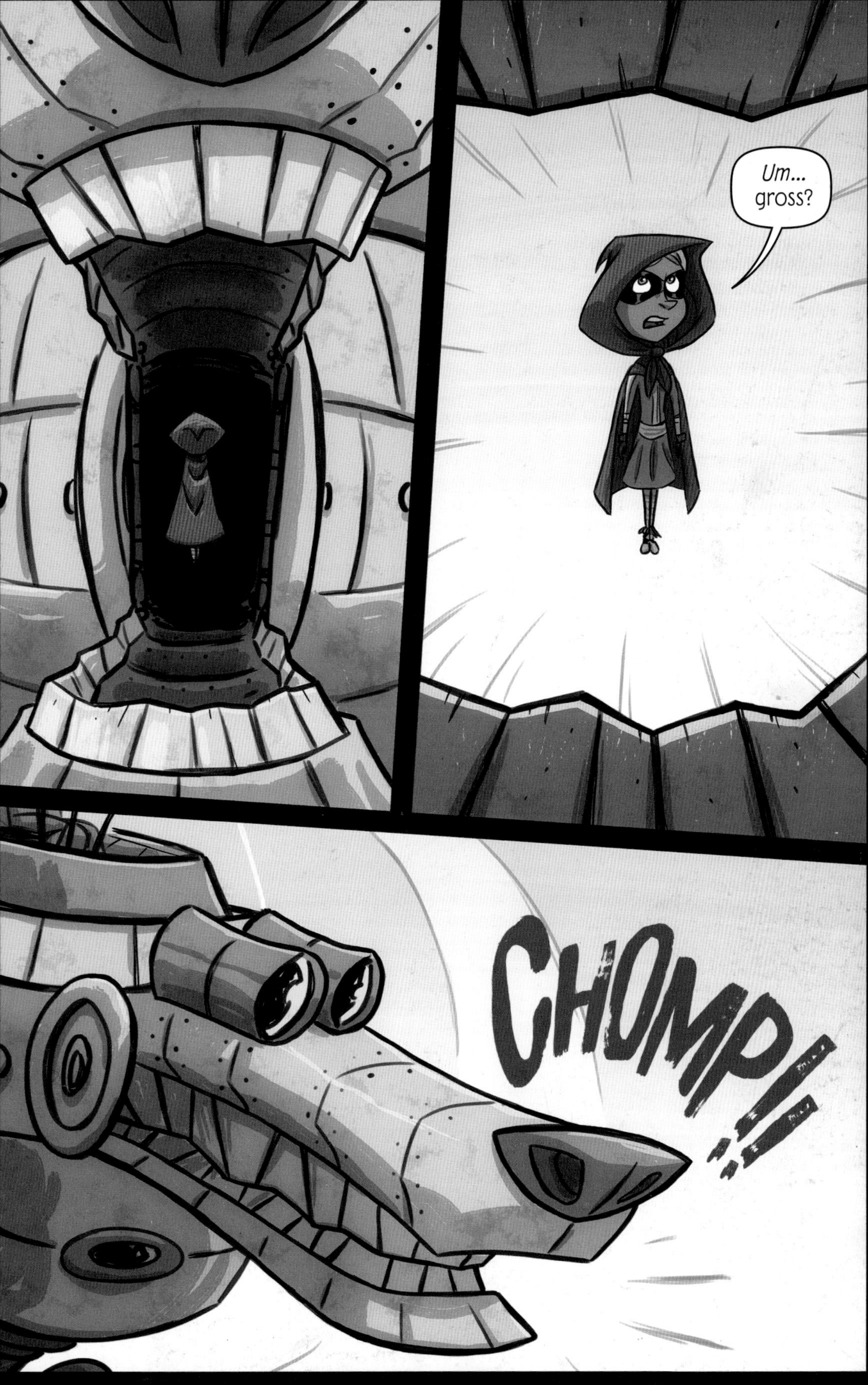
Um... gross?
CHOMP!!

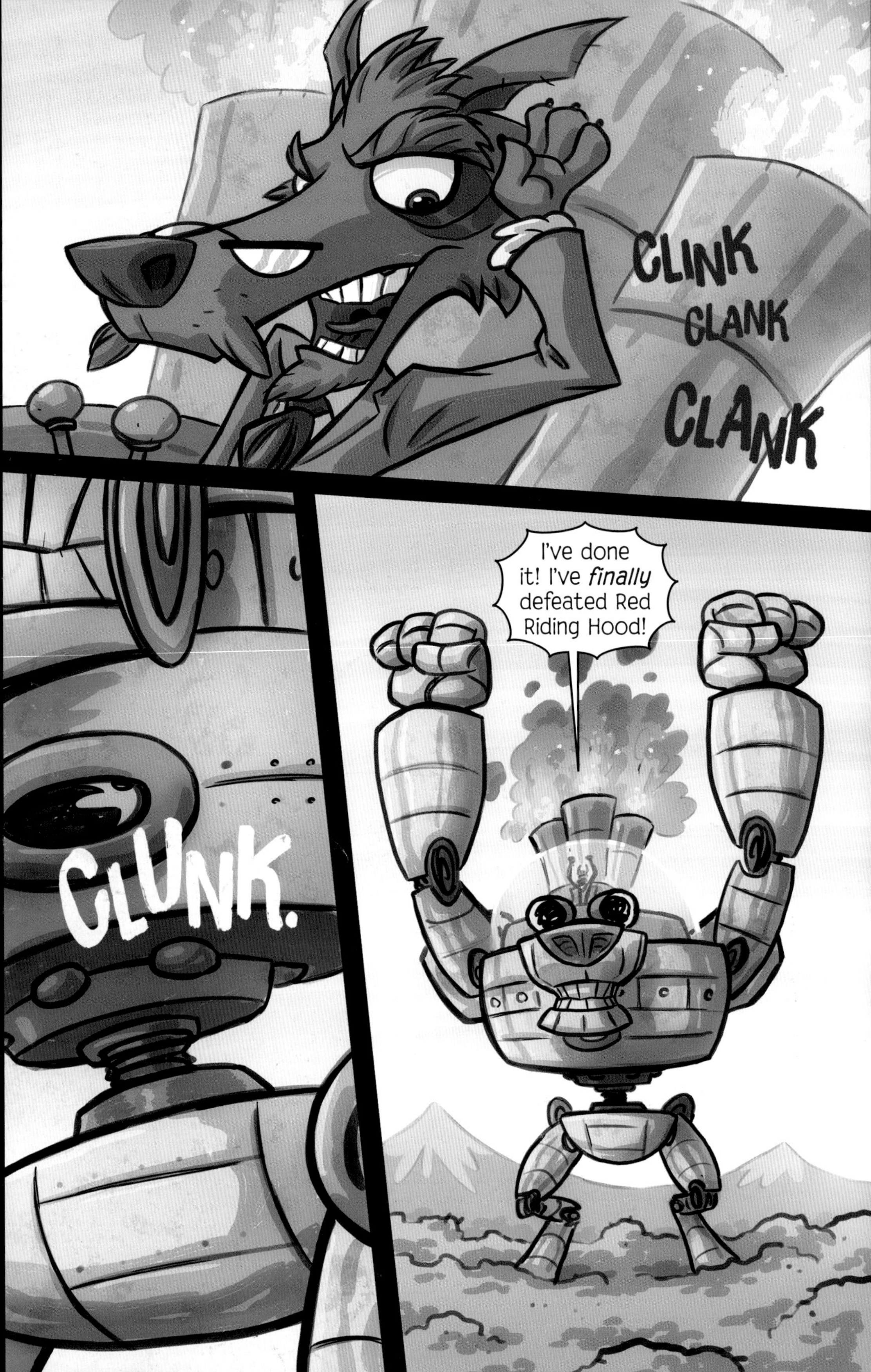
CLINK
CLANK
CLANK
CLUNK.
I've done it! I've *finally* defeated Red Riding Hood!

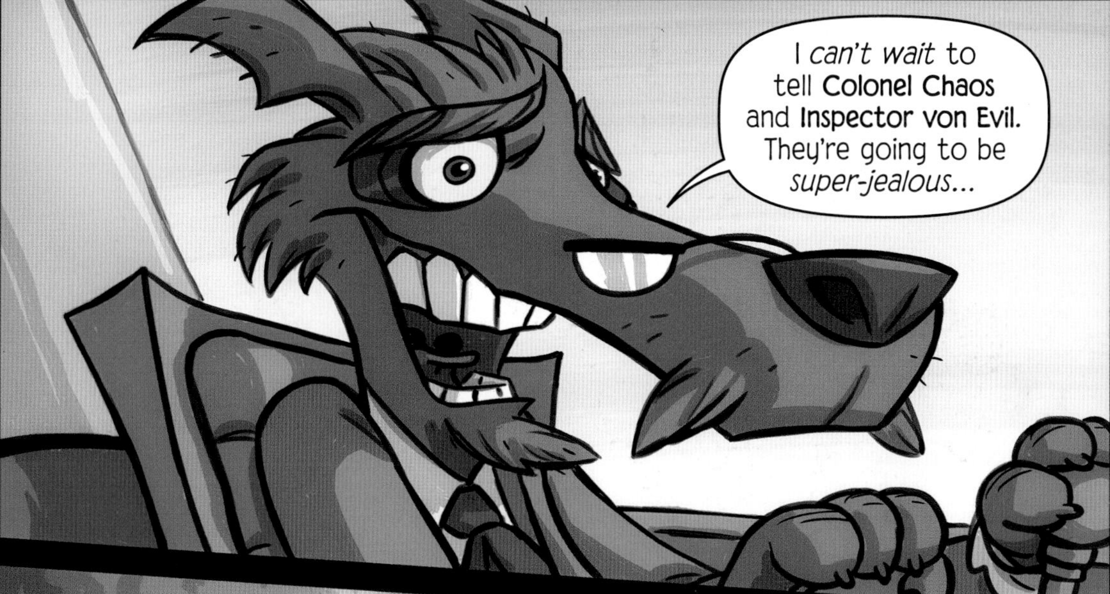
I *can't wait* to tell **Colonel Chaos** and **Inspector von Evil**. They're going to be *super-jealous...*

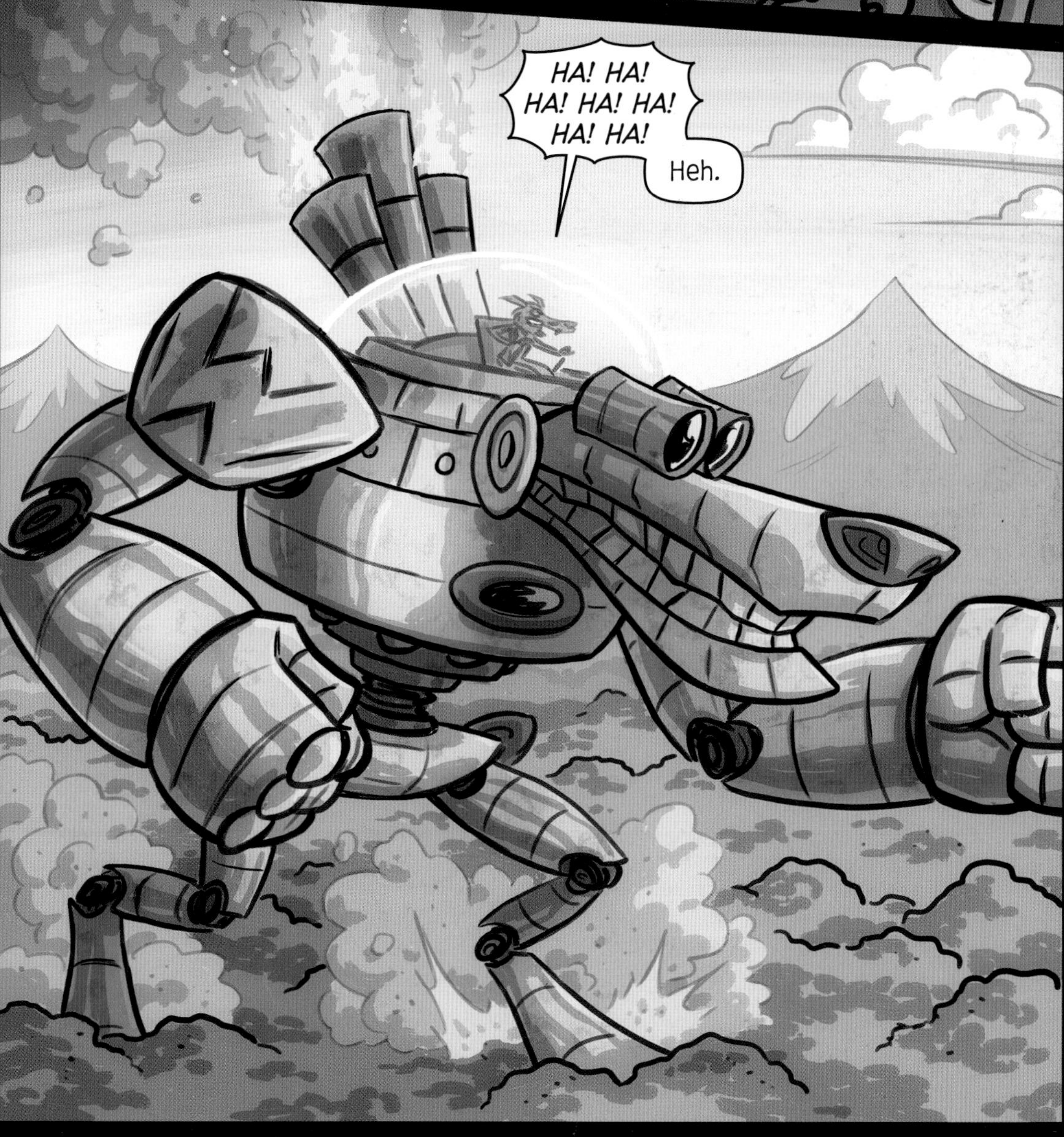
HA! HA! HA! HA! HA! HA! HA!
Heh.

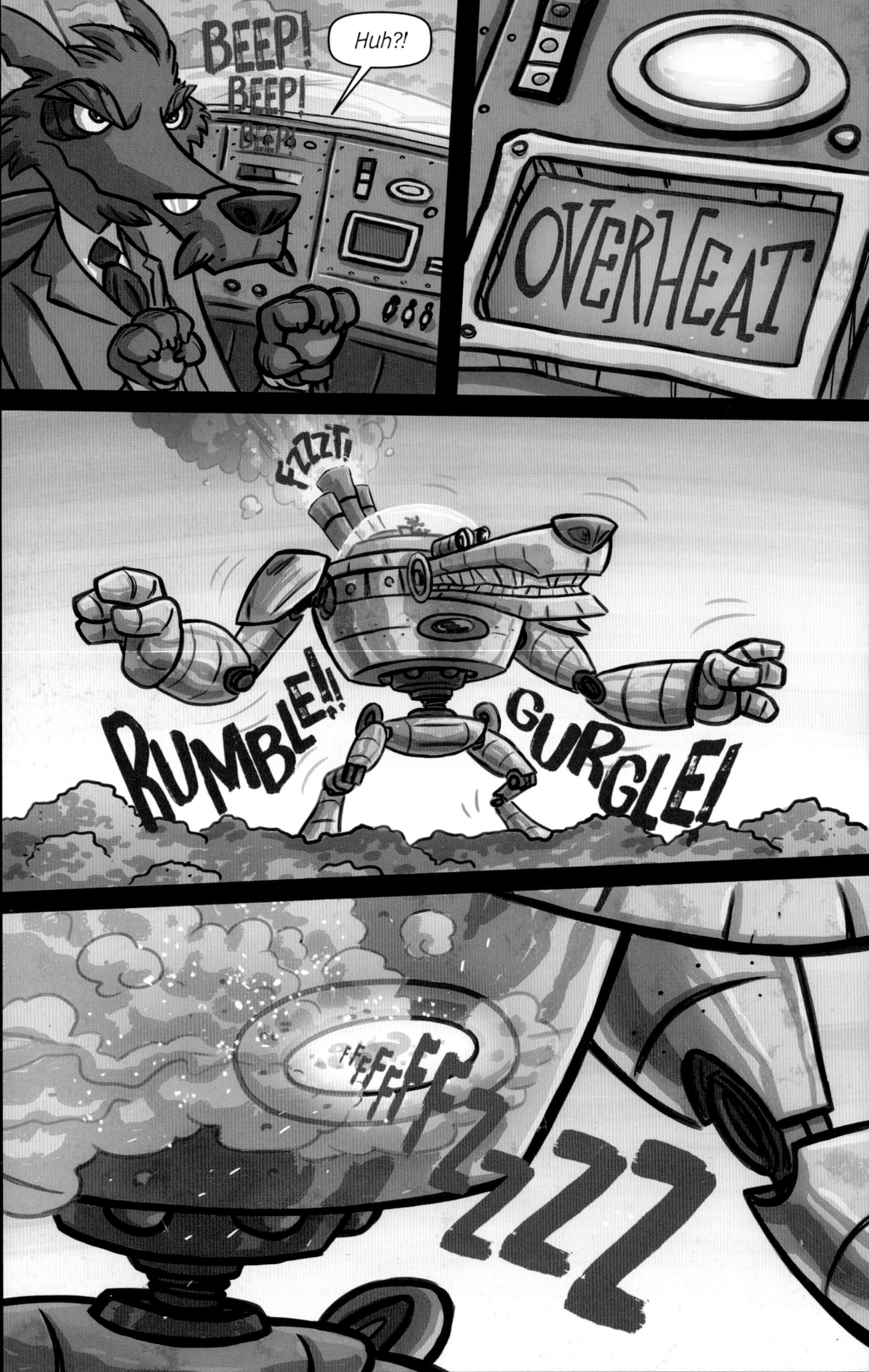
BEEP!
BEEP!
BEEP!
Huh?!
OVERHEAT
FZZZT!
RUMBLE!!
GURGLE!
FFFFFFF
ZZZZ

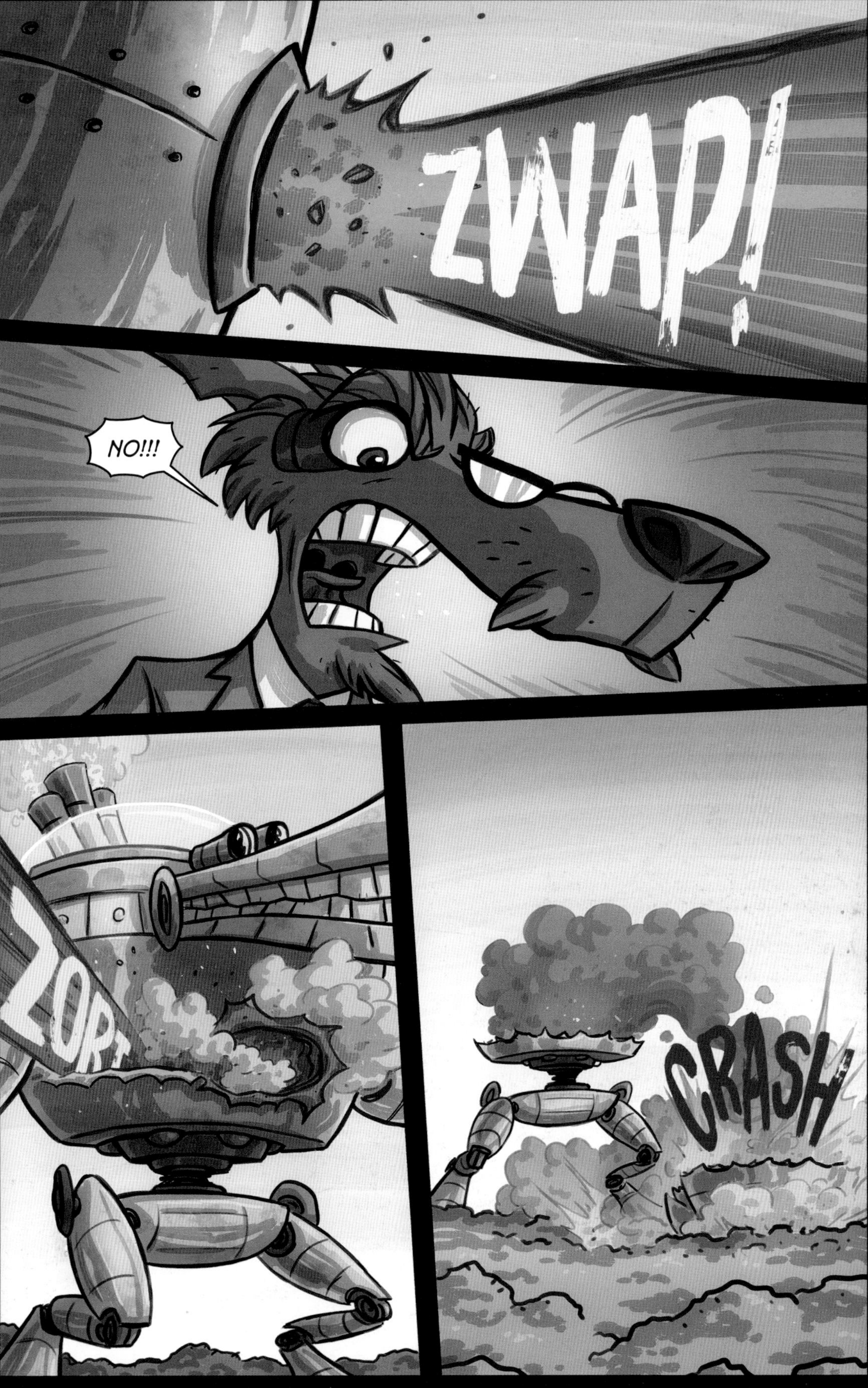
ZWAP!
NO!!!
ZORT
CRASH

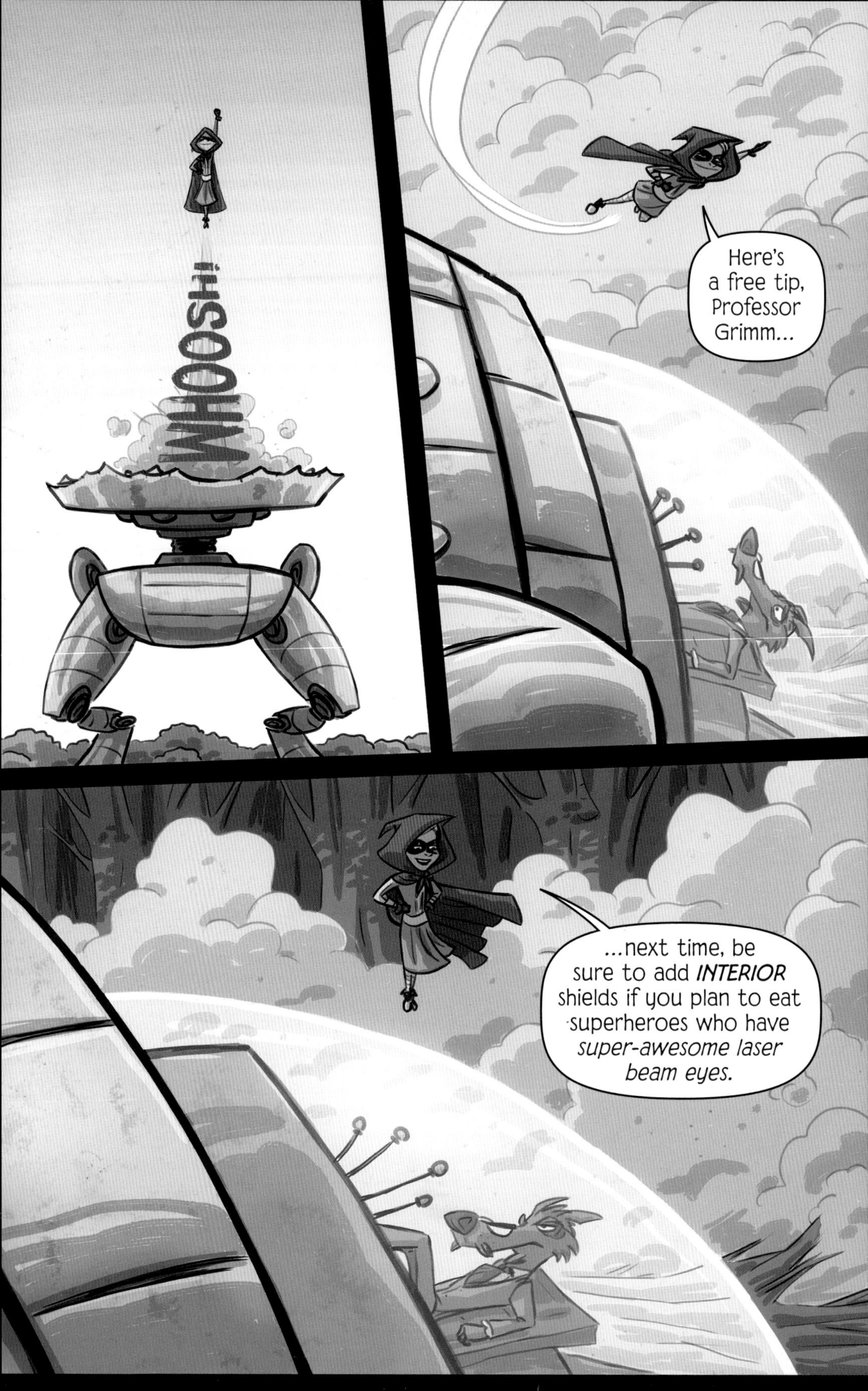
WHOOSH!
Here's a free tip, Professor Grimm...
...next time, be sure to add *INTERIOR* shields if you plan to eat superheroes who have *super-awesome laser beam eyes.*

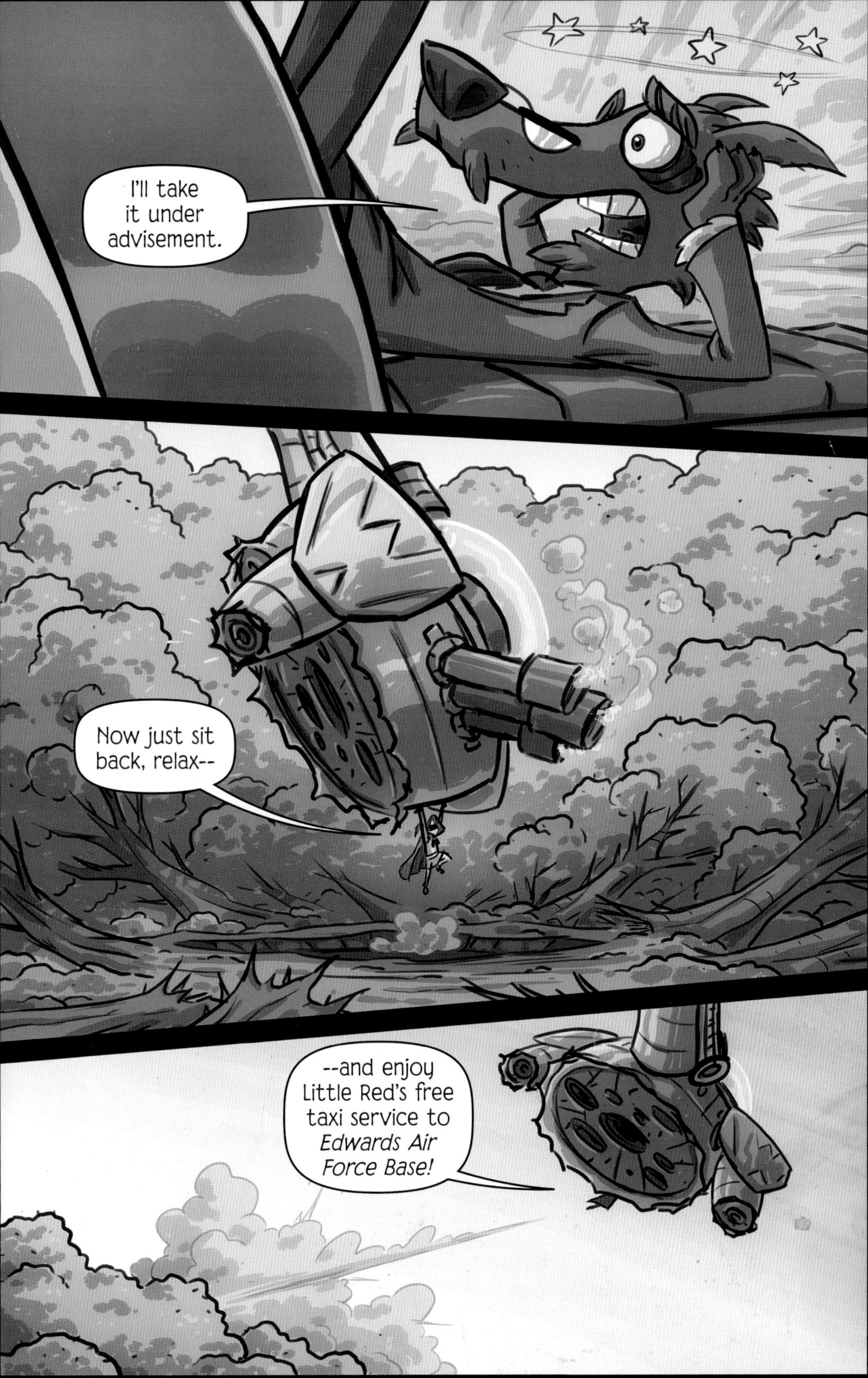
I'll take it under advisement.
Now just sit back, relax--
--and enjoy Little Red's free taxi service to *Edwards Air Force Base!*

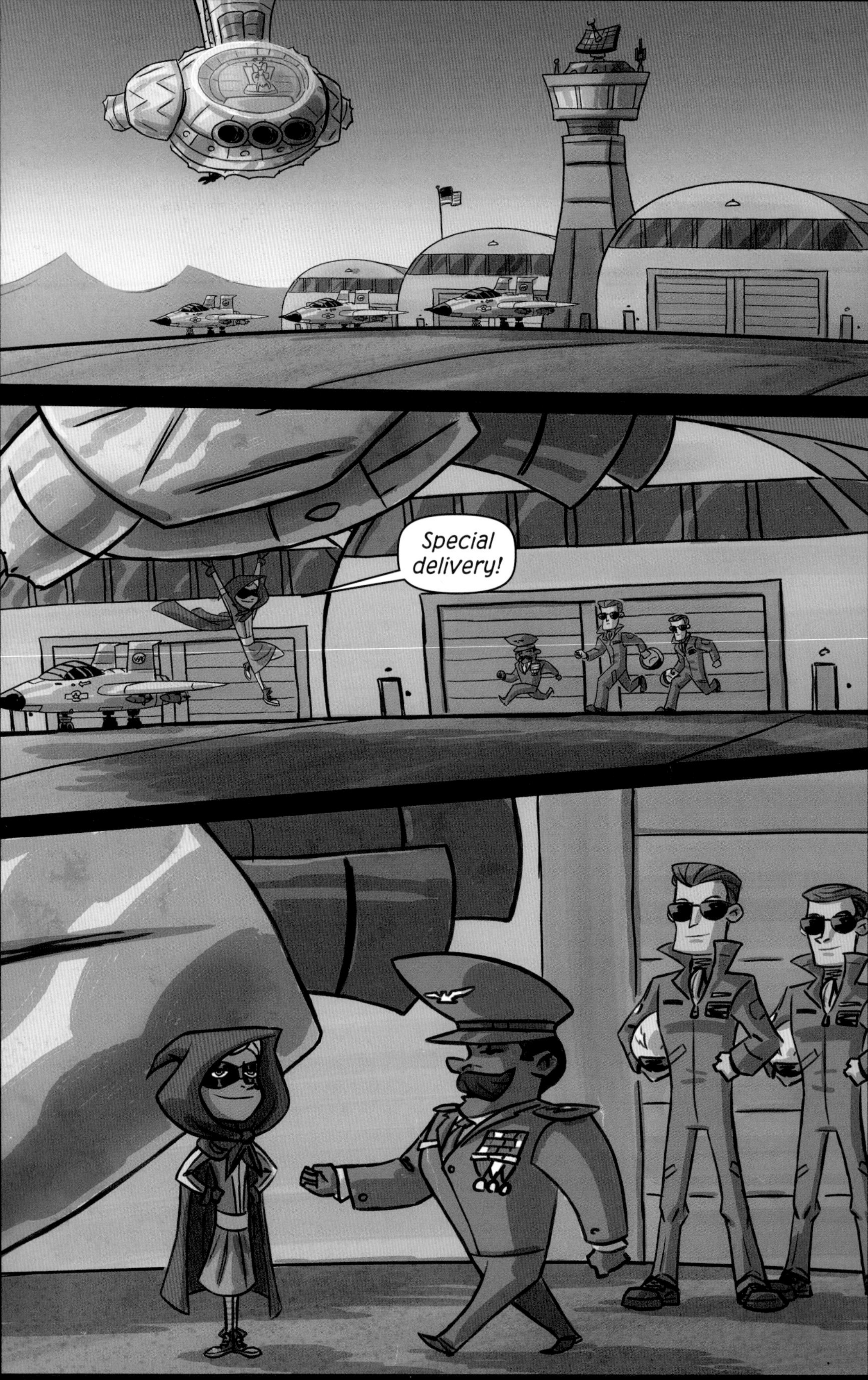
Special delivery!

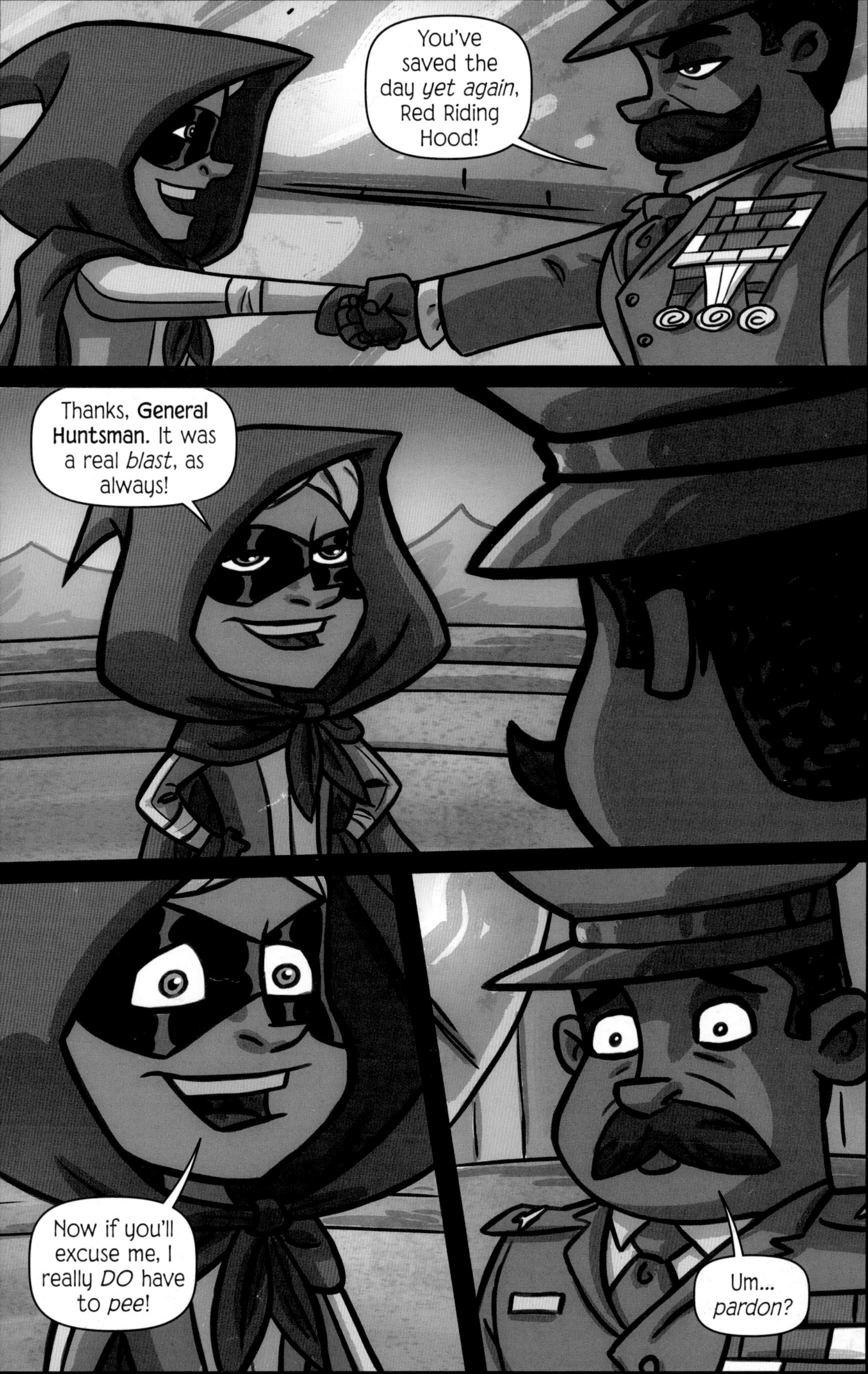
You've saved the day *yet again*, Red Riding Hood!
Thanks, **General Huntsman.** It was a real *blast*, as always!
Now if you'll excuse me, I really *DO* have to *pee*!
Um... *pardon*?

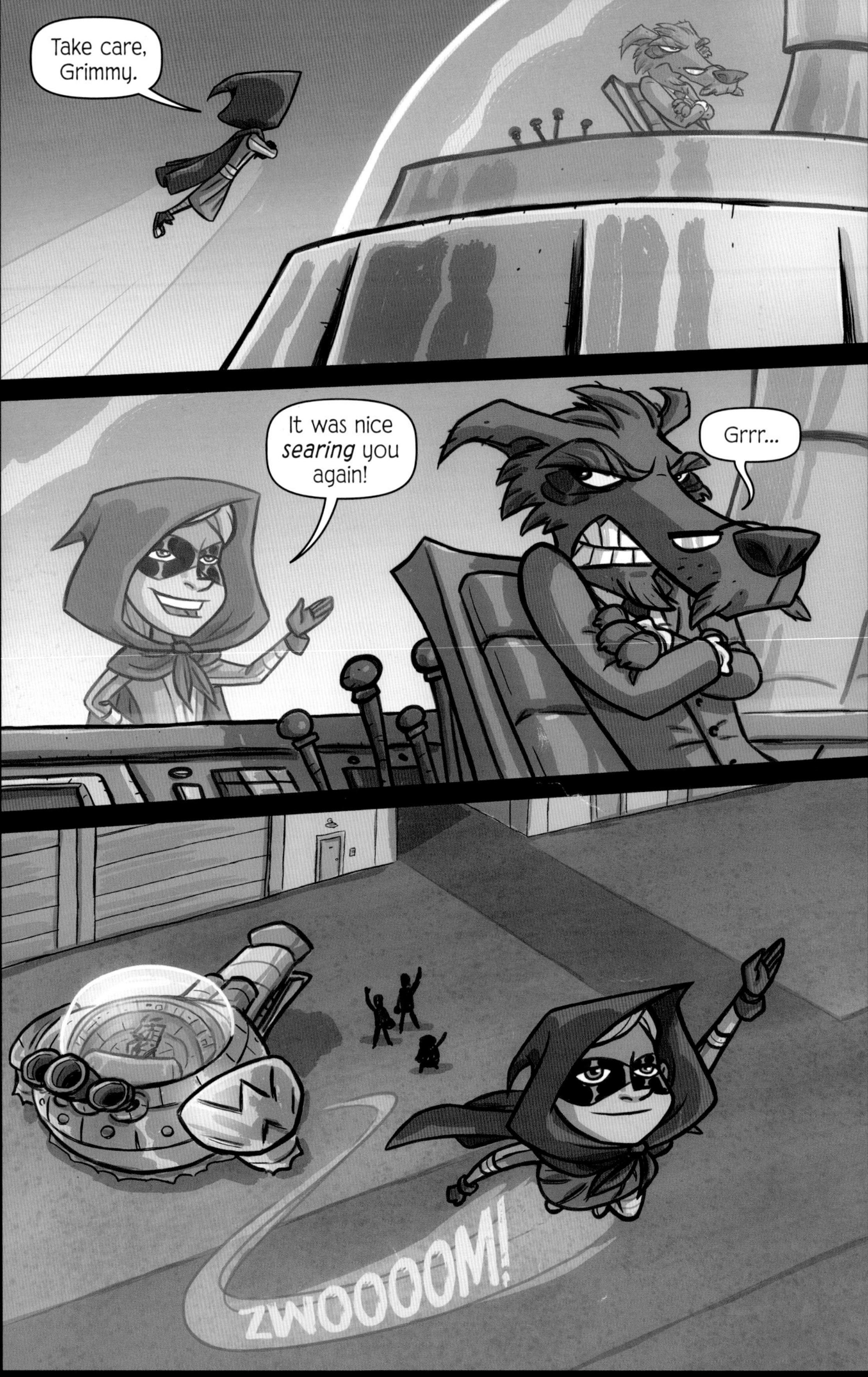

Take care, Grimmy.
It was nice *searing* you again!
Grrr...
ZWOOOOM!

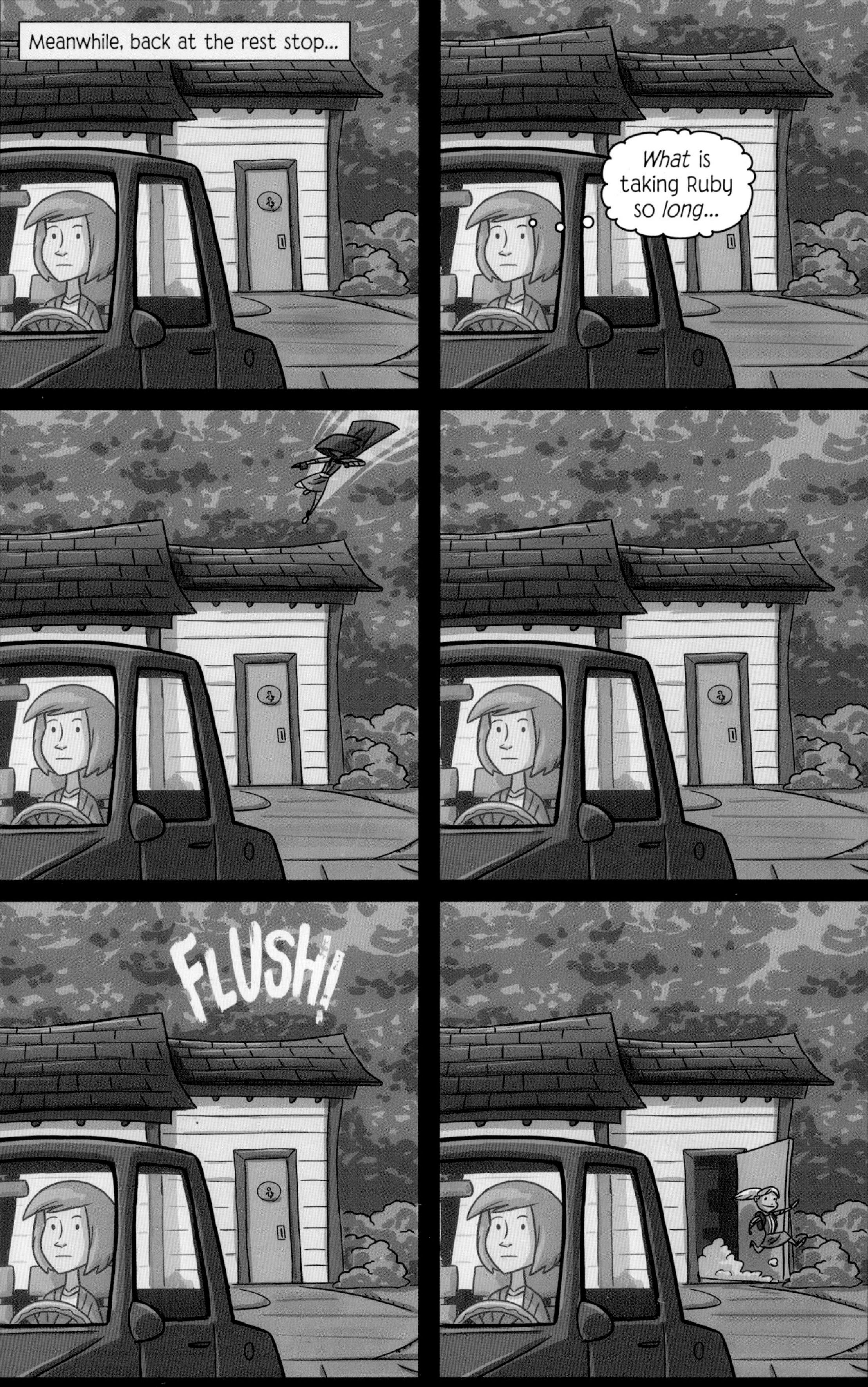
Meanwhile, back at the rest stop...
What is taking Ruby so long...
FLUSH!

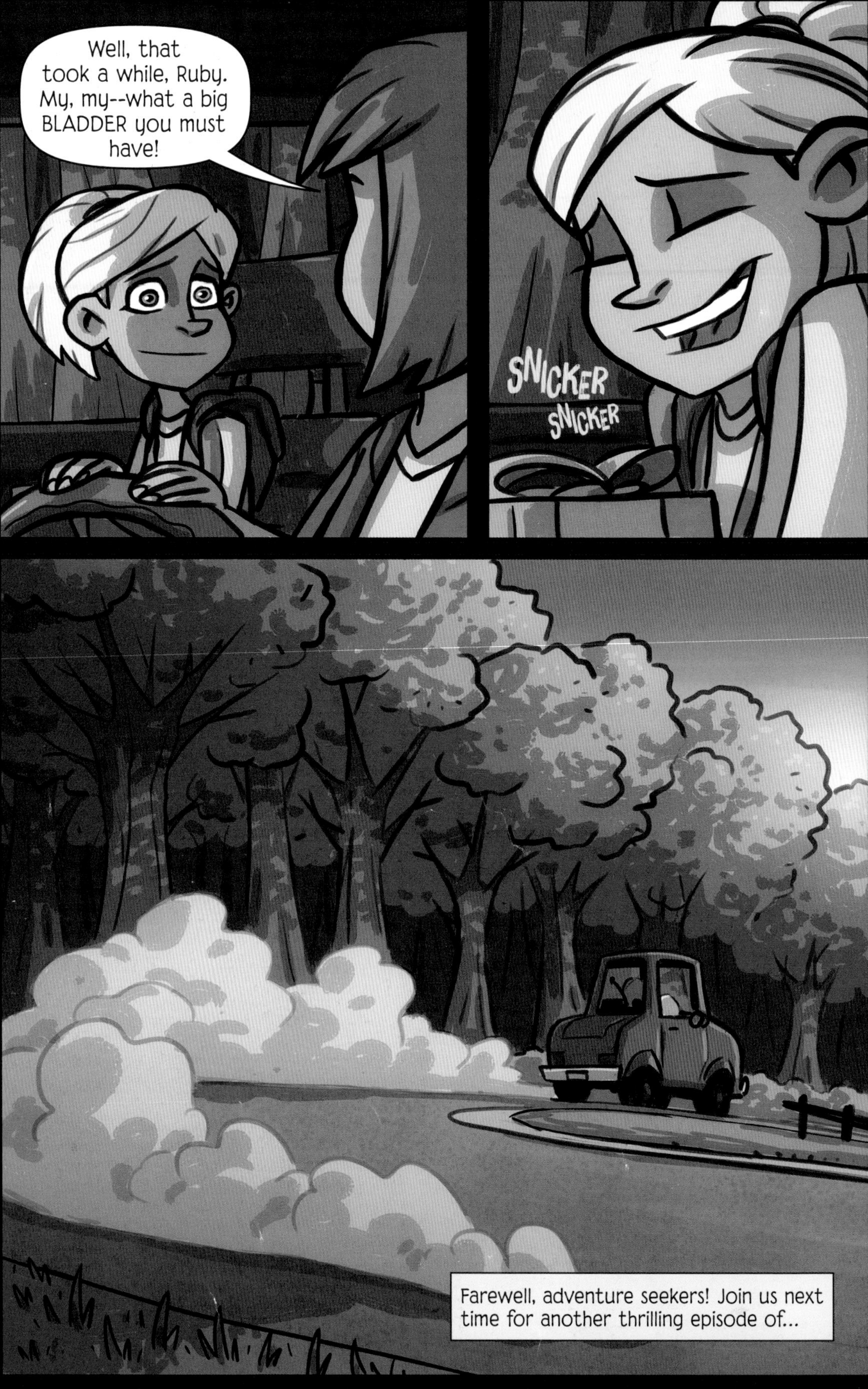
Well, that took a while, Ruby. My, my--what a big BLADDER you must have!
SNICKER
SNICKER
Farewell, adventure seekers! Join us next time for another thrilling episode of...

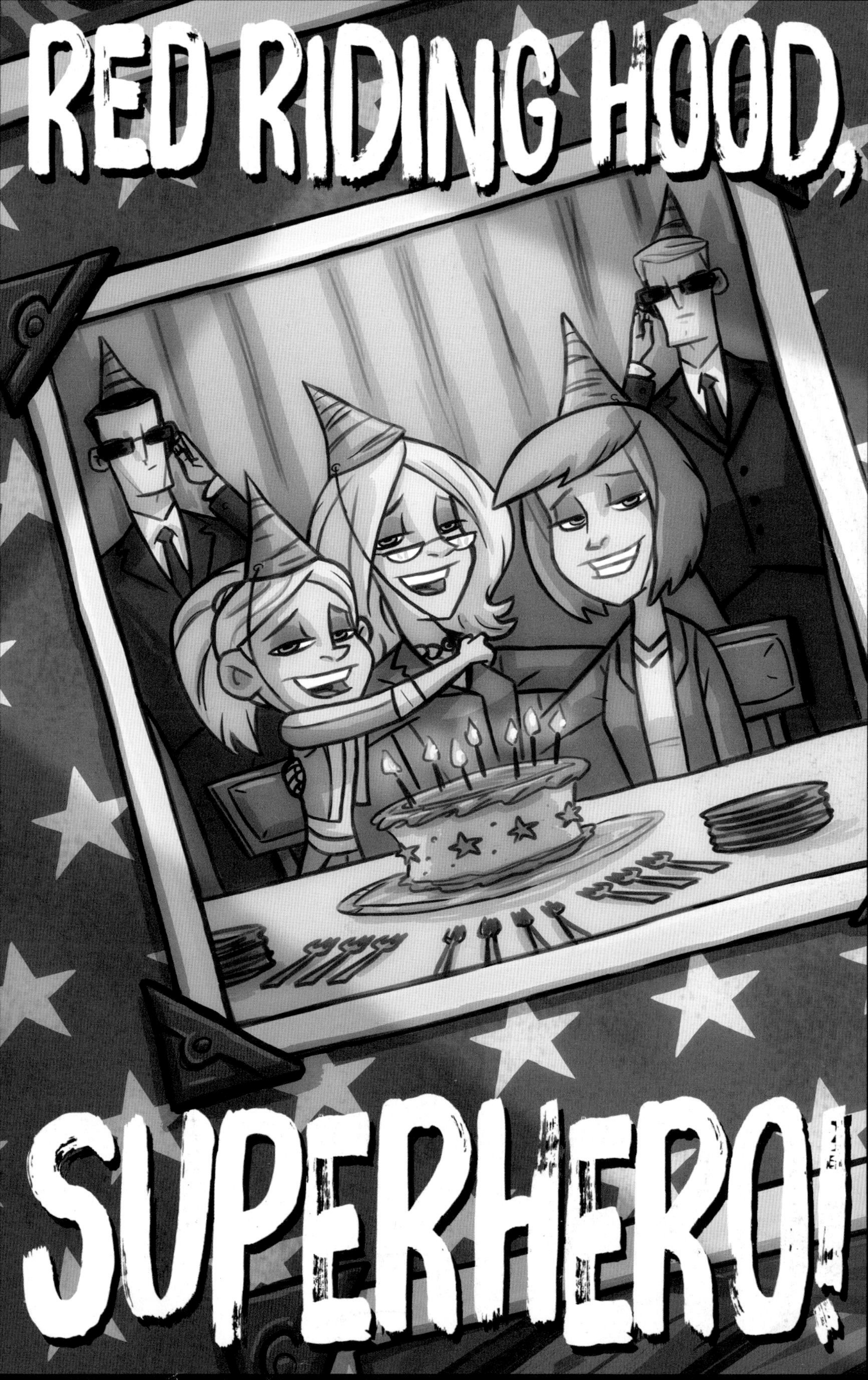
RED RIDING HOOD,
SUPERHERO!

ALL ABOUT THE ORIGINAL TALE!

The most popular version of this particular fairy tale was published in German by the Brothers Grimm in the 1800s. Translated as "Little Red Cap," the fairy tale tells the story of a young girl who receives a red cap (or cloak and hood) from her mother. Her mom then sends Little Red Cap to take food to her sick grandmother, warning her not to stop along the way.

As she travels, a hungry wolf sees the girl walking through the woods. The wolf asks the girl where she is headed, and she tells him. The wolf suggests that some freshly picked flowers might cheer up her grandmother, so Little Red Cap stops for a while to collect a bouquet. The wolf uses the delay to race to her grandmother's house. The wolf eats Little Red Cap's grandma, puts on her nightcap, and takes her place in her bed. When Little Red Cap arrives at her grandmother's house, she gets into bed with the wolf.

The wolf leaps upon the child and eats the girl. A woodcutter (sometimes referred to as the huntsman) arrives and cuts open the wolf's belly. He saves the grandmother and the girl, who are still alive in the wolf's stomach. Then the woodcutter crams stones into the wolf's belly and drowns the wolf.

In another version of the story, published by Charles Perrault, Red's encounter with the wolf goes a little differently. Red remarks to her grandmother (the wolf in disguise), "What big arms you have, Granny!" The wolf responds with, "The better to hug you with, my dear!" The conversation continues with the child remarking on other body parts until she notices the wolf's sharp teeth. "What big teeth you have, Granny!" Red cries. "The better to eat you with, my dear!" the wolf howls. And the wolf gobbles her all up. The end.

While Perrault's version of the tale ends badly for Little Red Riding Hood, this book has a much happier ending. Take a look at the far out twists made to this classic tale...

A FAR OUT GUIDE TO RED RIDING HOOD'S TALE TWISTS!

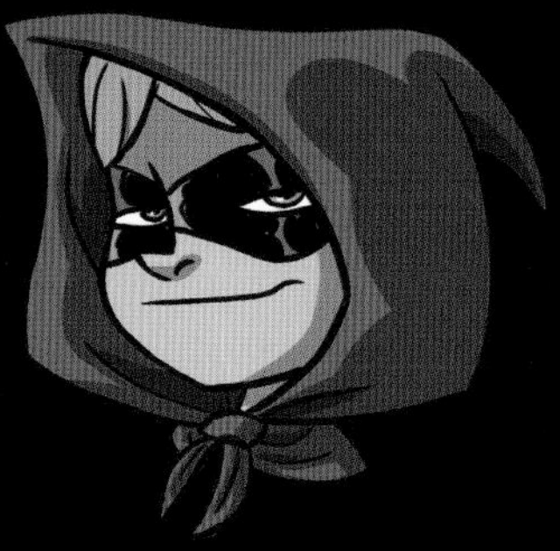

In some versions of the fairy tale, the red cloak given to Red Riding Hood is supposed to protect her from harm. In this book, it sort of does that too--by giving her superpowers! Red also takes her fate into her own hands instead of relying on a huntsman to save her and grandma.

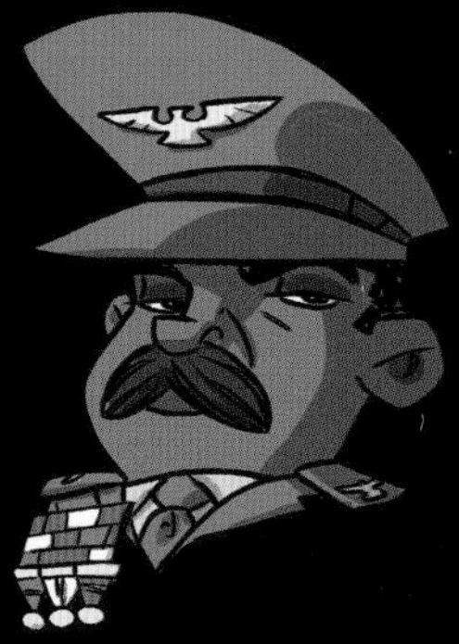

In the original tales, a woodcutter or huntsman saves Red from the Big Bad Wolf. In this version of the tale, he's a thankful General all too happy to have the superhero Red Riding Hood on his side!

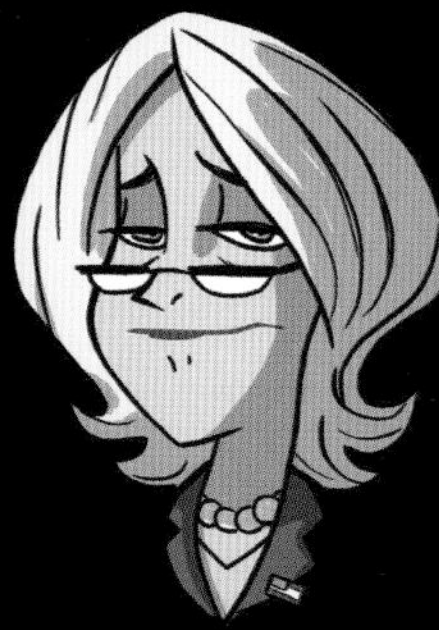

Most versions of Little Red Riding Hood feature a sickly grandmother in need of food and care. In this version, she's the President of the United States!

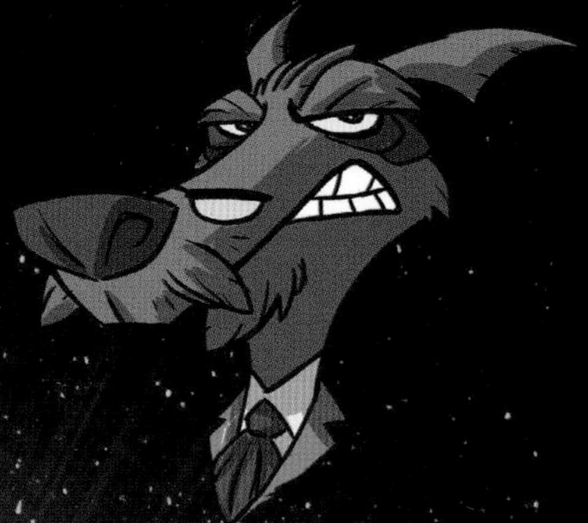

The Big Bad Wolf is in every version of Red Riding Hood--but this time he's a werewolf! And he wreaks havoc in his Big Bad Wolf-Bot. Only Red Riding Hood, Superhero, has what it takes to stop the menace from kidnapping the President of the United States.

FAR OUT FAIRY TALES

SUPER
BILLY GOATS
GRUFF

A GRAPHIC NOVEL

BY SEAN TULIEN
ILLUSTRATED BY FERNANDO CANO

INTRODUCING...

PLAYER 1:

LITTLE GRUFF,
THE NINJA-GOAT

STATS:
LEVEL: 10
INTELLIGENCE: 2
STRENGTH: 1
AGILITY: 5
LUCK: 2

STRENGTHS:
Quick-hoofed and competitive

WEAKNESSES:
Shiny objects, paying attention

PLAYER 2:

MIDDLE GRUFF,
THE WIZARD-GOAT

STATS:
LEVEL: 11
INTELLIGENCE: 6
STRENGTH: 1
AGILITY: 2
LUCK: 2

STRENGTHS:
Smart and observant

WEAKNESSES:
Bossy

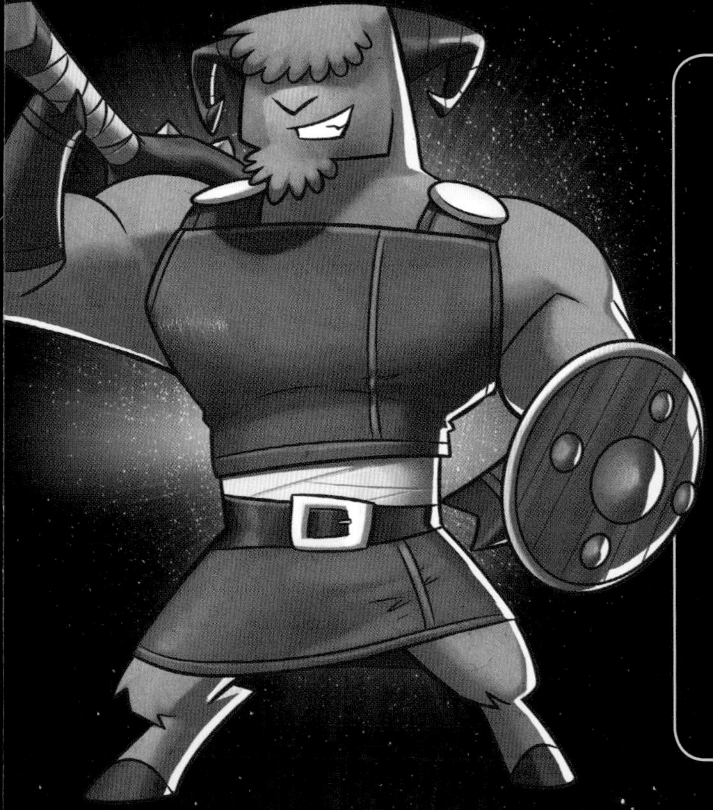

PLAYER 3:

BIG GRUFF,
THE WARRIOR-GOAT

STATS:
LEVEL: 12
INTELLIGENCE: 1
STRENGTH: 6
AGILITY: 3
LUCK: 2

STRENGTHS:
Determined

WEAKNESSES:
Stubborn

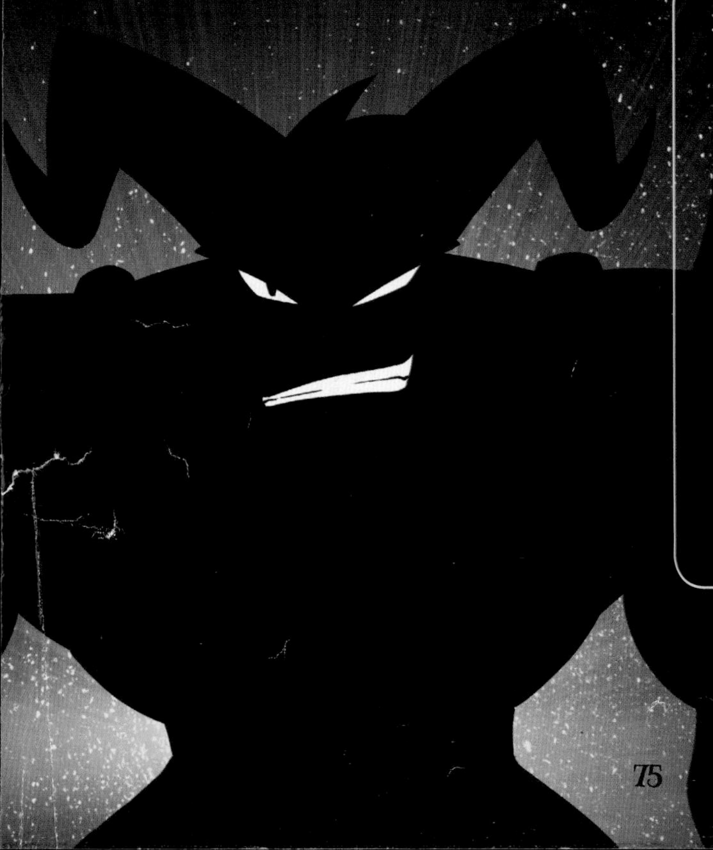

FINAL BOSS

STATS:
LEVEL: ☠
INTELLIGENCE: ??
STRENGTH: 99
AGILITY: ??
LUCK: ??

STRENGTHS:
Strength

WEAKNESSES:
??

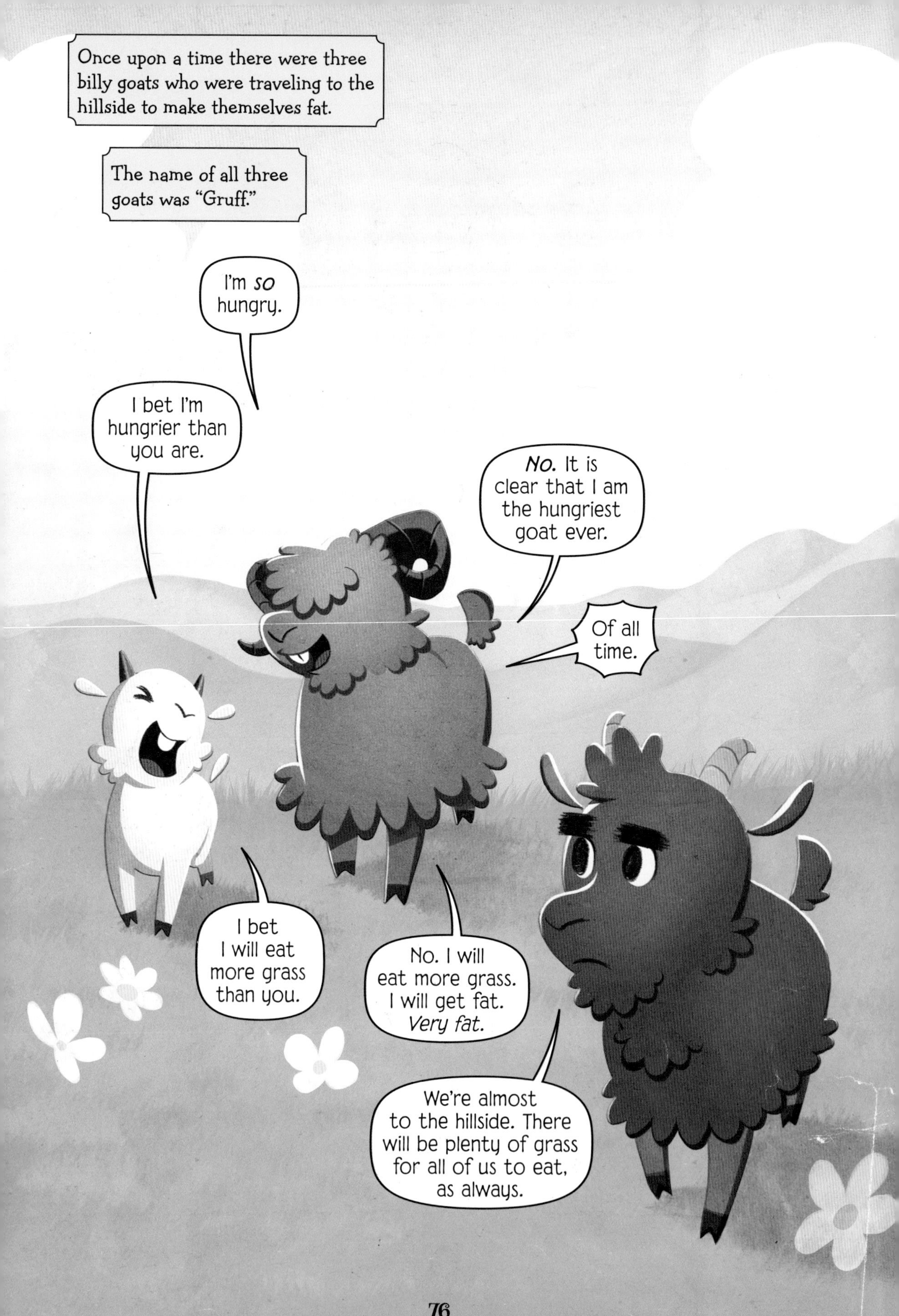
Once upon a time there were three billy goats who were traveling to the hillside to make themselves fat.
The name of all three goats was "Gruff."
I'm *so* hungry.
I bet I'm hungrier than you are.
No. It is clear that I am the hungriest goat ever.
Of all time.
I bet I will eat more grass than you.
No. I will eat more grass. I will get fat. *Very fat.*
We're almost to the hillside. There will be plenty of grass for all of us to eat, as always.

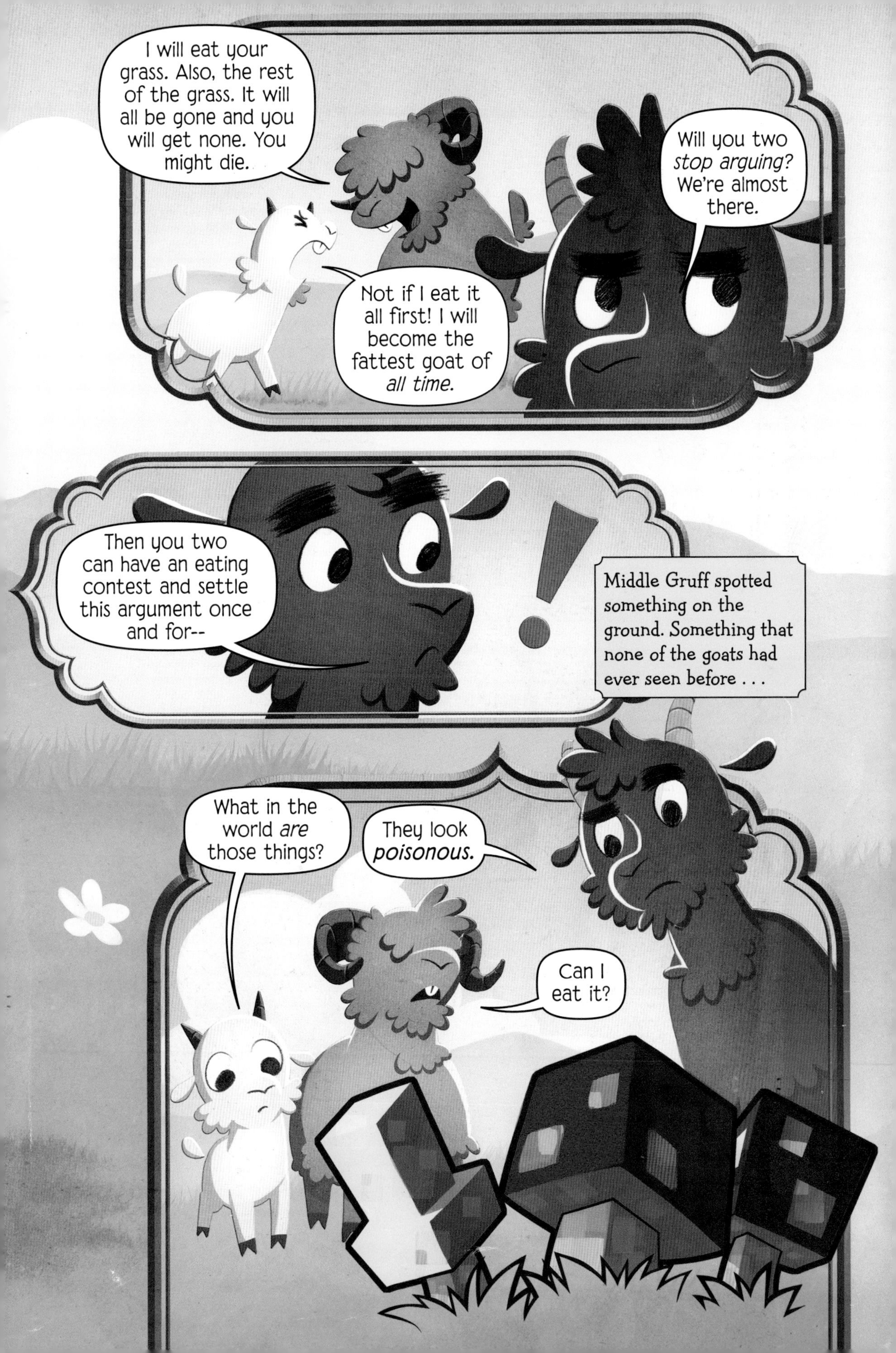
I will eat your grass. Also, the rest of the grass. It will all be gone and you will get none. You might die.
Will you two *stop arguing?* We're almost there.
Not if I eat it all first! I will become the fattest goat of *all time.*
Then you two can have an eating contest and settle this argument once and for--
!
Middle Gruff spotted something on the ground. Something that none of the goats had ever seen before . . .
What in the world *are* those things?
They look ***poisonous.***
Can I eat it?

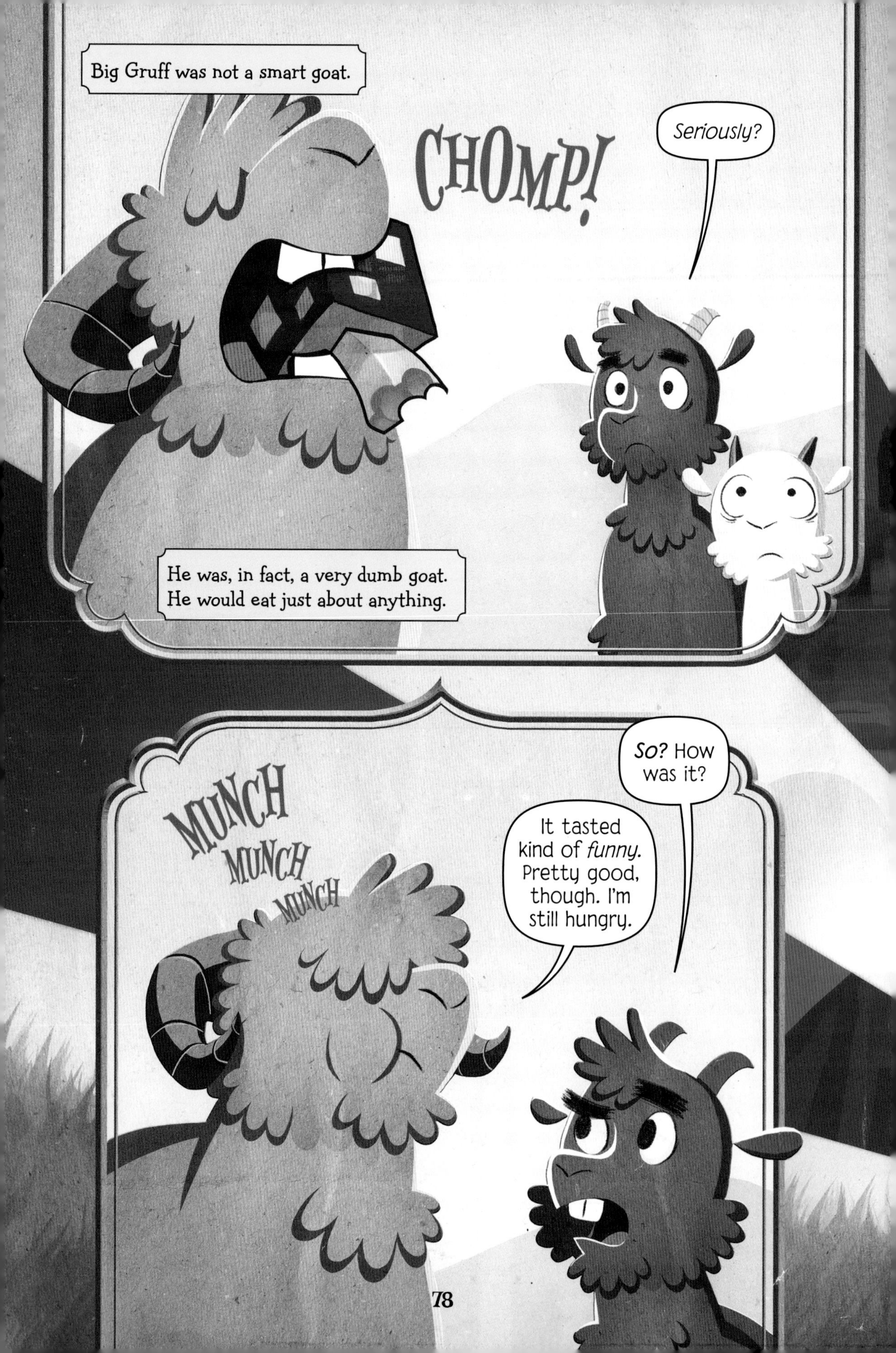

Big Gruff was not a smart goat.
CHOMP!
Seriously?
He was, in fact, a very dumb goat. He would eat just about anything.
MUNCH MUNCH MUNCH
So? How was it?
It tasted kind of *funny*. Pretty good, though. I'm still hungry.

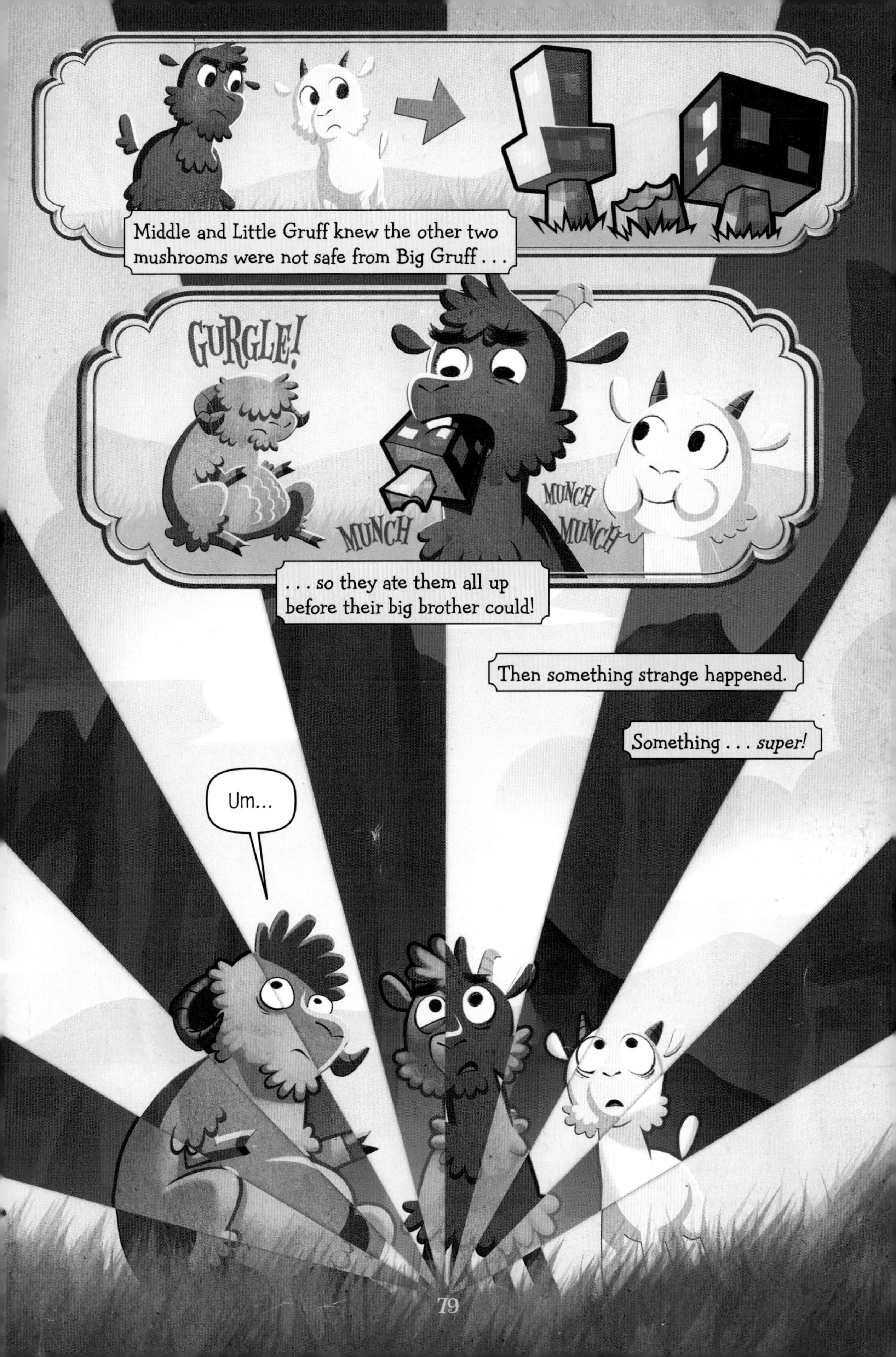
Middle and Little Gruff knew the other two mushrooms were not safe from Big Gruff . . .
GURGLE!
MUNCH
MUNCH
MUNCH
. . . so they ate them all up before their big brother could!
Then something strange happened.
Something . . . *super!*
Um...

SUPER BILLY GOATS GRUFF!

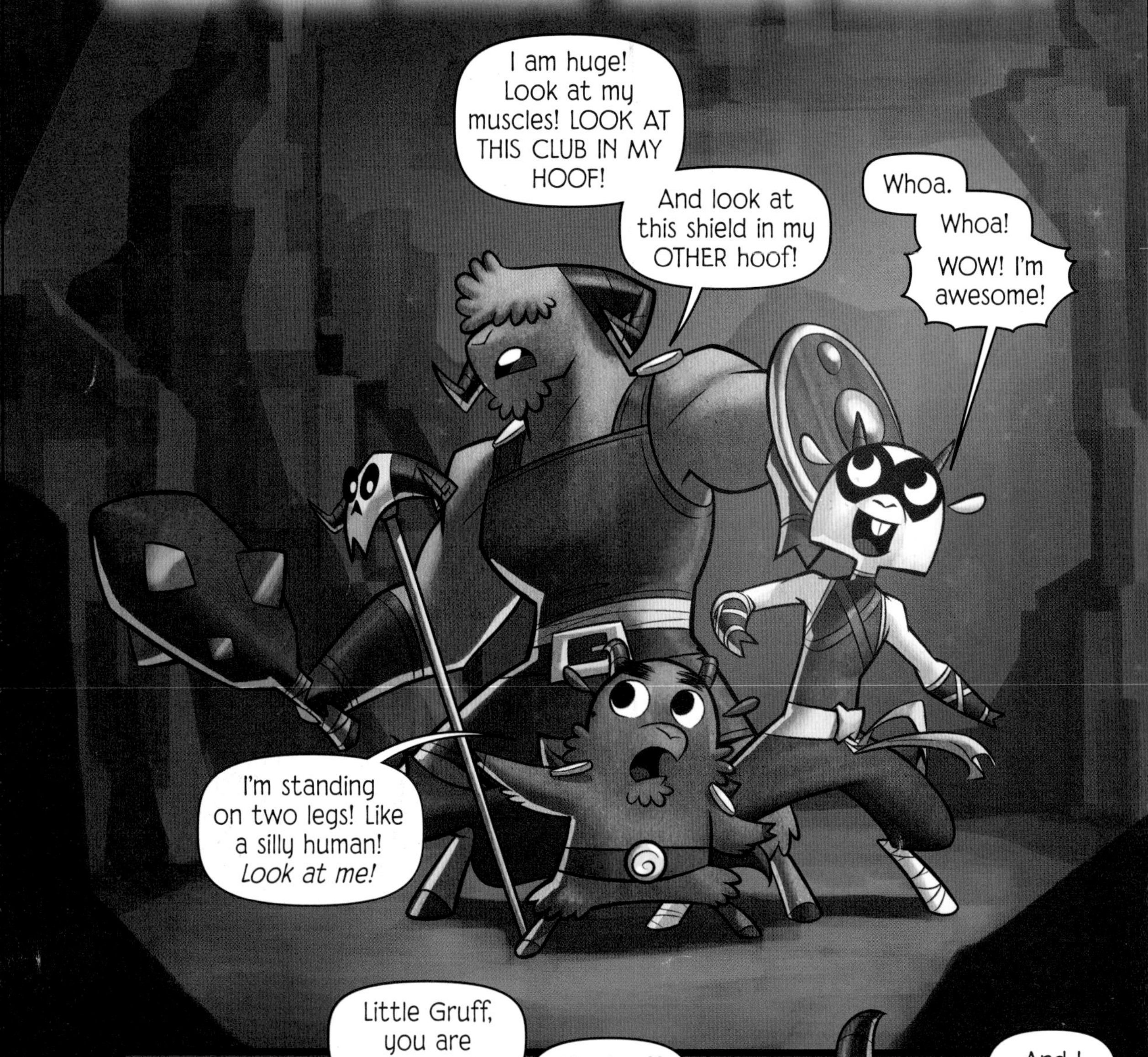
I am huge! Look at my muscles! LOOK AT THIS CLUB IN MY HOOF!
And look at this shield in my OTHER hoof!
Whoa.
Whoa!
WOW! I'm awesome!
I'm standing on two legs! Like a silly human! *Look at me!*

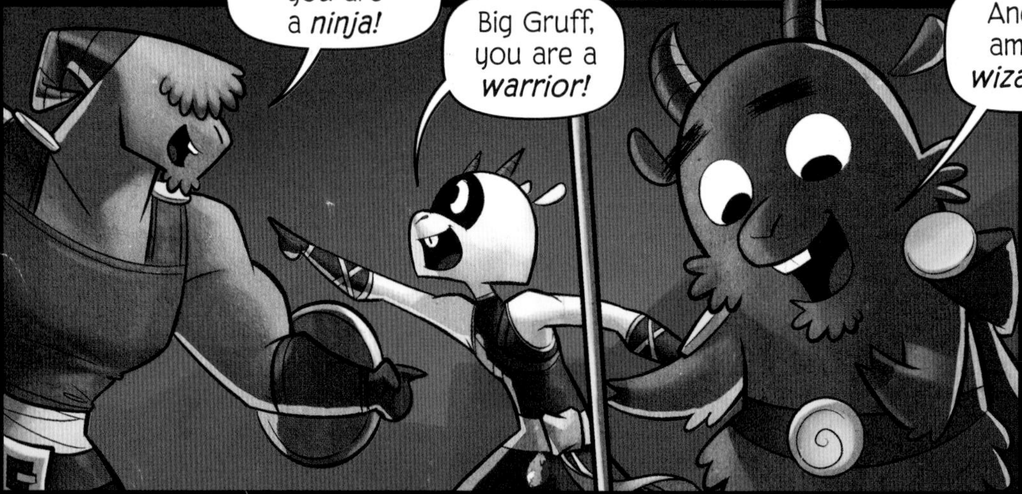
Little Gruff, you are a *ninja!*
Big Gruff, you are a *warrior!*
And I am a *wizard!*

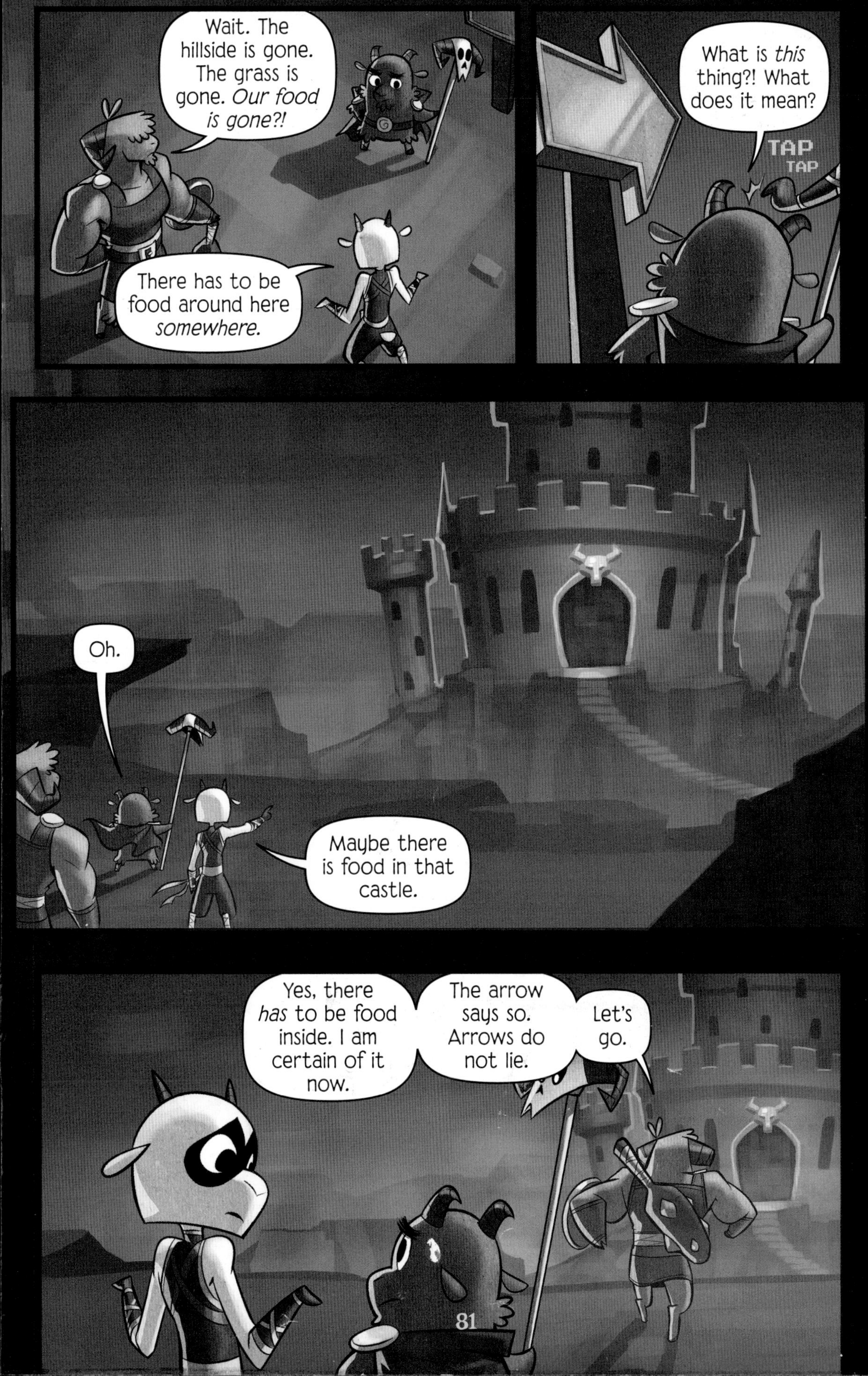
Wait. The hillside is gone. The grass is gone. *Our food is gone?!*
There has to be food around here *somewhere.*
What is *this* thing?! What does it mean?
TAP TAP
Oh.
Maybe there is food in that castle.
Yes, there *has* to be food inside. I am certain of it now.
The arrow says so. Arrows do not lie.
Let's go.

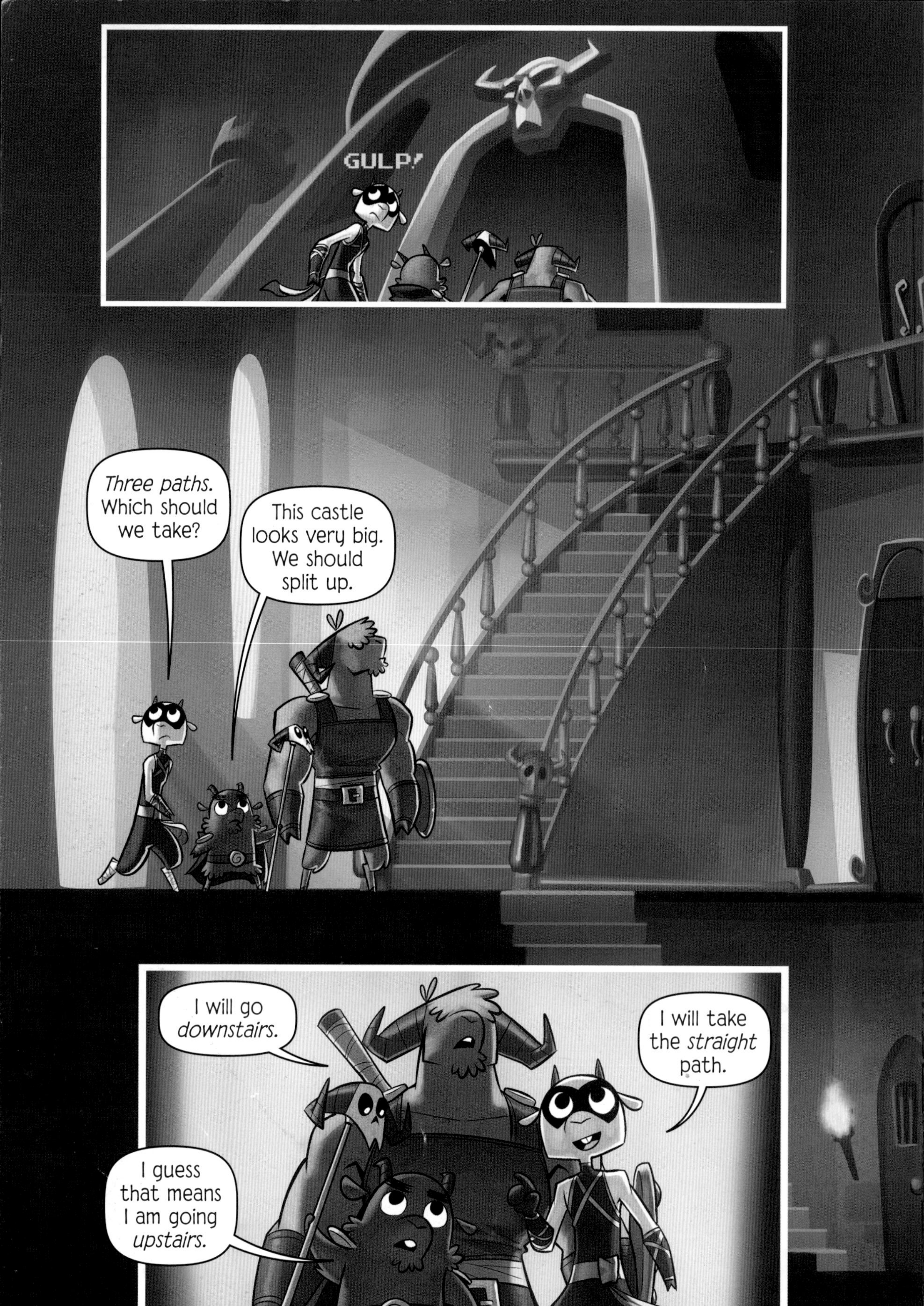
GULP!
Three paths. Which should we take?
This castle looks very big. We should split up.
I will go *downstairs.*
I will take the *straight* path.
I guess that means I am going *upstairs.*

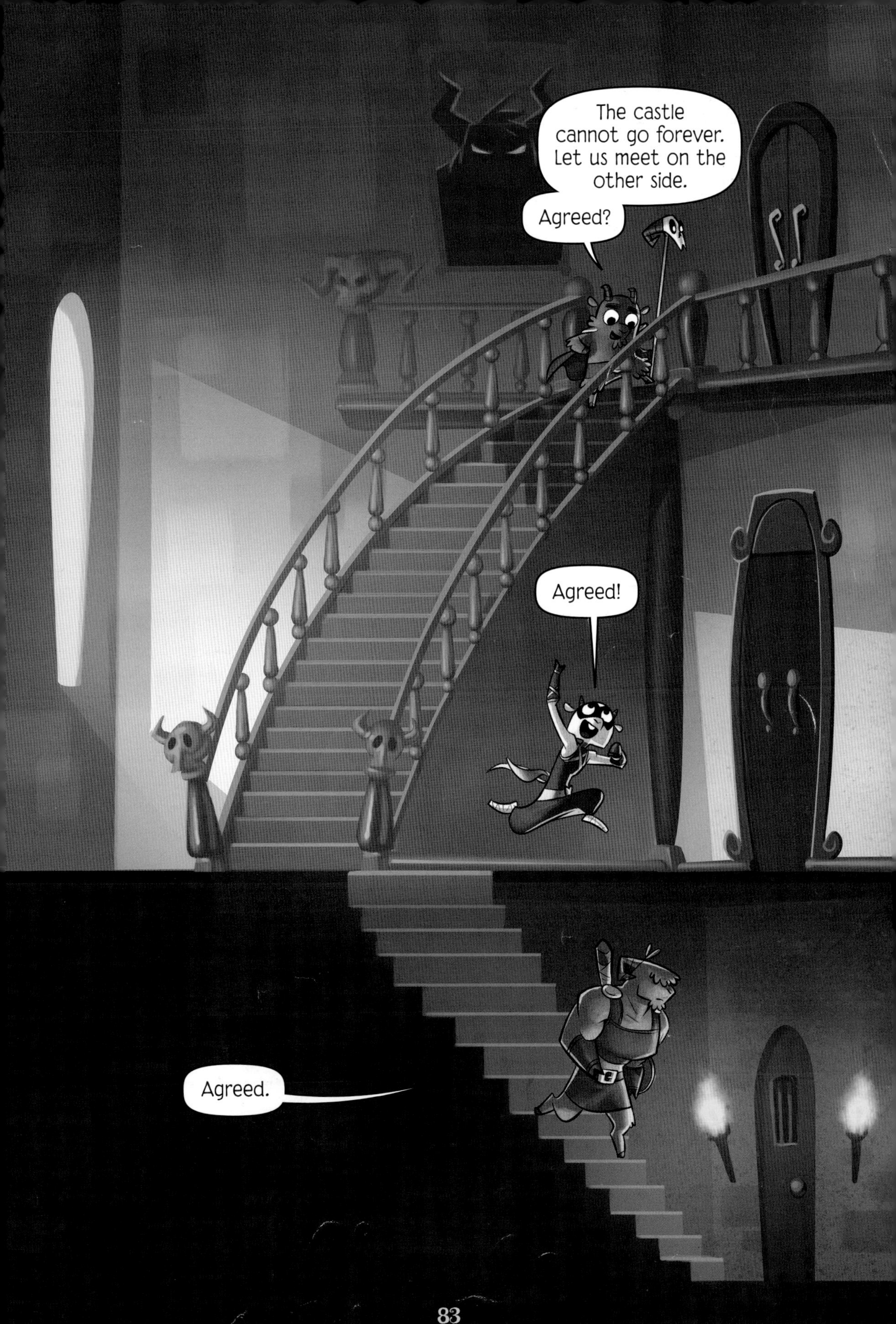
The castle cannot go forever. Let us meet on the other side.
Agreed?
Agreed!
Agreed.

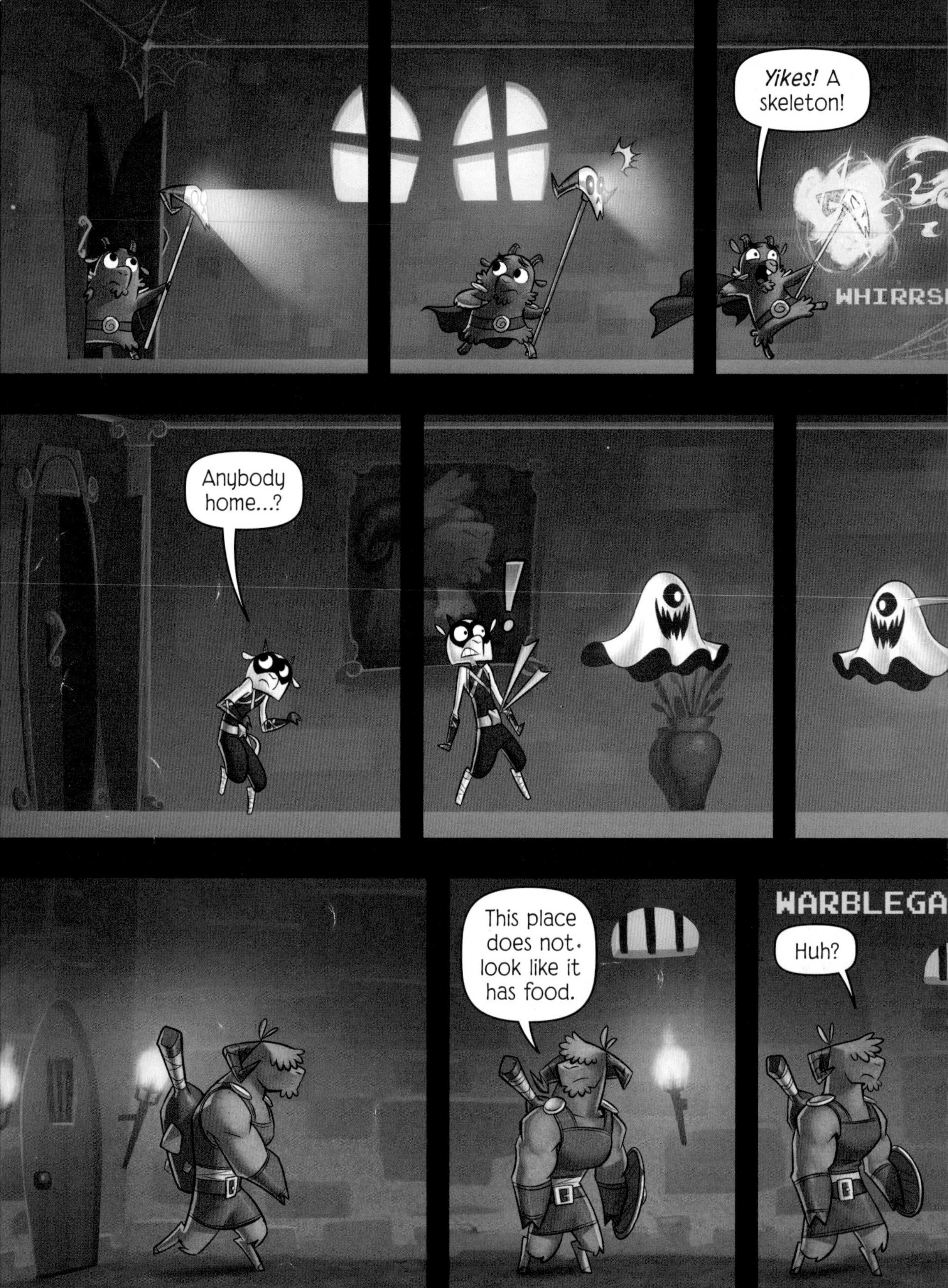
Yikes! A skeleton!
WHIRRSH
Anybody home...?
This place does not look like it has food.
WARBLEGA
Huh?

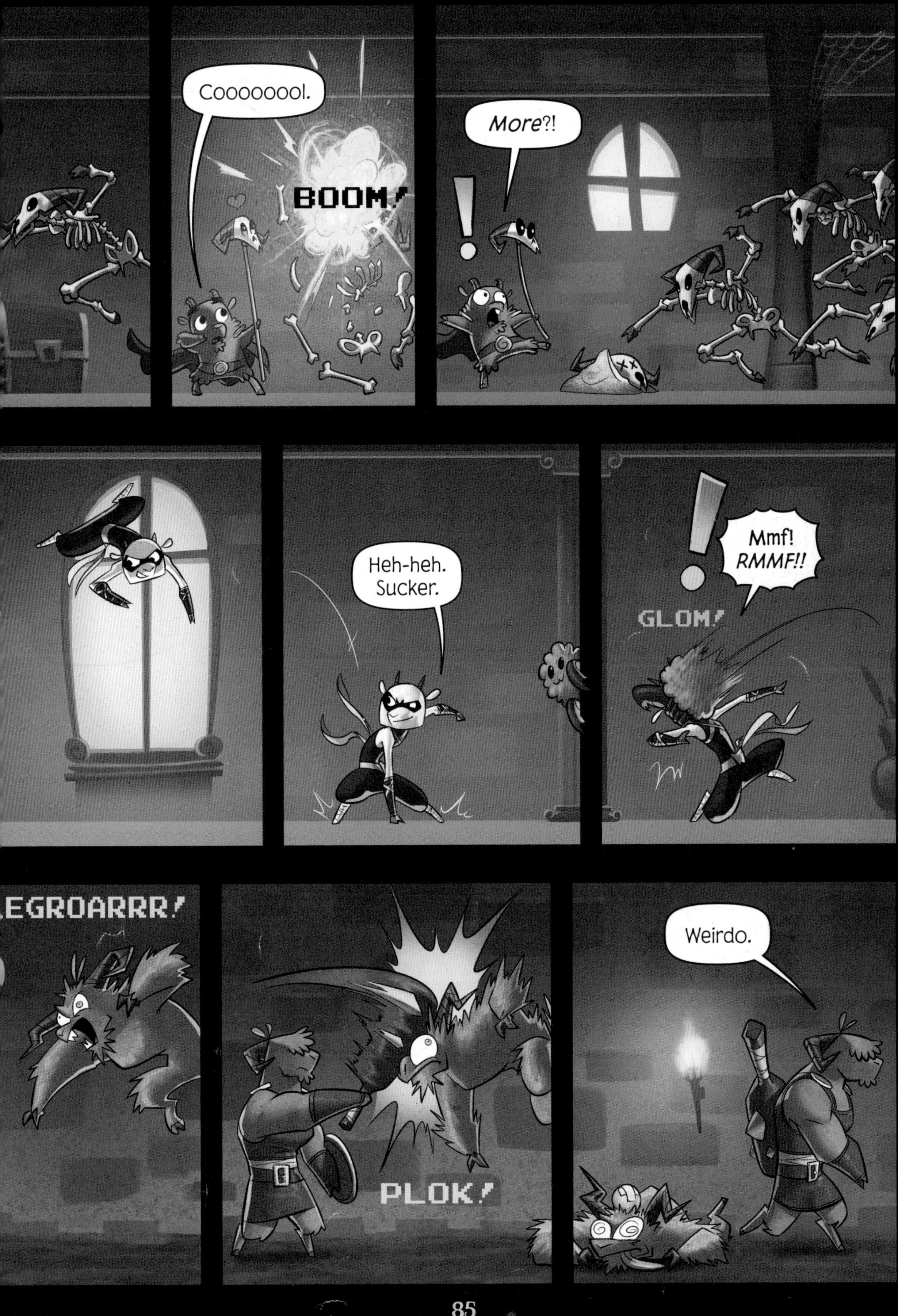
Cooooooool.
BOOM!
More?!
Heh-heh.
Sucker.
Mmf!
RMMF!!
GLOM!
EGROARRR!
PLOK!
Weirdo.

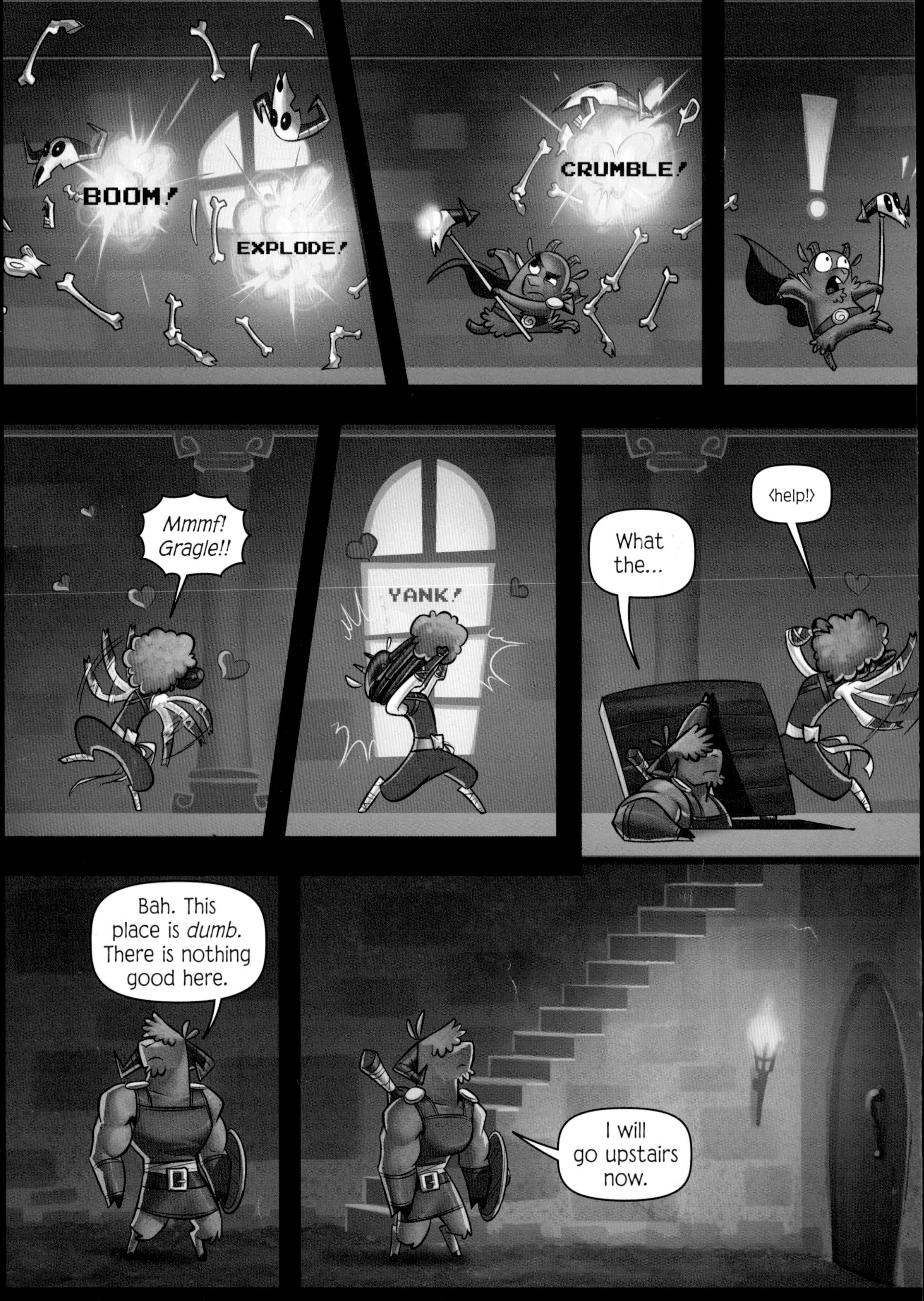
BOOM!
EXPLODE!
CRUMBLE!
!
Mmmf! Gragle!!
YANK!
What the...
<help!>
Bah. This place is *dumb*. There is nothing good here.
I will go upstairs now.

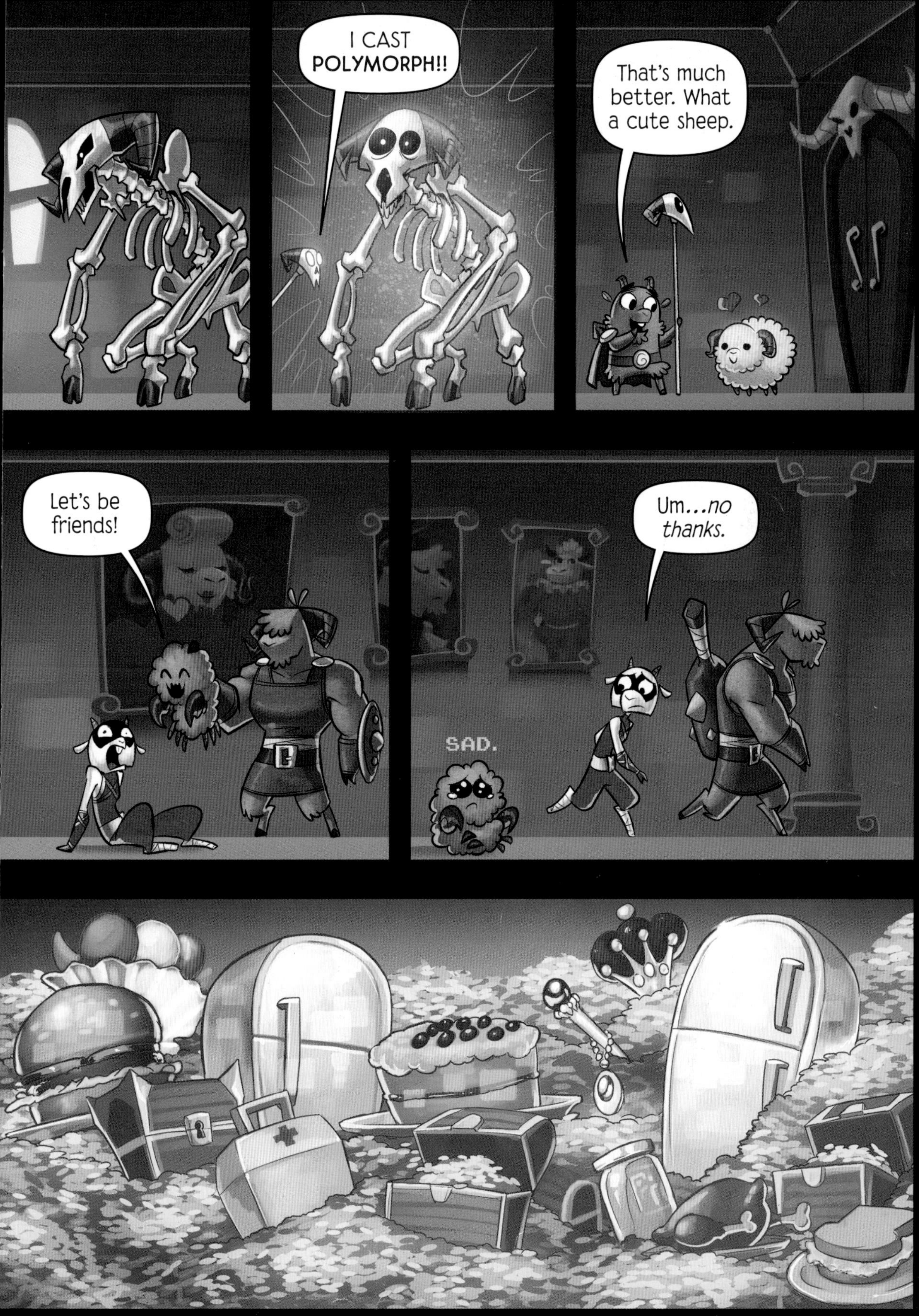
I CAST **POLYMORPH!!**
That's much better. What a cute sheep.
Let's be friends!
Um...*no thanks.*
SAD.

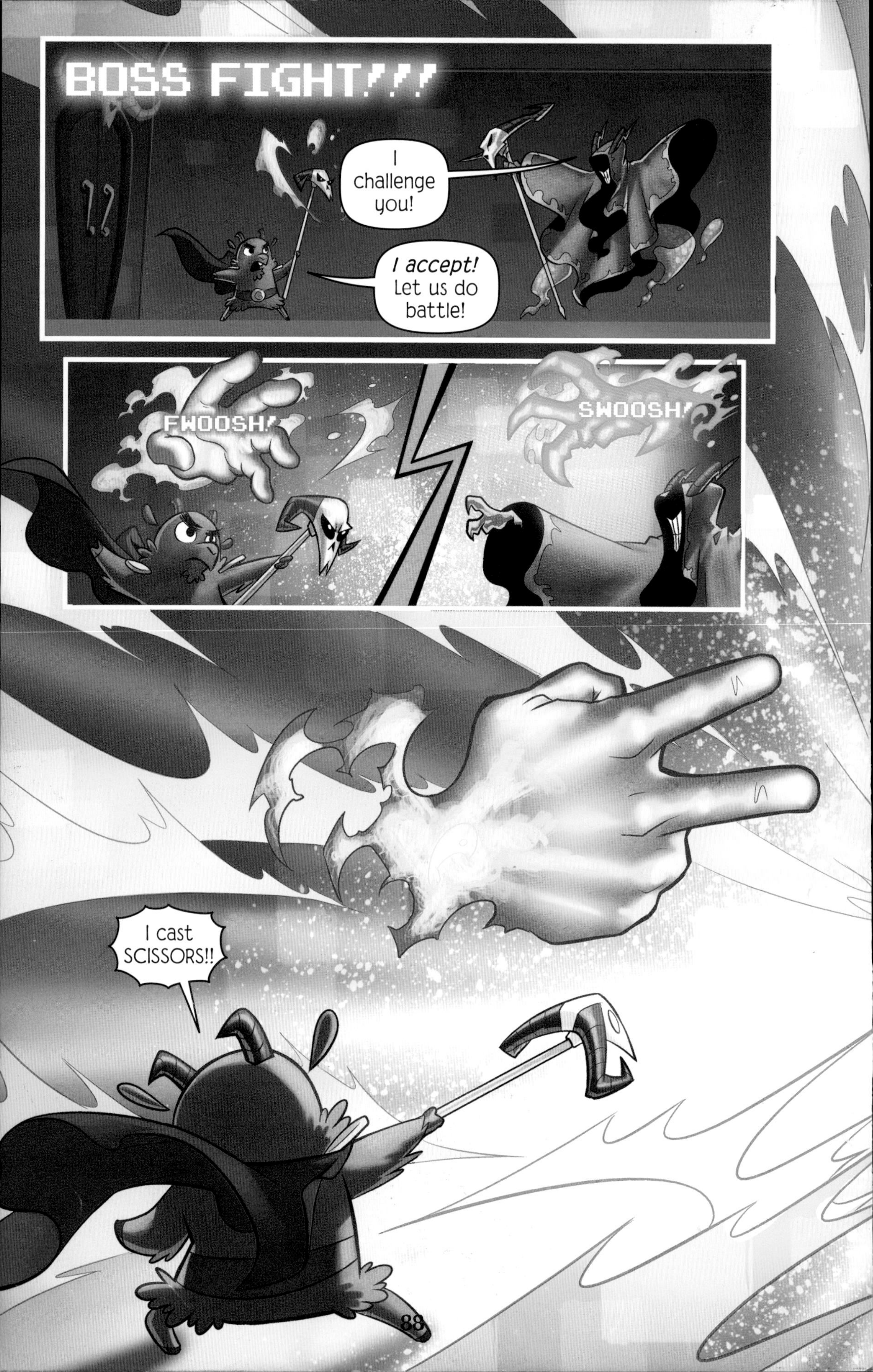
BOSS FIGHT!!!
I challenge you!
I accept! Let us do battle!
FWOOSH!
SWOOSH!
I cast SCISSORS!!

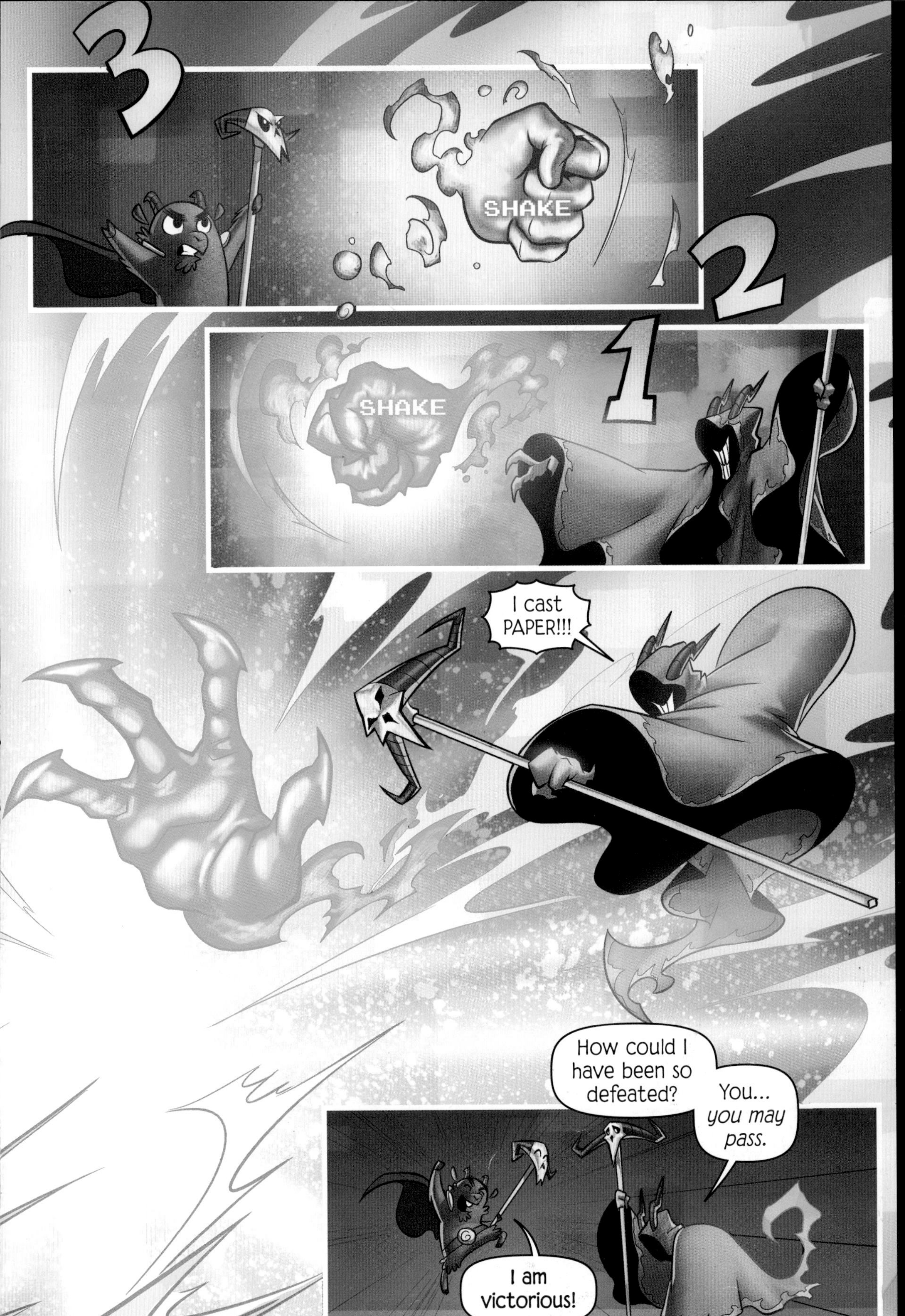
3
SHAKE
2
1
SHAKE
I cast PAPER!!!
How could I have been so defeated?
You... *you may pass.*
I am victorious!

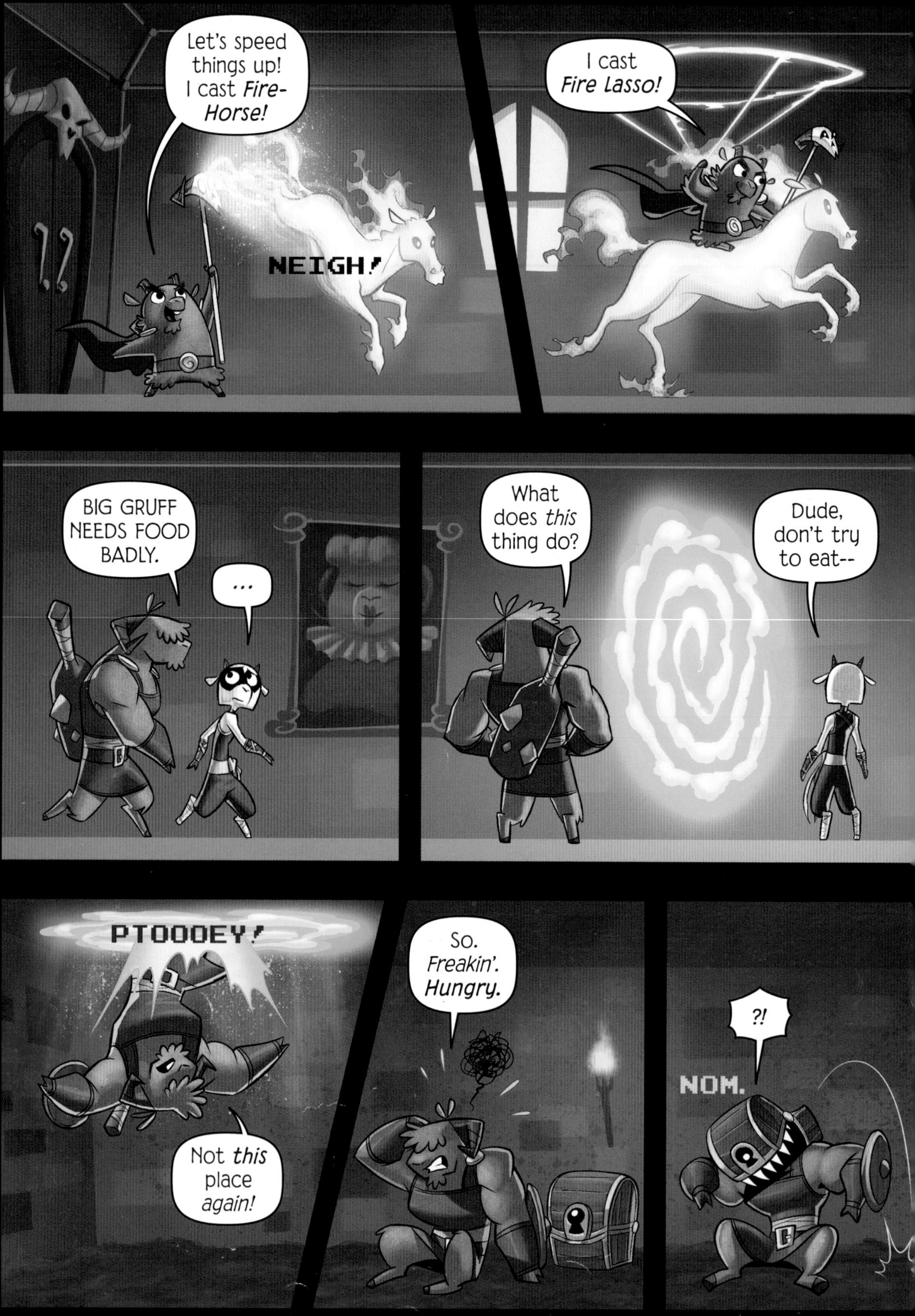
Let's speed things up! I cast *Fire-Horse!*
NEIGH!
I cast *Fire Lasso!*
BIG GRUFF NEEDS FOOD BADLY.
...
What does *this* thing do?
Dude, don't try to eat--
PTOOOEY!
Not *this* place *again!*
So. *Freakin'. Hungry.*
?!
NOM.

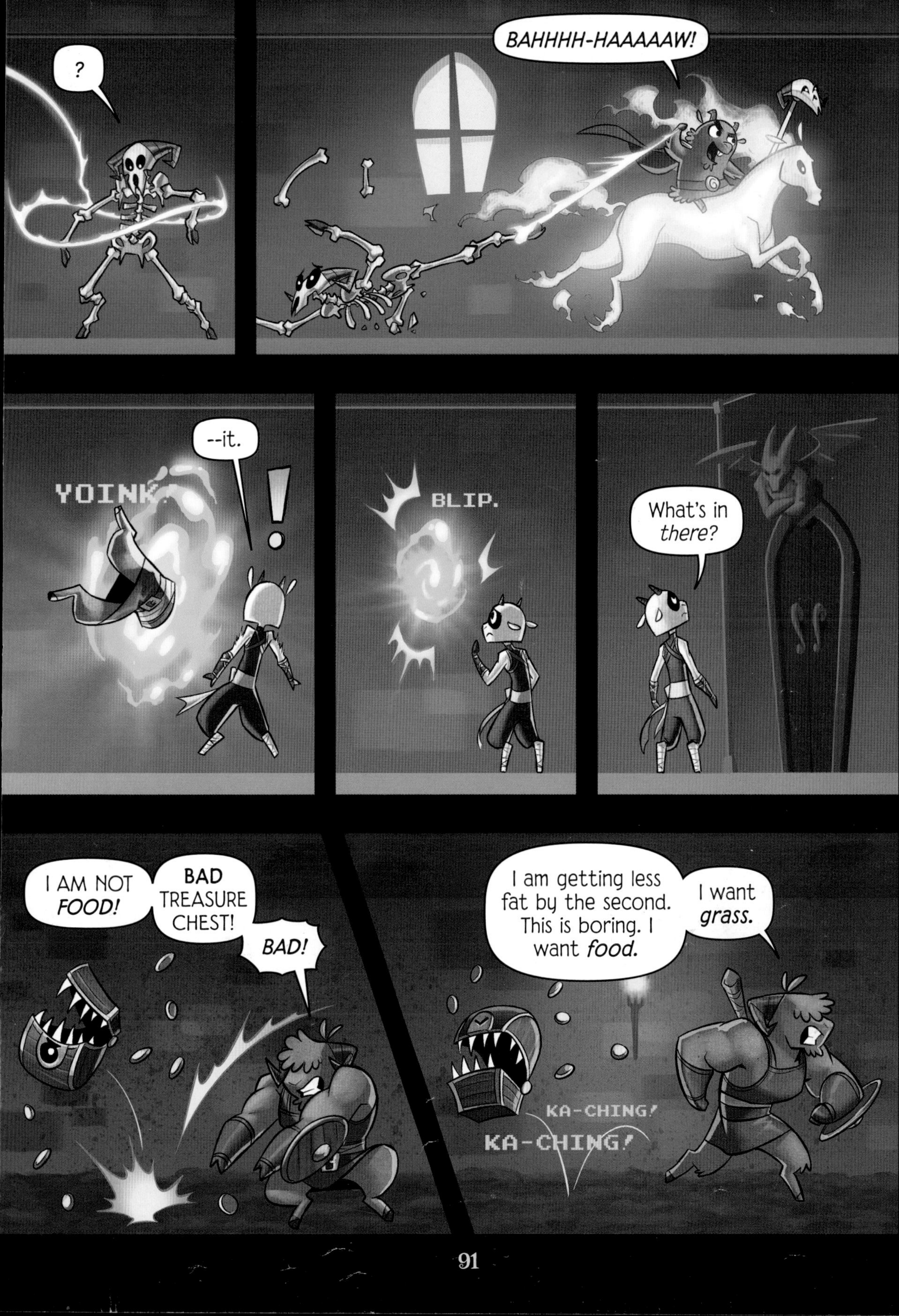
?
BAHHHH-HAAAAAW!
YOINK!
--it.
!
BLIP.
What's in *there*?
I AM NOT *FOOD!*
BAD TREASURE CHEST!
BAD!
I am getting less fat by the second. This is boring. I want *food.*
I want *grass.*
KA-CHING!
KA-CHING!

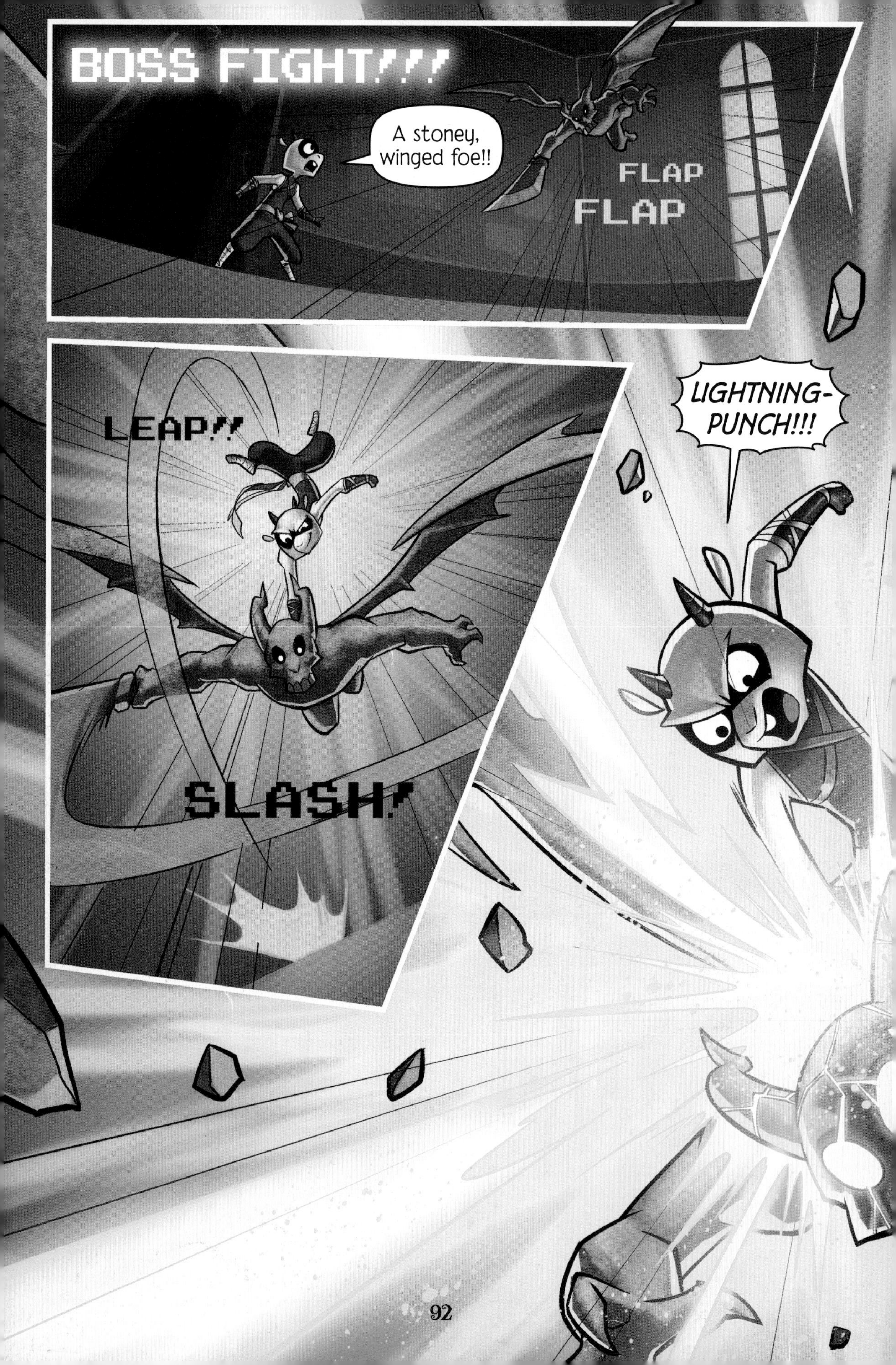
BOSS FIGHT!!!
A stoney, winged foe!!
FLAP
FLAP
LEAP!!
SLASH!
LIGHTNING-PUNCH!!!

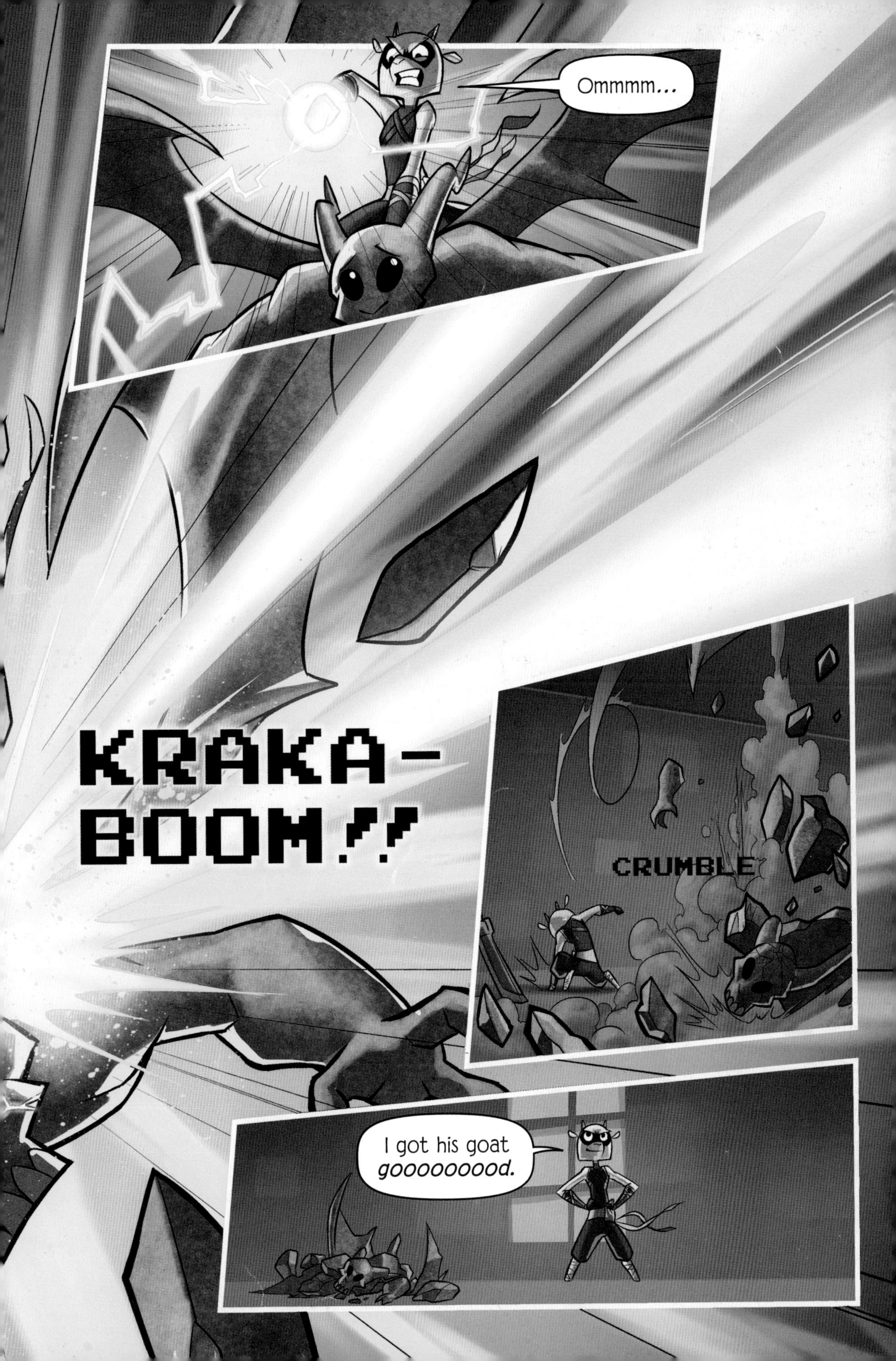
Ommmm...
KRAKA-
BOOM!!
CRUMBLE
I got his goat
gooooooood.

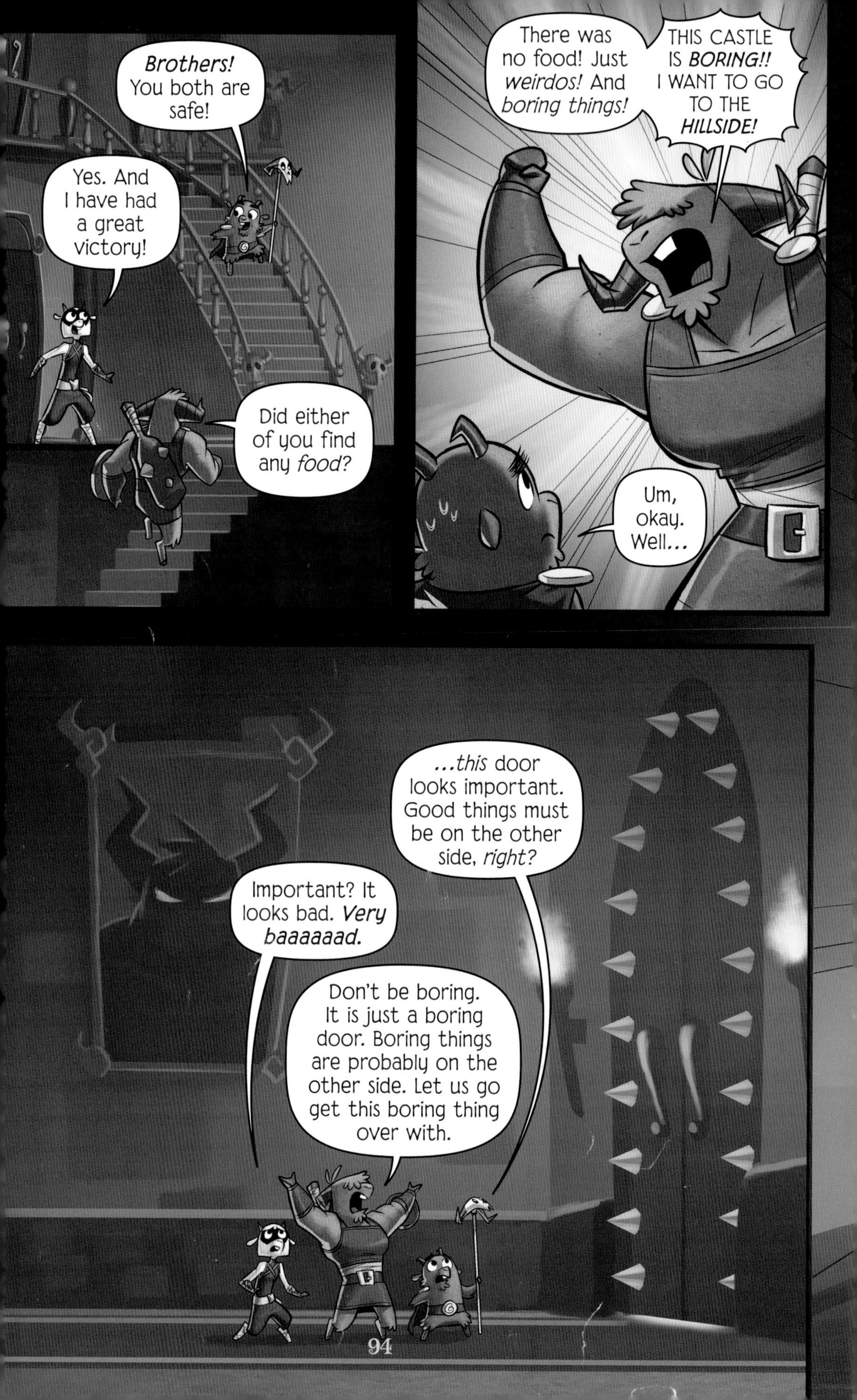

Brothers! You both are safe!
Yes. And I have had a great victory!
Did either of you find any *food?*
There was no food! Just *weirdos!* And *boring things!*
THIS CASTLE IS ***BORING!!*** I WANT TO GO TO THE ***HILLSIDE!***
Um, okay. Well…
…*this* door looks important. Good things must be on the other side, *right?*
Important? It looks bad. ***Very baaaaaad.***
Don't be boring. It is just a boring door. Boring things are probably on the other side. Let us go get this boring thing over with.

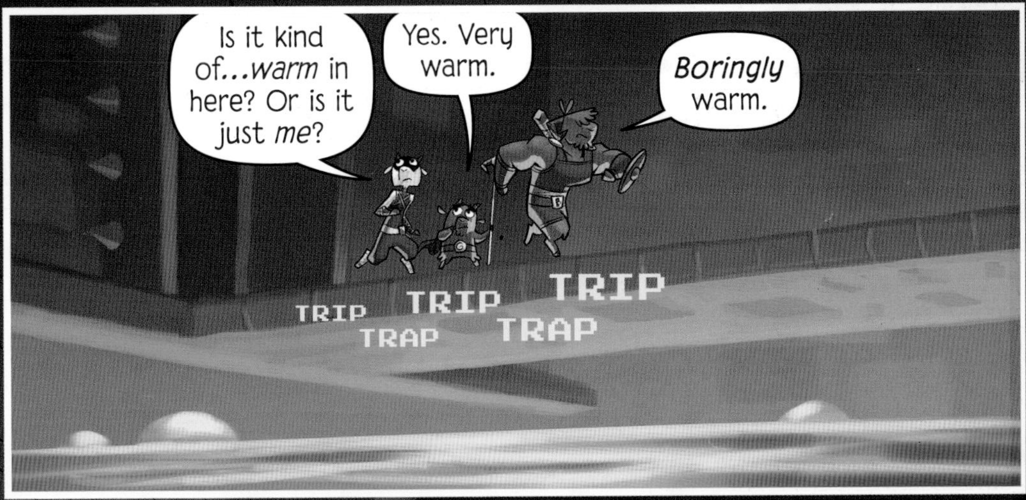

Is it kind of...*warm* in here? Or is it just *me*?
Yes. Very warm.
Boringly warm.
TRIP TRIP TRIP
TRAP TRAP

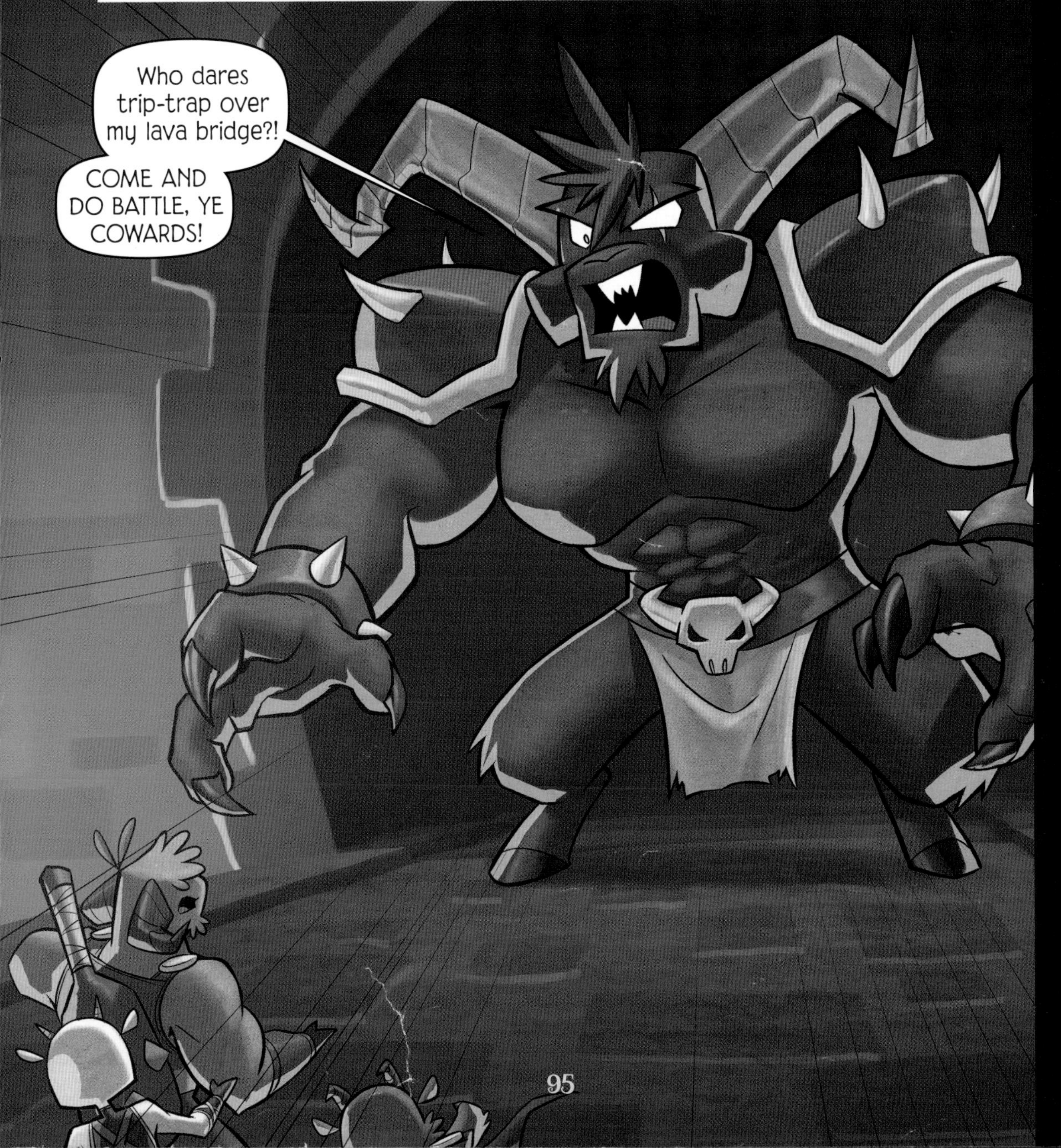

Who dares trip-trap over my lava bridge?!
COME AND DO BATTLE, YE COWARDS!

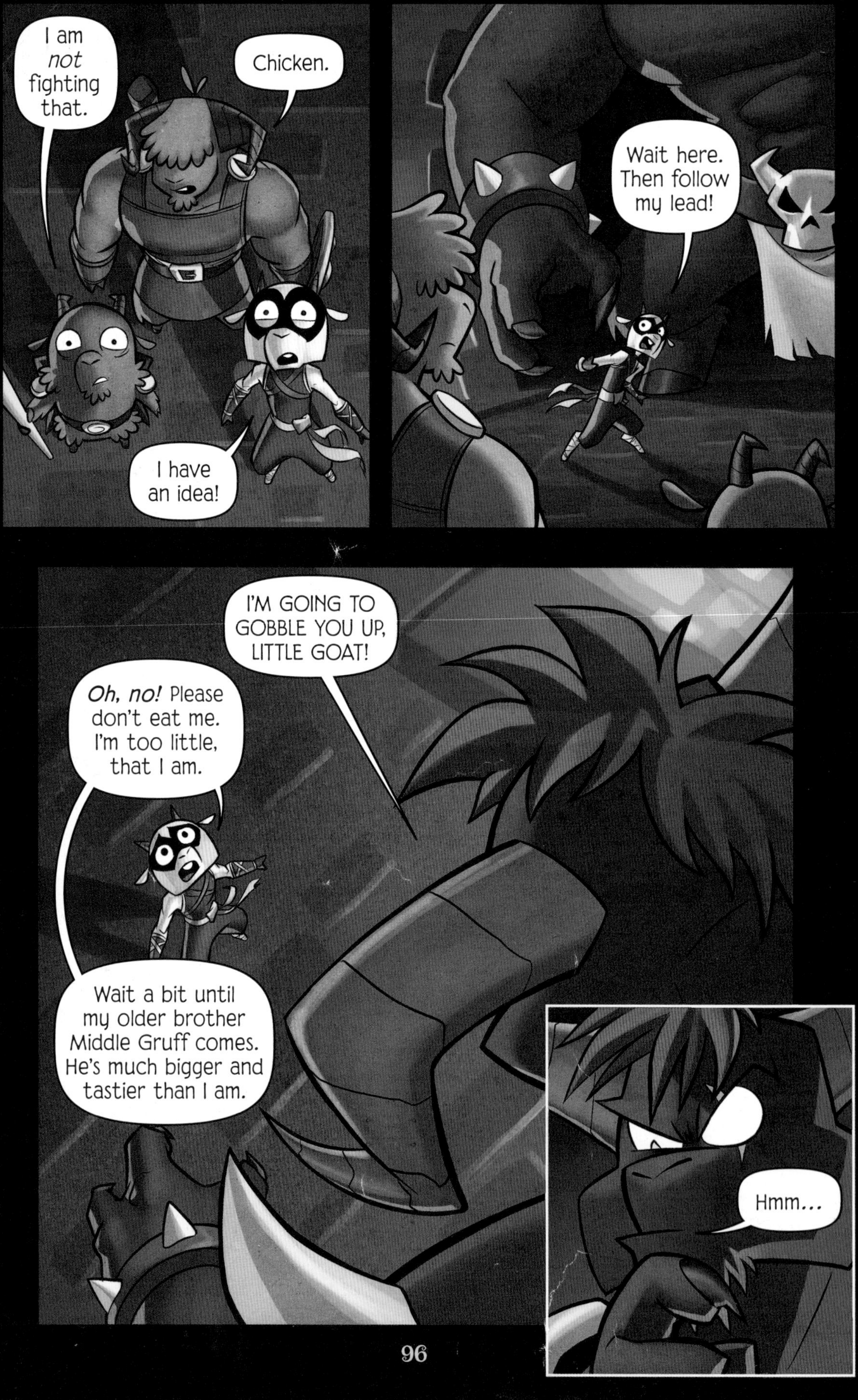
I am *not* fighting that.
Chicken.
I have an idea!
Wait here. Then follow my lead!
I'M GOING TO GOBBLE YOU UP, LITTLE GOAT!
Oh, no! Please don't eat me. I'm too little, that I am.
Wait a bit until my older brother Middle Gruff comes. He's much bigger and tastier than I am.
Hmm...

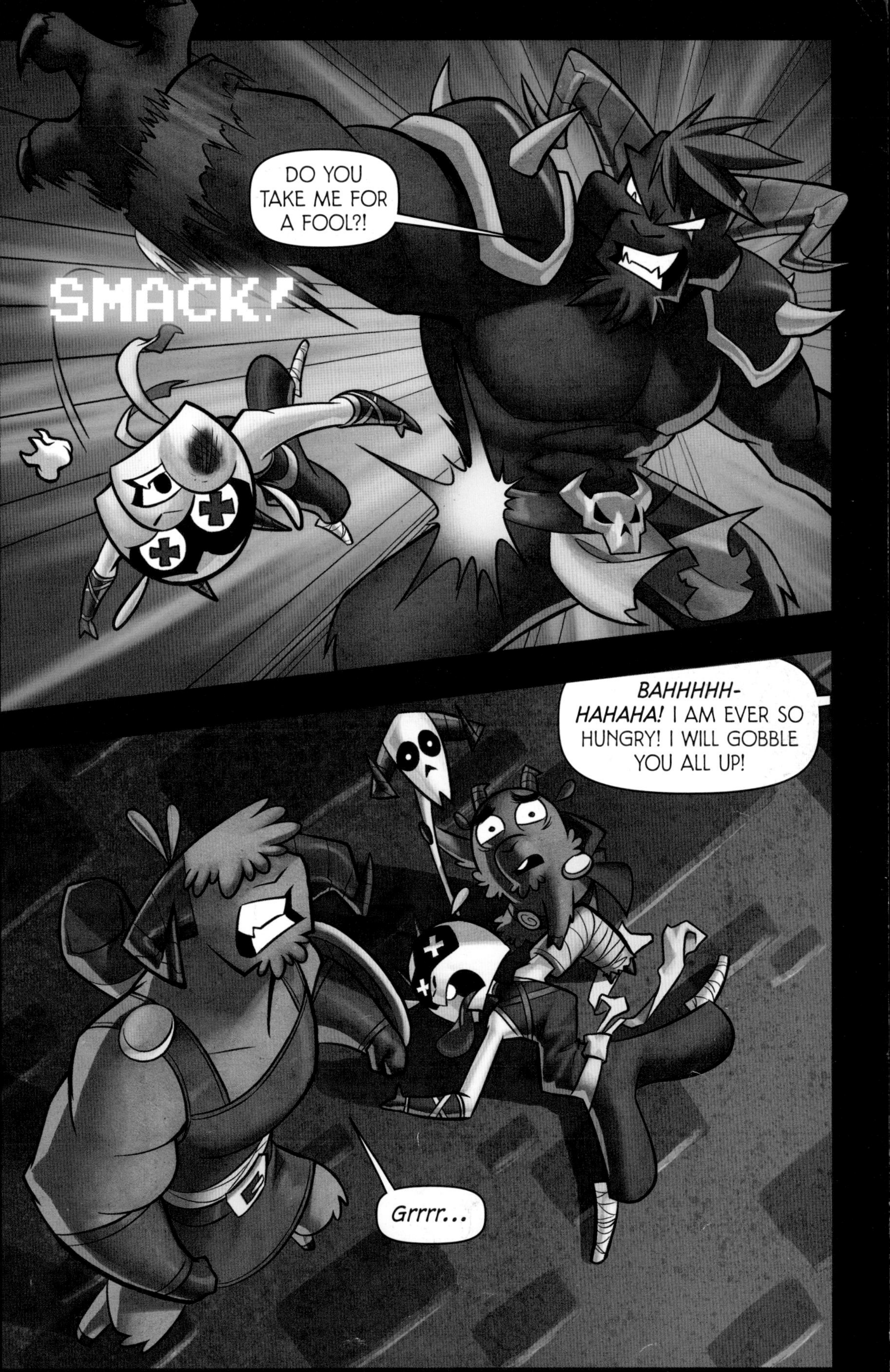
DO YOU TAKE ME FOR A FOOL?!
SMACK!
BAHHHHH-HAHAHA! I AM EVER SO HUNGRY! I WILL GOBBLE YOU ALL UP!
Grrrr...

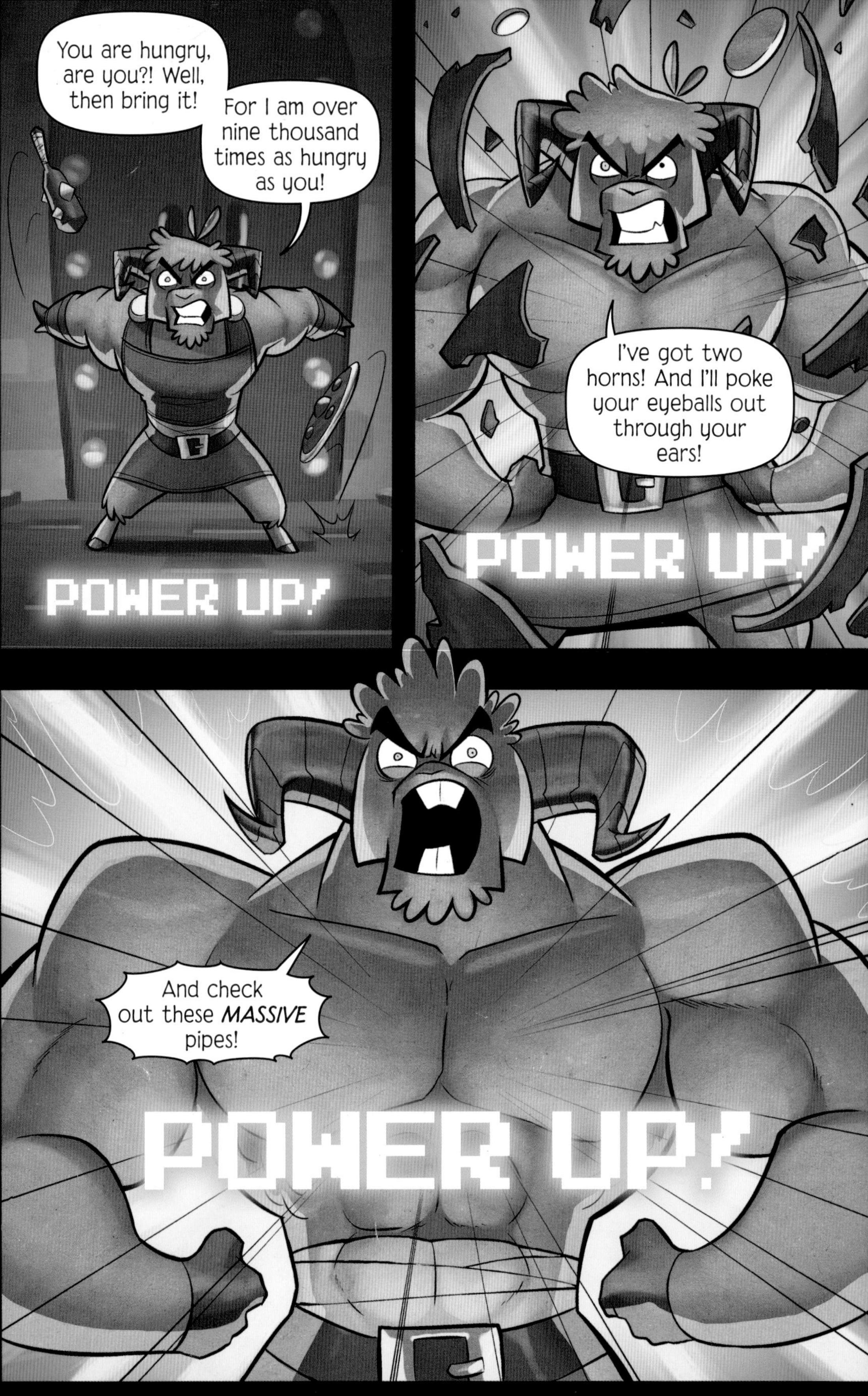
You are hungry, are you?! Well, then bring it!
For I am over nine thousand times as hungry as you!
POWER UP!
I've got two horns! And I'll poke your eyeballs out through your ears!
POWER UP!
And check out these *MASSIVE* pipes!
POWER UP!

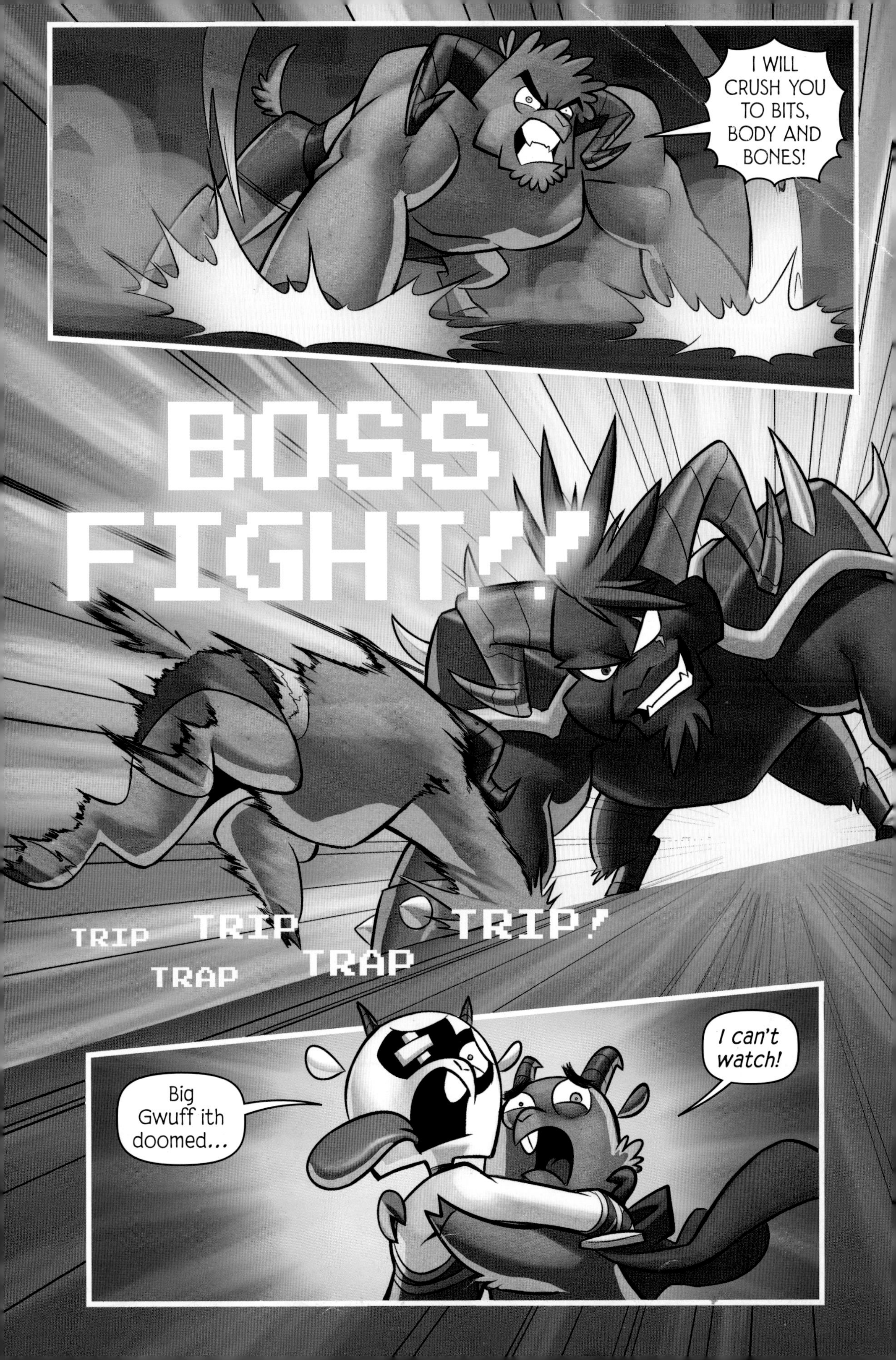
I WILL CRUSH YOU TO BITS, BODY AND BONES!
BOSS FIGHT!!
TRIP
TRIP
TRIP!
TRAP
TRAP
Big Gwuff ith doomed...
I can't watch!

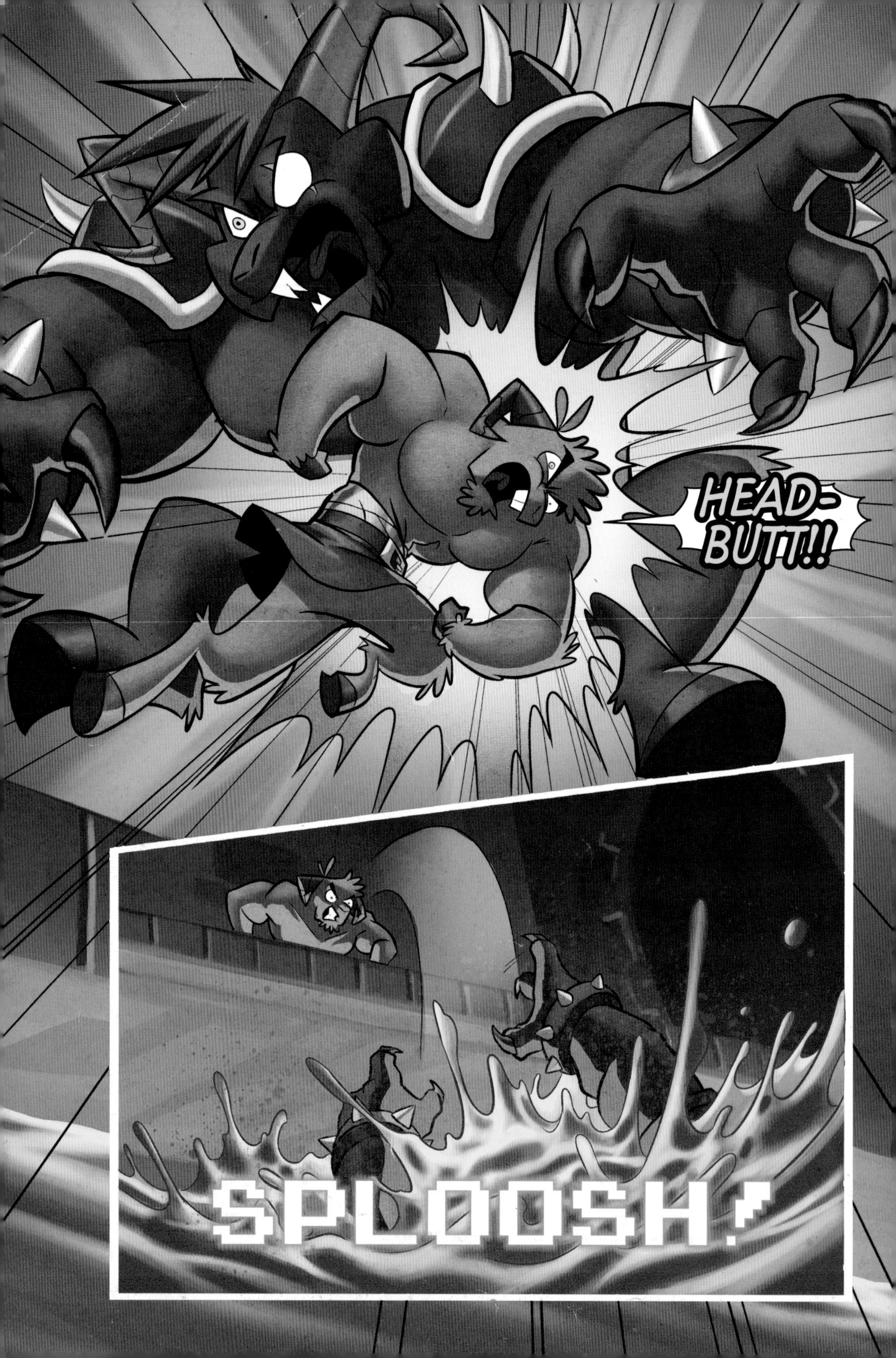
HEAD-
BUTT!!
SPLOOSH!

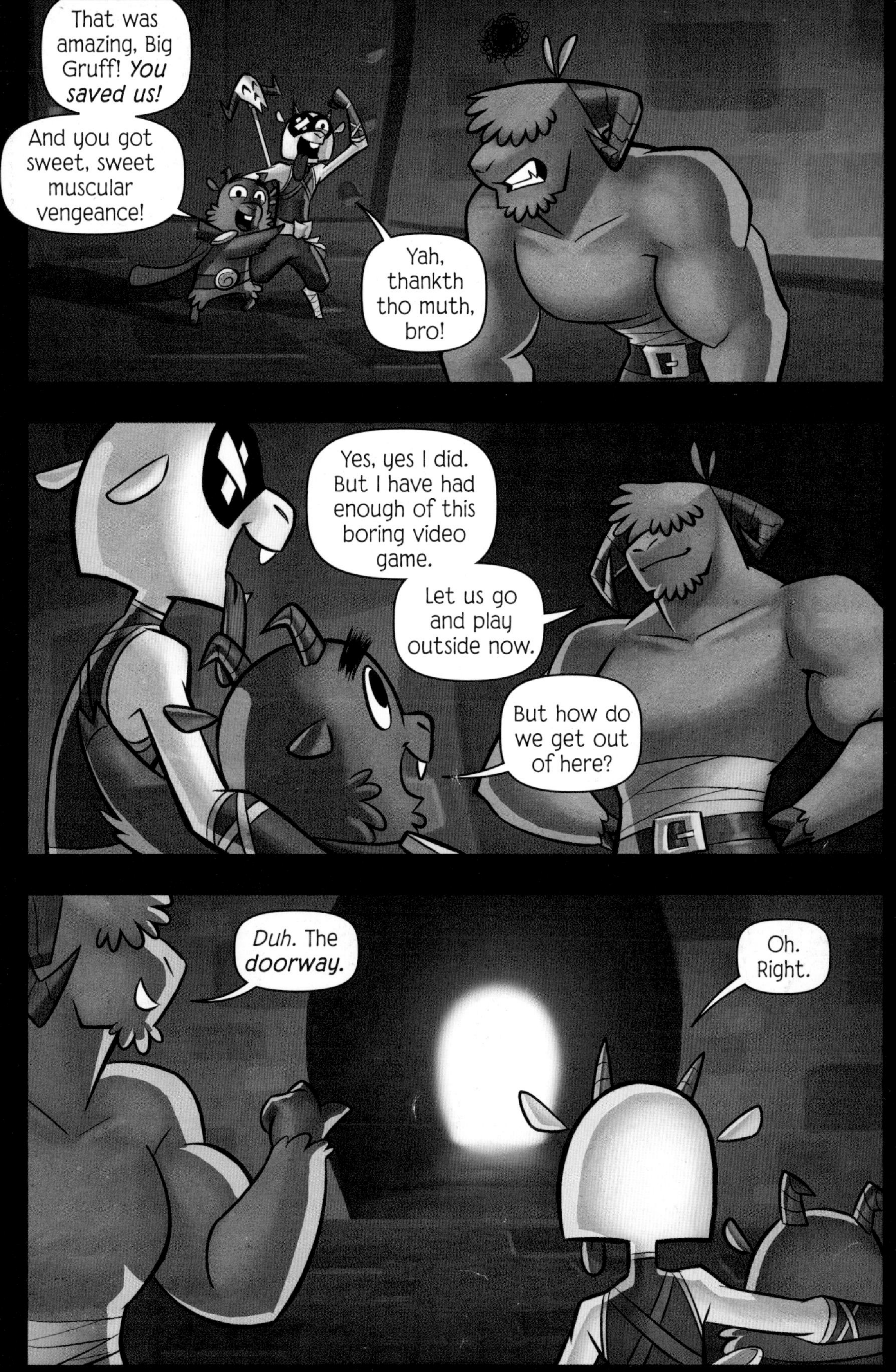

That was amazing, Big Gruff! *You saved us!*
And you got sweet, sweet muscular vengeance!
Yah, thankth tho muth, bro!
Yes, yes I did. But I have had enough of this boring video game.
Let us go and play outside now.
But how do we get out of here?
Duh. The ***doorway.***
Oh. Right.

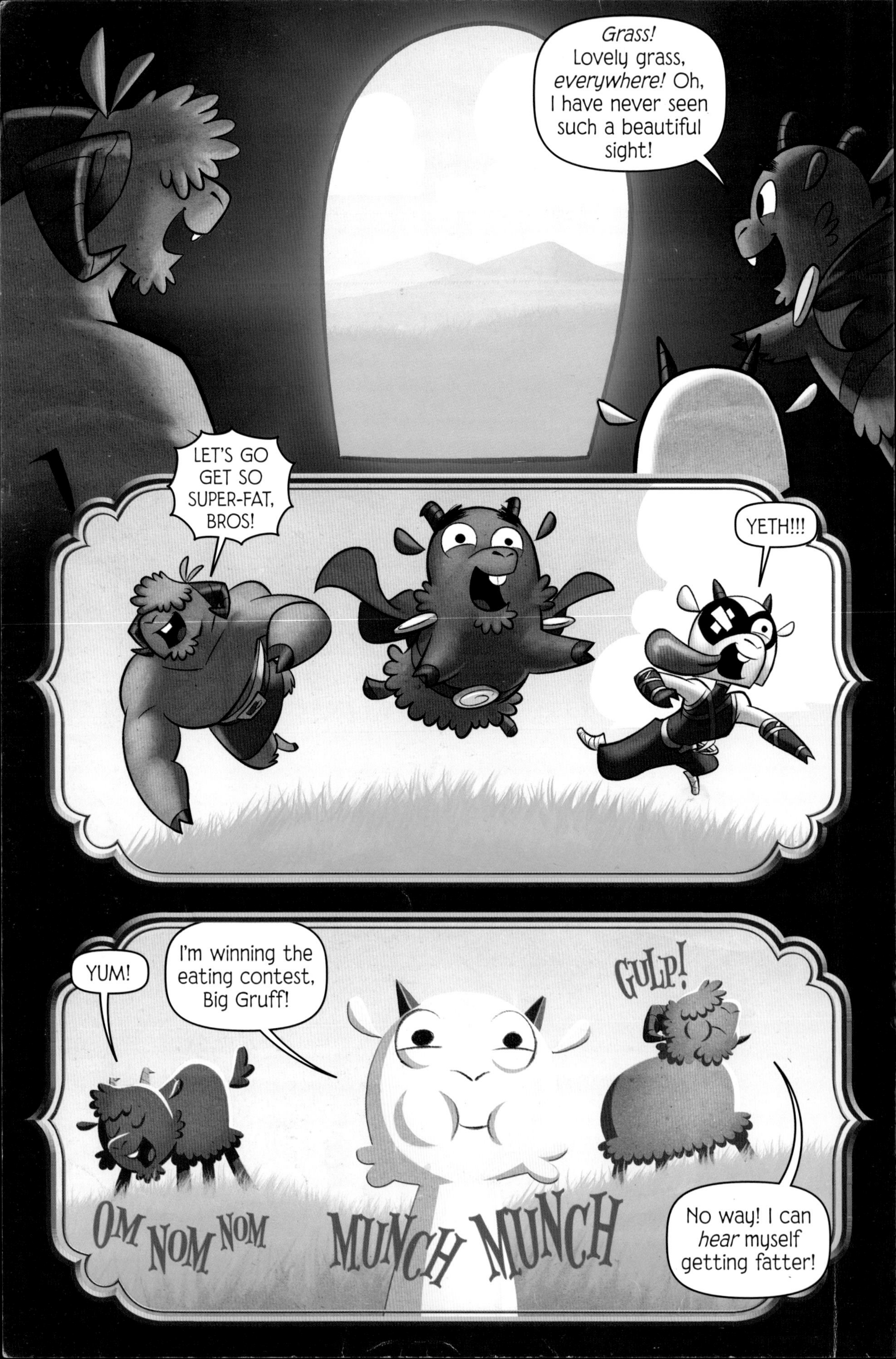

Grass! Lovely grass, *everywhere!* Oh, I have never seen such a beautiful sight!
LET'S GO GET SO SUPER-FAT, BROS!
YETH!!!
YUM!
I'm winning the eating contest, Big Gruff!
GULP!
No way! I can *hear* myself getting fatter!
OM NOM NOM
MUNCH MUNCH

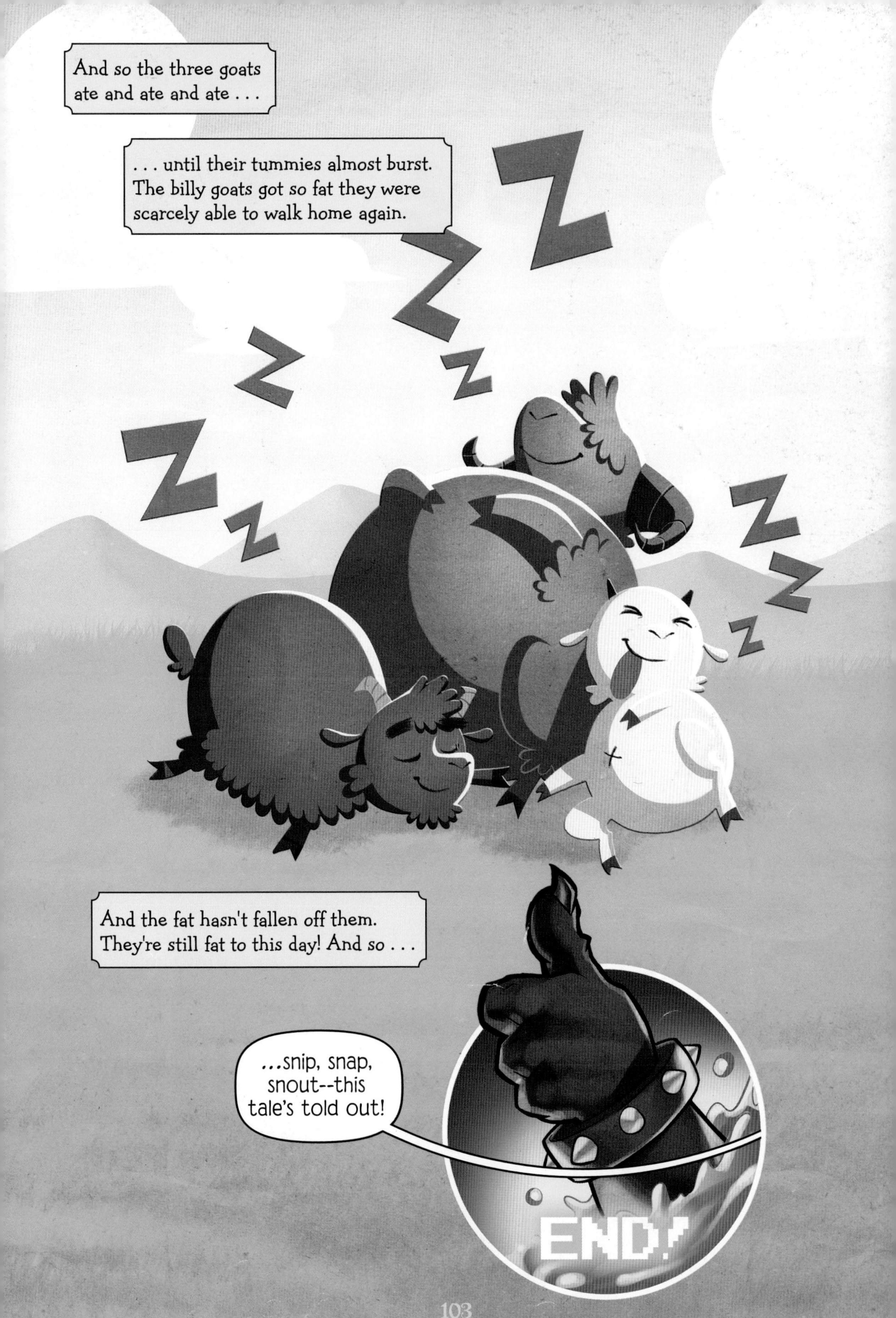
And so the three goats ate and ate and ate . . .
. . . until their tummies almost burst. The billy goats got so fat they were scarcely able to walk home again.
And the fat hasn't fallen off them. They're still fat to this day! And so . . .
...snip, snap, snout--this tale's told out!
END!

ALL ABOUT THE ORIGINAL TALE!

"Three Billy Goats Gruff" is a Norwegian fairy tale first published sometime between 1841 and 1844. While this version has a video game twist to it, the original version has its own far out elements!

The original story introduces three billy goats of different sizes. They are usually referred to as brothers. Hungry for grass, they decide to travel to the hillside across a river in order to eat and get fatter. However, a fearsome troll lives under the bridge and eats anyone who tries to cross.

The smallest billy goat crosses first. When the troll threatens to gobble him up, the little goat tricks him by saying his older, slightly bigger brother would make a better snack and that the troll should wait for him to cross. The greedy troll allows the little goat to pass in hopes of a bigger, better meal.

The middle-sized, slightly larger goat then crosses the bridge. He uses the same trick to get the troll to let him pass, saying that his older, even bigger brother is on his way. It works again.

The third, largest goat is then stopped by the troll, who threatens to gobble him up. But the third goat is so big that he simply kicks the troll off the bridge and into the river! (In some versions of the tale, he bashes the troll to bits with his horns and hooves.)

With the bridge clear, all three goats venture to the hillside, eat their fill of grass, and live happily ever after. The troll continues to live under the bridge but he never bothers anyone ever again.

Super Billy Goats Gruff adds its own weird twists to this timeless tale, including enemies the goats fight before the big battle on the bridge with the Final Boss...

A FAR OUT GUIDE TO HILLSIDE CASTLE!

GRIN-SNEER 💀

BOSS

A shadowy sorcerer, Grin-Sneer summons the skele-goats on the top level of Hillside Castle to fight for him. His father, Tanngrisnir, was one of the Norse god Thor's pet goats. He pulled Thor's chariot and was known for his scary, toothy sneer.

MIMIC 💲

MINION

It has long been said that greed will lead to the downfall of even the greatest adventurers--and the Mimic is living proof. This hungry chest may appear to hold valuable treasure, but its only contents are the bones of careless adventurers.

GOATGOYLE 💀

BOSS

While most gargoyles serve as rain spouts for buildings, the Goatgoyle only pretends to be a statue. This granite guardian perches atop the roof of the exterior of the castle and serves as the first line of defense against intruders.

FACE-HUGGER 🖤

MINION

Some foes are actually friends who just don't understand how to respect personal space. He may mean well, but the Face-Hugger is so needy that he makes it a little hard to breathe-- literally.

SNOW WHITE
AND THE
SEVEN ROBOTS

A GRAPHIC NOVEL

BY LOUISE SIMONSON

ILLUSTRATED BY JIMENA SÁNCHEZ

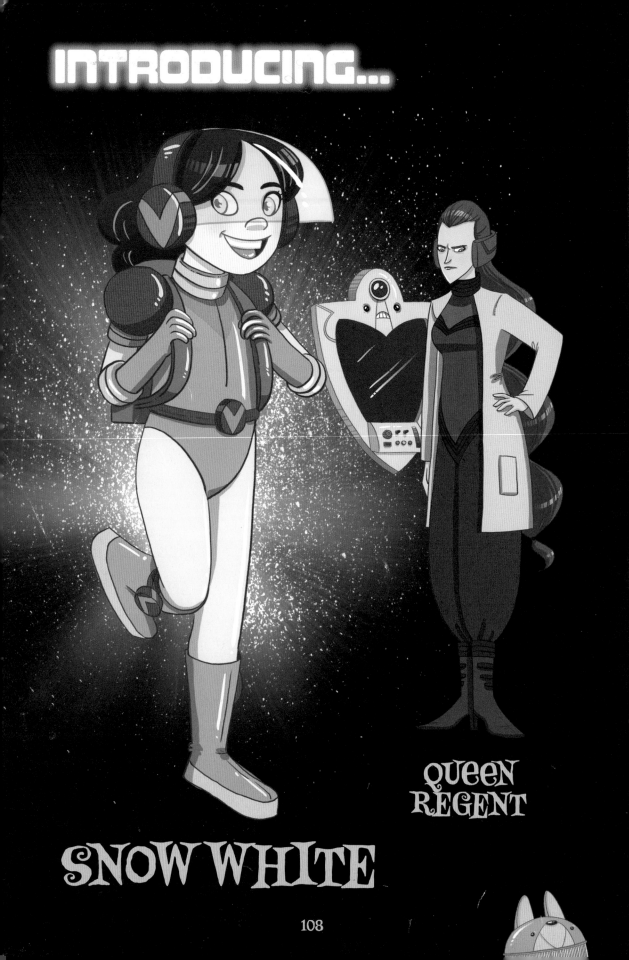

INTRODUCING...

QUEEN
REGENT

SNOW WHITE

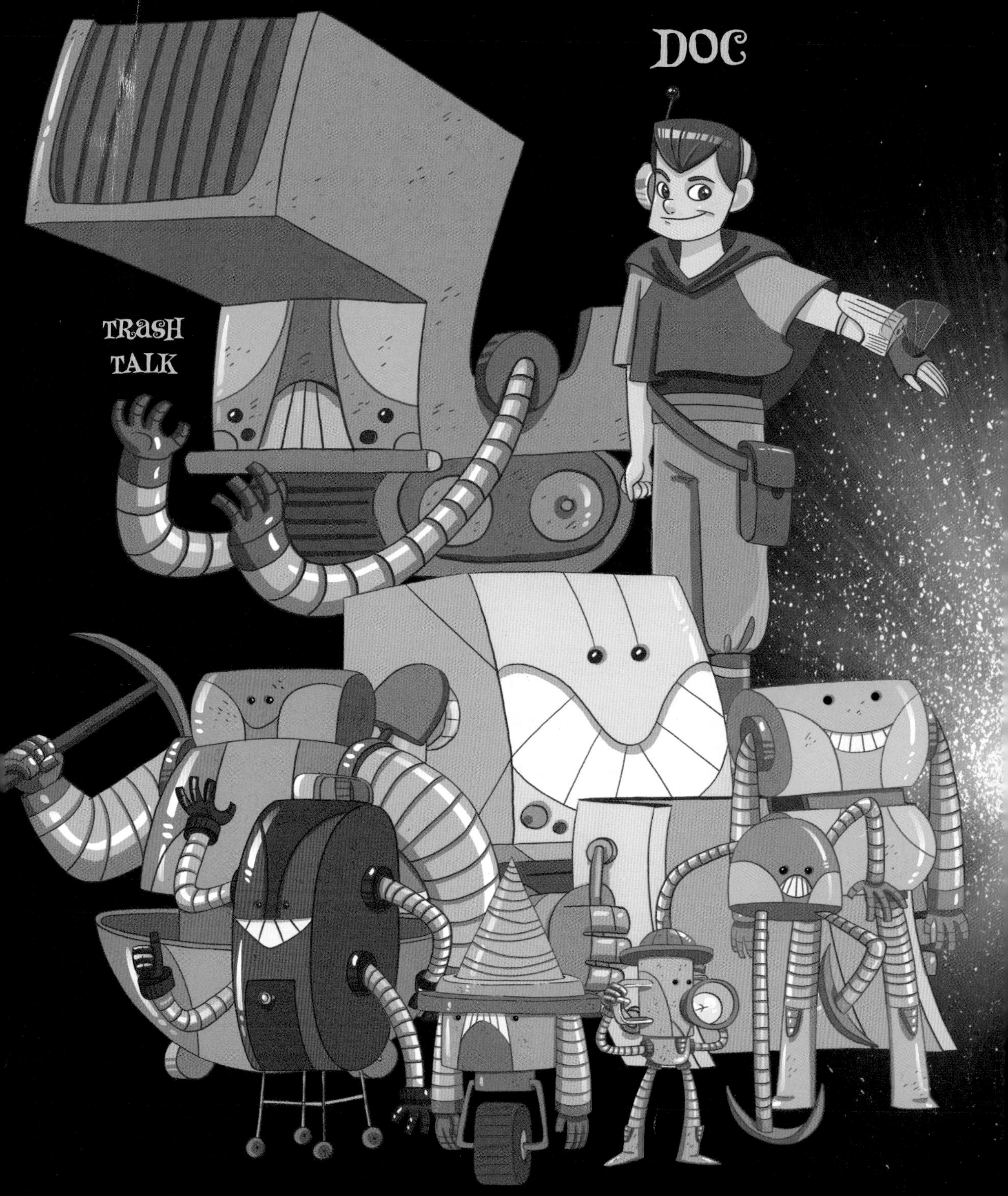
DOC
TRASH TALK

THE SEVEN ROBOTS

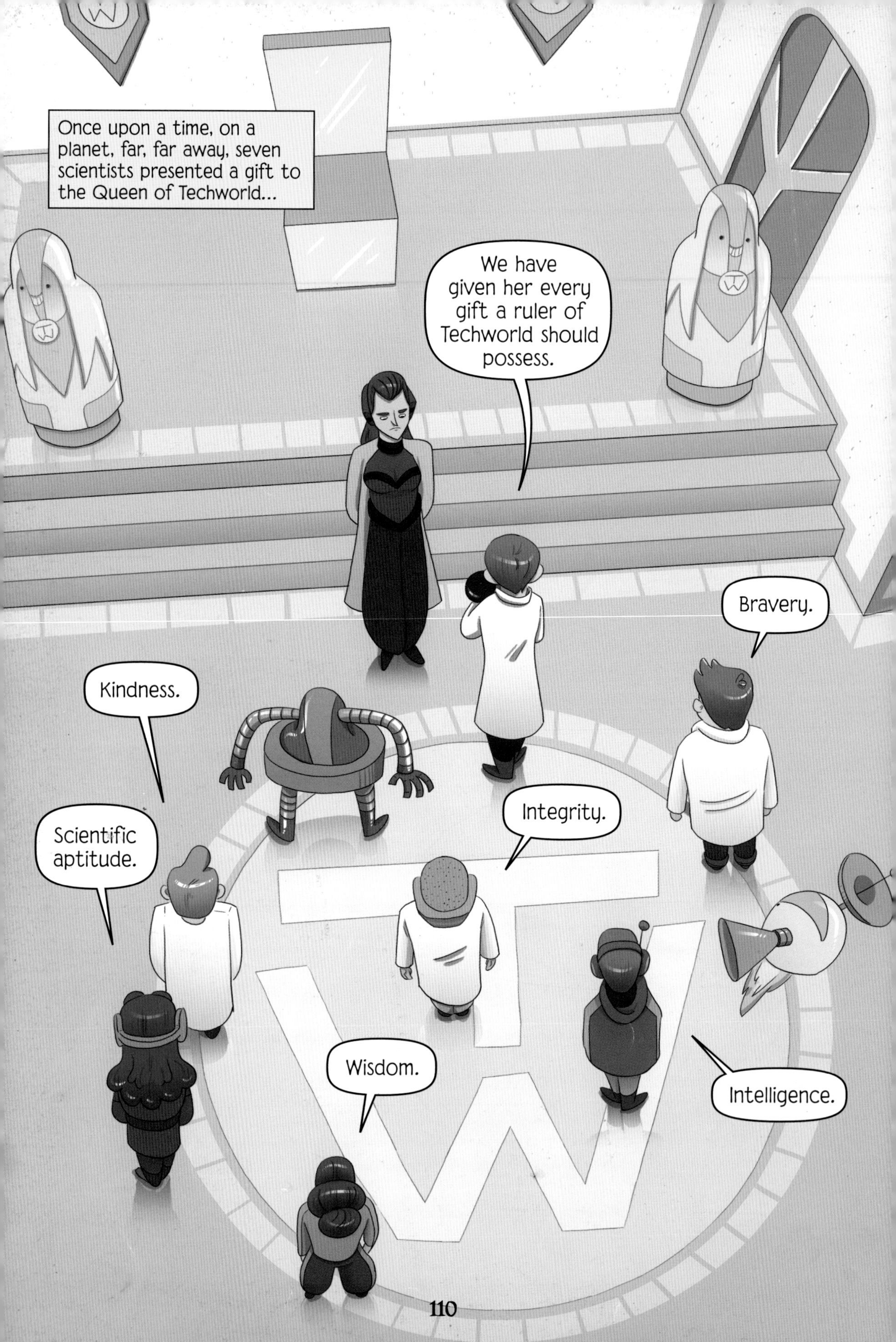
Once upon a time, on a planet, far, far away, seven scientists presented a gift to the Queen of Techworld...
We have given her every gift a ruler of Techworld should possess.
Bravery.
Kindness.
Integrity.
Scientific aptitude.
Wisdom.
Intelligence.

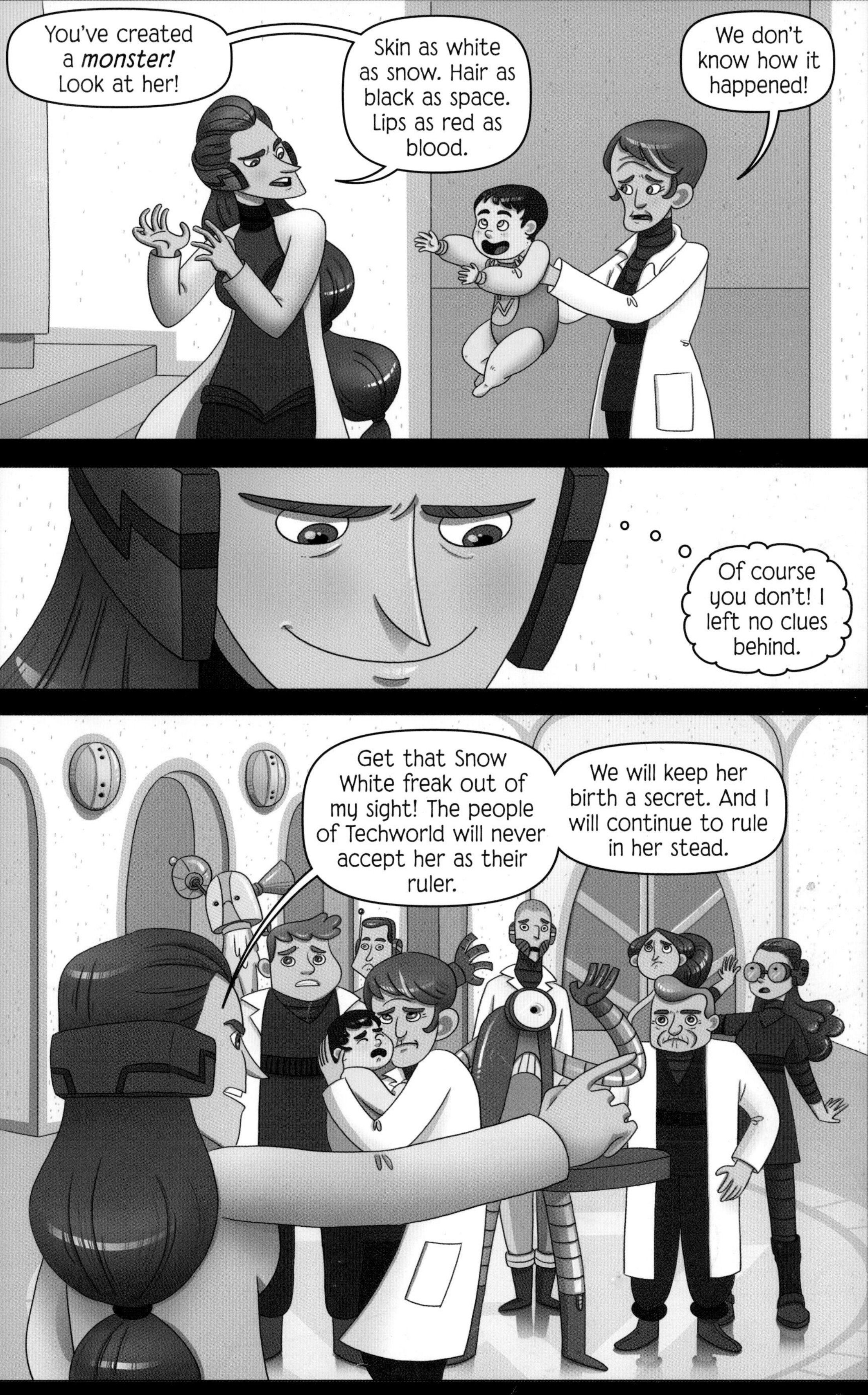
You've created a *monster!* Look at her!
Skin as white as snow. Hair as black as space. Lips as red as blood.
We don't know how it happened!
Of course you don't! I left no clues behind.
Get that Snow White freak out of my sight! The people of Techworld will never accept her as their ruler.
We will keep her birth a secret. And I will continue to rule in her stead.

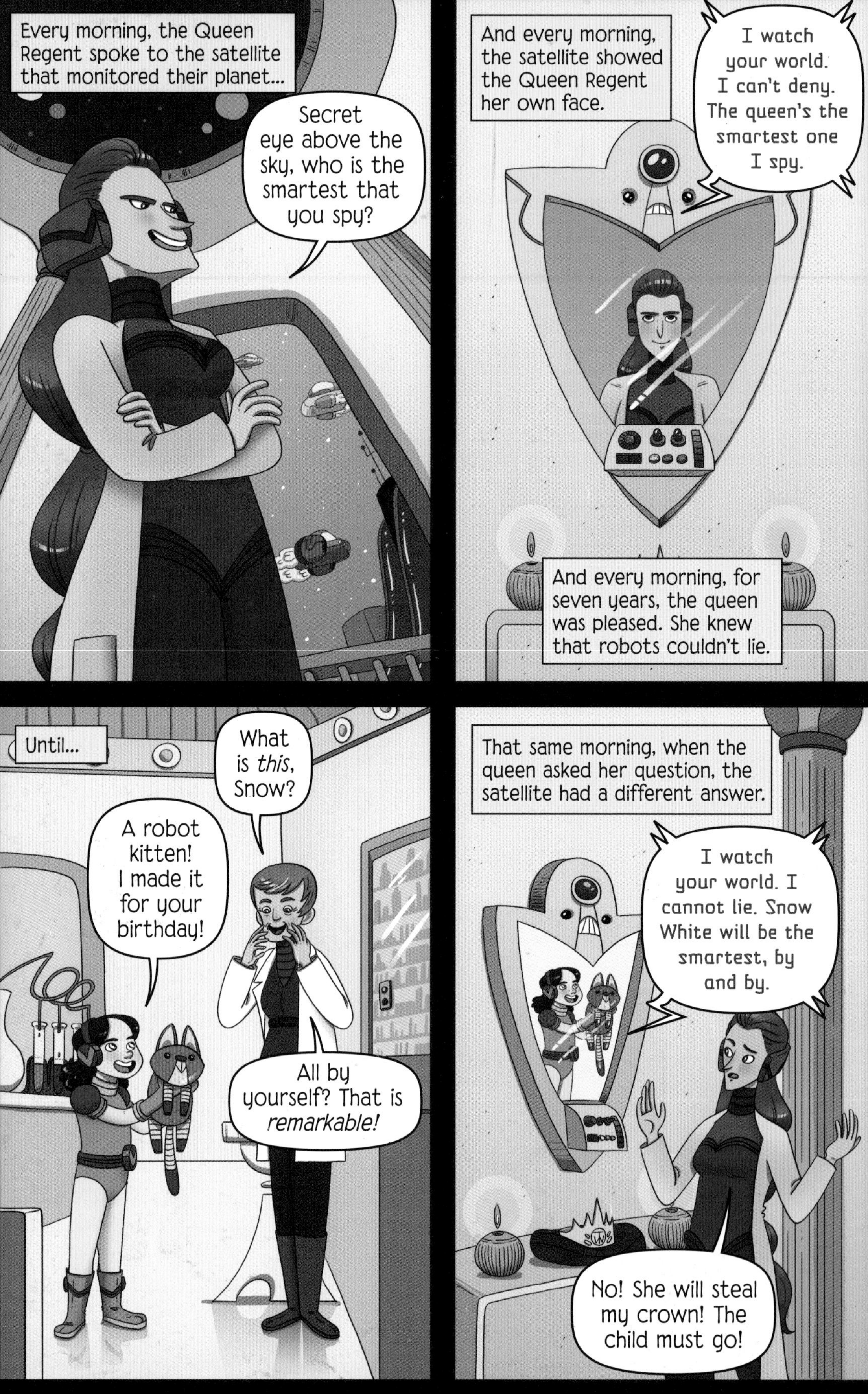
Every morning, the Queen Regent spoke to the satellite that monitored their planet...
Secret eye above the sky, who is the smartest that you spy?
And every morning, the satellite showed the Queen Regent her own face.
I watch your world. I can't deny. The queen's the smartest one I spy.
And every morning, for seven years, the queen was pleased. She knew that robots couldn't lie.
Until...
What is *this*, Snow?
A robot kitten! I made it for your birthday!
All by yourself? That is *remarkable!*
That same morning, when the queen asked her question, the satellite had a different answer.
I watch your world. I cannot lie. Snow White will be the smartest, by and by.
No! She will steal my crown! The child must go!

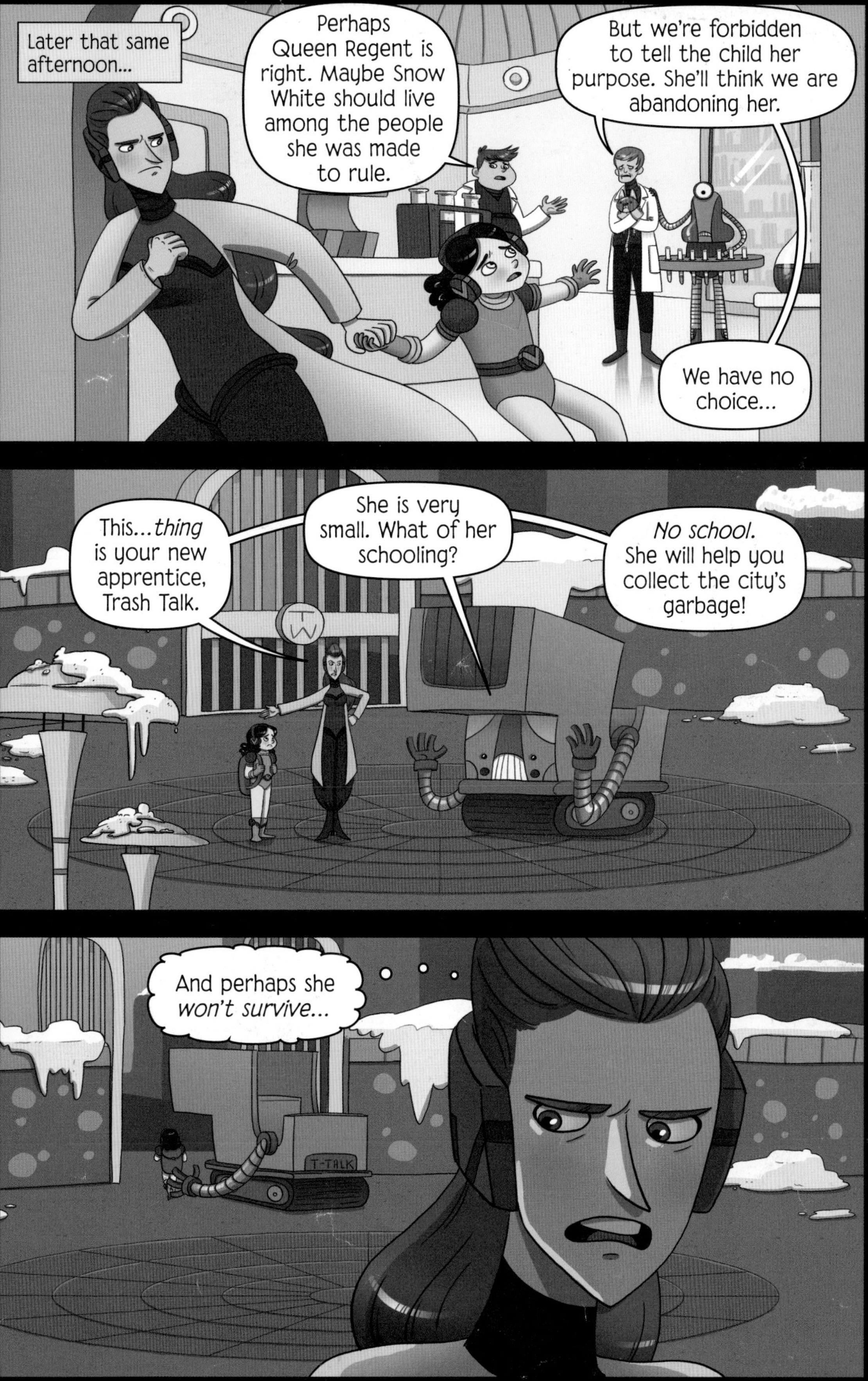
Later that same afternoon...
Perhaps Queen Regent is right. Maybe Snow White should live among the people she was made to rule.
But we're forbidden to tell the child her purpose. She'll think we are abandoning her.
We have no choice...
This...*thing* is your new apprentice, Trash Talk.
She is very small. What of her schooling?
No school. She will help you collect the city's garbage!
TW
And perhaps she *won't survive...*
T-TALK

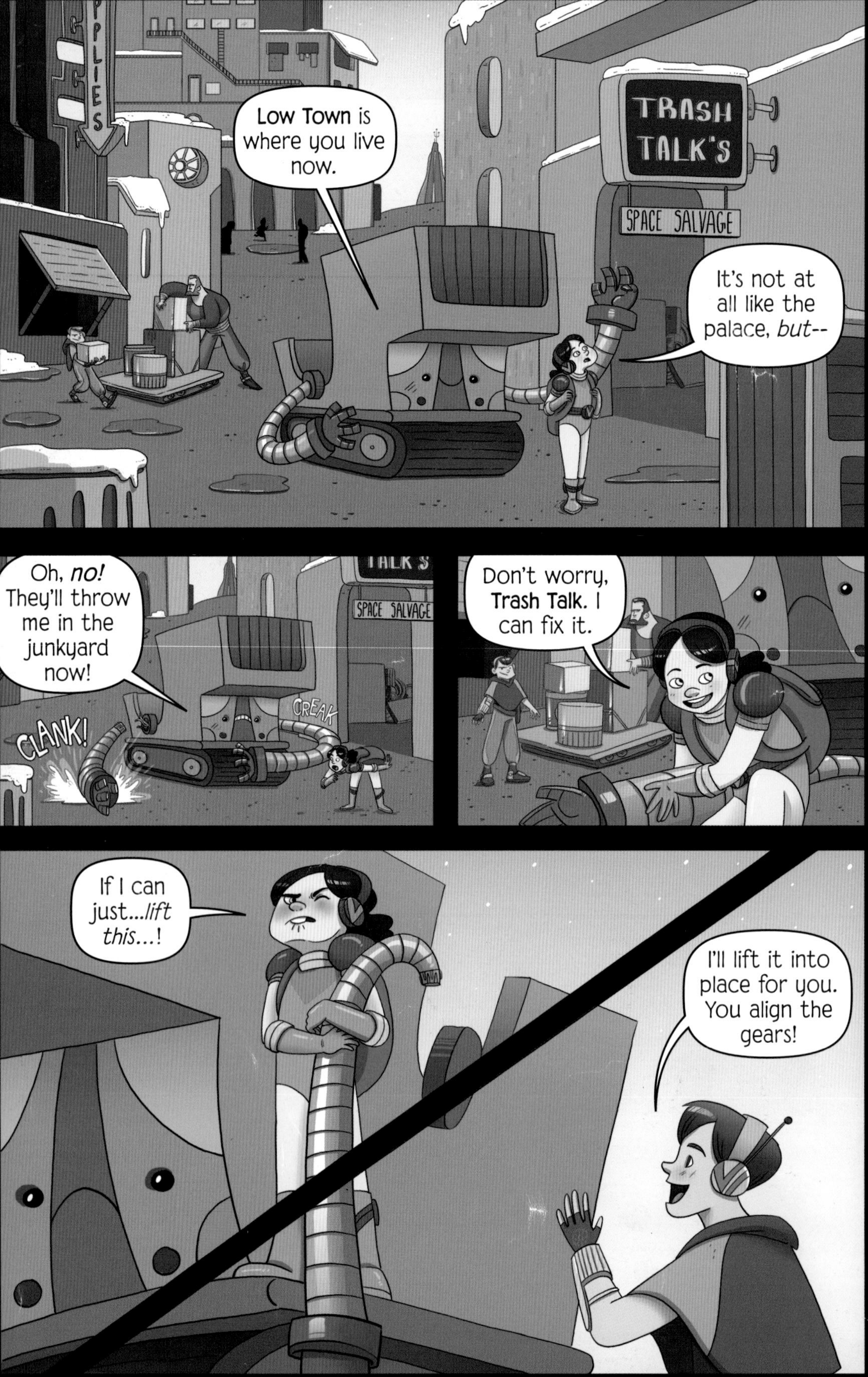

PPLIES
Low Town is where you live now.
TRASH TALK'S
SPACE SALVAGE
It's not at all like the palace, *but*--
SPACE SALVAGE
Oh, *no!* They'll throw me in the junkyard now!
CLANK!
CREAK
Don't worry, **Trash Talk**. I can fix it.
If I can just...*lift this*...!
I'll lift it into place for you. You align the gears!

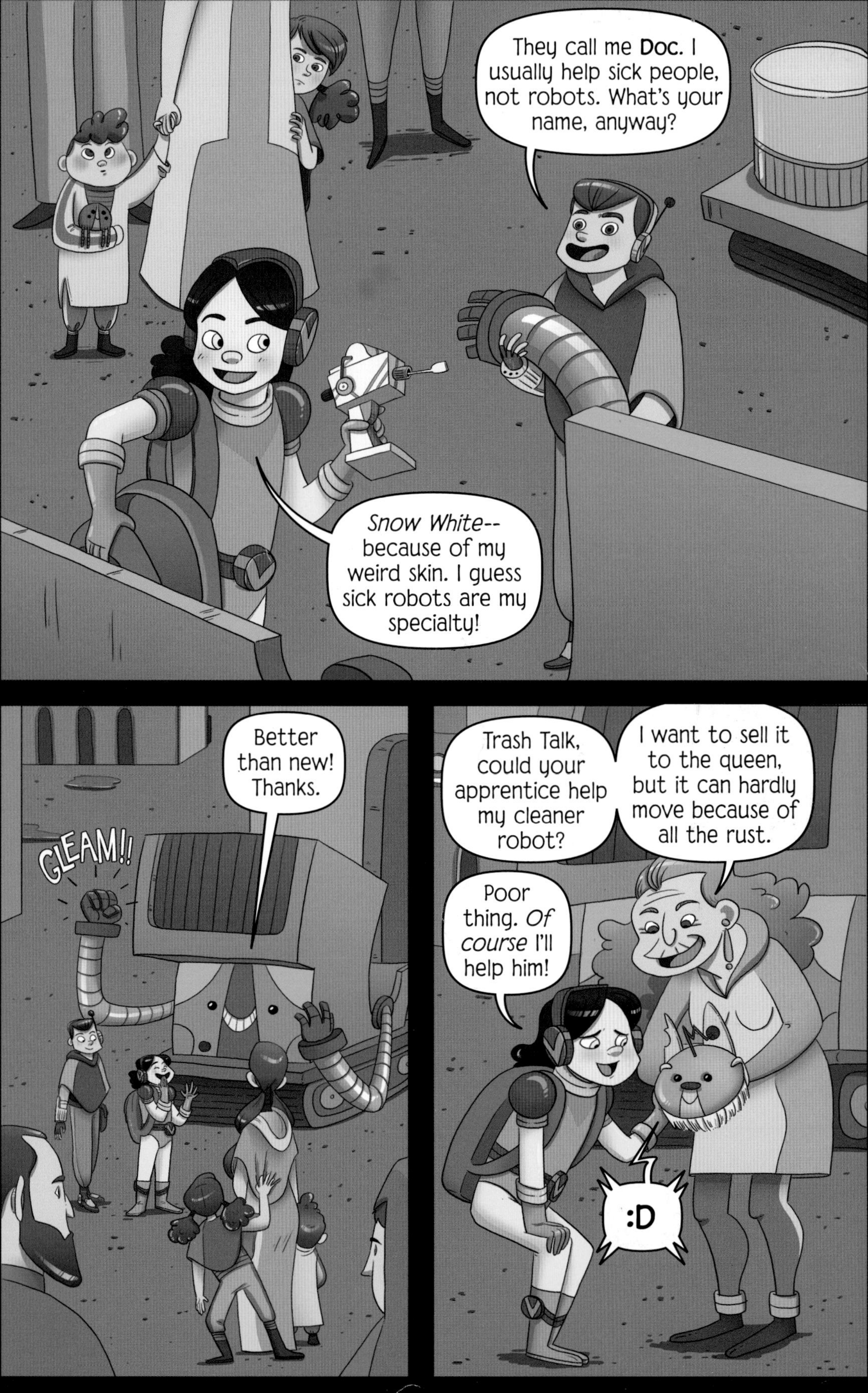
They call me **Doc**. I usually help sick people, not robots. What's your name, anyway?
Snow White-- because of my weird skin. I guess sick robots are my specialty!
GLEAM!!
Better than new! Thanks.
Trash Talk, could your apprentice help my cleaner robot?
I want to sell it to the queen, but it can hardly move because of all the rust.
Poor thing. *Of course* I'll help him!
:D

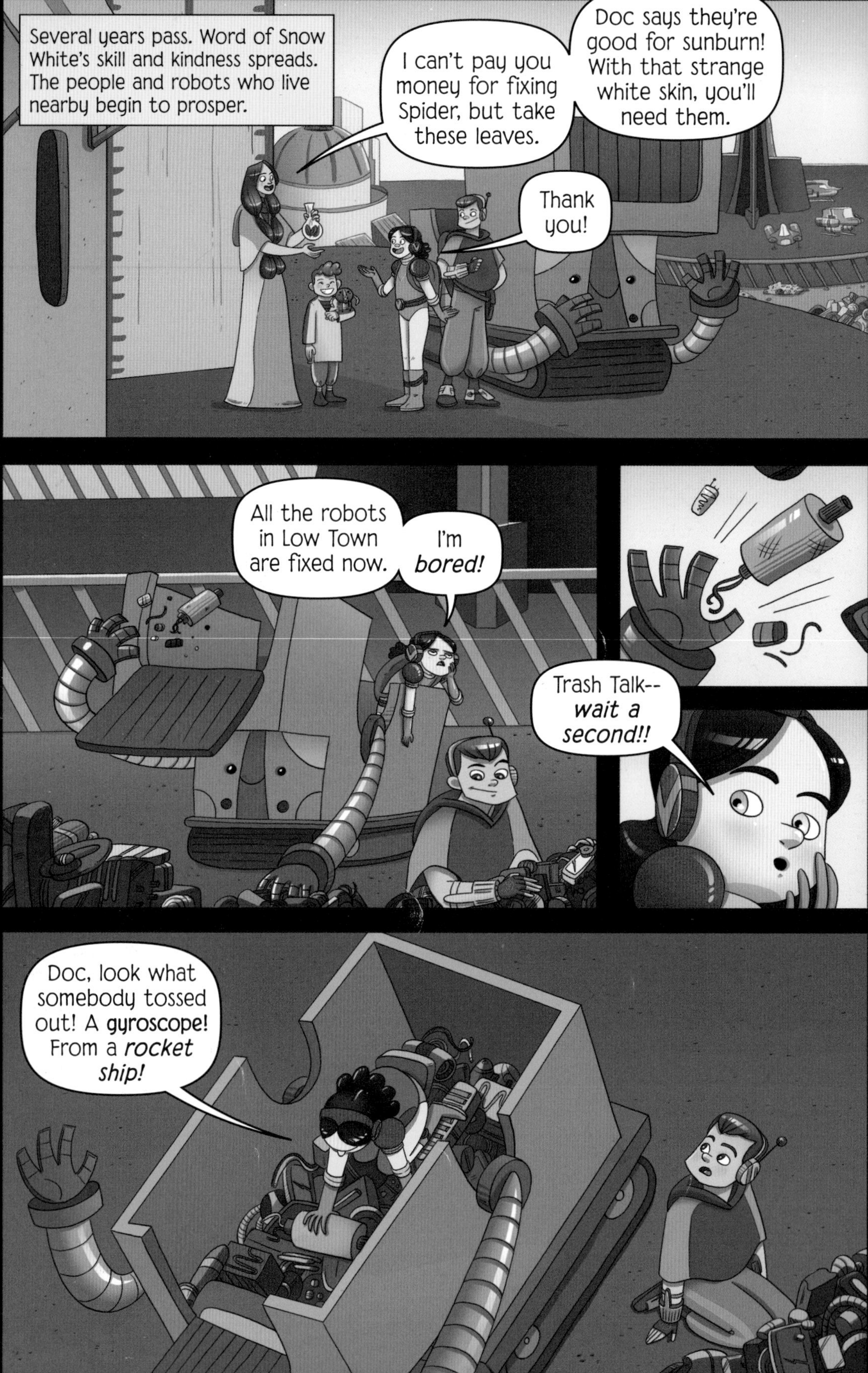
Several years pass. Word of Snow White's skill and kindness spreads. The people and robots who live nearby begin to prosper.
I can't pay you money for fixing Spider, but take these leaves.
Doc says they're good for sunburn! With that strange white skin, you'll need them.
Thank you!
All the robots in Low Town are fixed now.
I'm *bored!*
Trash Talk-- *wait a second!!*
Doc, look what somebody tossed out! A **gyroscope!** From a *rocket ship!*

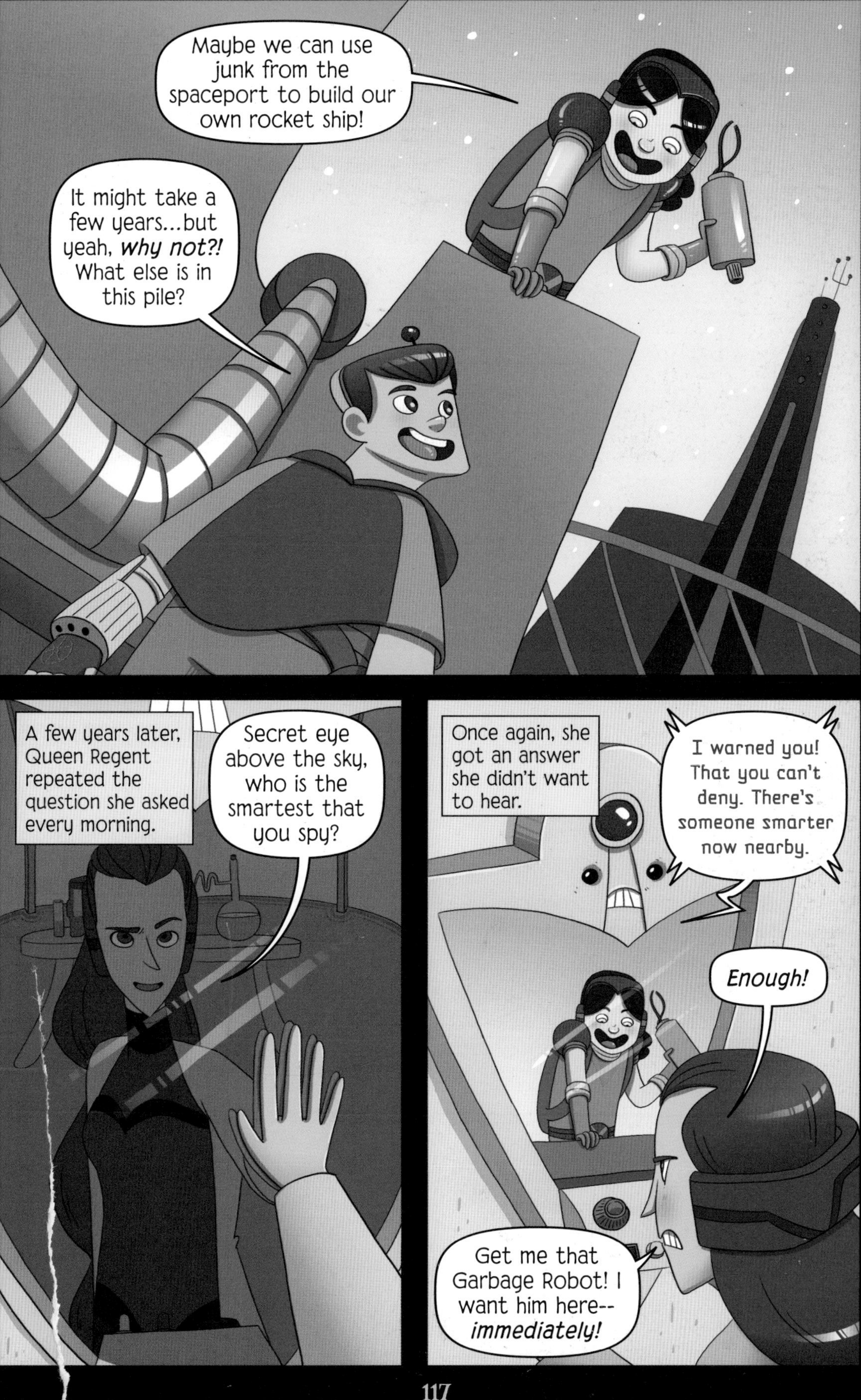

Maybe we can use junk from the spaceport to build our own rocket ship!
It might take a few years...but yeah, *why not?!* What else is in this pile?
A few years later, Queen Regent repeated the question she asked every morning.
Secret eye above the sky, who is the smartest that you spy?
Once again, she got an answer she didn't want to hear.
I warned you! That you can't deny. There's someone smarter now nearby.
Enough!
Get me that Garbage Robot! I want him here-- *immediately!*

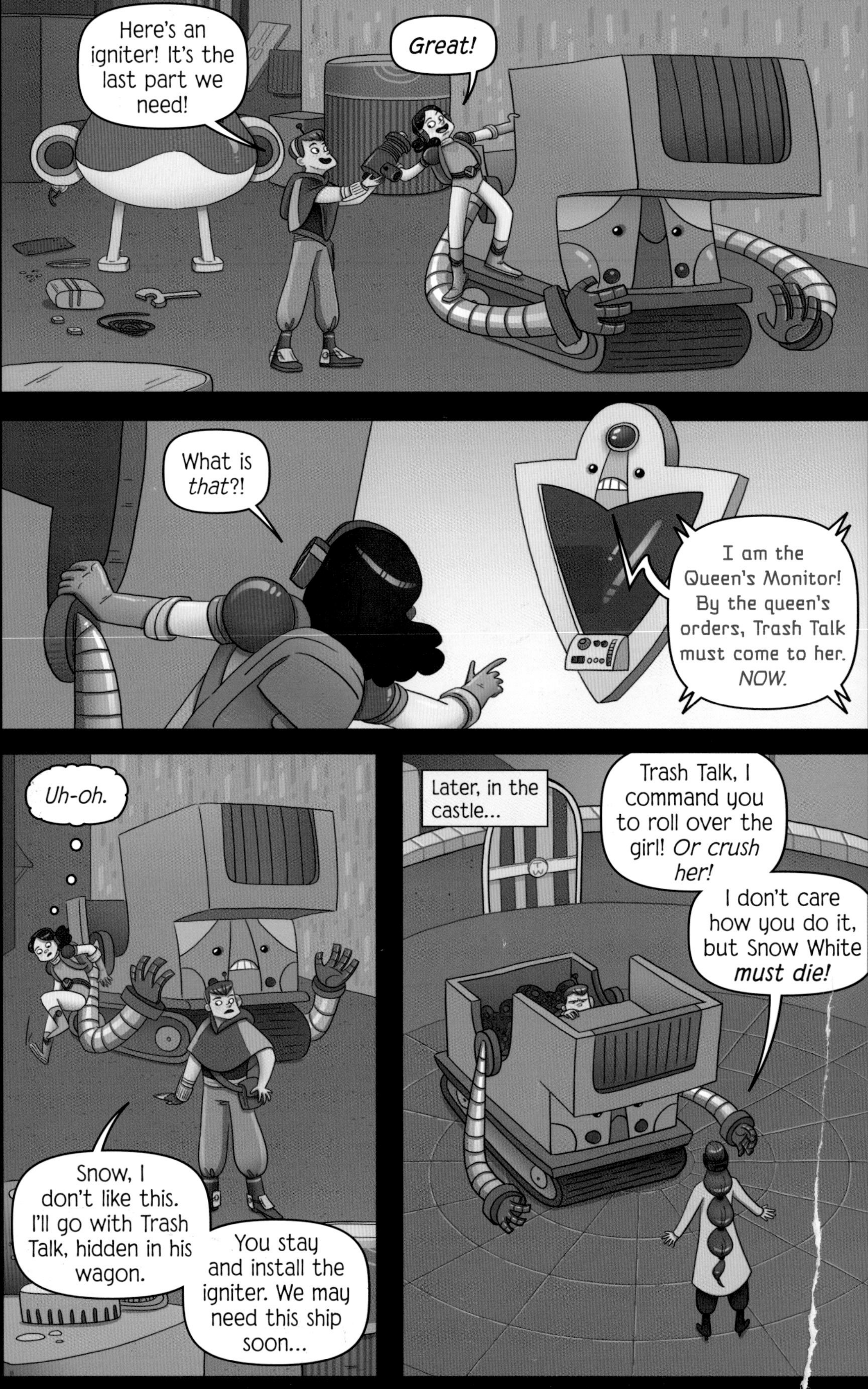

Here's an igniter! It's the last part we need!
Great!
What is *that*?!
I am the Queen's Monitor! By the queen's orders, Trash Talk must come to her. *NOW.*
Uh-oh.
Snow, I don't like this. I'll go with Trash Talk, hidden in his wagon.
You stay and install the igniter. We may need this ship soon...
Later, in the castle...
Trash Talk, I command you to roll over the girl! *Or crush her!*
I don't care how you do it, but Snow White ***must die!***

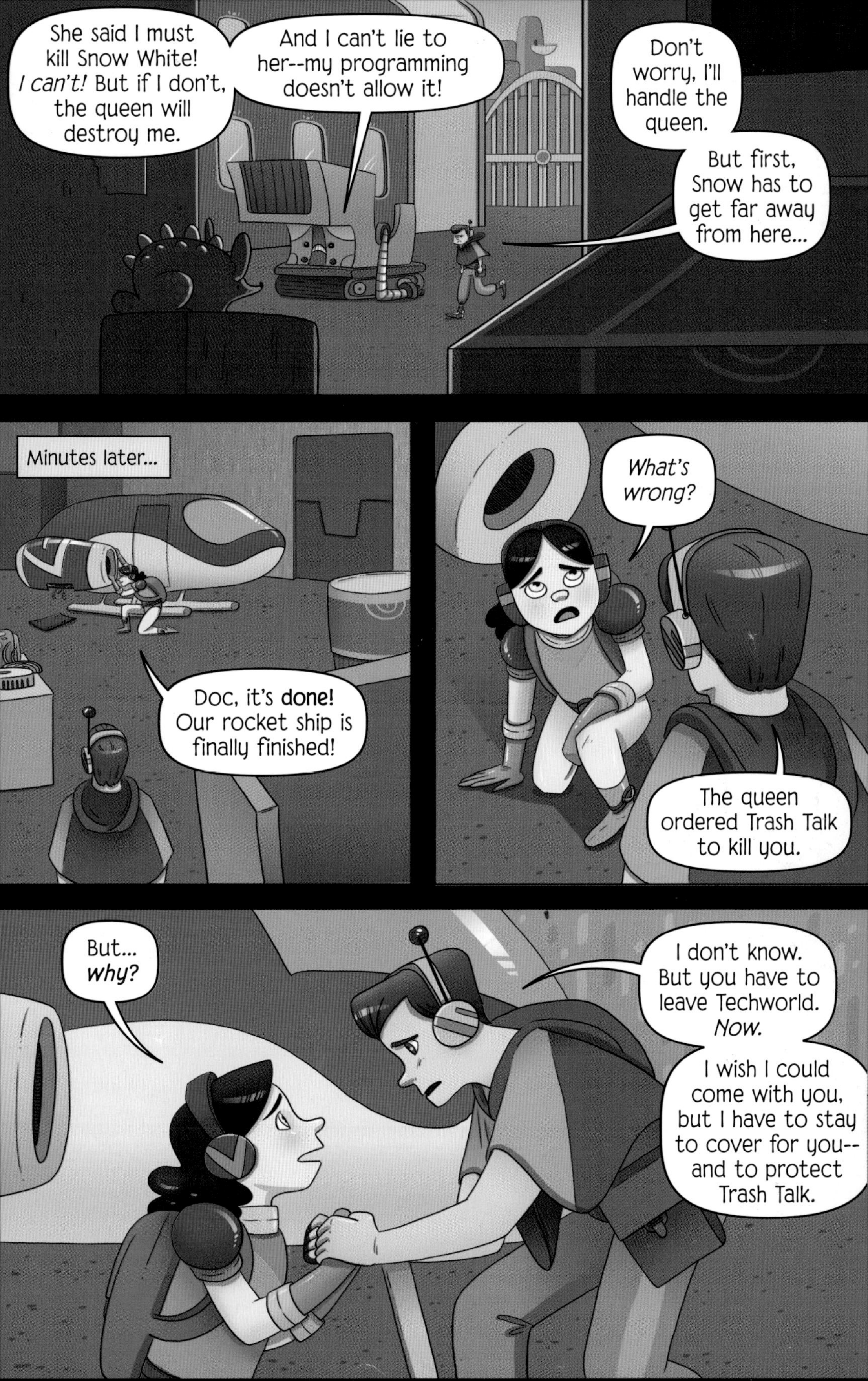
She said I must kill Snow White! *I can't!* But if I don't, the queen will destroy me.
And I can't lie to her--my programming doesn't allow it!
Don't worry, I'll handle the queen.
But first, Snow has to get far away from here...
Minutes later...
Doc, it's **done!** Our rocket ship is finally finished!
What's wrong?
The queen ordered Trash Talk to kill you.
But... *why?*
I don't know. But you have to leave Techworld. *Now.*
I wish I could come with you, but I have to stay to cover for you--and to protect Trash Talk.

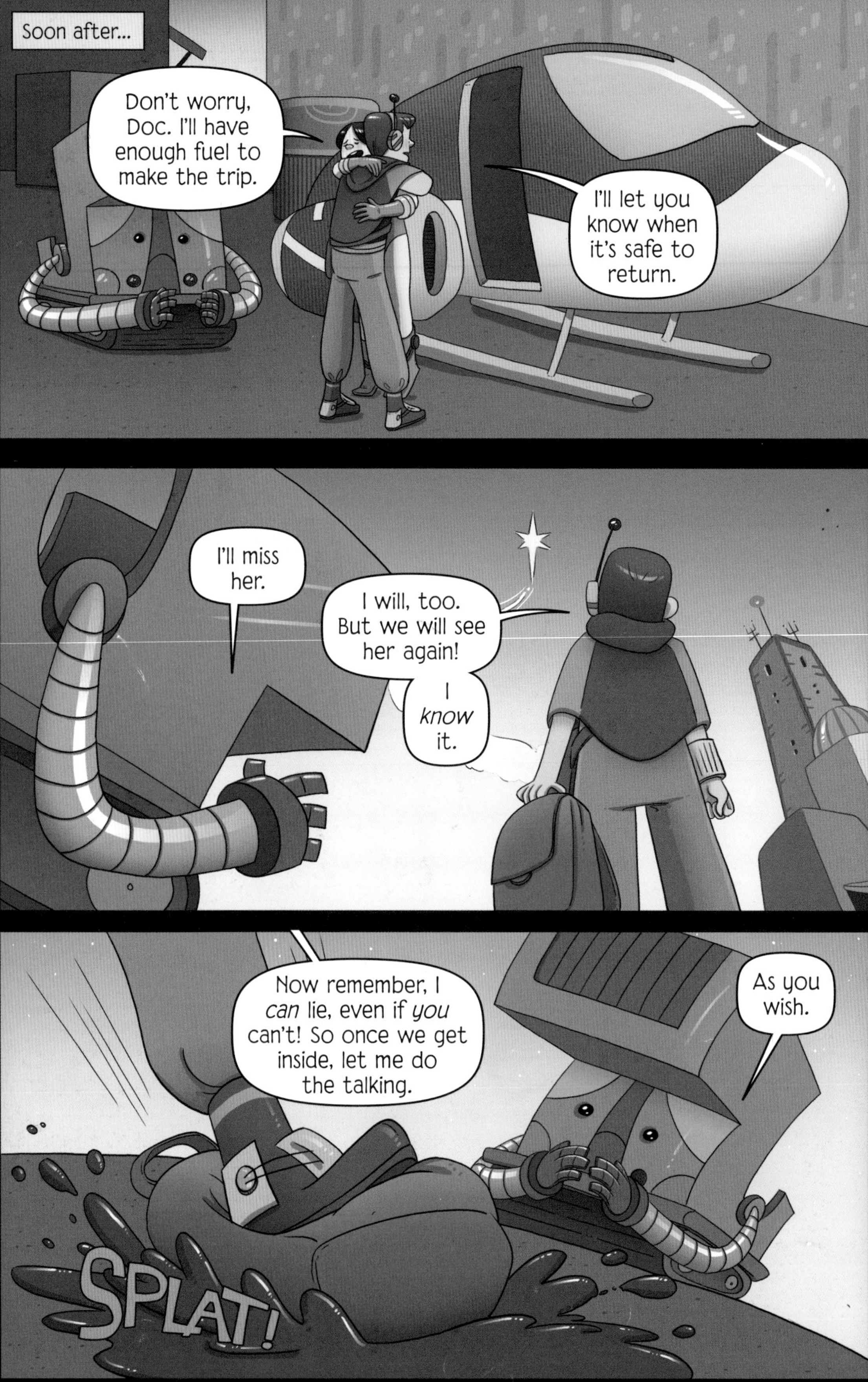
Soon after...
Don't worry, Doc. I'll have enough fuel to make the trip.
I'll let you know when it's safe to return.
I'll miss her.
I will, too. But we will see her again!
I *know* it.
Now remember, I *can* lie, even if *you* can't! So once we get inside, let me do the talking.
As you wish.
SPLAT!

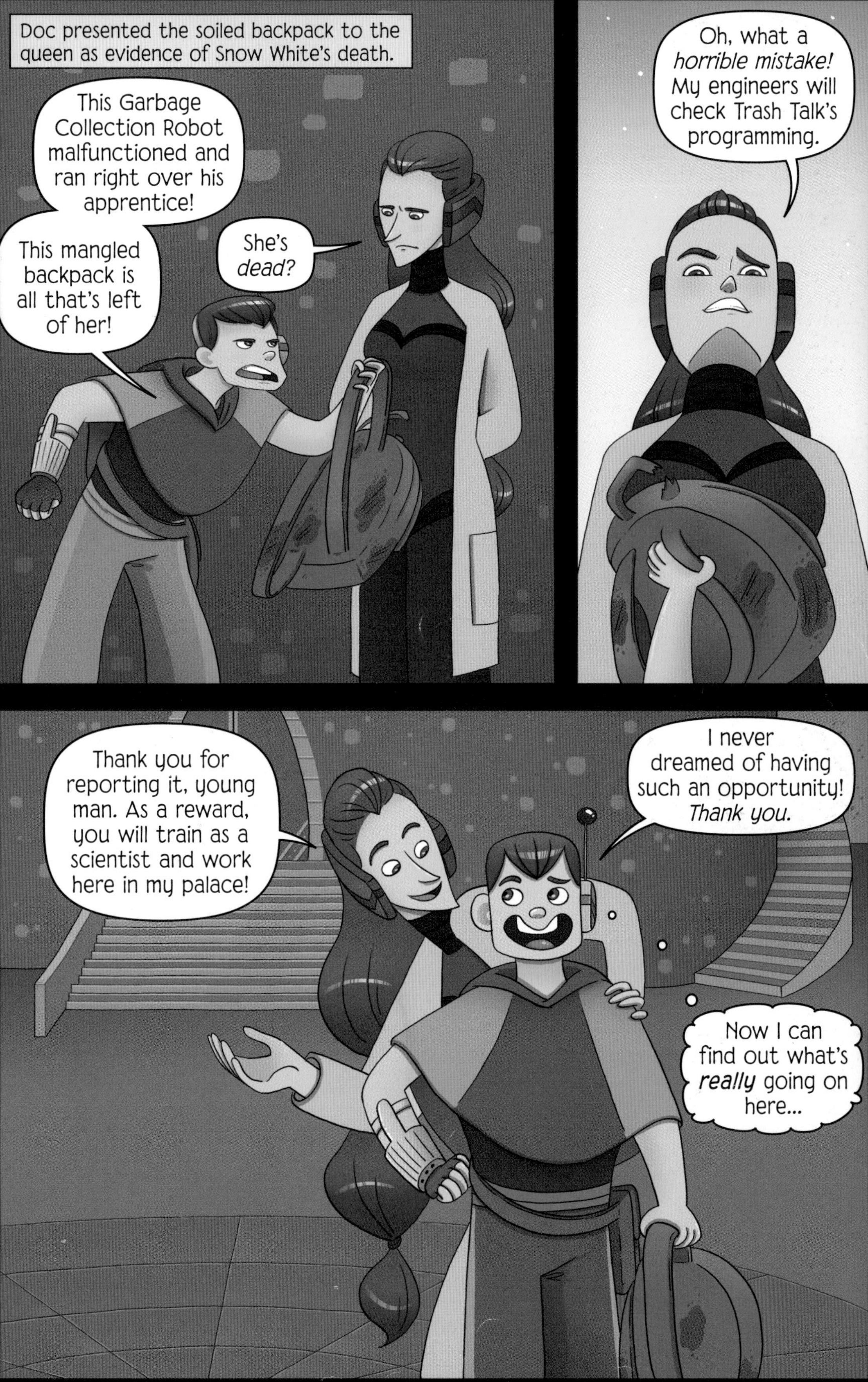

Doc presented the soiled backpack to the queen as evidence of Snow White's death.
This Garbage Collection Robot malfunctioned and ran right over his apprentice!
This mangled backpack is all that's left of her!
She's *dead?*
Oh, what a *horrible mistake!* My engineers will check Trash Talk's programming.
Thank you for reporting it, young man. As a reward, you will train as a scientist and work here in my palace!
I never dreamed of having such an opportunity! *Thank you.*
Now I can find out what's *really* going on here...

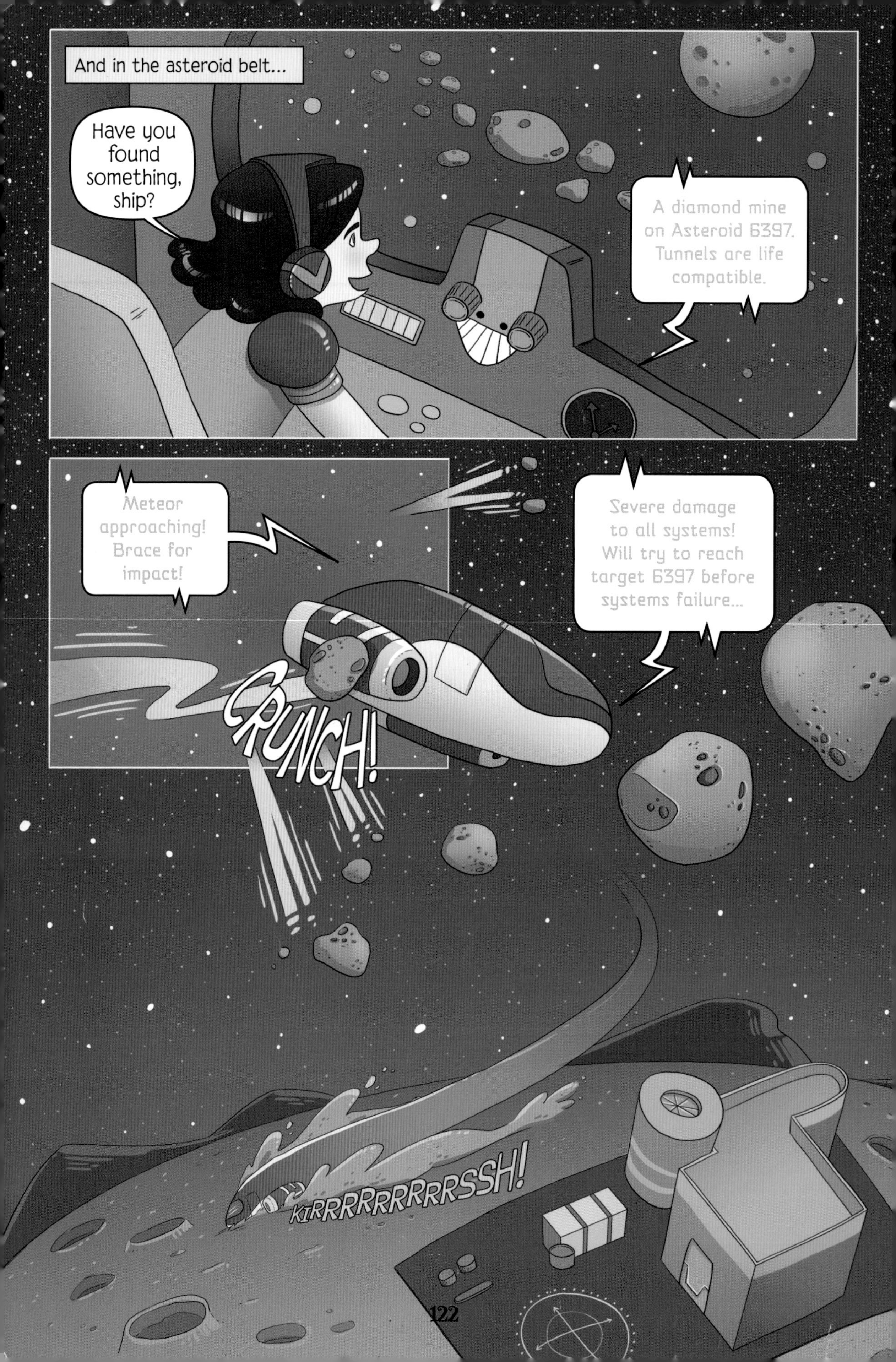

And in the asteroid belt...
Have you found something, ship?
A diamond mine on Asteroid 6397. Tunnels are life compatible.
Meteor approaching! Brace for impact!
CRUNCH!
Severe damage to all systems! Will try to reach target 6397 before systems failure...
KIRRRRRRRRRSSH!

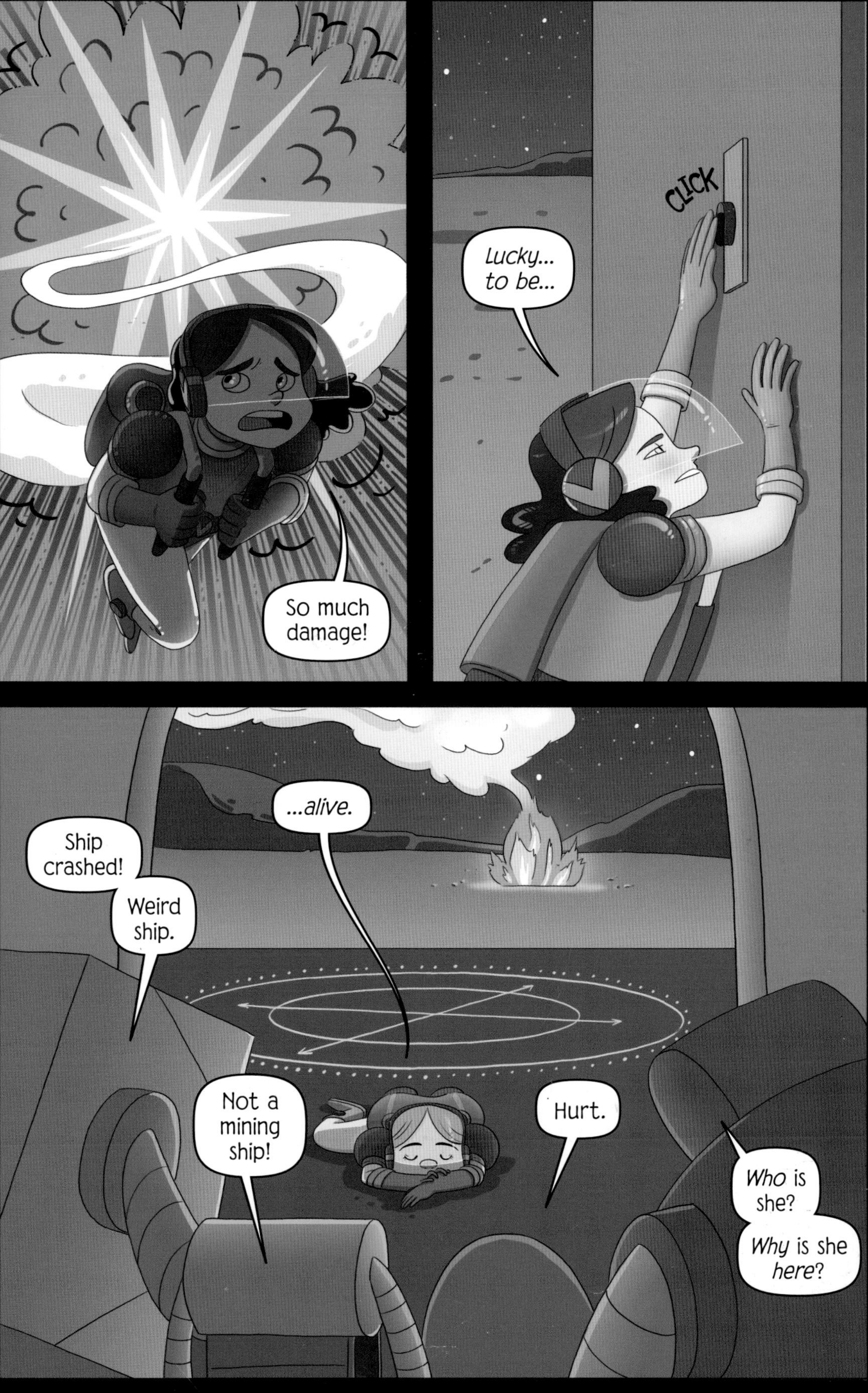
So much damage!
CLICK
Lucky... to be...
...alive.
Ship crashed!
Weird ship.
Not a mining ship!
Hurt.
Who is she?
Why is she here?

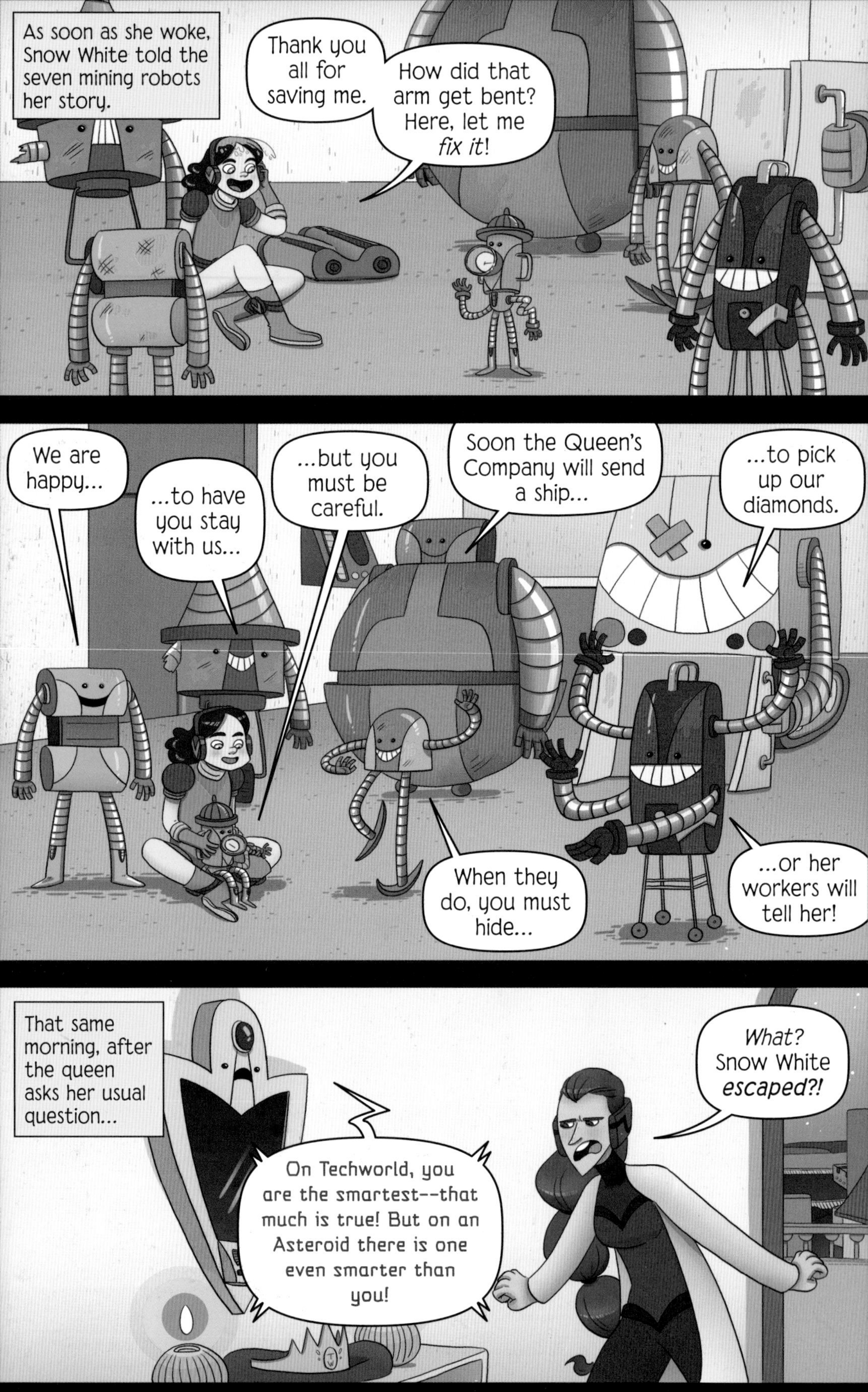

As soon as she woke, Snow White told the seven mining robots her story.
Thank you all for saving me.
How did that arm get bent? Here, let me *fix it*!
We are happy...
...to have you stay with us...
...but you must be careful.
Soon the Queen's Company will send a ship...
...to pick up our diamonds.
When they do, you must hide...
...or her workers will tell her!
That same morning, after the queen asks her usual question...
On Techworld, you are the smartest--that much is true! But on an Asteroid there is one even smarter than you!
What? Snow White *escaped?!*

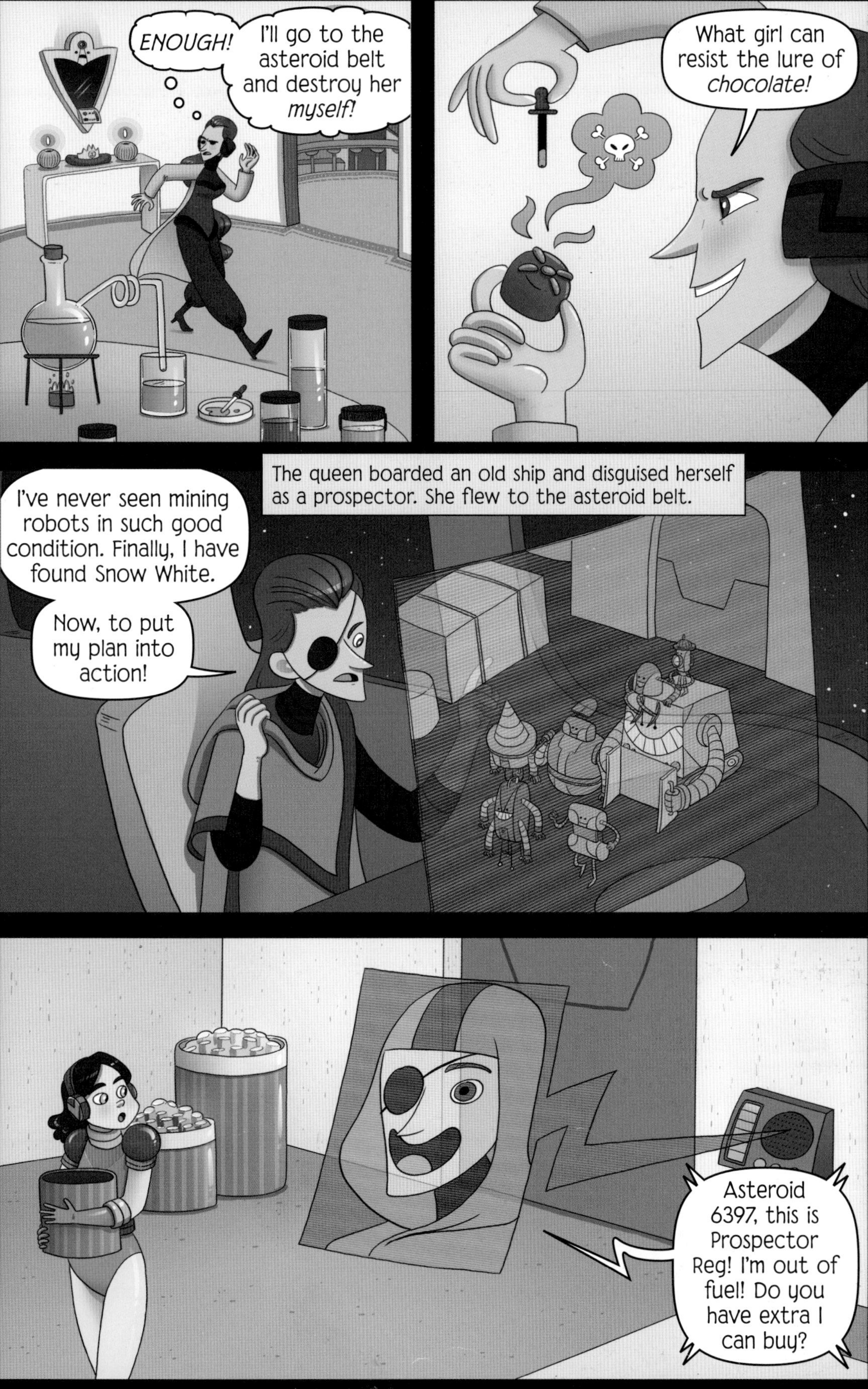
ENOUGH!
I'll go to the asteroid belt and destroy her *myself!*
What girl can resist the lure of *chocolate!*
The queen boarded an old ship and disguised herself as a prospector. She flew to the asteroid belt.
I've never seen mining robots in such good condition. Finally, I have found Snow White.
Now, to put my plan into action!
Asteroid 6397, this is Prospector Reg! I'm out of fuel! Do you have extra I can buy?

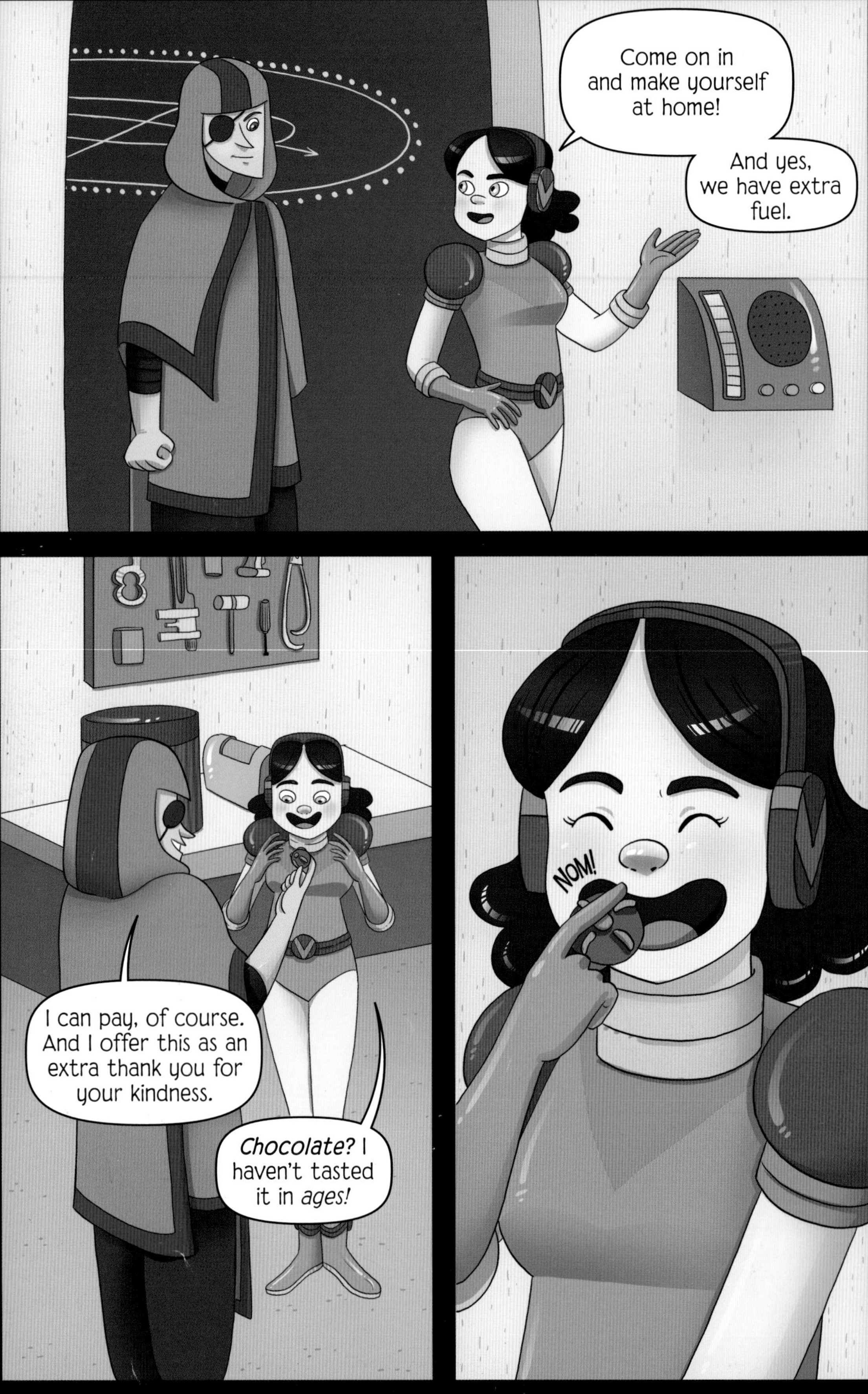

Come on in and make yourself at home!
And yes, we have extra fuel.
I can pay, of course. And I offer this as an extra thank you for your kindness.
Chocolate? I haven't tasted it in *ages!*
NOM!

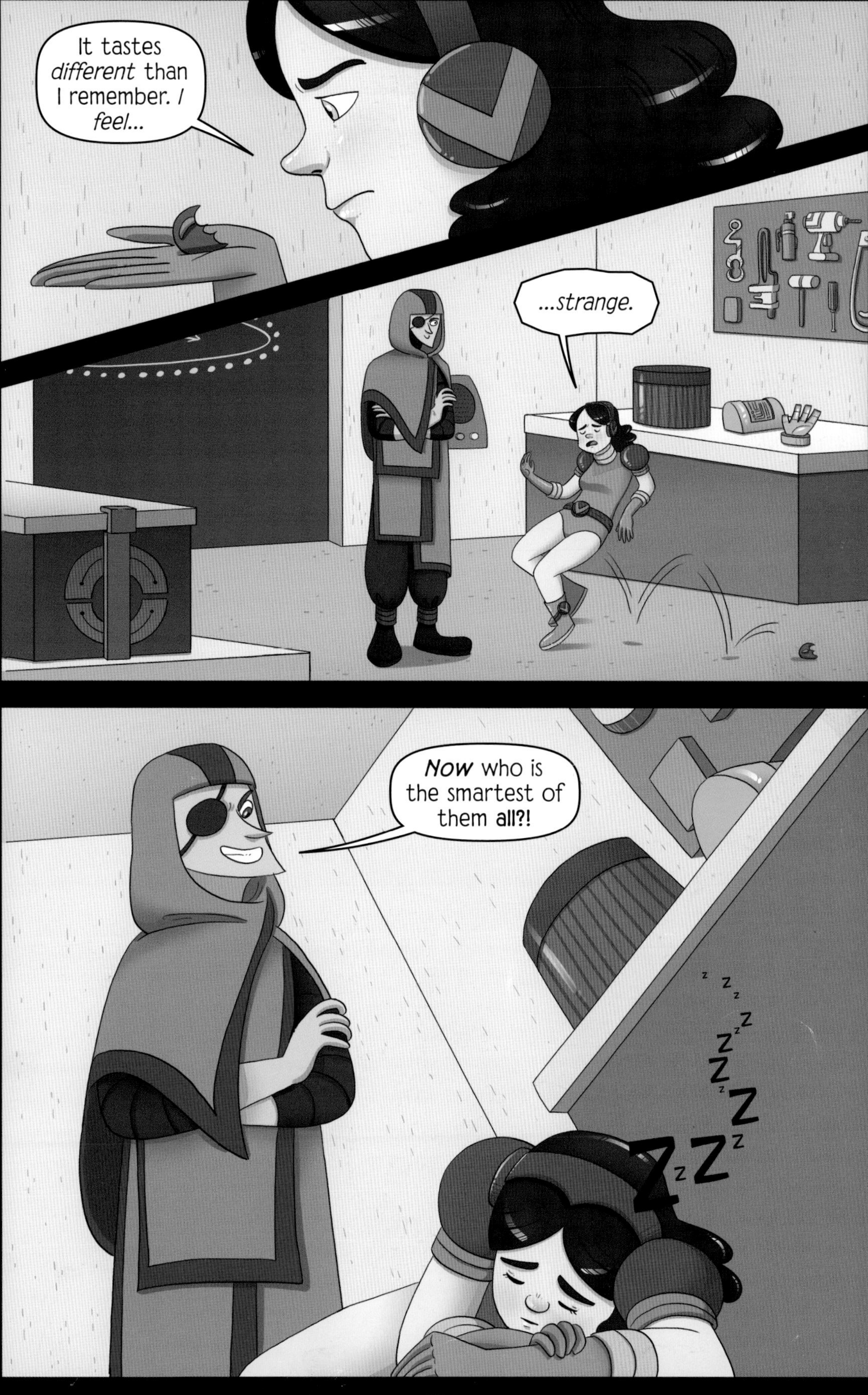
It tastes *different* than I remember. *I feel...*
...strange.
Now who is the smartest of them **all?!**
Z Z Z Z Z Z Z Z Z Z Z Z Z

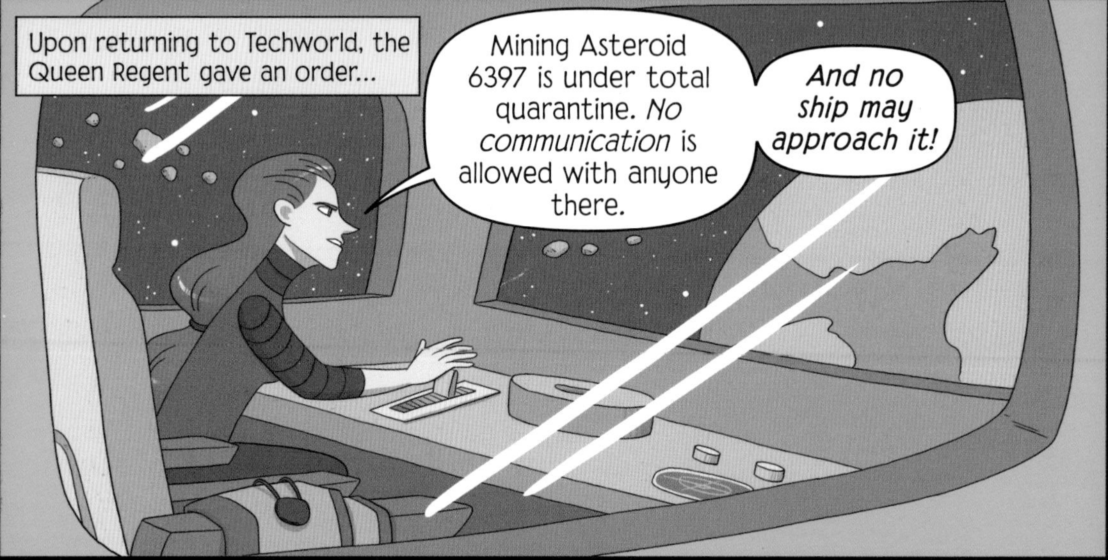
Upon returning to Techworld, the Queen Regent gave an order...
Mining Asteroid 6397 is under total quarantine. *No communication* is allowed with anyone there.
And no ship may approach it!

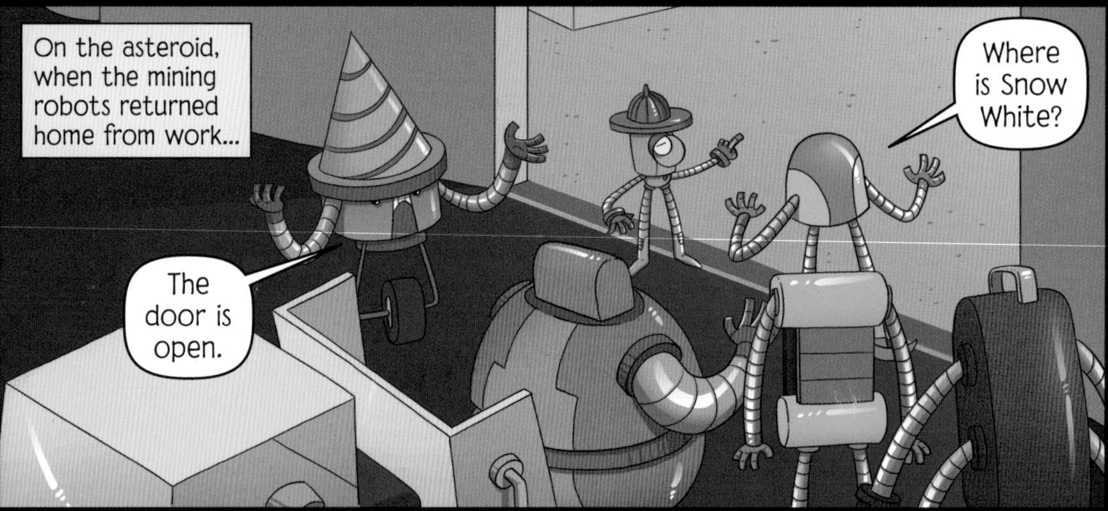
On the asteroid, when the mining robots returned home from work...
Where is Snow White?
The door is open.

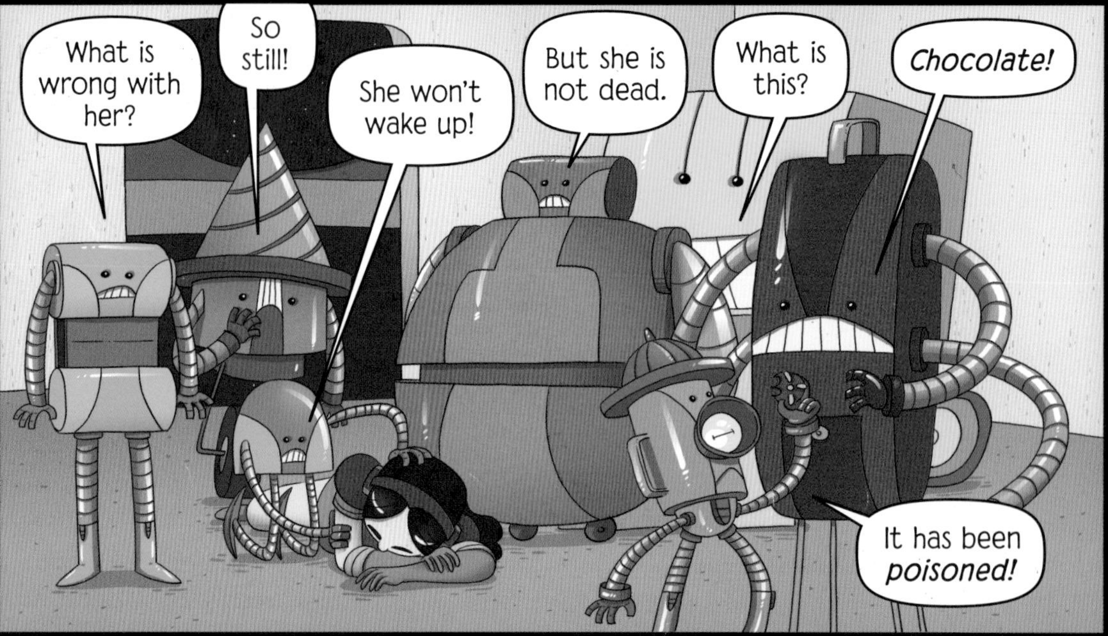
What is wrong with her?
So still!
She won't wake up!
But she is not dead.
What is this?
Chocolate!
It has been *poisoned!*

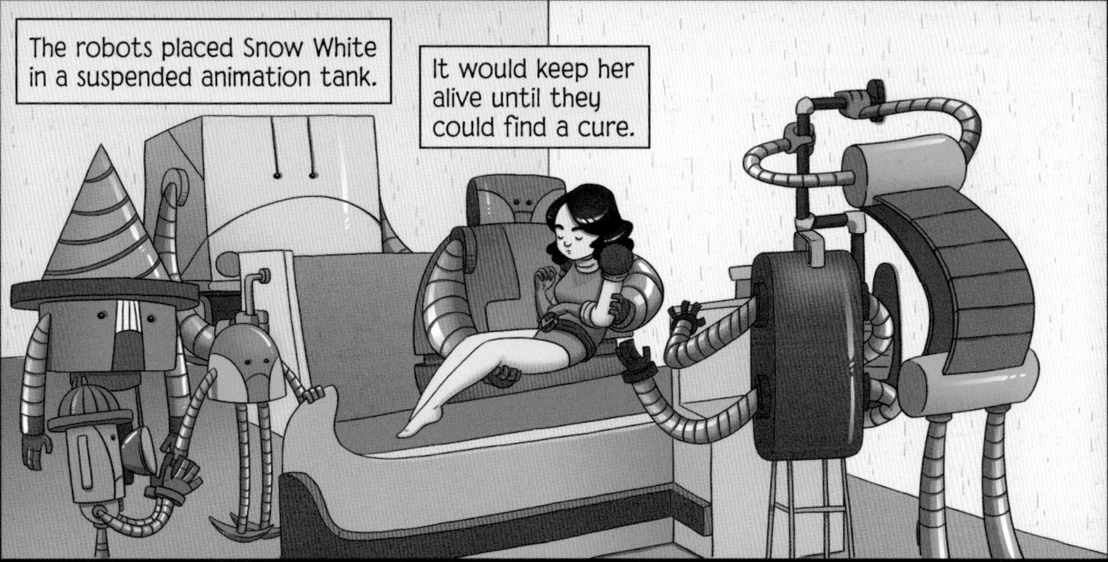
The robots placed Snow White in a suspended animation tank.
It would keep her alive until they could find a cure.

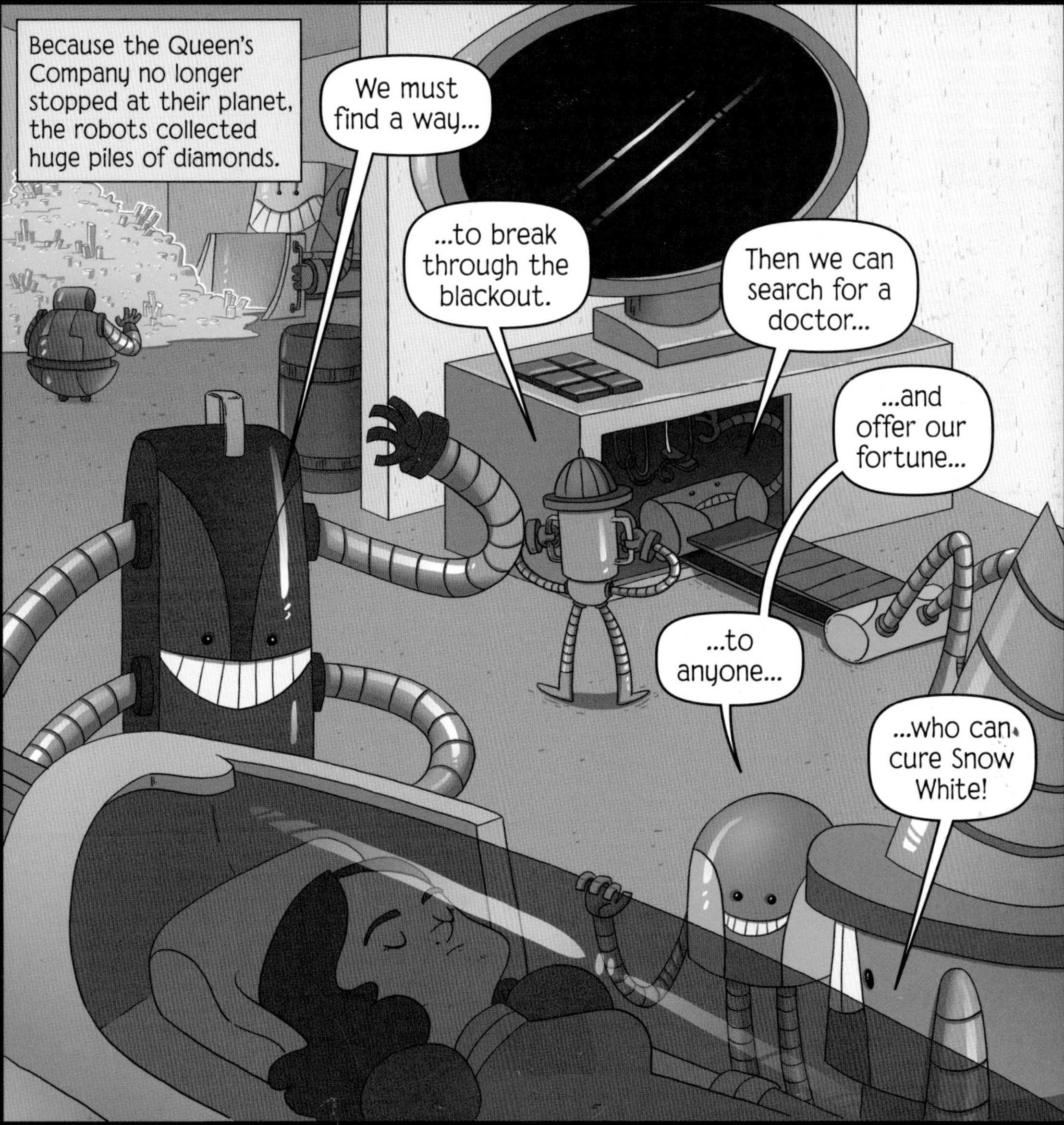
Because the Queen's Company no longer stopped at their planet, the robots collected huge piles of diamonds.
We must find a way...
...to break through the blackout.
Then we can search for a doctor...
...and offer our fortune...
...to anyone...
...who can cure Snow White!

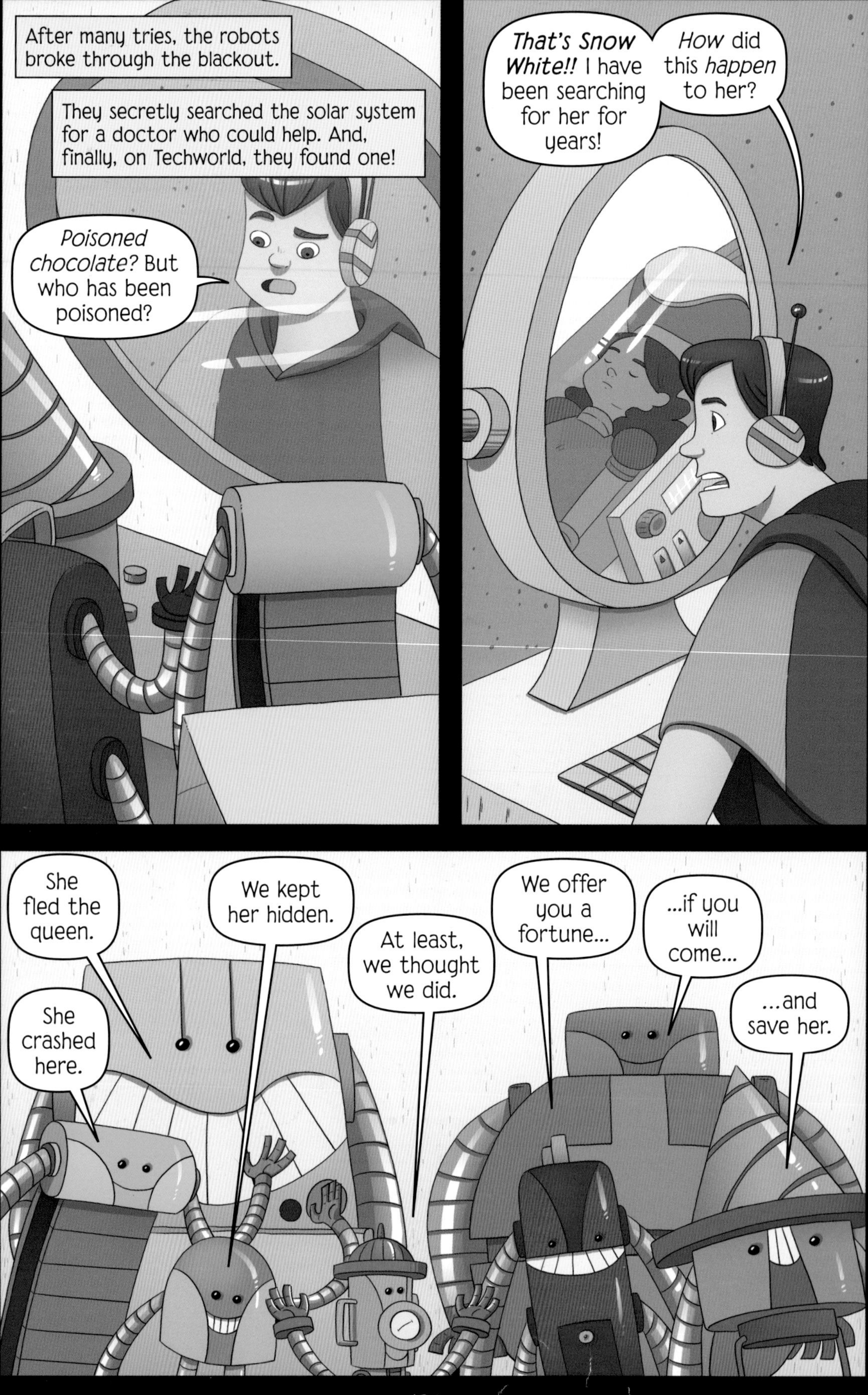
After many tries, the robots broke through the blackout.
They secretly searched the solar system for a doctor who could help. And, finally, on Techworld, they found one!
Poisoned chocolate? But who has been poisoned?
That's Snow White!! I have been searching for her for years!
How did this *happen* to her?
She fled the queen.
She crashed here.
We kept her hidden.
At least, we thought we did.
We offer you a fortune...
...if you will come...
...and save her.

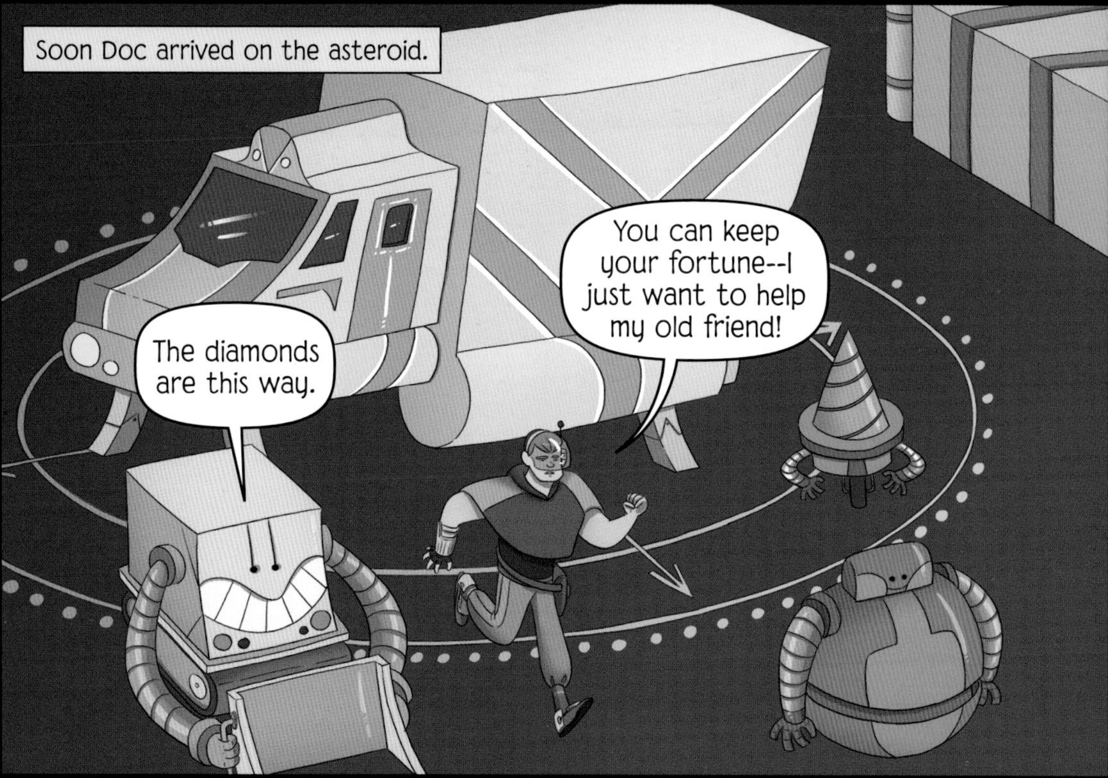
Soon Doc arrived on the asteroid.
The diamonds are this way.
You can keep your fortune--I just want to help my old friend!

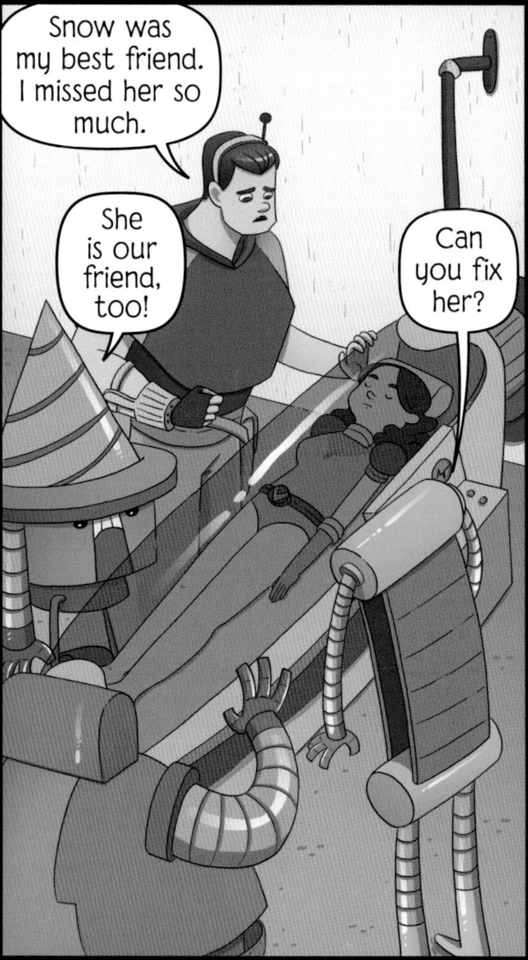
Snow was my best friend. I missed her so much.
She is our friend, too!
Can you fix her?

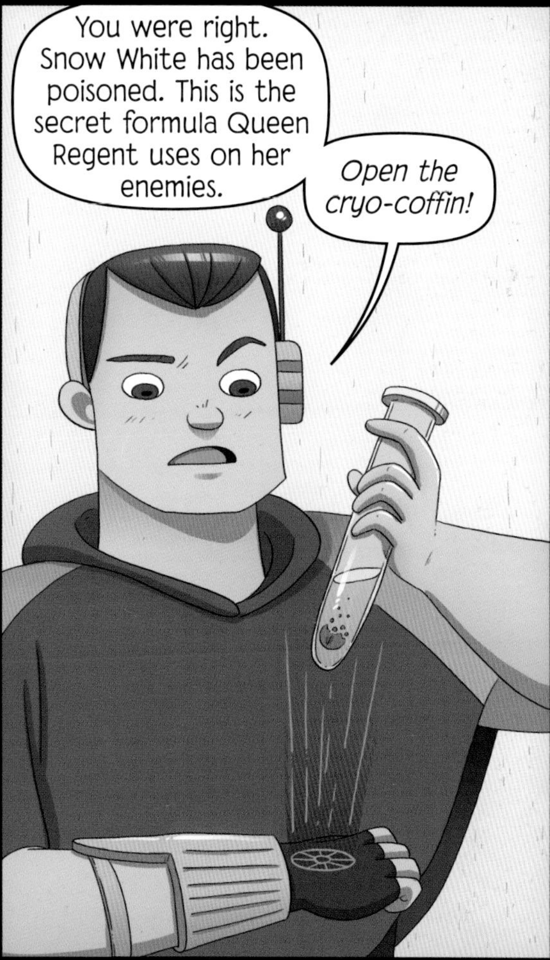
You were right. Snow White has been poisoned. This is the secret formula Queen Regent uses on her enemies.
Open the cryo-coffin!

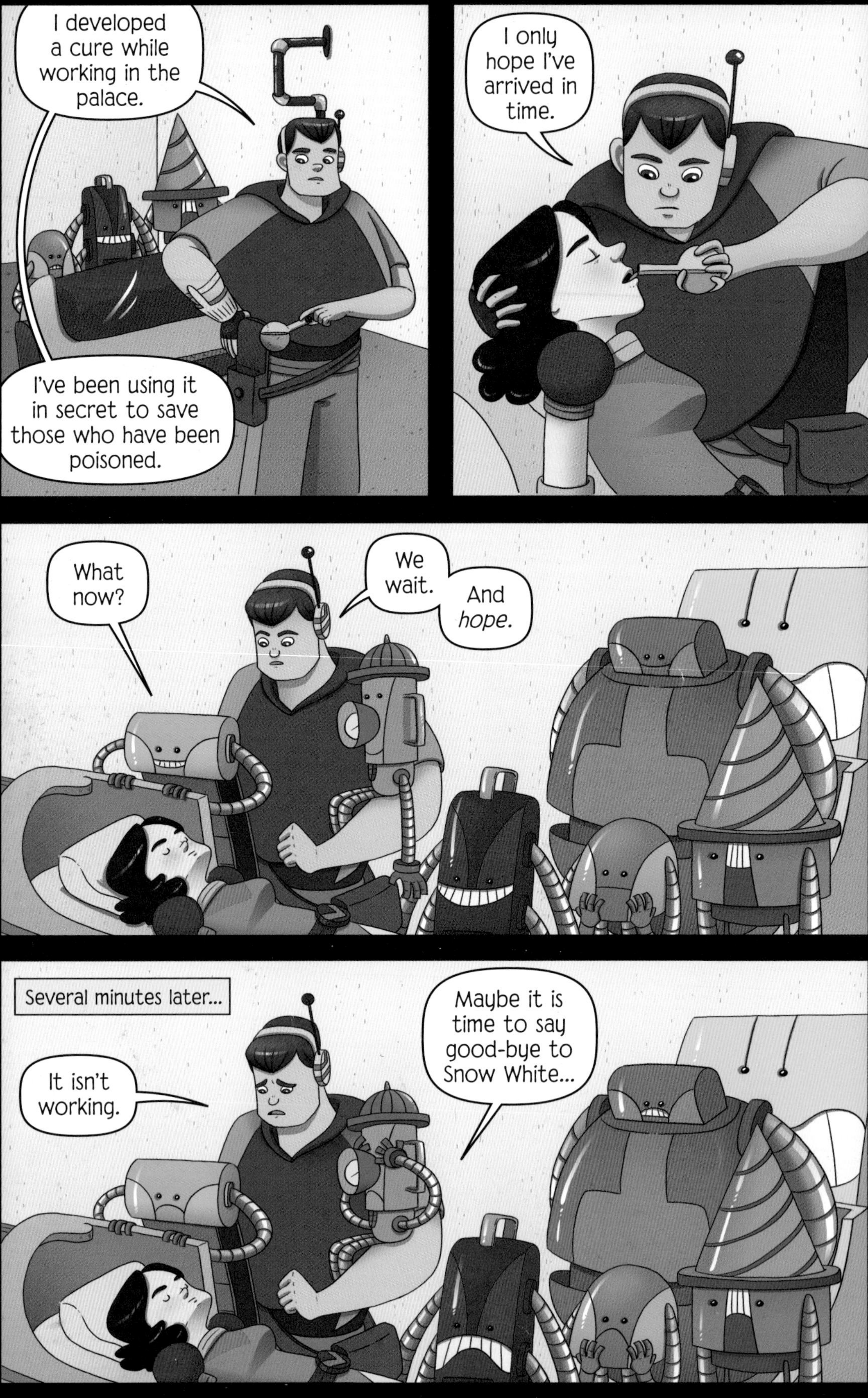
I developed a cure while working in the palace.
I've been using it in secret to save those who have been poisoned.
I only hope I've arrived in time.
What now?
We wait.
And *hope.*
Several minutes later...
It isn't working.
Maybe it is time to say good-bye to Snow White...

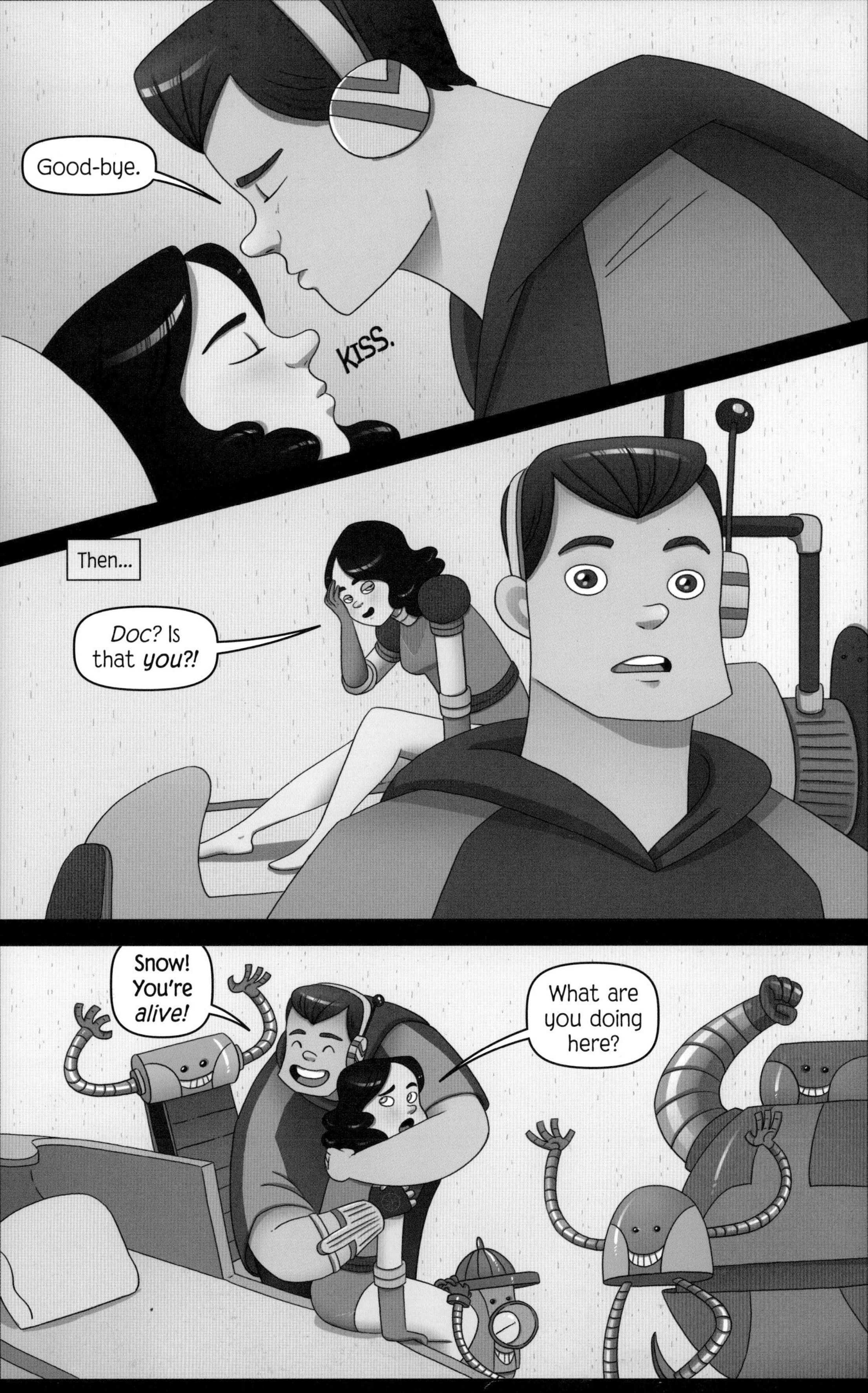
Good-bye.
KISS.
Then...
Doc? Is that *you?!*
Snow! You're *alive!*
What are you doing here?

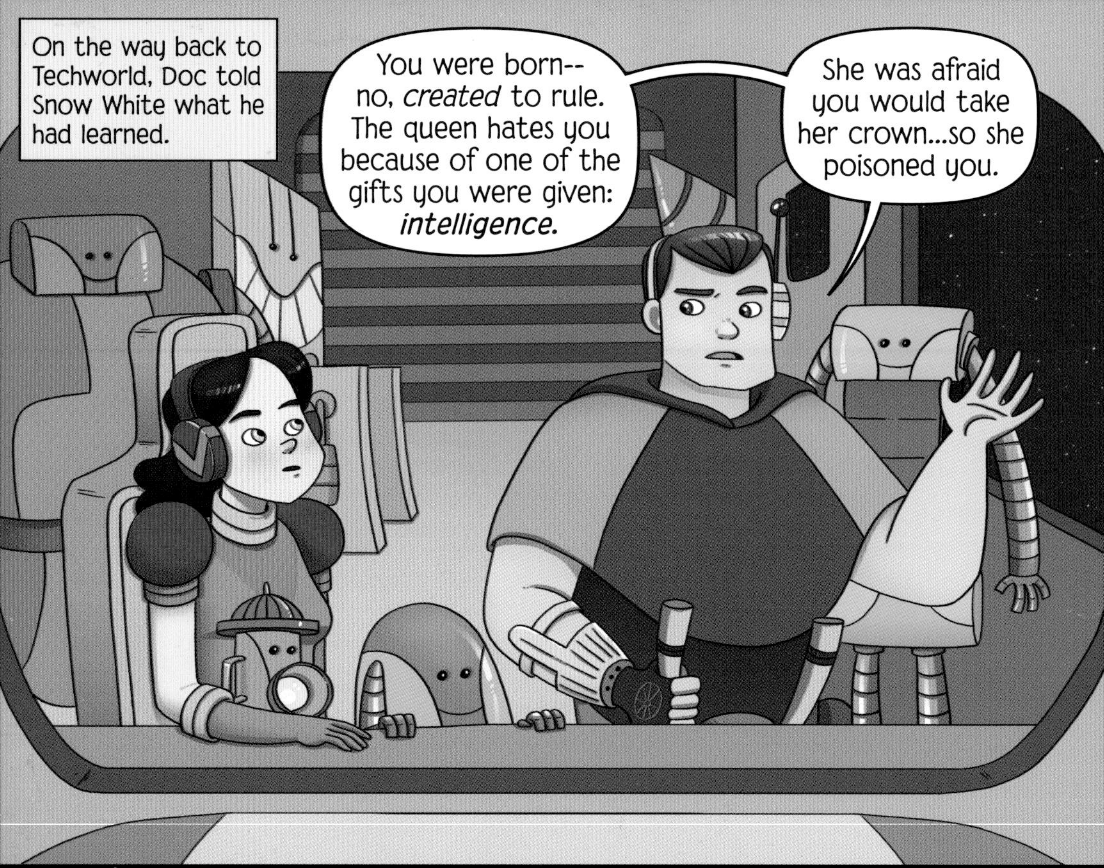
On the way back to Techworld, Doc told Snow White what he had learned.
You were born--no, *created* to rule. The queen hates you because of one of the gifts you were given: *intelligence.*
She was afraid you would take her crown...so she poisoned you.

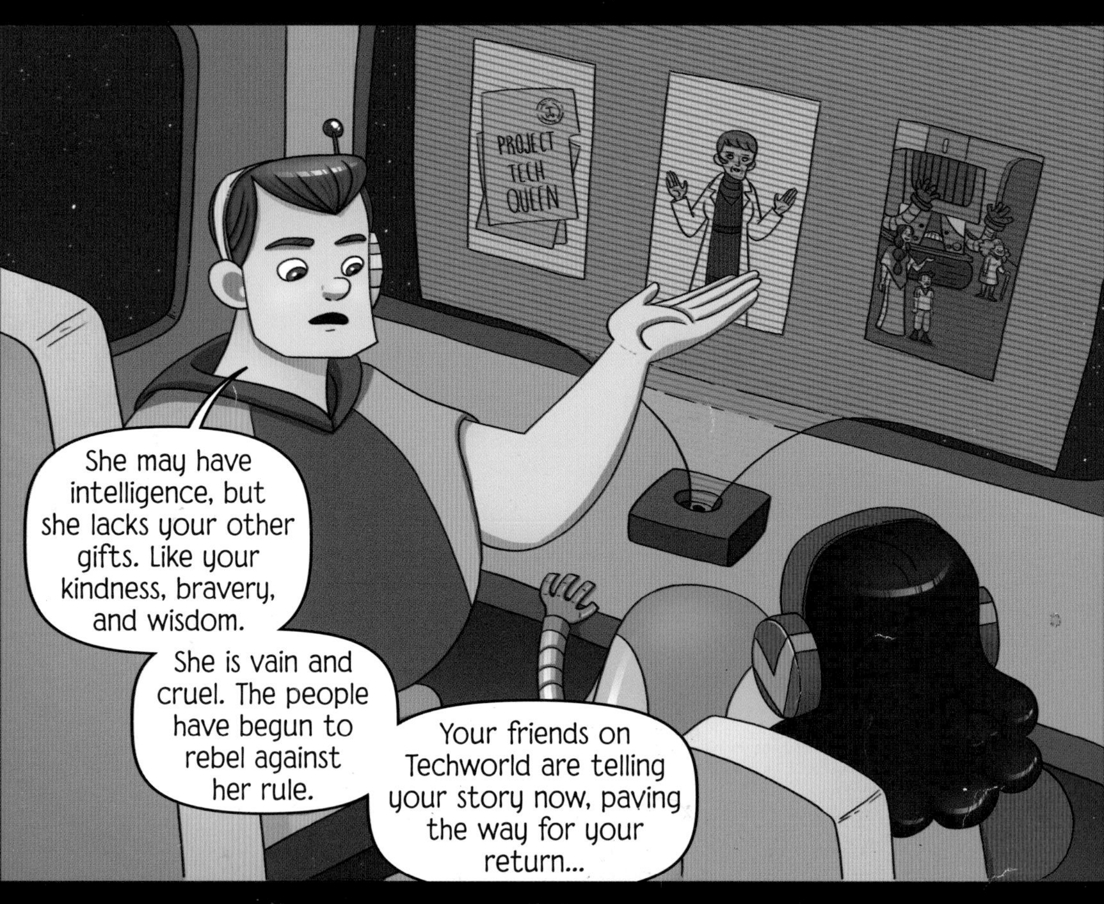
PROJECT TECH QUEEN
She may have intelligence, but she lacks your other gifts. Like your kindness, bravery, and wisdom.
She is vain and cruel. The people have begun to rebel against her rule.
Your friends on Techworld are telling your story now, paving the way for your return...

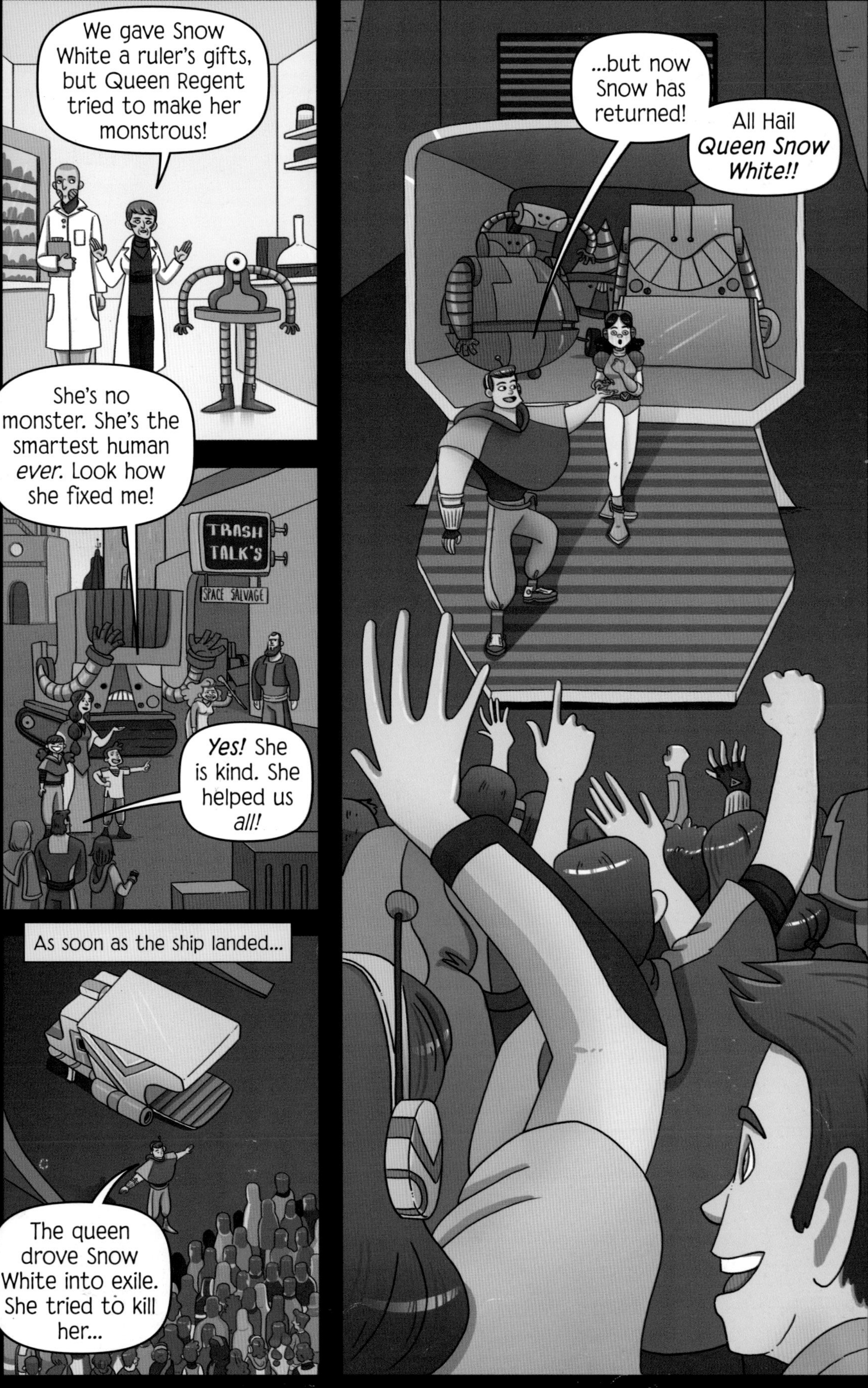
We gave Snow White a ruler's gifts, but Queen Regent tried to make her monstrous!
She's no monster. She's the smartest human *ever*. Look how she fixed me!
TRASH TALK'S
SPACE SALVAGE
Yes! She is kind. She helped us *all!*
As soon as the ship landed...
The queen drove Snow White into exile. She tried to kill her...
...but now Snow has returned!
All Hail *Queen Snow White!!*

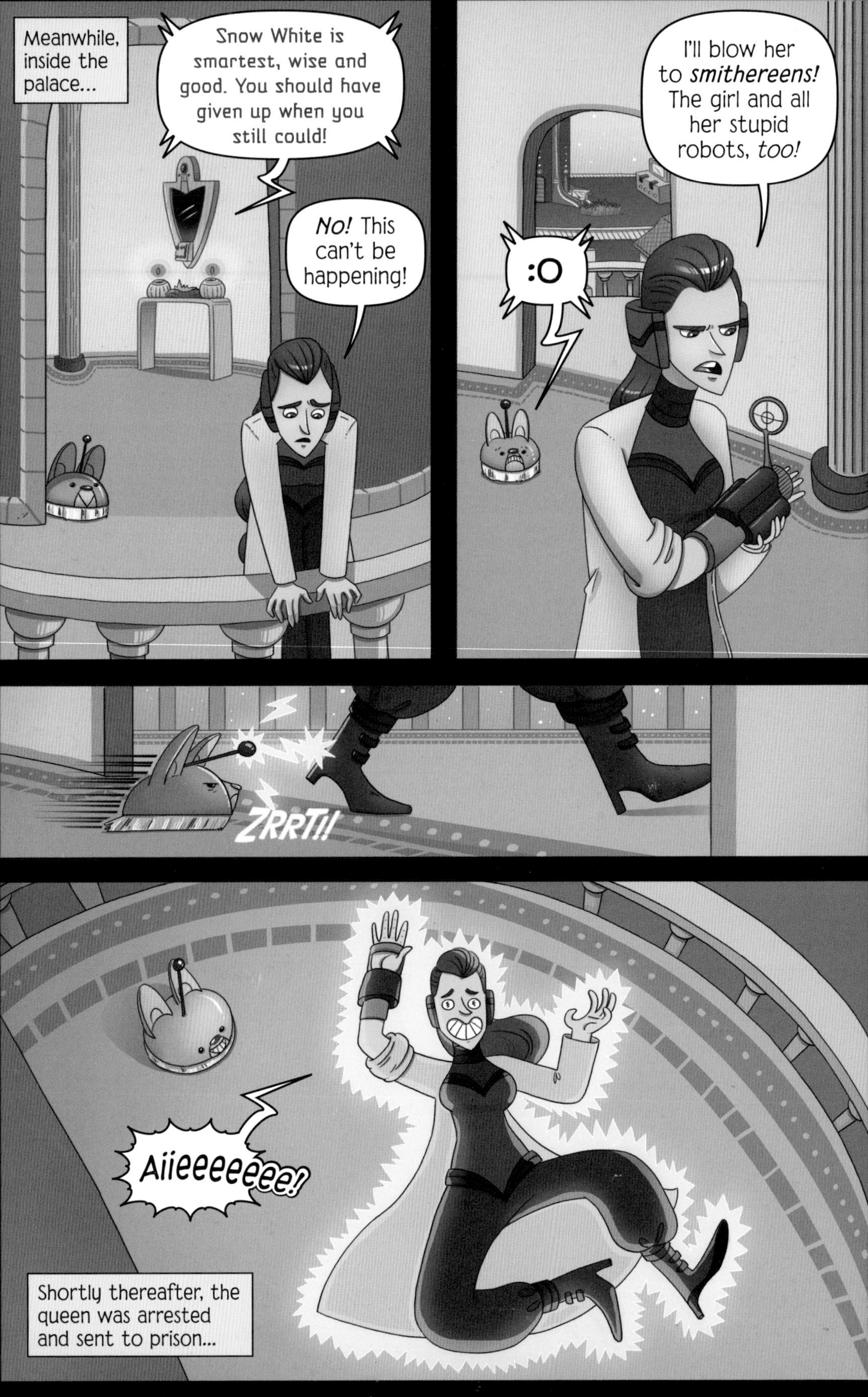
Meanwhile, inside the palace...
Snow White is smartest, wise and good. You should have given up when you still could!
No! This can't be happening!
I'll blow her to smithereens! The girl and all her stupid robots, too!
:O
ZRRT!!
Aiieeeeeeee!
Shortly thereafter, the queen was arrested and sent to prison...

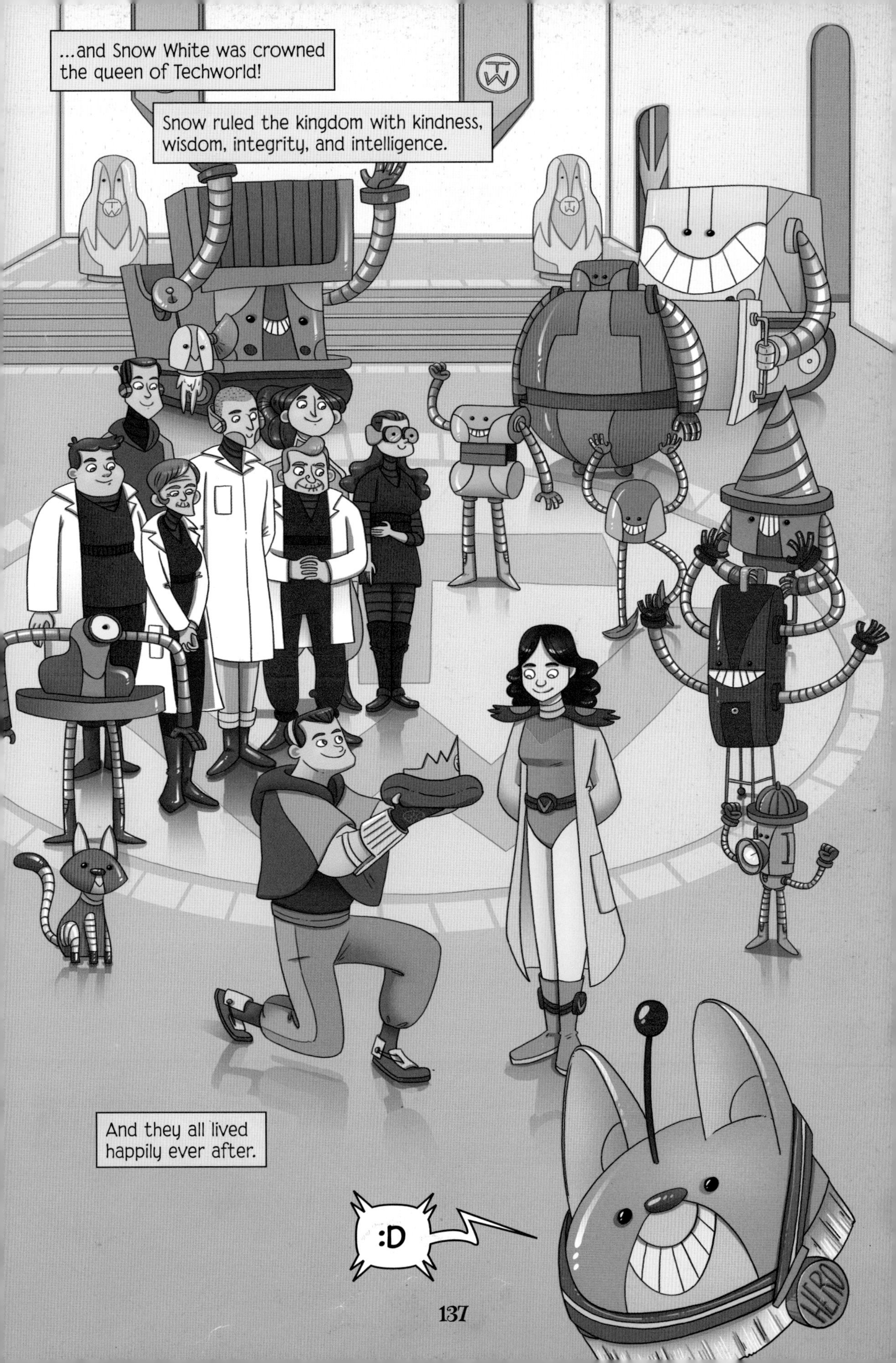
...and Snow White was crowned the queen of Techworld!
Snow ruled the kingdom with kindness, wisdom, integrity, and intelligence.
And they all lived happily ever after.
:D
HERO

ALL ABOUT THE ORIGINAL TALE!

The story of Snow White was first published by the Brothers Grimm in 1812. This fairy tale tells the story of a queen who wishes for a daughter with skin as white as snow, lips as red as blood, and jet-black hair. She gets her wish, but tragically dies during childbirth.

Snow White's father then marries a beautiful but selfish woman. Each day, the new queen asks a magic mirror who the most beautiful woman alive is. And each day, the mirror says it's the queen--until one day the mirror names Snow White instead.

The queen decides to have Snow killed. She orders a huntsman to murder her, but he can't make himself do the deed so he abandons her in the forest instead. Snow comes across a tiny cottage with seven small beds. As it turns out, seven dwarves live there, and they let her stay with them in exchange for keeping their home tidy and making their meals.

Soon after, the magic mirror tells the queen where Snow is hiding. The queen arrives disguised as a farmer's wife and offers Snow a poisoned apple, which puts Snow into a permanent state of sleep. When the dwarves return from work, they think Snow is dead, so they place her in a glass coffin.

One day, a prince comes along and is struck by Snow White's beauty. The dwarves let the prince take the coffin, presumably so she can have a proper burial. As the dwarves carry the coffin away, they trip and drop it. The bump dislodges the chunk of apple that was caught in Snow's throat, and she awakens! (In some versions of the tale, it's the prince's kiss that wakes Snow White from her endless sleep.) Either way, Snow falls in love with the prince at first sight. They marry, live happily ever after, and the evil queen is punished for her misdeeds.

In this far out version of the fairy tale, it's Snow White's inner beauty and intelligence that the queen fears. Check out this book's other twists to the timeless tale...

A **FAR OUT** GUIDE TO SNOW WHITE'S TALE TWISTS!

The all-knowing magic mirror is replaced by an all-seeing space satellite!

Dwarves helped the original Snow White. In this tale, robots come to her aid!

Instead of a poisoned apple putting Snow to sleep, poisoned chocolate is the culprit.

This cryo-tank preserves Snow White instead of the glass coffin in the original tale.

FAR OUT FAIRY TALES

HANSEL & GRETEL & ZOMBIES

A GRAPHIC NOVEL

BY BENJAMIN HARPER

ILLUSTRATED BY FERNANDO CANO

INTRODUCING...

HANSEL & GRETEL

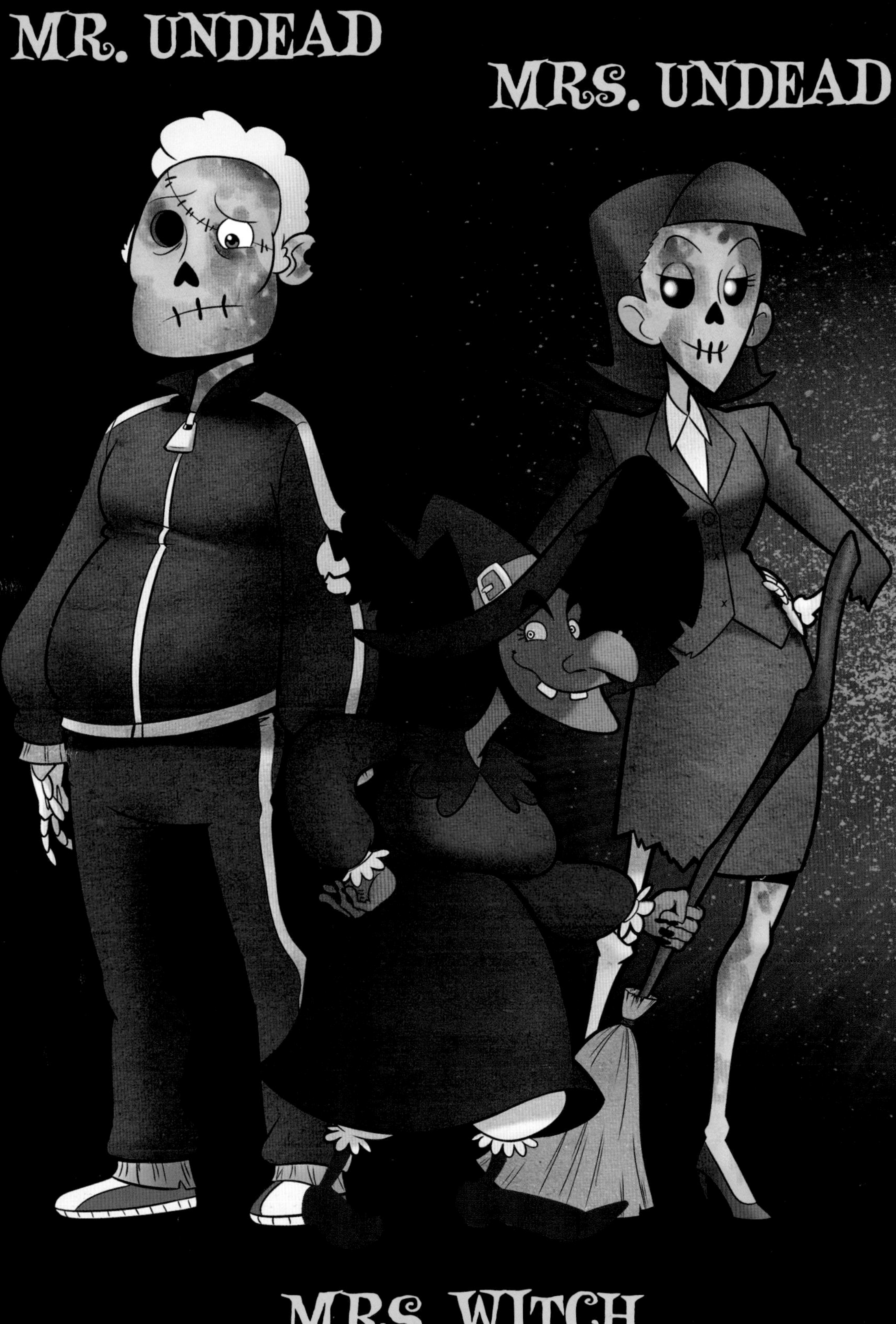
MR. UNDEAD
MRS. UNDEAD
MRS. WITCH

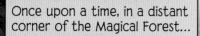

Once upon a time, in a distant corner of the Magical Forest...

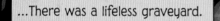

...There was a lifeless graveyard.

CEMETERY

It had long been abandoned. No one had been buried there in years. No one visited.

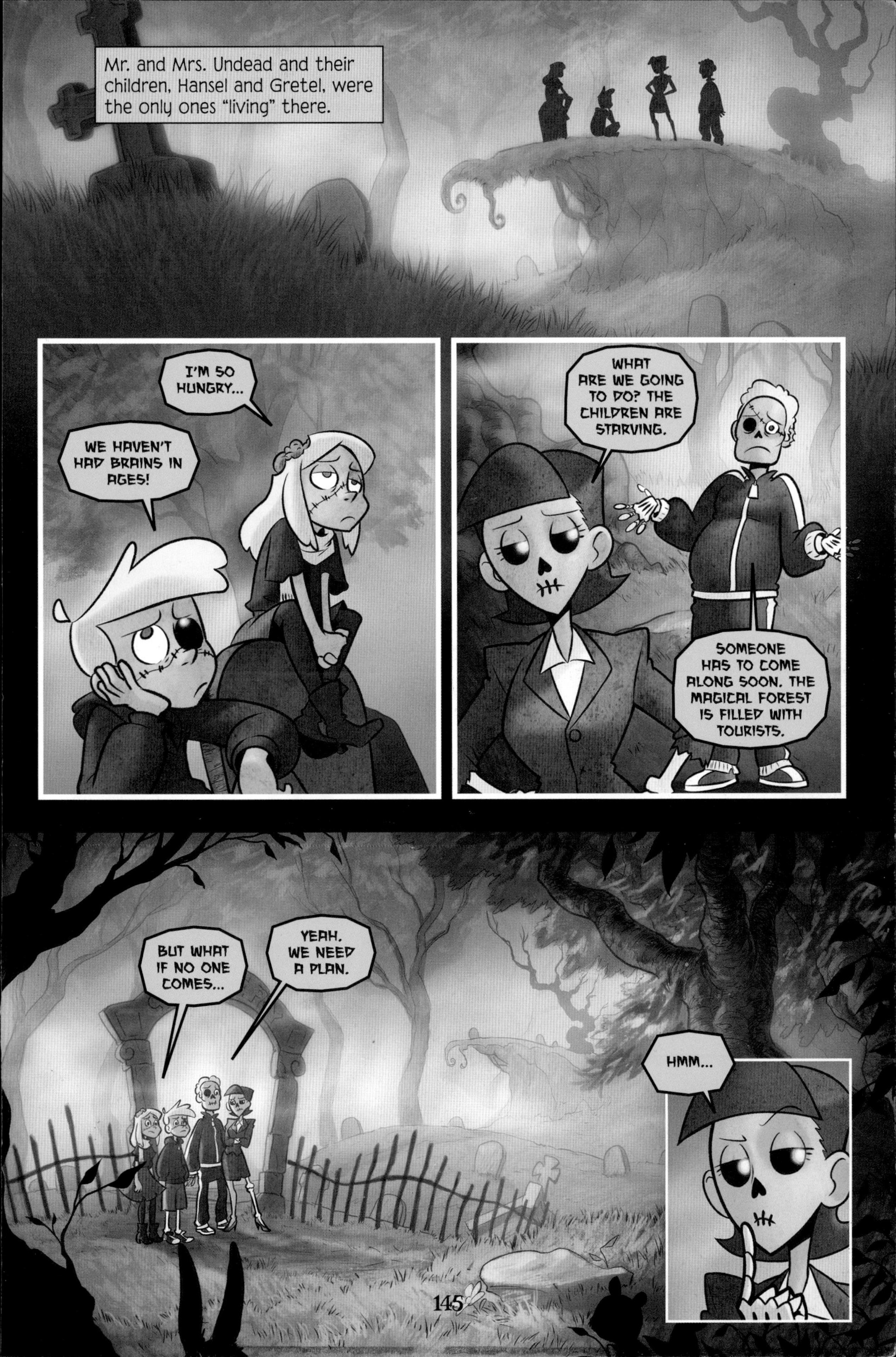
Mr. and Mrs. Undead and their children, Hansel and Gretel, were the only ones "living" there.
I'M SO HUNGRY...
WE HAVEN'T HAD BRAINS IN AGES!
WHAT ARE WE GOING TO DO? THE CHILDREN ARE STARVING.
SOMEONE HAS TO COME ALONG SOON. THE MAGICAL FOREST IS FILLED WITH TOURISTS.
BUT WHAT IF NO ONE COMES...
YEAH, WE NEED A PLAN.
HMM...

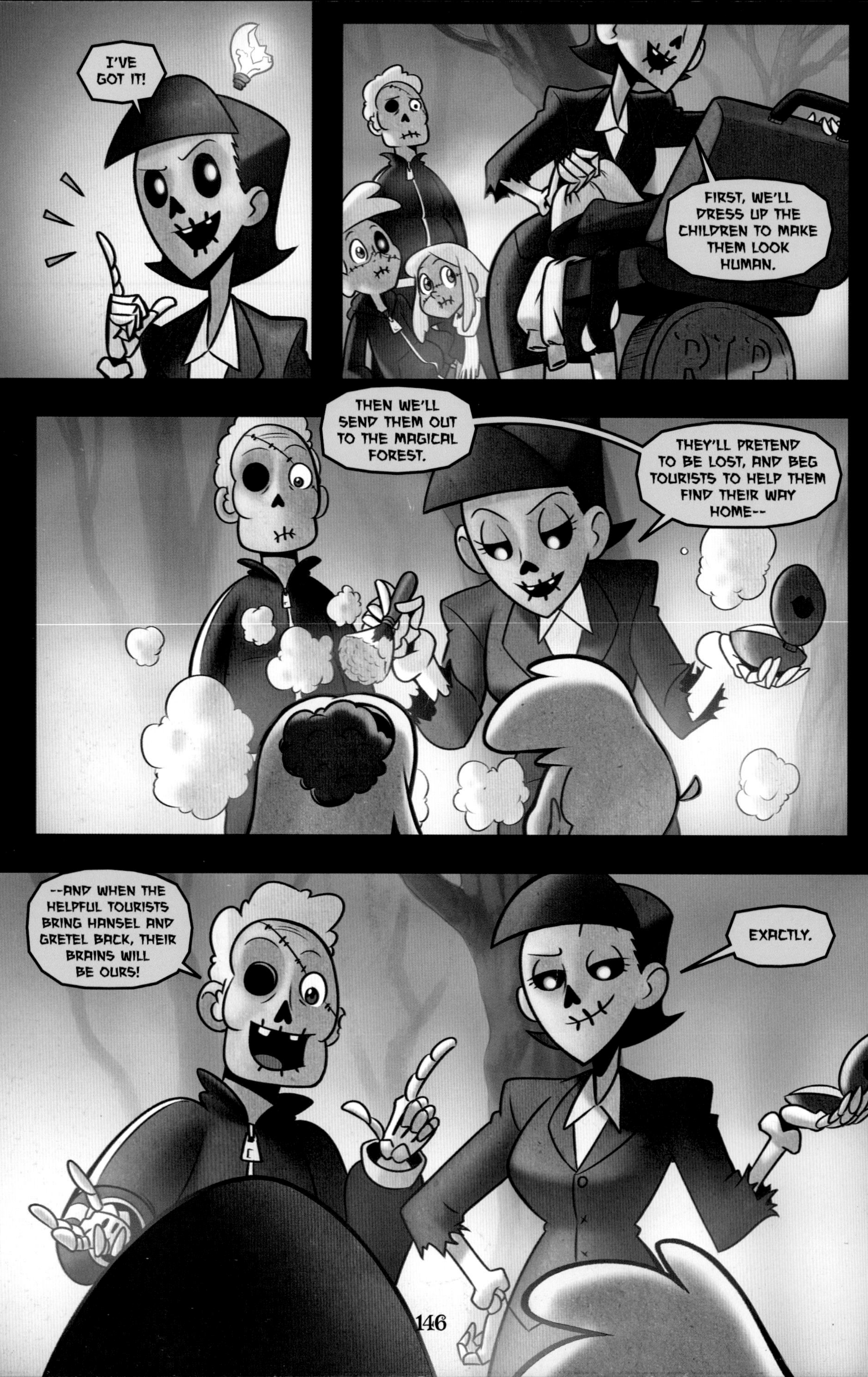
I'VE GOT IT!
FIRST, WE'LL DRESS UP THE CHILDREN TO MAKE THEM LOOK HUMAN.
R.I.P.
THEN WE'LL SEND THEM OUT TO THE MAGICAL FOREST.
THEY'LL PRETEND TO BE LOST, AND BEG TOURISTS TO HELP THEM FIND THEIR WAY HOME--
--AND WHEN THE HELPFUL TOURISTS BRING HANSEL AND GRETEL BACK, THEIR BRAINS WILL BE OURS!
EXACTLY.

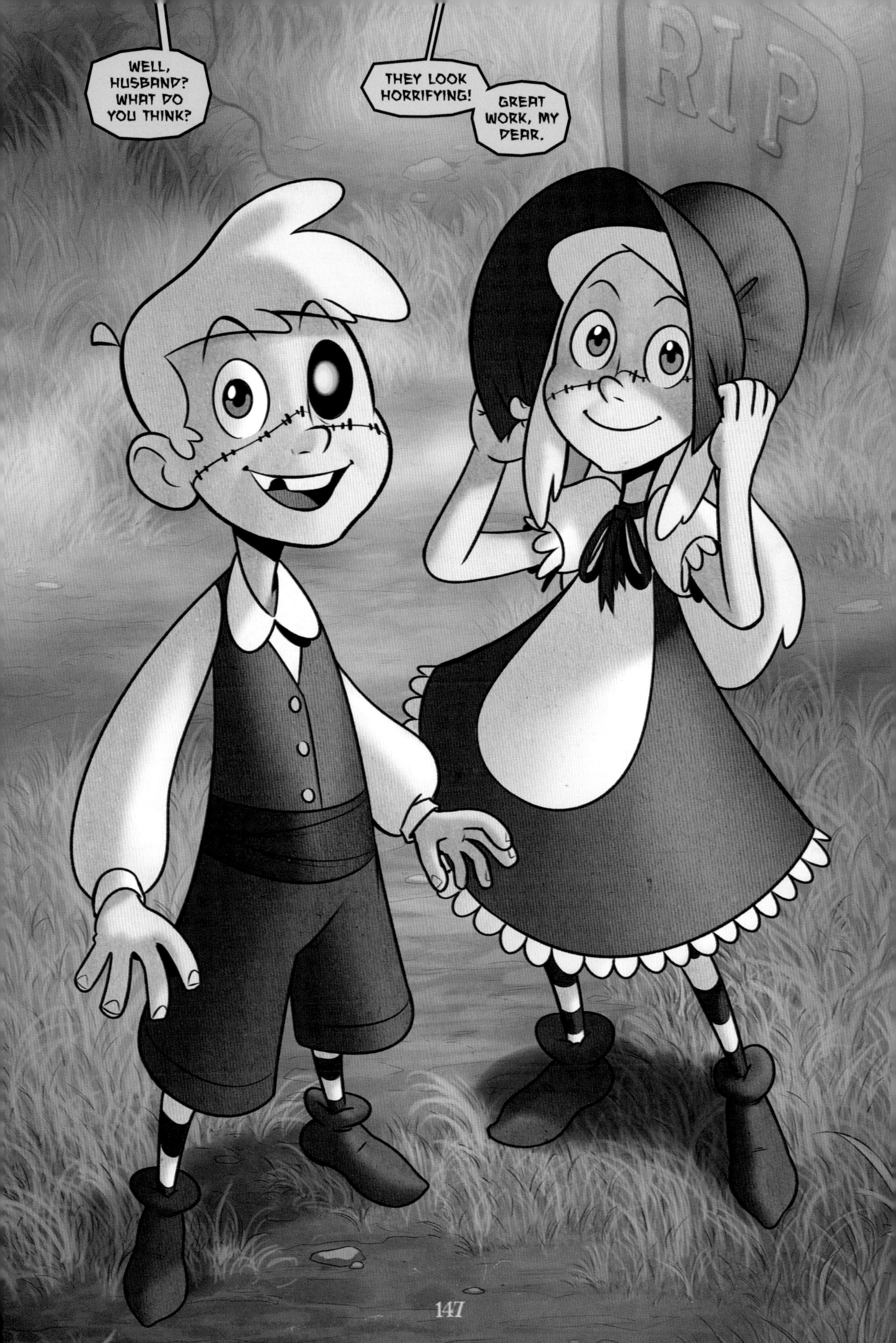
WELL, HUSBAND? WHAT DO YOU THINK?
THEY LOOK HORRIFYING!
GREAT WORK, MY DEAR.
RIP

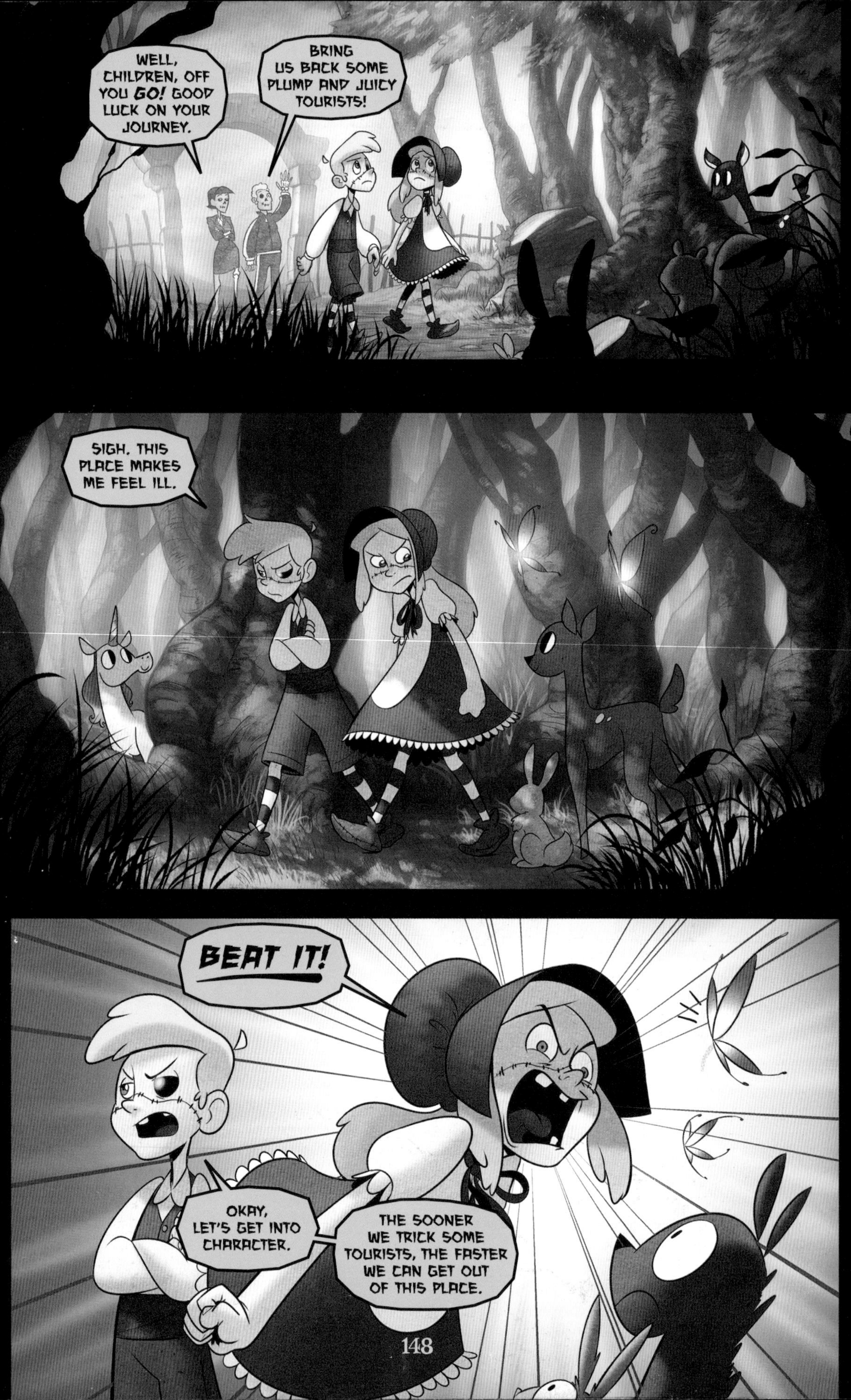
WELL, CHILDREN, OFF YOU GO! GOOD LUCK ON YOUR JOURNEY.
BRING US BACK SOME PLUMP AND JUICY TOURISTS!
SIGH. THIS PLACE MAKES ME FEEL ILL.
BEAT IT!
OKAY, LET'S GET INTO CHARACTER.
THE SOONER WE TRICK SOME TOURISTS, THE FASTER WE CAN GET OUT OF THIS PLACE.

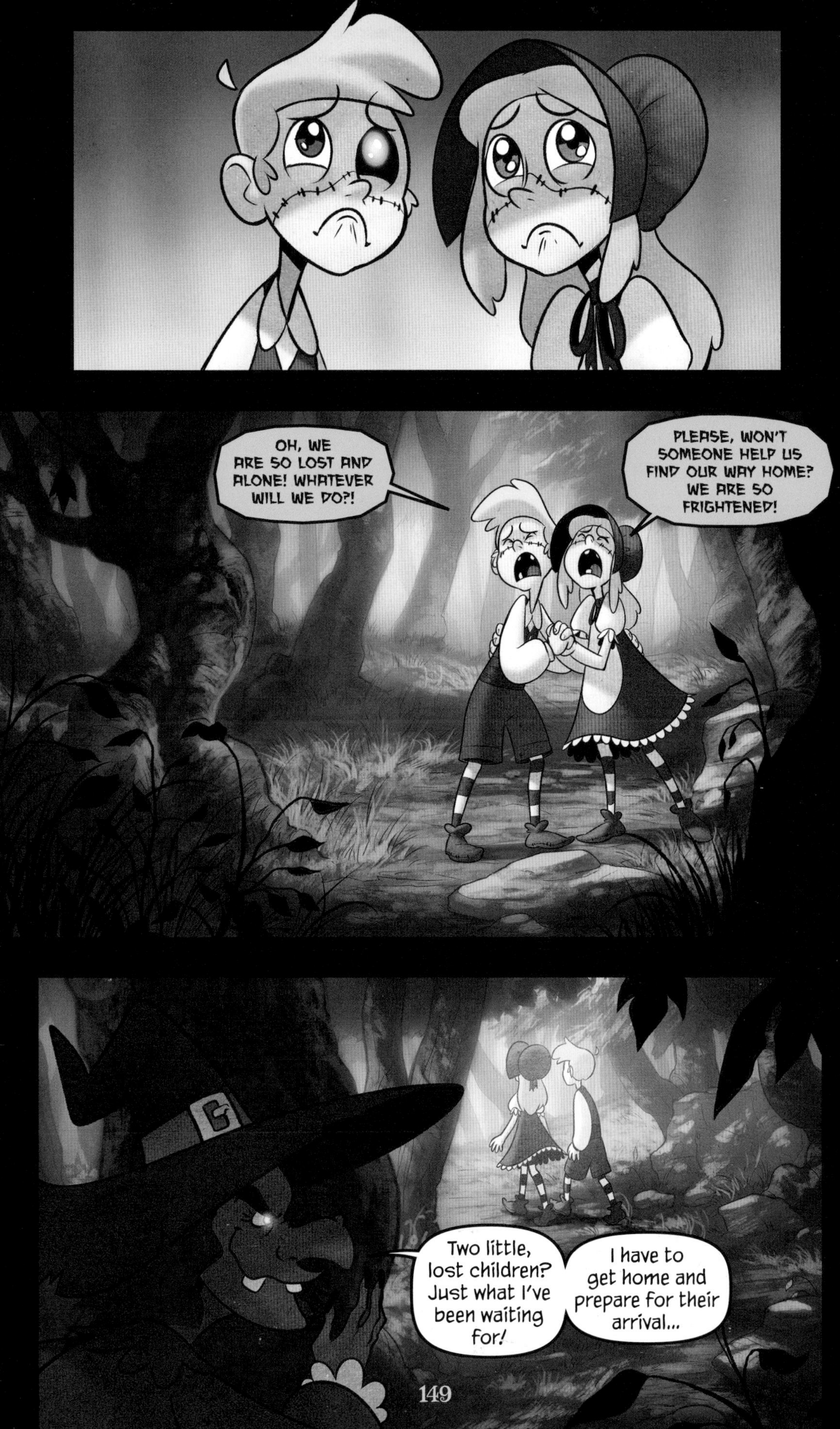

OH, WE ARE SO LOST AND ALONE! WHATEVER WILL WE DO?!
PLEASE, WON'T SOMEONE HELP US FIND OUR WAY HOME? WE ARE SO FRIGHTENED!
Two little, lost children? Just what I've been waiting for!
I have to get home and prepare for their arrival...

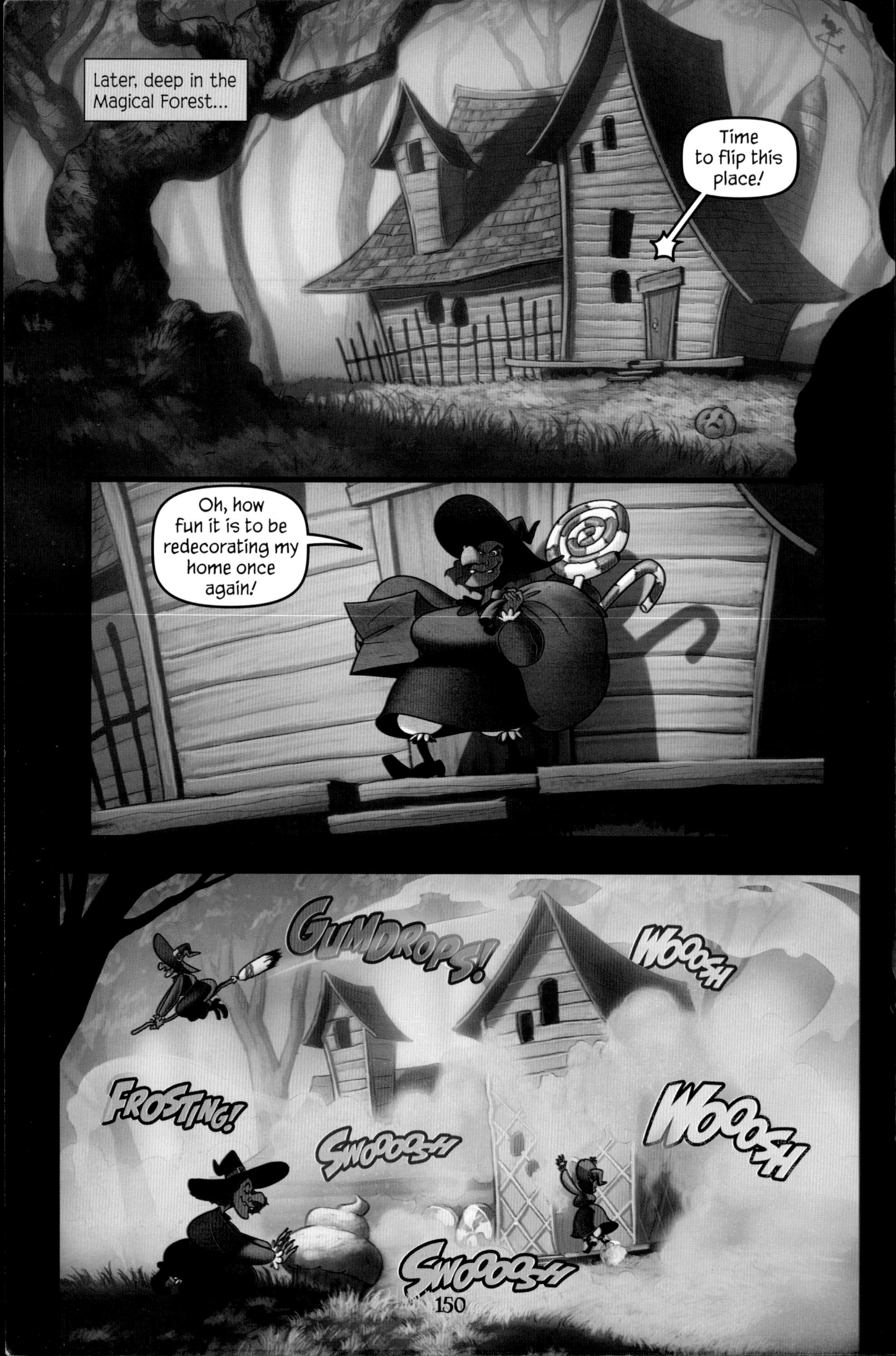
Later, deep in the Magical Forest...
Time to flip this place!
Oh, how fun it is to be redecorating my home once again!
GUMDROPS!
WOOOSH
FROSTING!
SWOOOSH
WOOOSH
SWOOOSH

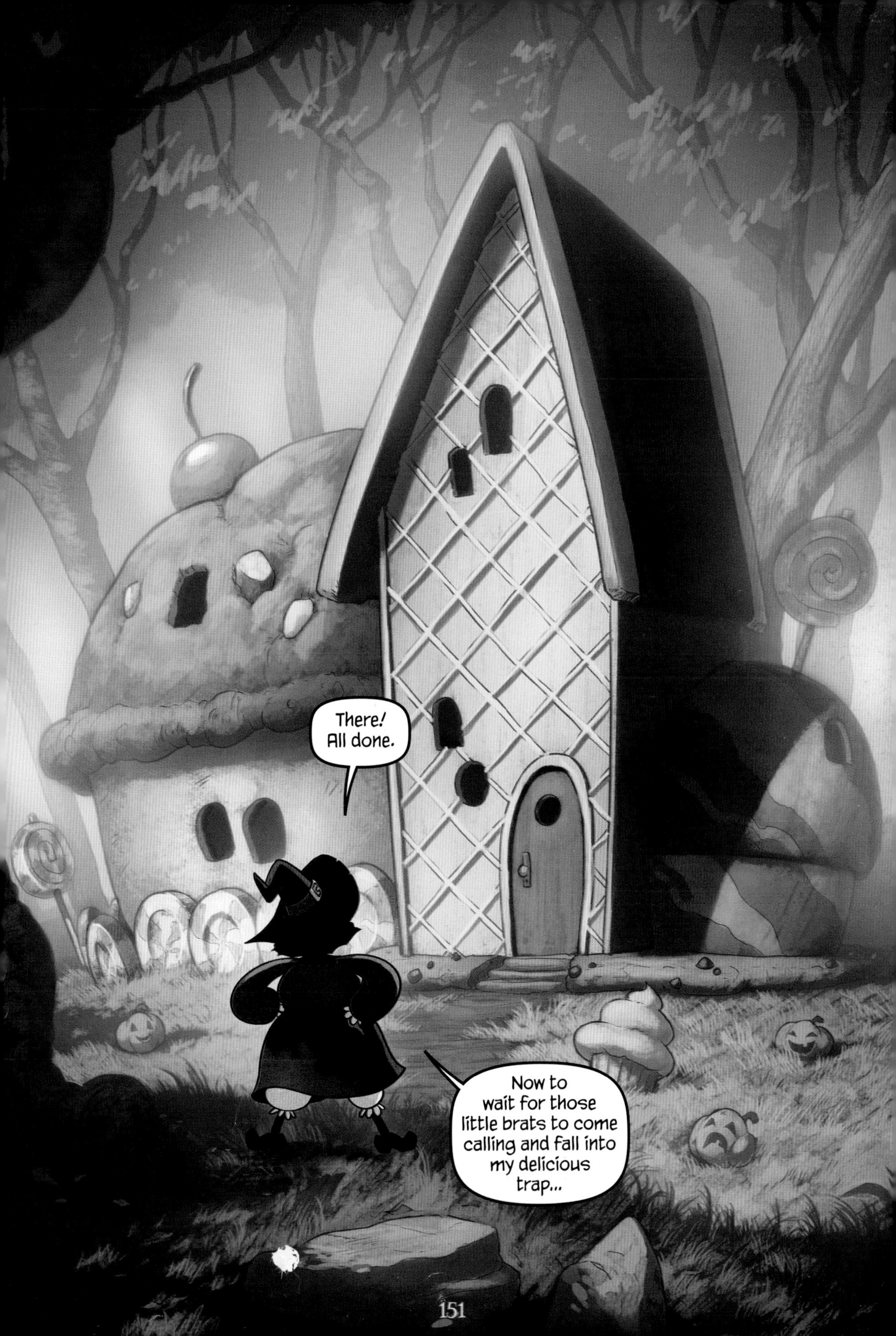
There! All done.
Now to wait for those little brats to come calling and fall into my delicious trap...

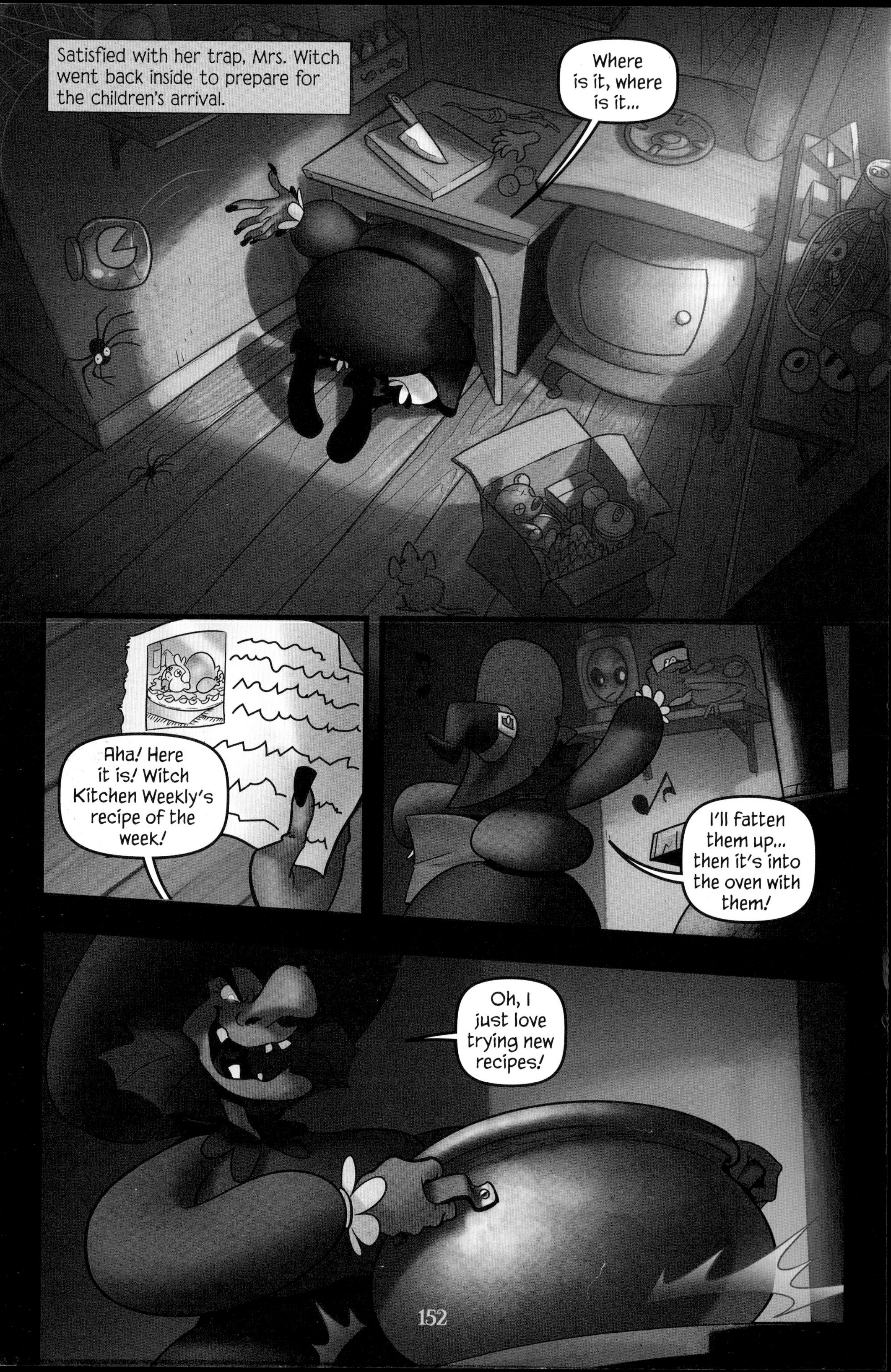
Satisfied with her trap, Mrs. Witch went back inside to prepare for the children's arrival.
Where is it, where is it...
Aha! Here it is! Witch Kitchen Weekly's recipe of the week!
I'll fatten them up... then it's into the oven with them!
Oh, I just love trying new recipes!

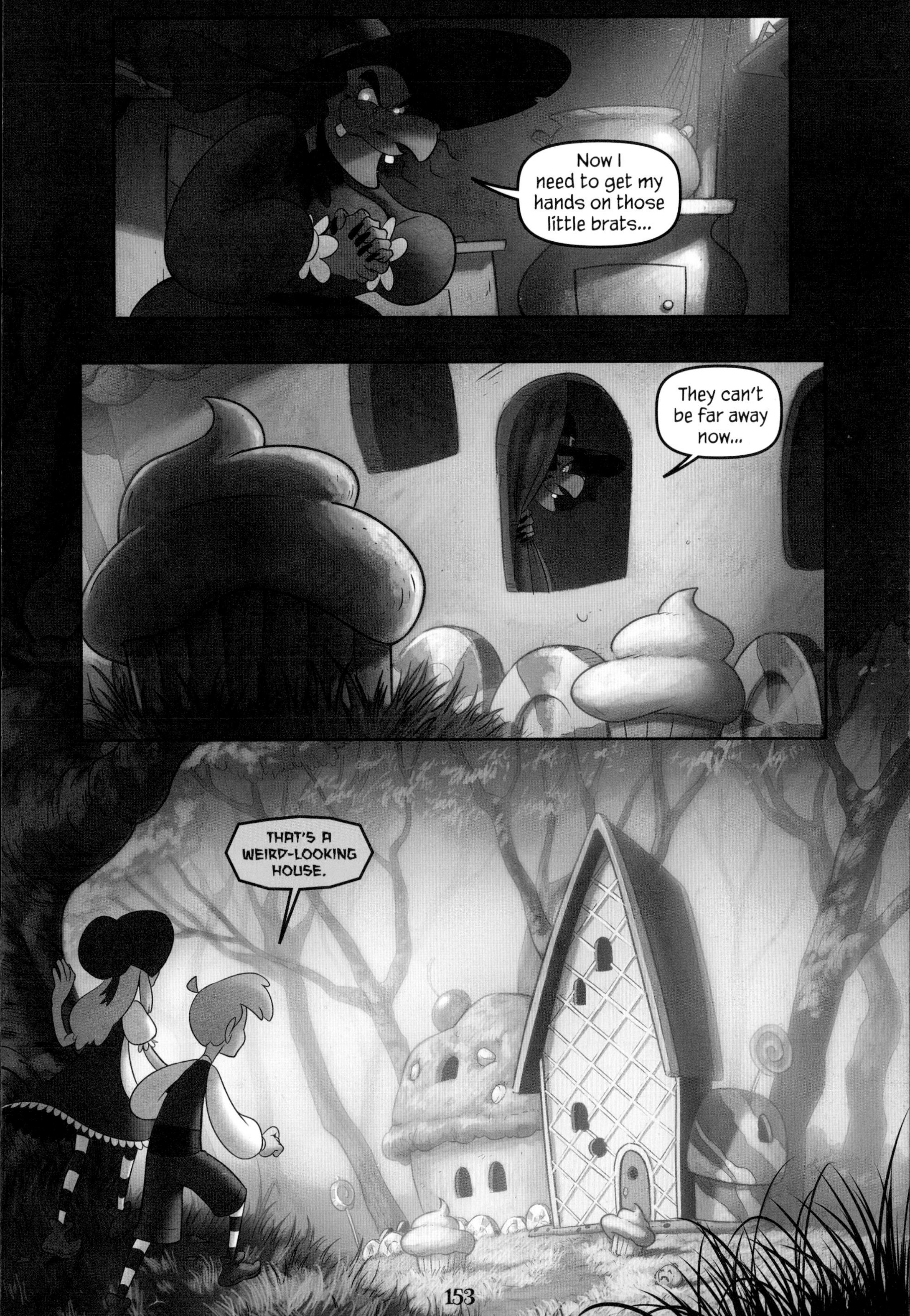

Now I need to get my hands on those little brats...
They can't be far away now...
THAT'S A WEIRD-LOOKING HOUSE.

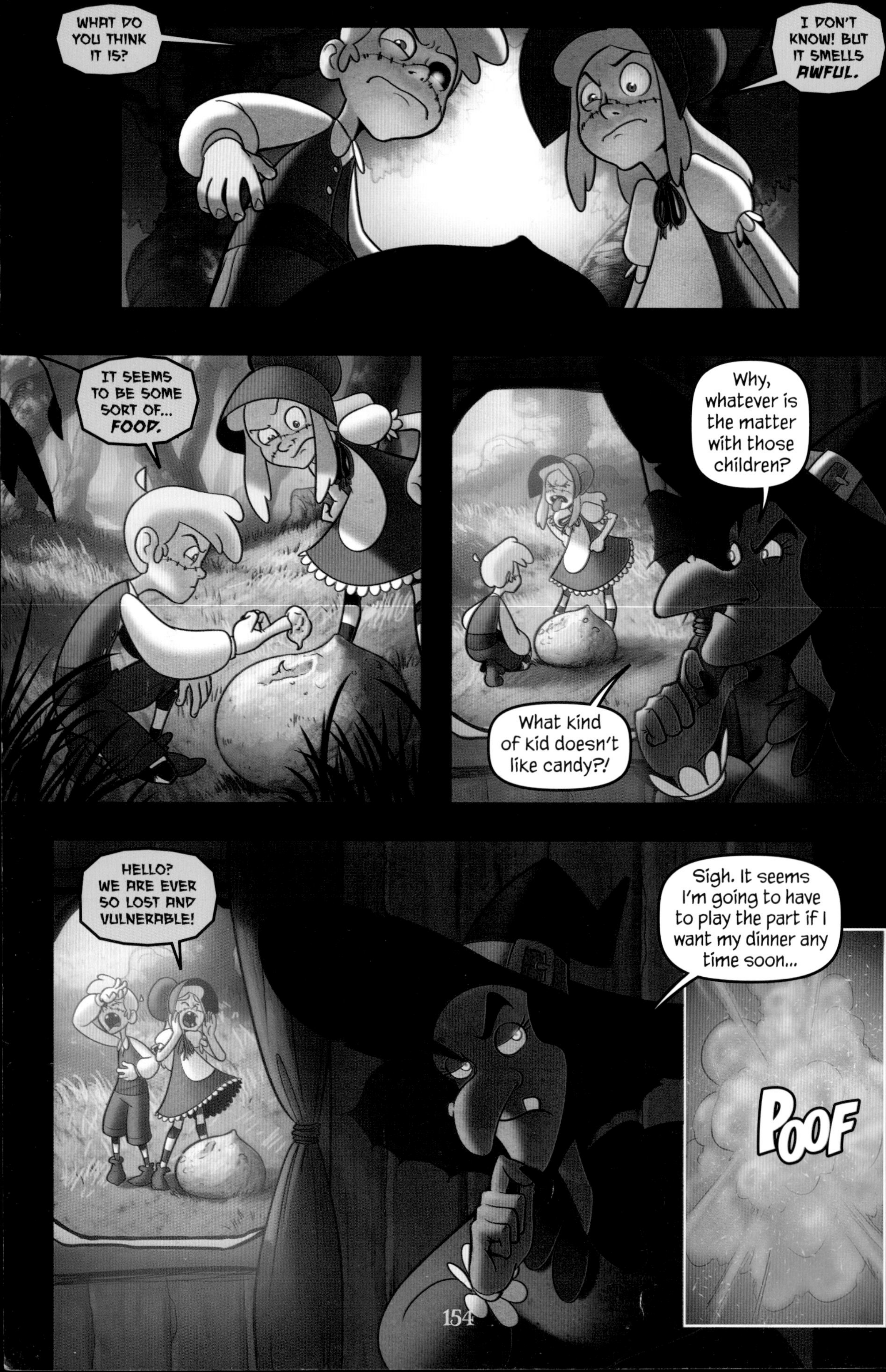

WHAT DO YOU THINK IT IS?
I DON'T KNOW! BUT IT SMELLS AWFUL.
IT SEEMS TO BE SOME SORT OF... FOOD.
Why, whatever is the matter with those children?
What kind of kid doesn't like candy?!
HELLO? WE ARE EVER SO LOST AND VULNERABLE!
Sigh. It seems I'm going to have to play the part if I want my dinner any time soon...
POOF

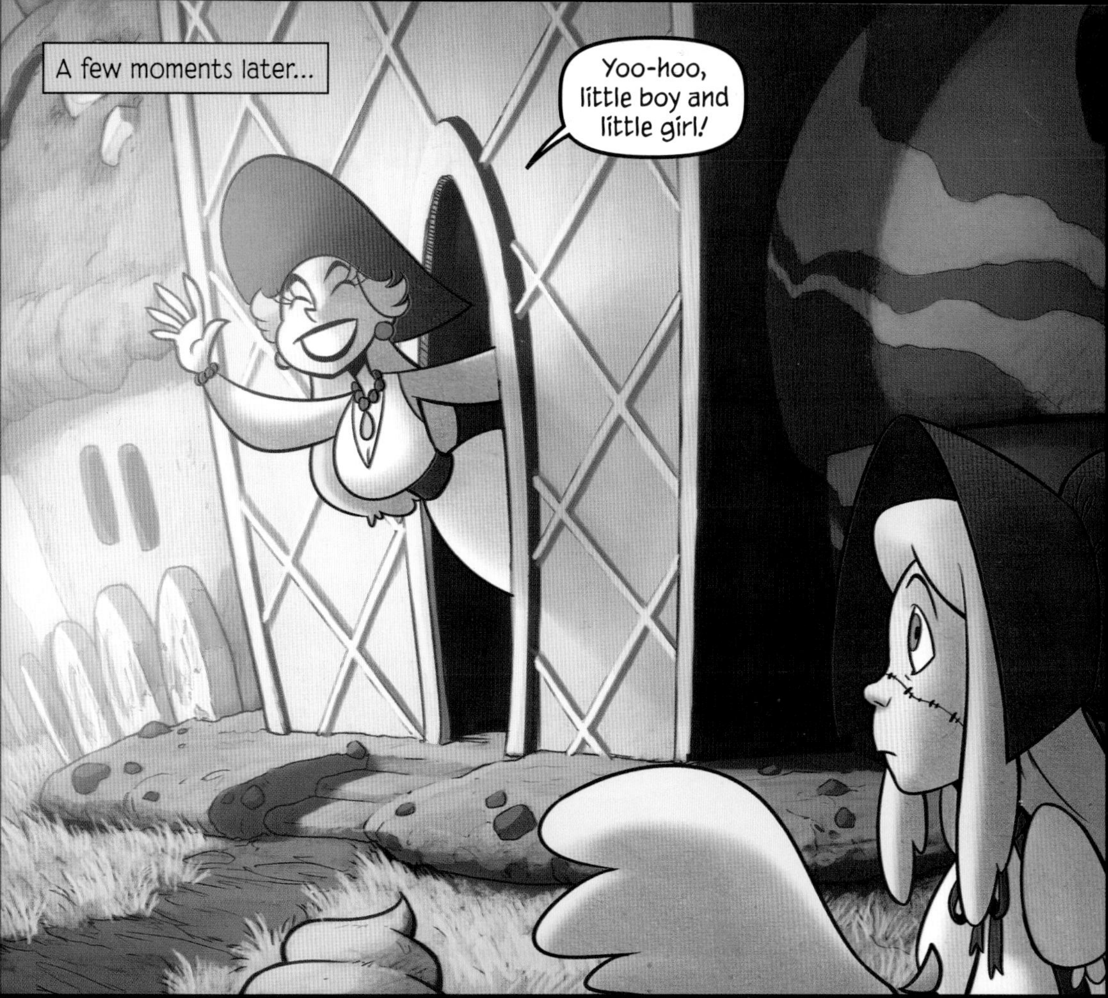
A few moments later...
Yoo-hoo, little boy and little girl!

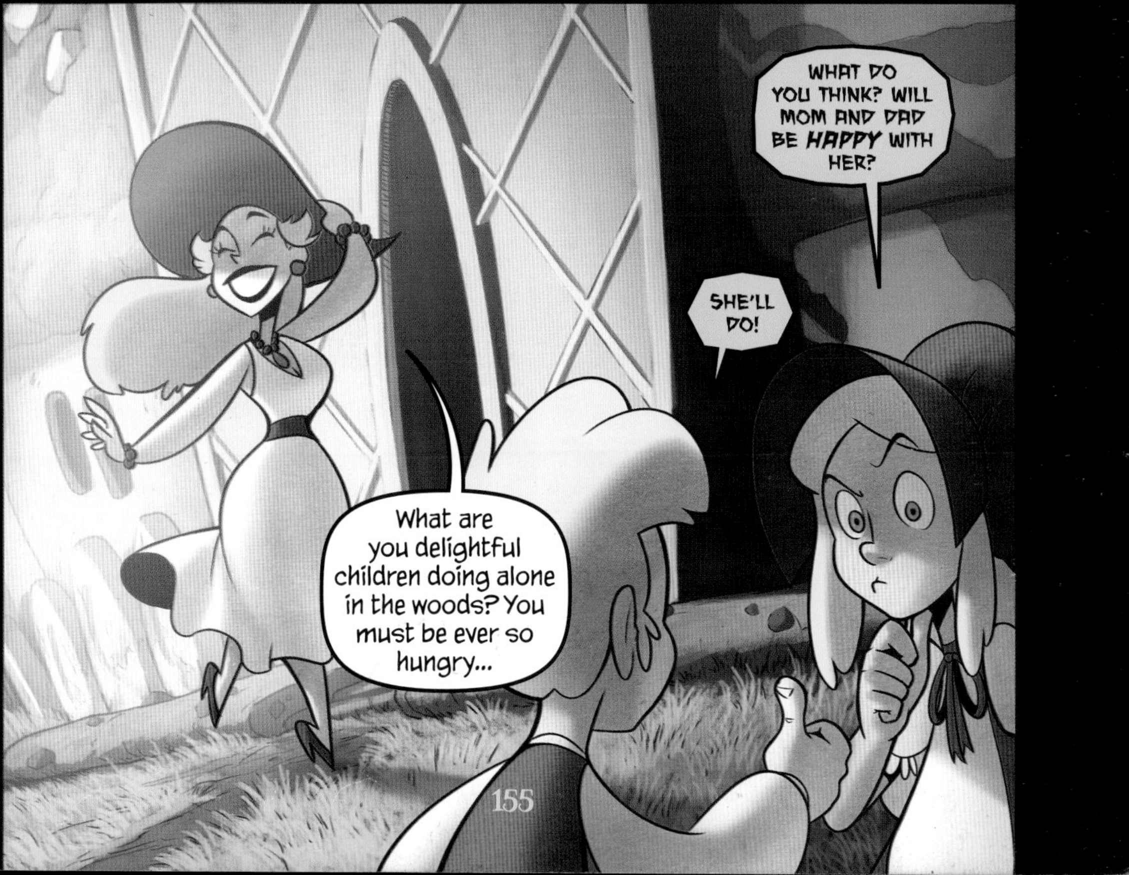
WHAT DO YOU THINK? WILL MOM AND DAD BE *HAPPY* WITH HER?
SHE'LL DO!
What are you delightful children doing alone in the woods? You must be ever so hungry...

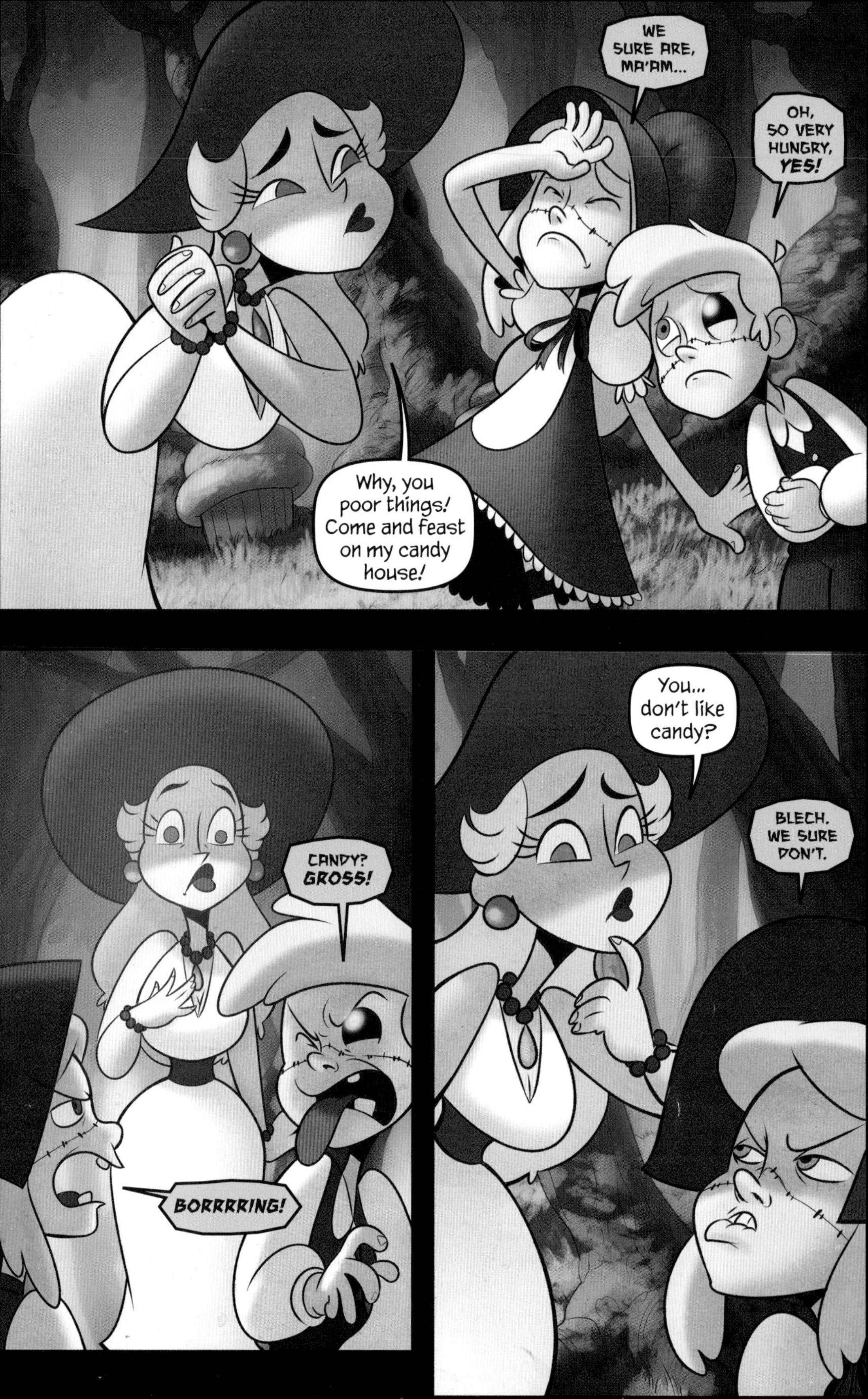
WE SURE ARE, MA'AM...
OH, SO VERY HUNGRY, YES!
Why, you poor things! Come and feast on my candy house!
CANDY? GROSS!
BORRRRING!
You... don't like candy?
BLECH. WE SURE DON'T.

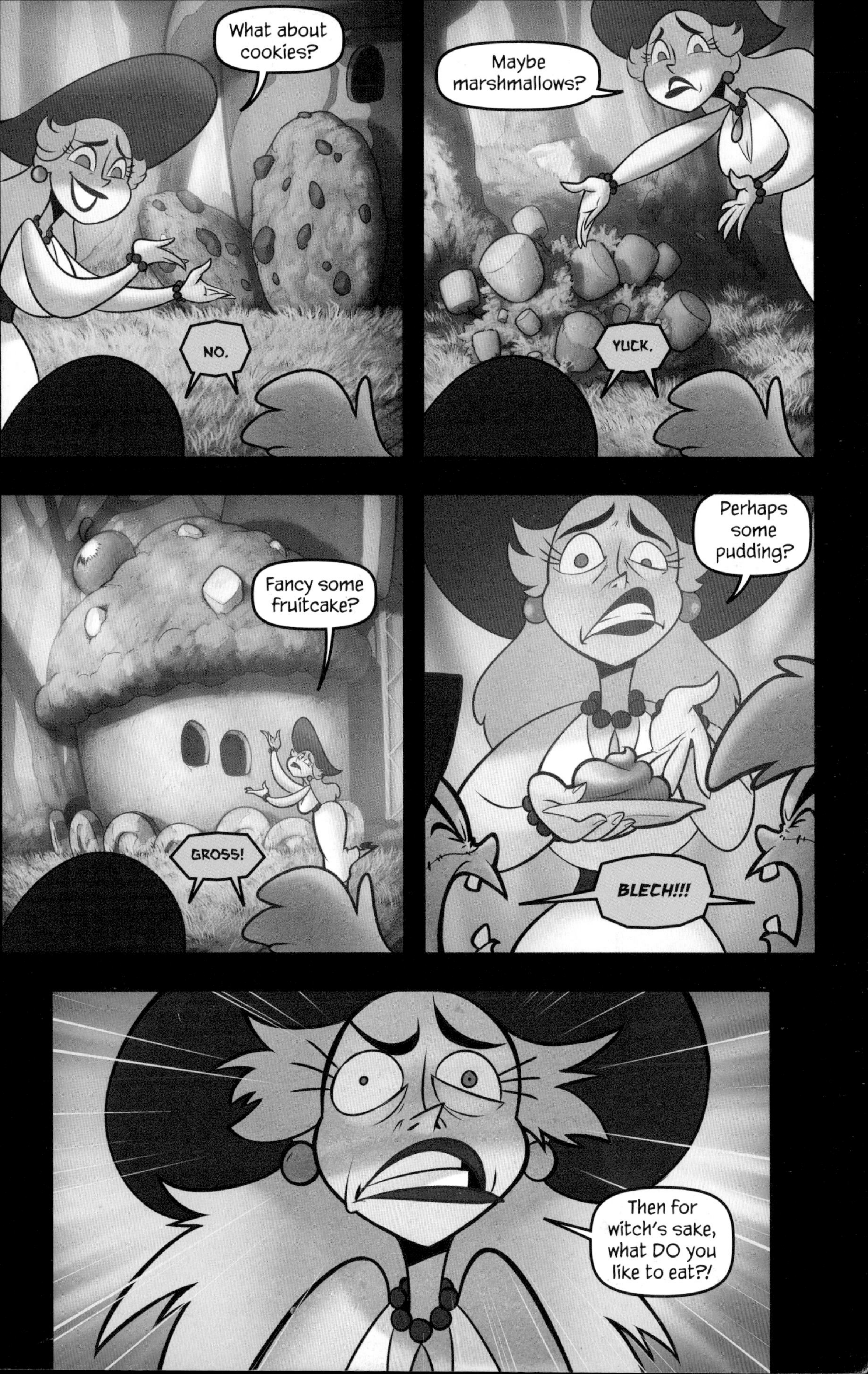
What about cookies?
NO.
Maybe marshmallows?
YUCK.
Fancy some fruitcake?
GROSS!
Perhaps some pudding?
BLECH!!!
Then for witch's sake, what DO you like to eat?!

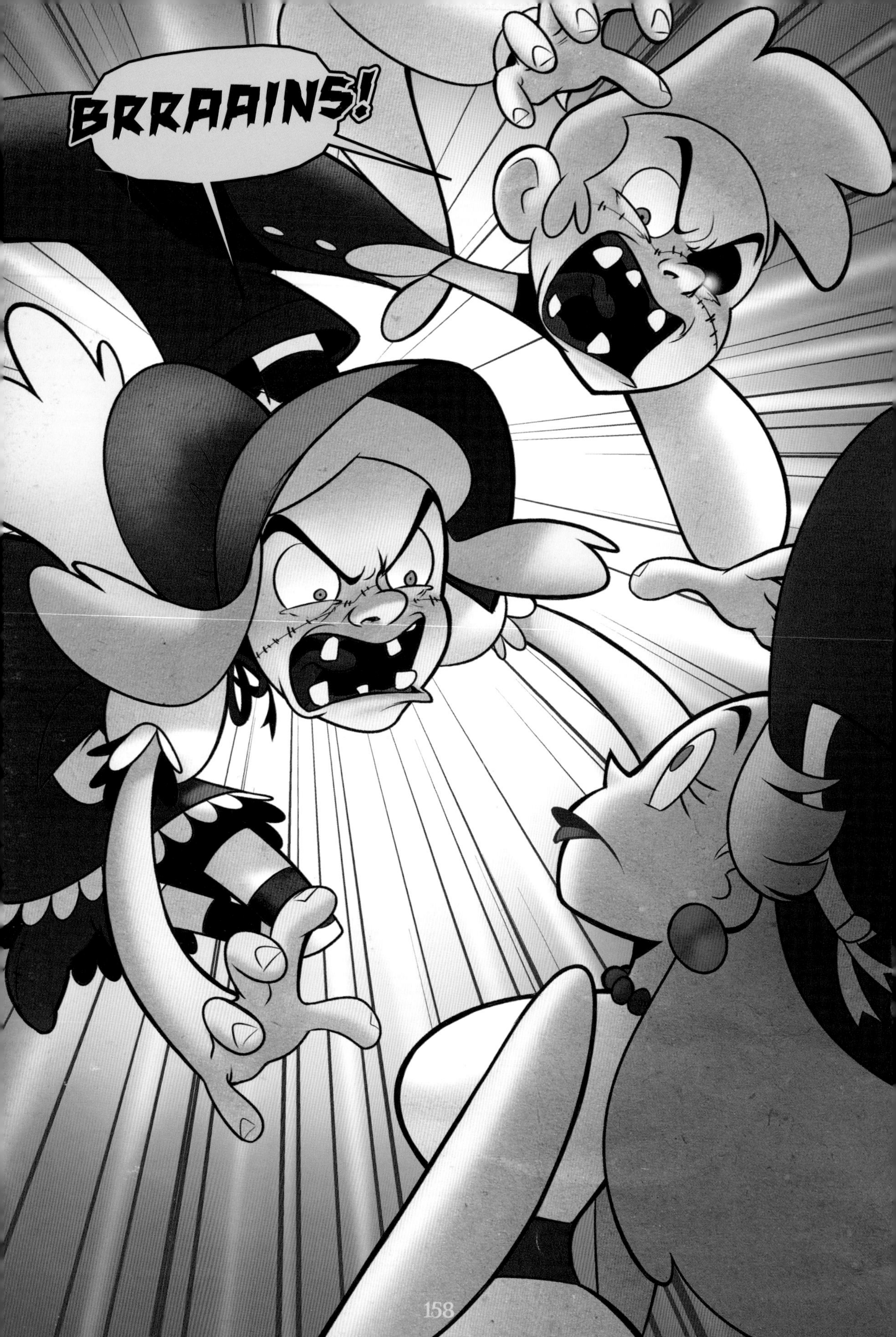
BRRAAINS!

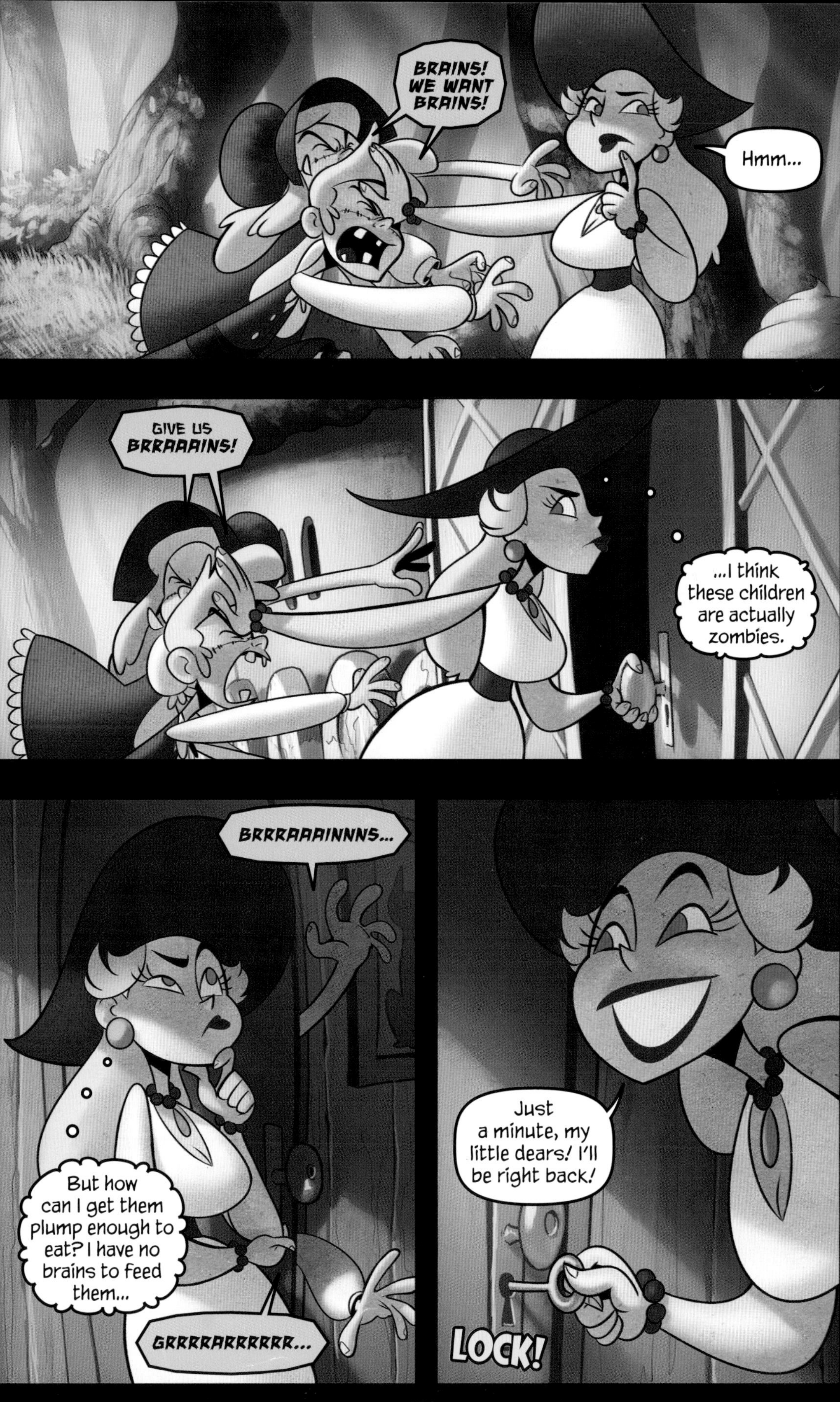
BRAINS! WE WANT BRAINS!
Hmm...
GIVE US BRRAAAINS!
...I think these children are actually zombies.
BRRRAAAINNNS...
But how can I get them plump enough to eat? I have no brains to feed them...
GRRRRARRRRRR...
Just a minute, my little dears! I'll be right back!
LOCK!

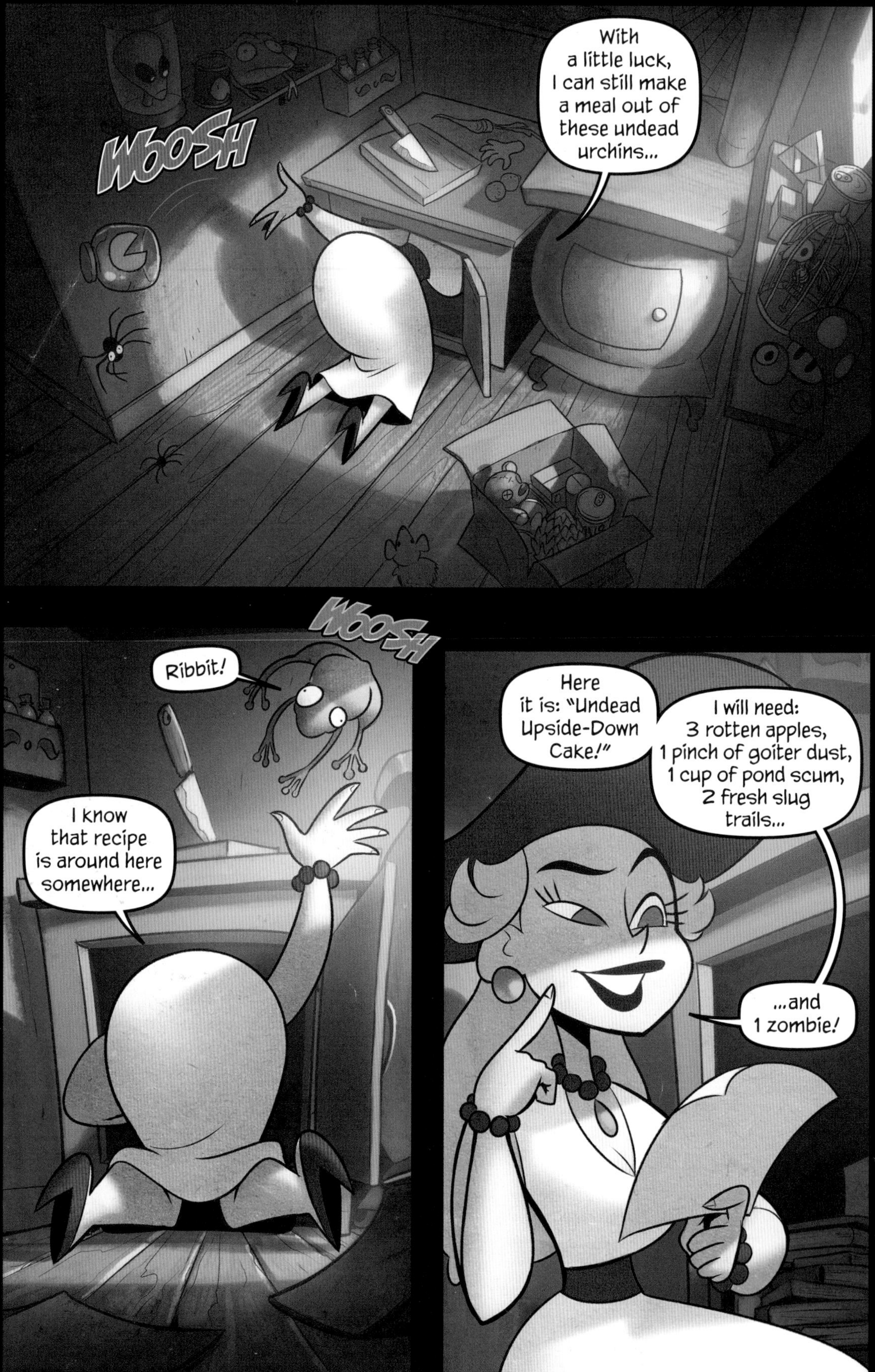
WOOSH
With a little luck, I can still make a meal out of these undead urchins...
WOOSH
Ribbit!
I know that recipe is around here somewhere...
Here it is: "Undead Upside-Down Cake!"
I will need: 3 rotten apples, 1 pinch of goiter dust, 1 cup of pond scum, 2 fresh slug trails...
...and 1 zombie!

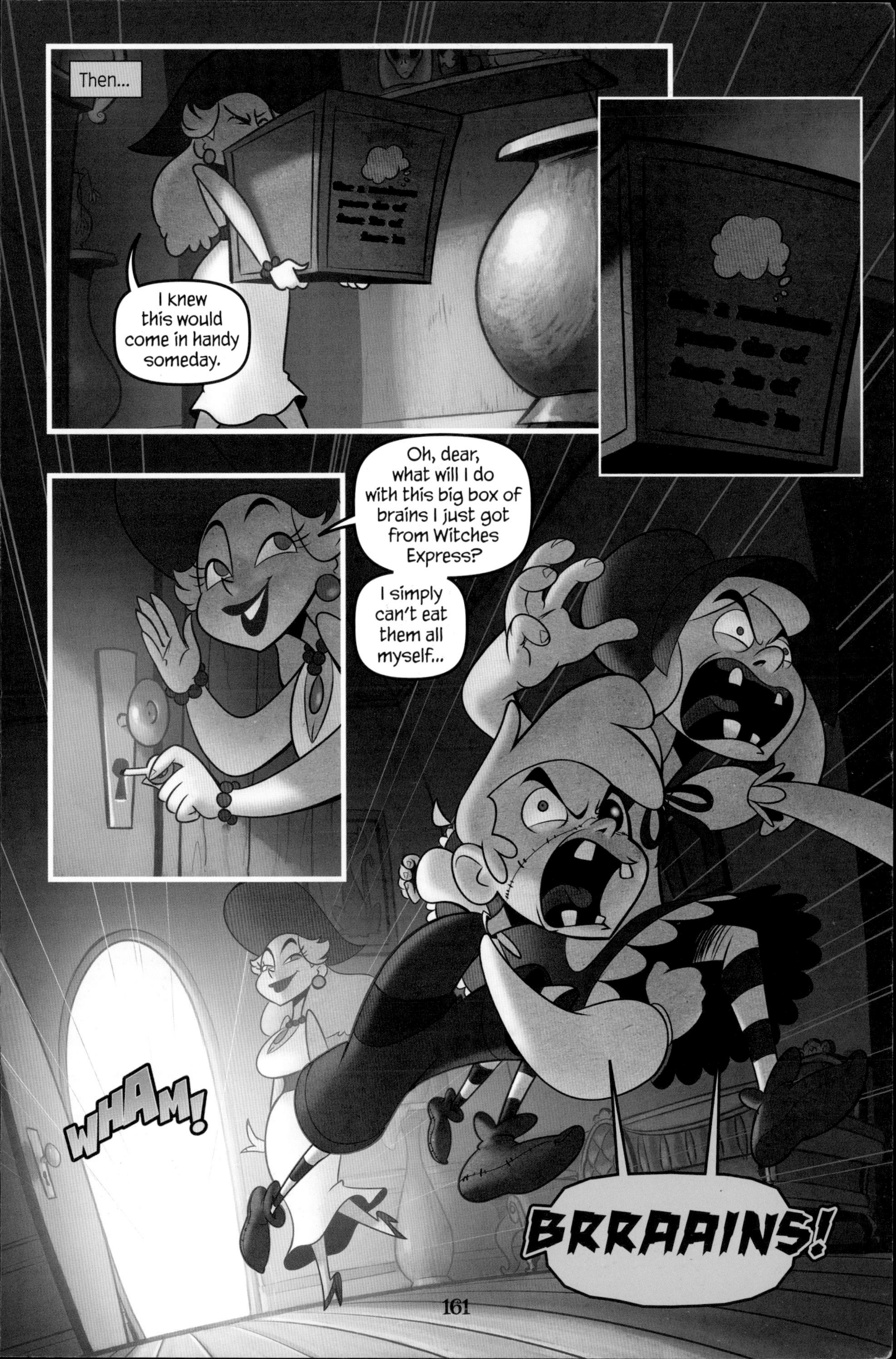
Then...
I knew this would come in handy someday.
Oh, dear, what will I do with this big box of brains I just got from Witches Express?
I simply can't eat them all myself...
WHAM!
BRRAAINS!

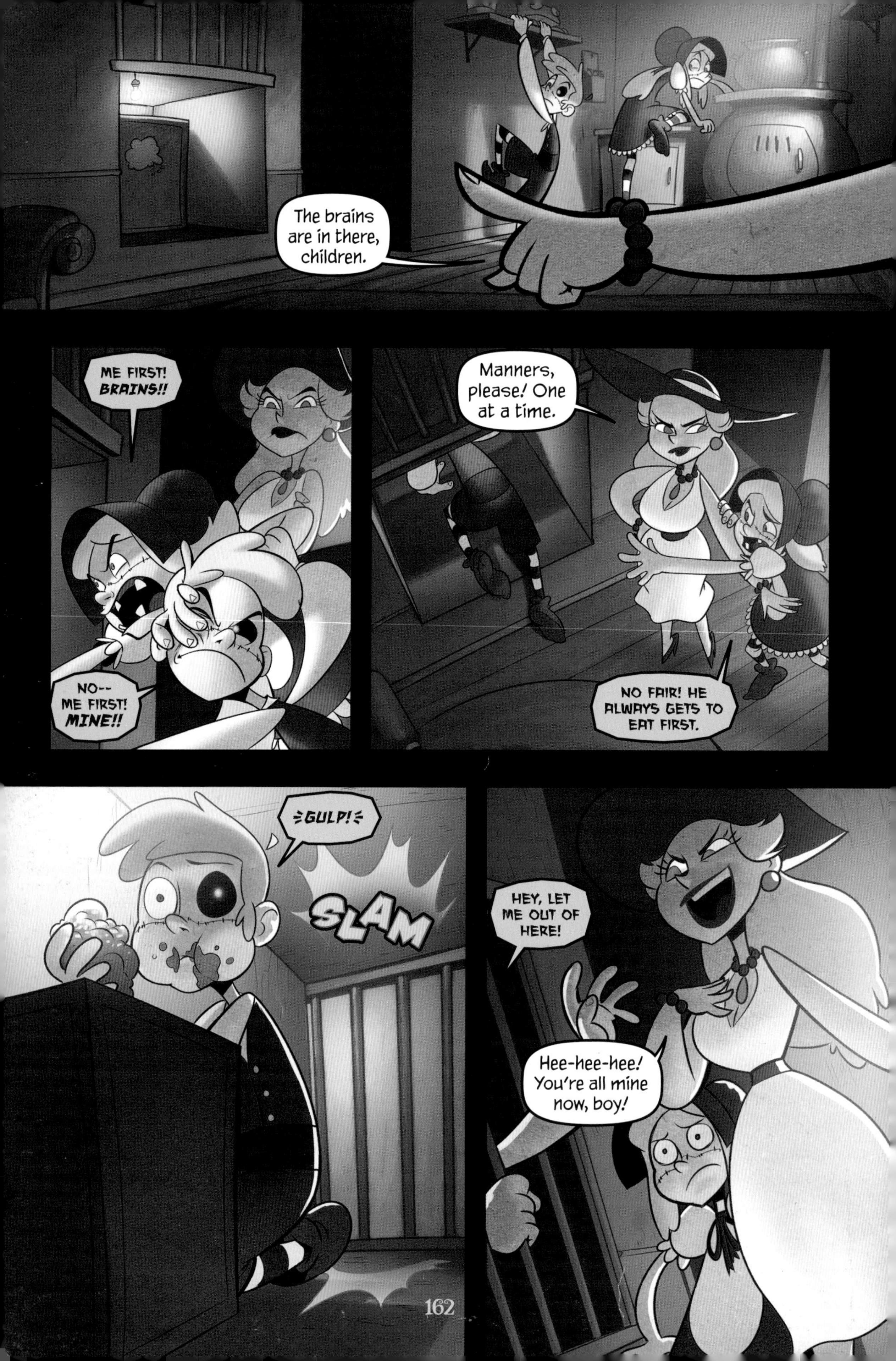
The brains are in there, children.
ME FIRST! BRAINS!!
NO-- ME FIRST! MINE!!
Manners, please! One at a time.
NO FAIR! HE ALWAYS GETS TO EAT FIRST.
GULP!
SLAM
HEY, LET ME OUT OF HERE!
Hee-hee-hee! You're all mine now, boy!

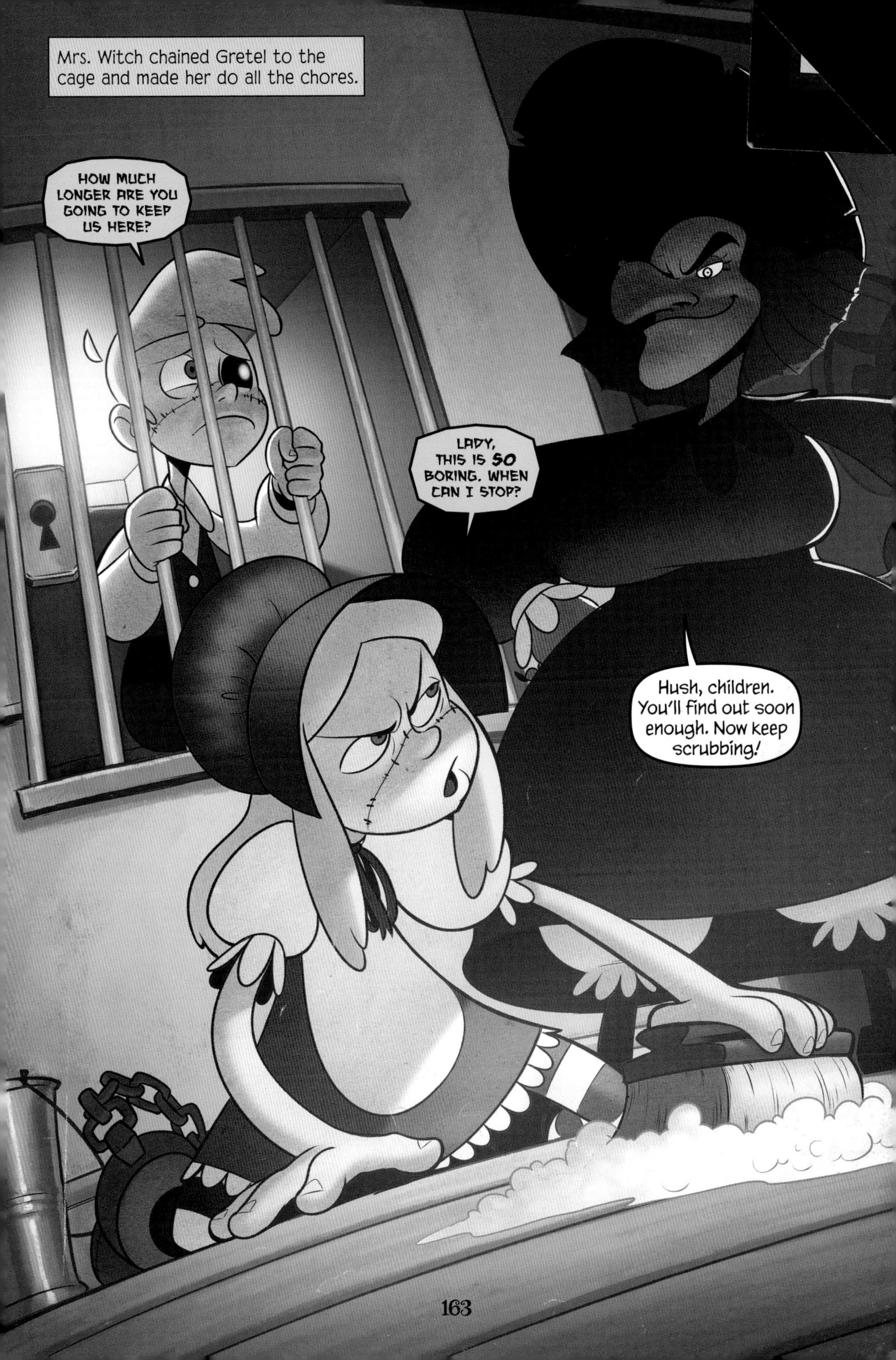
Mrs. Witch chained Gretel to the cage and made her do all the chores.
HOW MUCH LONGER ARE YOU GOING TO KEEP US HERE?
LADY, THIS IS SO BORING. WHEN CAN I STOP?
Hush, children. You'll find out soon enough. Now keep scrubbing!

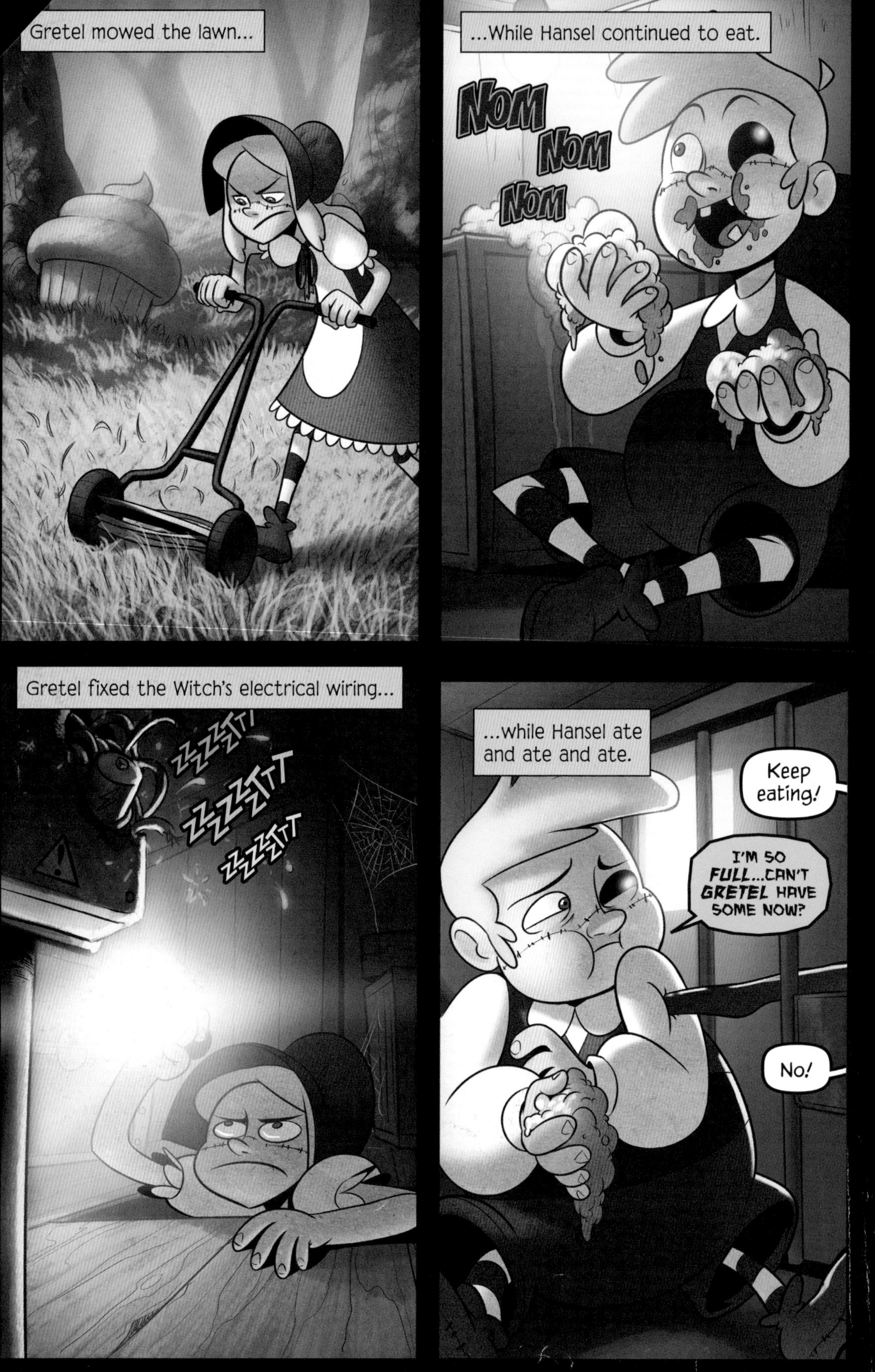
Gretel mowed the lawn...
...While Hansel continued to eat.
NOM
NOM
NOM
Gretel fixed the Witch's electrical wiring...
ZZZZZTTT
ZZZZZTTT
ZZZZZTTT
...while Hansel ate and ate and ate.
Keep eating!
I'M SO FULL...CAN'T GRETEL HAVE SOME NOW?
No!

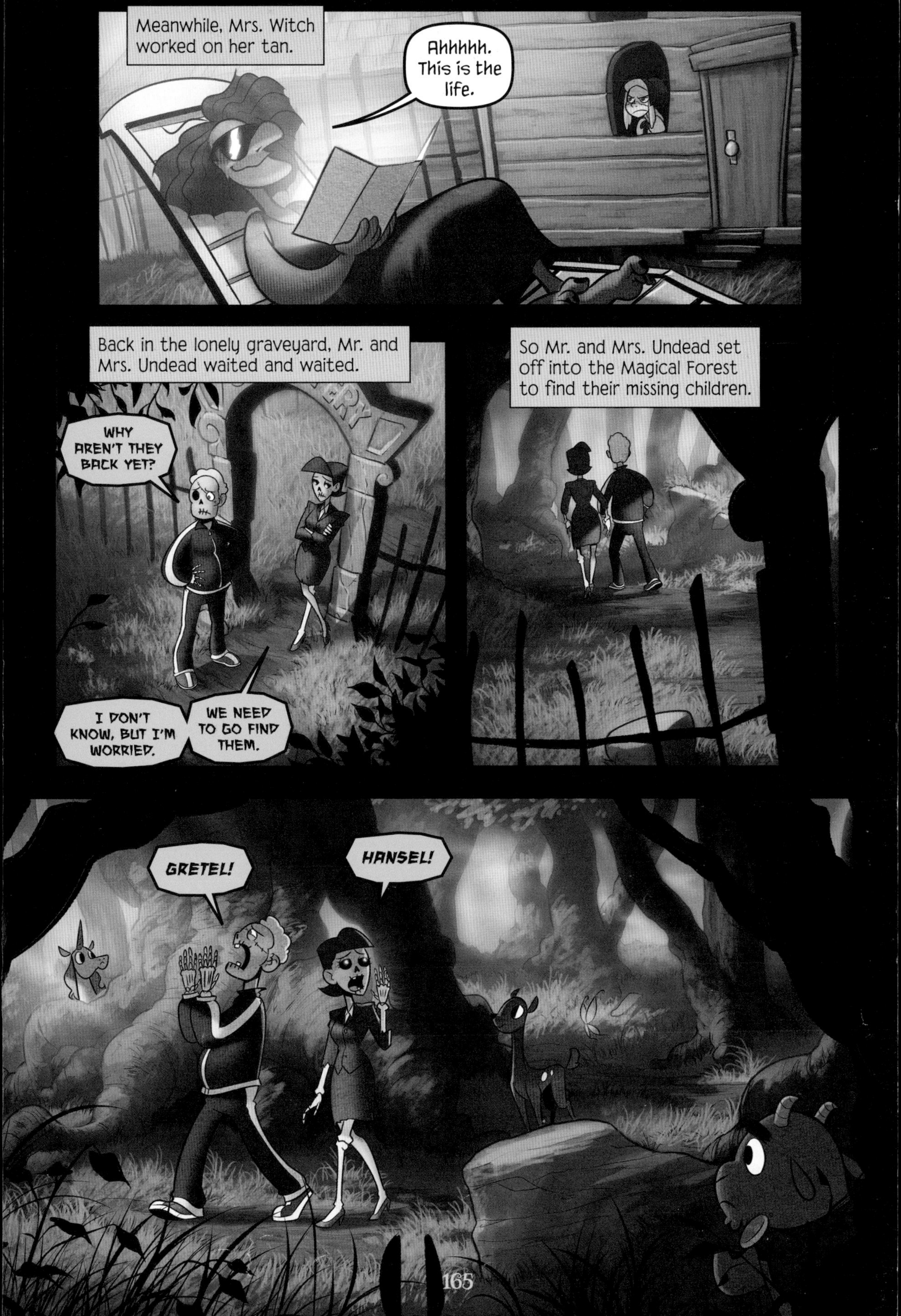
Meanwhile, Mrs. Witch worked on her tan.
Ahhhhh. This is the life.
Back in the lonely graveyard, Mr. and Mrs. Undead waited and waited.
WHY AREN'T THEY BACK YET?
I DON'T KNOW, BUT I'M WORRIED.
WE NEED TO GO FIND THEM.
So Mr. and Mrs. Undead set off into the Magical Forest to find their missing children.
GRETEL!
HANSEL!

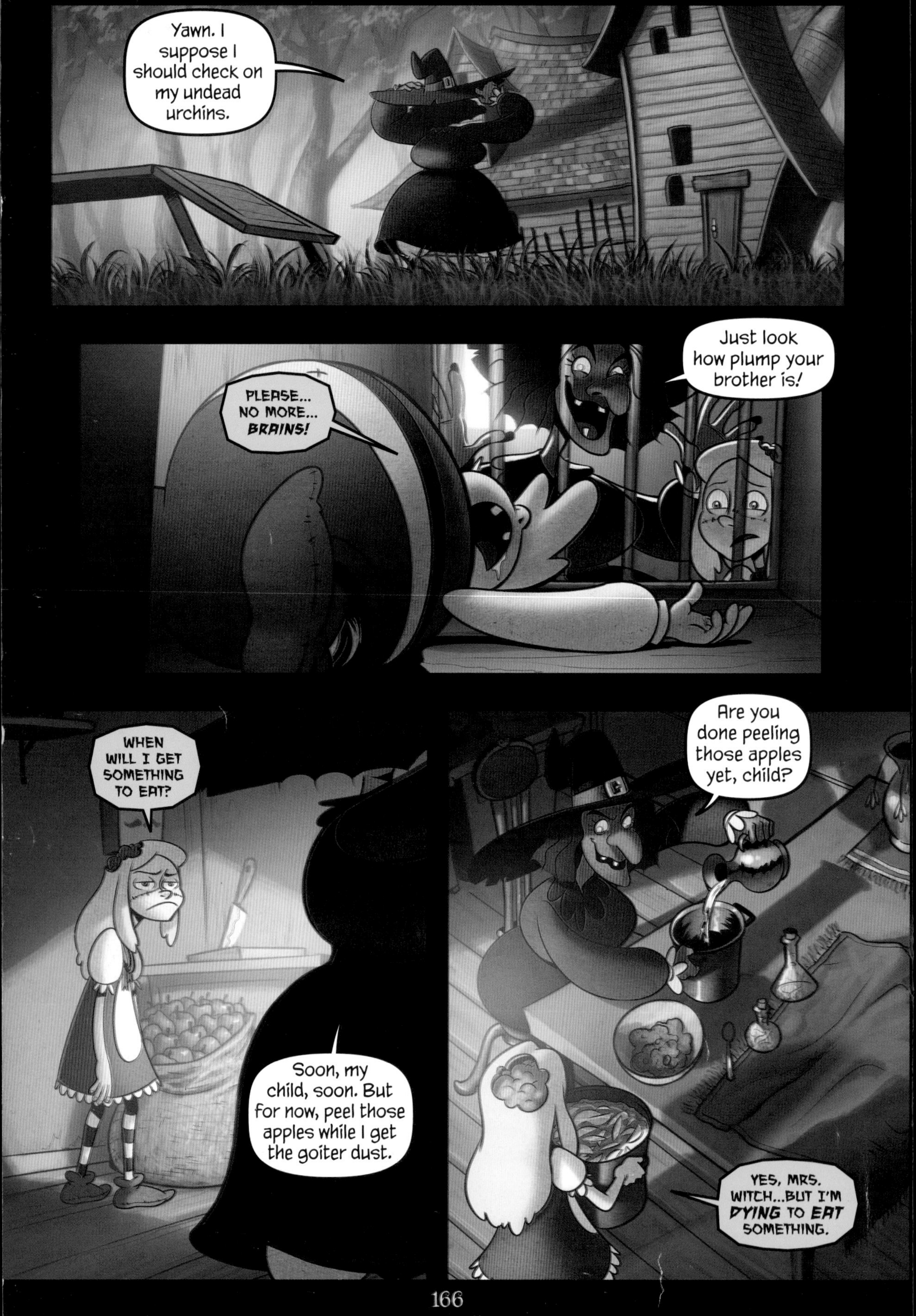
Yawn. I suppose I should check on my undead urchins.
PLEASE... NO MORE... BRAINS!
Just look how plump your brother is!
WHEN WILL I GET SOMETHING TO EAT?
Soon, my child, soon. But for now, peel those apples while I get the goiter dust.
Are you done peeling those apples yet, child?
YES, MRS. WITCH...BUT I'M DYING TO EAT SOMETHING.

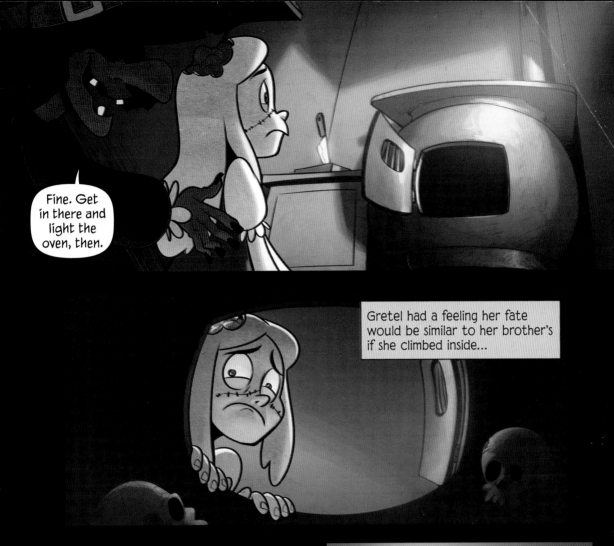

Fine. Get in there and light the oven, then.

Gretel had a feeling her fate would be similar to her brother's if she climbed inside...

...so she wracked her undead brain for a way out.

IDEA!

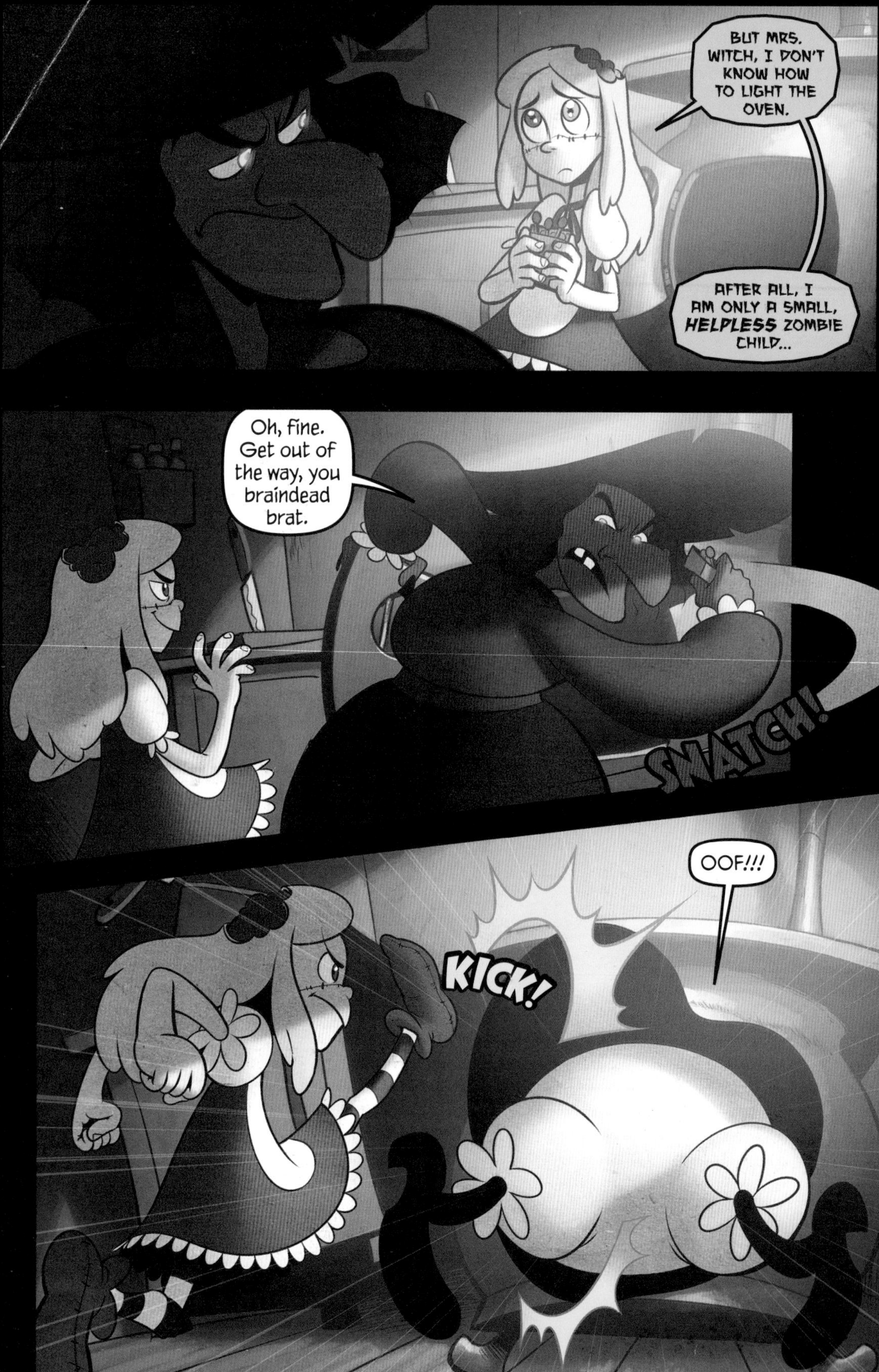
BUT MRS. WITCH, I DON'T KNOW HOW TO LIGHT THE OVEN.
AFTER ALL, I AM ONLY A SMALL, HELPLESS ZOMBIE CHILD...
Oh, fine. Get out of the way, you braindead brat.
SNATCH!
KICK!
OOF!!!

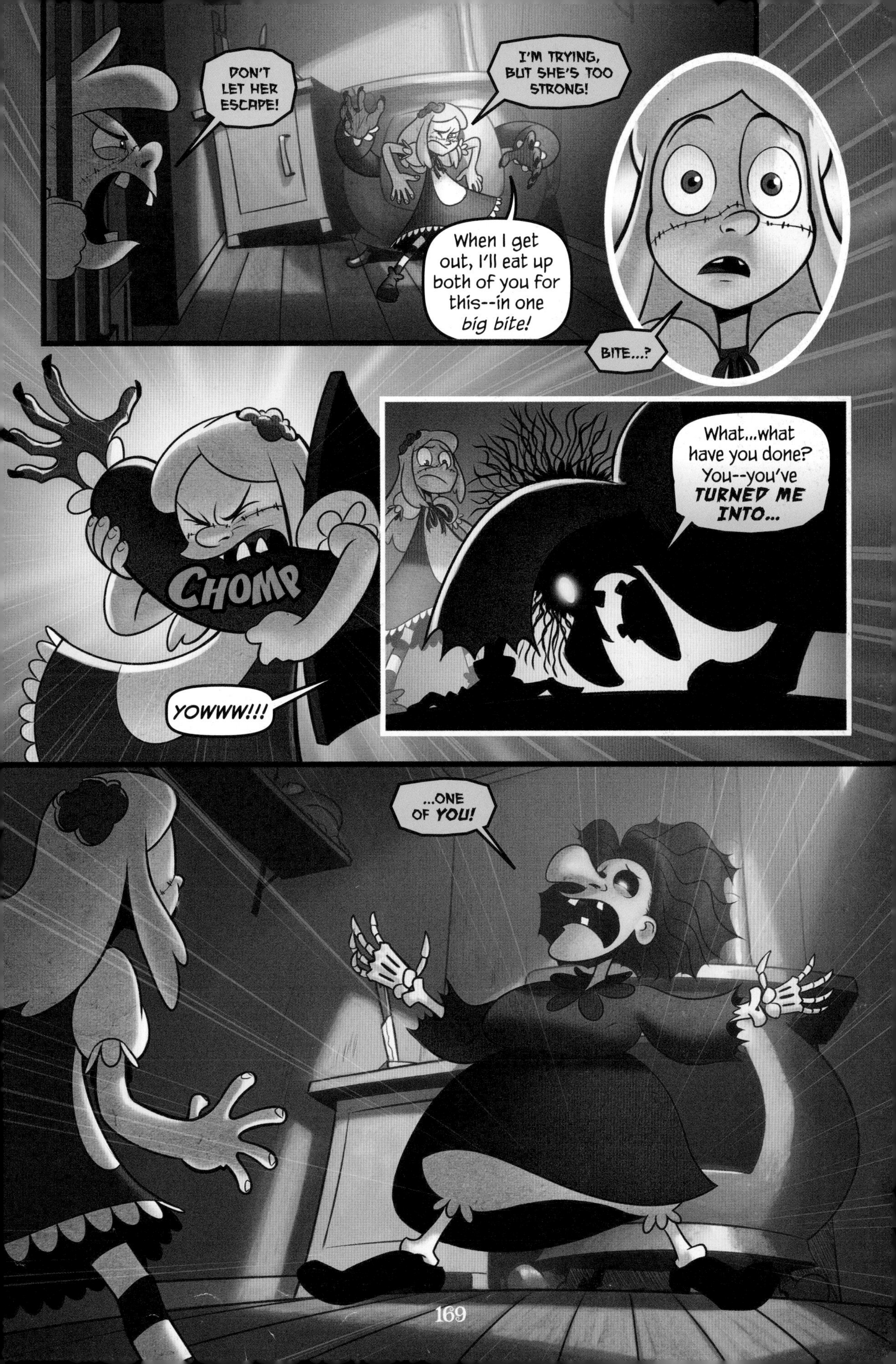

DON'T LET HER ESCAPE!
I'M TRYING, BUT SHE'S TOO STRONG!
When I get out, I'll eat up both of you for this--in one *big bite!*
BITE...?
CHOMP
YOWWW!!!
What...what have you done? You--you've **TURNED ME INTO...**
...ONE OF **YOU!**

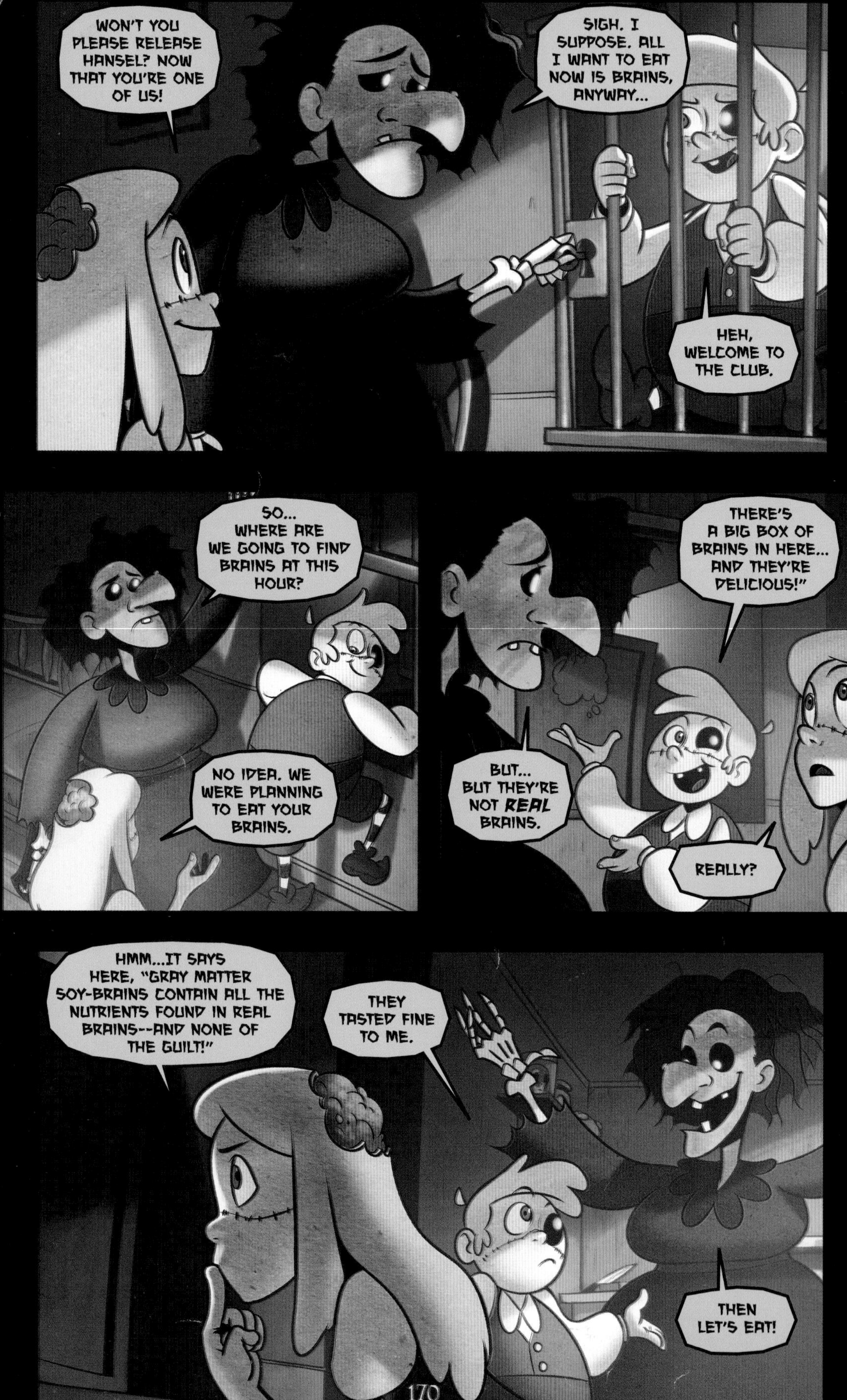
WON'T YOU PLEASE RELEASE HANSEL? NOW THAT YOU'RE ONE OF US!
SIGH. I SUPPOSE. ALL I WANT TO EAT NOW IS BRAINS, ANYWAY...
HEH, WELCOME TO THE CLUB.
SO... WHERE ARE WE GOING TO FIND BRAINS AT THIS HOUR?
NO IDEA. WE WERE PLANNING TO EAT YOUR BRAINS.
THERE'S A BIG BOX OF BRAINS IN HERE... AND THEY'RE DELICIOUS!"
BUT... BUT THEY'RE NOT *REAL* BRAINS.
REALLY?
HMM...IT SAYS HERE, "GRAY MATTER SOY-BRAINS CONTAIN ALL THE NUTRIENTS FOUND IN REAL BRAINS--AND NONE OF THE GUILT!"
THEY TASTED FINE TO ME.
THEN LET'S EAT!

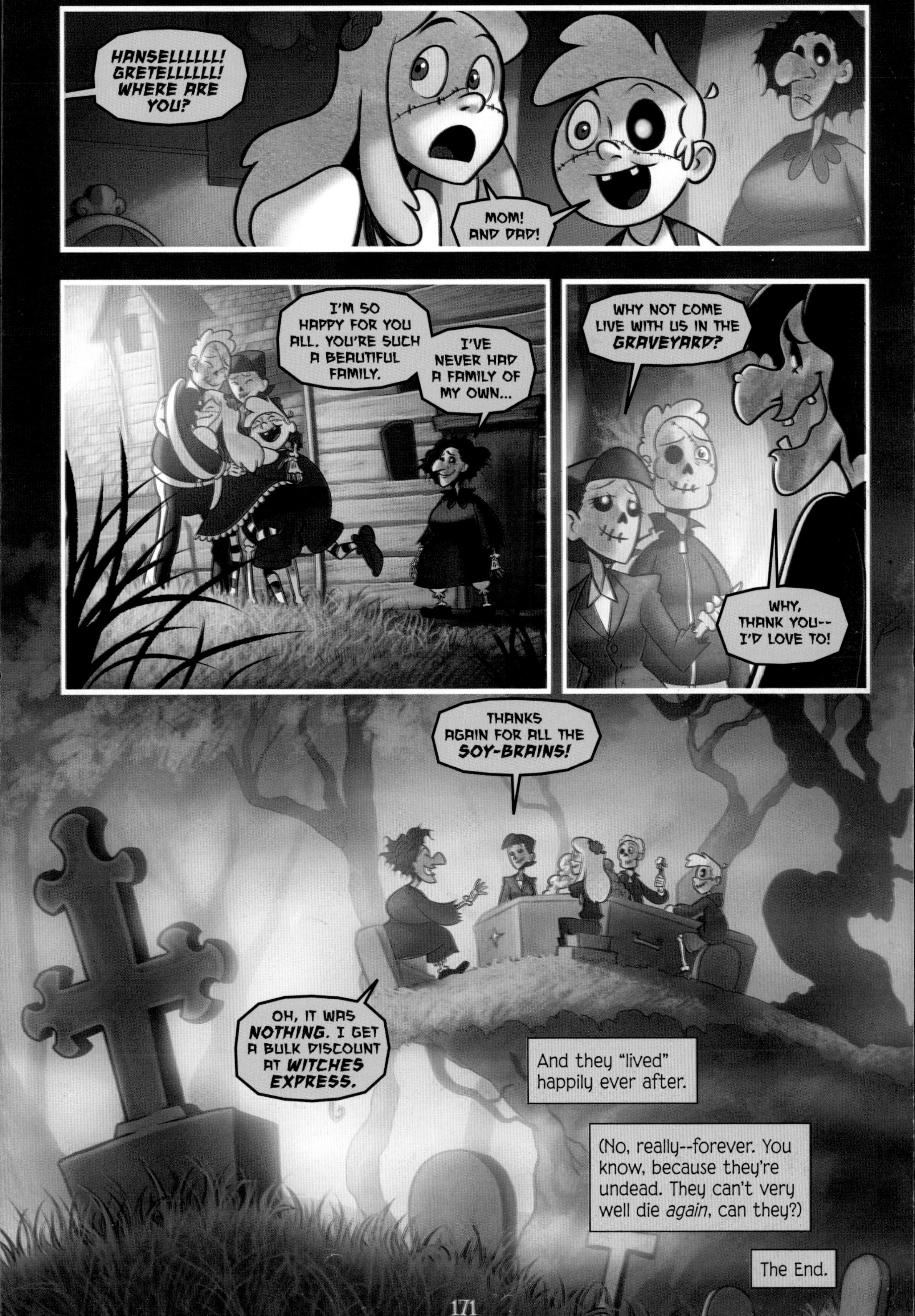
HANSELLLLLLL! GRETELLLLLLL! WHERE ARE YOU?
MOM! AND DAD!
I'M SO HAPPY FOR YOU ALL. YOU'RE SUCH A BEAUTIFUL FAMILY.
I'VE NEVER HAD A FAMILY OF MY OWN...
WHY NOT COME LIVE WITH US IN THE GRAVEYARD?
WHY, THANK YOU-- I'D LOVE TO!
THANKS AGAIN FOR ALL THE SOY-BRAINS!
OH, IT WAS NOTHING. I GET A BULK DISCOUNT AT WITCHES EXPRESS.
And they "lived" happily ever after.
(No, really--forever. You know, because they're undead. They can't very well die again, can they?)
The End.

ALL ABOUT THE ORIGINAL TALE!

Zombies didn't appear in
the original Brothers Grimm
version of "Hansel and Gretel."
However, Hansel and Gretel's
parents were pretty *monstrous*.

You see, they tried not once--but twice--to
abandon their children in the forest so they couldn't return home.
The parents succeeded the second time, leaving Hansel and Gretel
lost in the woods. In fact, their mother was so monstrous that she
led them even farther into the woods, ensuring they would never
find their way home.

Lost and alone in the woods, Hansel and Gretel wandered aimlessly until
they felt the need to lie down and sleep. Several days passed like this,
until they grew so hungry they could scarcely bear it. However, they
soon came upon a strange sight: a house's walls made entirely of bread,
and the roof was made of cakes and other sweets.

The siblings, desperately hungry at this point, started snacking on the
gingerbread house. Soon, the house's owner spotted them and welcomed
them inside. To their surprise, the woman turned out to be a hungry
witch who eats children!

The witch plumped up Hansel, hoping to make him nice and fat so he
would be a bigger meal for her to eat. Meanwhile, the witch forced
Gretel to work--and fed her nothing but crab shells.

One morning, the witch told Gretel to climb inside the hot oven to see
if it was warm enough to bake bread. Gretel knew the witch was up
to something, so she asked her to climb inside instead--and kicked the
witch into the oven. The witch was never seen again.

Gretel freed her brother. In a room next to the kitchen, they found
boxes of precious gems! When they finally found their way home,
they discovered their father alone. While they'd
been gone, their evil mother had died.
Gretel tugged on her apron,
releasing all the gems. The
three of them lived richly
and happily ever after.

A **FAR OUT** GUIDE TO HANSEL & GRETEL'S TALE TWISTS!

Two innocent, human siblings star in the original tale. In this version, they're zombies!

Hansel & Gretel get nabbed by the witch when they nibble on her house. Zombie Hansel & Gretel get kidnapped because they *won't* eat the candy-house!

In the original tale, a witch tries to eat the children, but they burn her to cinders. (Yikes!) In this book, Zombie Gretel bites the witch, transforming her into one of them!

In the Brothers Grimm version of the story, the mother and the witch die. But in this far out version, everyone lives happily ever after--even the witch!

AUTHORS

Louise Simonson writes about monsters, science fiction and fantasy characters, and superheroes. She wrote the award-winning Power Pack series, several best-selling X-Men titles, Web of Spider-man for Marvel Comics, and Superman: Man of Steel and Steel for DC Comics. She has also written many books for kids. She is married to comic artist and writer Walter Simonson and lives in the suburbs of New York City.

Sean Tulien is a children's book editor and writer living and working in Minnesota. In his spare time, he likes to read, play video games, eat sushi, exercise outdoors, spend time with his lovely wife, Nicolle, listen to loud music, and play with his pets Buddy and Habibi (a hamster and rabbit).

Otis Frampton is a comic book writer *and* illustrator. He is also one of the character and background artists on the popular animated web series "How It Should Have Ended." His comic book series *Oddly Normal* was published by Image Comics.

Joey Comeau is a writer! He lives in Toronto, which is where he wrote the all-ages space-adventure comic *Bravest Warriors*. He also wrote the young adult zombie novel *One Bloody Thing After Another*. It's pretty spooky.

Benjamin Harper has worked as an editor at Lucasfilm LTD. and DC Comics. He currently works at Warner Bros. Consumer Products in Burbank, California. He has written many books, including *Obsessed with Star Wars* and *Thank You, Superman!*

ILLUSTRATORS

Jimena Sánchez was born in Mexico City, Mexico, in 1980. She studied illustration in the Escuela Nacional de Artes Plásticas (National School of Arts) and has since worked and lived in the United States as well as Spain. Jimena now lives in Mexico City again, working as an illustrator and comic book artist. Her art has appeared in many children's books and magazines.

Fernando Cano is an illustrator born in Mexico City, Mexico. He currently resides in Monterrey, Mexico, where he makes a living as an illustrator and colorist. He has done work for Marvel, DC Comics, and role-playing games like Pathfinder from Paizo Publishing. In his spare time, he enjoys hanging out with friends, singing, rowing, and drawing!

Omar Lozano lives in Monterrey, Mexico. He has always been crazy for illustration and is constantly on the lookout for awesome things to draw. In his free time, he watches lots of movies, reads fantasy and sci-fi books, and draws! Omar has done work for Marvel, DC, IDW, Capstone, and several other publishing companies.

FAR OUT
FAIRY TALES

Far Out Fairy Tales is published by
Stone Arch Books
A Capstone Imprint
1710 Roe Crest Drive, North Mankato,
Minnesota 56003
www.mycapstone.com

Cataloging-in-Publication Data is
available at the Library of Congress
website.
ISBN: 978-1-4965-2511-6 (paperback)
ISBN: 978-1-4965-2514-7 (eBook PDF)

Summary: What do you get when
classic fairy tales are twisted about,
turned inside out, and reworked for
the graphic novel format? Far Out
Fairy Tales! Discover what Snow White
would be like if she were raised by
robots. Chase down the Big Bad Wolf
with the help of a superpowered Red
Riding Hood! Experience fairy tales like
never before in this innovative series
of full-color comic books for kids!

Designer: Bob Lentz & Hilary Wacholz
Editor: Sean Tulien
Lettering: Jaymes Reed

Printed and bound in the USA. 1885